BRINGER OF LIGHT

BRINGER OF LIGHT

JAINE FENN

GOLLANCZ

LONDON

First published in Great Britain in 2011 by Gollancz
An imprint of the Orion Publishing Group
Orion House, 5 Upper St Martin's Lane, London WC2H 9EA
An Hachette UK Company

A CIP catalogue record for this book
is available from the British Library.

ISBN 978 0 575 09694 3 (Cased)
ISBN 978 0 575 09695 0 (Trade Paperback)

1 3 5 7 9 10 8 6 4 2

Typeset by Deltatype Ltd, Birkenhead, Merseyside

Printed in Great Britain by
CPI Mackays, Chatham, Kent

The Orion Publishing Group's policy is to use papers
that are natural, renewable and recyclable products and
made from wood grown in sustainable forests. The logging
and manufacturing processes are expected to conform to
the environmental regulations of the country of origin.

www.jainefenn.com
www.orionbooks.co.uk

To everyone in the Tripod writers' group, past, present and future – especially Jim, for asking so many awkward questions.

'Touch the divine
As we fall in line'

'City of Delusion', Muse

'Who can in reason then or right assume
Monarchy over such as live by right
His equals, if in power and splendour less,
In freedom equal?'

Paradise Lost, John Milton

CHAPTER ONE

This was no way to save the universe. Taro fiddled with the sauce dispenser on the table and tried to look inconspicuous. Business like this should be going down in a dingy bar, with a scowling barkeep and shadowy booths where trigger-happy space-dogs were striking smoky deals. And here was he, in a family diner full of grizzling brats, wipe-clean surfaces and eye-searing ceiling lights. So much for the glamorous freetrader lifestyle.

His attempt to act casual was rewarded by a trickle of yellowish goo from the dispenser. He snatched his hand back, resisting the instinct to lick the sauce off his fingers. He'd made that mistake once already. Instead he wiped it on the edge of the table, warily eyeing the garish menu emblazoned across the tabletop. Now he'd finished his bowl of crunchy-deep-fried-whatever he expected he'd be asked to order more food or shove off. He probably shouldn't have eaten so fast, but even the local junk was a pleasant change from his usual diet. No matter how good a ship's reclamation unit was, shit was still shit.

When the menu display didn't light up and try to sell him more food he risked a glance at the nearest diner, who was tucking into a plate of orange rice-type-stuff using one of the oversized spoons that passed for cutlery around here. Nual had arrived a few minutes after Taro, because they didn't want anyone getting the idea she was with him – which, of course, she was, in every way. She must have sensed him watching her because a warm spark blossomed briefly inside his head. He looked away reluctantly. Mustn't let himself get distracted.

Taro checked the door for what had to be the twentieth time. Still no sign of the contact.

The only reason they'd agreed to this meeting was credit – or rather, lack of it. Perhaps they should've refused the request from a local freight service asking if they could transport a box of 'biological samples' – but whilst they'd got themselves a paying passenger for the trip back to the shipping lanes, they had a half-empty cargo-hold, and half-empty cargo-holds made customs officers suspicious. Plus, the freight company had offered nearly as much as 'Apian Lamark' (almost certainly not his real name) was paying for his ride. Freetrading might be just what they did as cover for their *real* mission – the important, *secret* one – but if they didn't score some heavy credit soon, they wouldn't have a ship with which to carry out that mission. Jarek had still been sorting their ongoing cargo when Taro had commed him, but he'd agreed it was worth following up the request.

Rather than watch the animated woodland critters on happy drugs dancing around the walls, Taro looked out of the diner's picture window; the view was filled with flying people, locals and tourists alike in neon-bright wing-suits, swooping and gliding through whirling vortexes of multi-coloured petals against the pale mauve sky. The imaginatively named Star City sprawled up and along a ridge of pink-grey rock of the sort that was apparently common in this particular region of this particular continent on this particular world. (The world was called Hetarey, he remembered that much; he'd looked it up on the way here, but the details hadn't stuck. They didn't need to. It wasn't like they planned to be here more than a few hours.) The starport itself was on the flat top of the ridge; the other flat land, at the bottom, was for the rich coves who liked houses with flat floors and big rooms. In between, built into a slope that varied from inconvenient to impossible, were the houses of the average folks, plus all the diversions and entertainments that went with being the only place on this backwater planet where the universe came to call. The slope was extra-steep just here, and heavy-duty grav-units and massive fans had been

installed at the bottom to give those without Nual and Taro's un-
natural advantages a chance to fly.

When he saw movement out of the corner of his eye, Taro turned
his head quickly enough to blow any pretence of being a casual cus-
tomer. That *had* to be his contact. The locals had a thing about hair
– everyone wore theirs long, and shaving was against their religion
or something – and while that wasn't such a prime look on the
men, especially combined with their preference for short trousers
and stupid hats, on a good-looking woman waist-length red curls
were pure blade. And this was a good-looking woman.

Even if he wasn't currently gawking at her, she'd have no
trouble spotting him. Hetarey didn't see many offworlders – in a
busy week, they might get two whole shiftships landing. Taro was
unfeasibly tall and thin, and dressed the way he knew he looked
good – big boots, tight leggings, vest top and black jacket – he had
already attracted the attention of the other diners ('Eat your greens
darling or you'll grow up *like that*' – not in this gravity you won't,
kid). Nual had also drawn looks, though for a different reason: she
was beautiful, probably the most beautiful woman they'd ever set
eyes on – though Taro was biased. People looked at her like they
wanted or admired her, and the same people looked at him like he
was an alien who shouldn't be allowed. Which was funny, really,
given he was the human one, and she was the alien.

The woman smiled and headed straight over. She had a sense
of style most of the locals lacked, and she moved well. Her body
wasn't bad, either, from what he could see of it under that flouncy
top.

He felt a tickle of amusement in the back of his mind. He resisted the temptation to look in Nual's direction. Instead he smiled
at the newcomer, and gestured to the chair opposite. She ignored
the offer and instead took the seat at the end of the table, which
put her immediately to Taro's right. More annoyingly, it meant she
had her back to Nual.

'Thank you for coming, Medame Klirin,' he said. 'Did you, uh,
want anything to drink? Or eat?'

'No. Thank you.' She tapped a dark spot on the table – so that was how you turned the damn thing off – then leant forward and gave him a sideways look. 'La, not meaning any offence, but why do we need to meet in person? Can you take the shipment? Or not?'

'We – I – just like to meet potential customers.' The gappy-sounding question thing was just how they spoke around here, so he added, 'Right?'

'Sirrah sanMalia, are you actually the captain of the *Heart of Glass*?'

Taro didn't need Nual to tell him what she was thinking: she was wondering why someone who'd yet to survive his second decade was making deals on interstellar cargo. 'No, I'm the junior partner. The captain is tied up elsewhere.' He spread his hands. 'If you'd got in contact sooner, I'm sure he could have met you, but at this short notice, I'm afraid you'll have to make do with me. All right?'

In the brief pause while she digested his apology he sent a silent query in Nual's direction. Her reply came through at once: <*She doesn't mean you harm, but I can't pick up more than that from here. Try some leading questions ...*>

'Sorry,' Medame Klirin was saying, 'No offence taken, right?'

'Er, right. Really, we just wanna know more about this cargo you want us to ship. And why the sudden rush?'

She brushed back a stray strand of hair, and Taro tried not to be distracted. 'It's a matter of commercial confidentiality, see?' she said quietly. 'A delicate and perishable product which we need to get to a company in Perilat. All sealed and safe; and we'll provide the permits and specs to keep customs sweet, la. We've been watching the listings for a ship heading out to Perilat, haven't we? So when you registered that as your next destination we got in contact.'

Before Taro could query Nual her comment arrived in his head: <*I think she's lying.*>

<*Can't you be sure? And which bit's a lie?*> he sent back.

<*No, I can't, not when I'm looking at the back of her head! I'm only getting this much because I'm in* your *head when you hear her words.*>

4

Which was, Taro had to admit, somewhat freaky. Oops, Nual would pick that thought up too, of course.

'Are you all right?'

He realised Medame Klirin was staring at him. 'Yeah, I'm— Let's just say you were right to avoid the food here. Um, when you say "we", who d'you represent?'

'A corporate interest.'

<Definitely a lie.> This time Nual was sure.

'That's a bit vague,' said Taro. 'Can I have some details?'

'I can provide them, la.' She held up a hand to show her com; like his it was a slap-com on the back of her hand, not an implant. Jarek had advised them against getting implanted coms – not that he could afford one right now – because they could cause issues with their not-entirely-accurate-and-subject-to-future-change IDs; that she also hadn't an implant was another point against Medame Klirin. Then again, what did he know? He was pretty new to this whole freetrading lark. Madam Klirin continued, 'Did you want details of the company at Perilat who'll eventually receive the goods? Given the confidential nature of our research, we'd rather you just dealt with their agents, you know?'

<All lies.>

Taro projected, *<You certain? She's coming over all confident and helpful.>*

<She's deceiving you. I just can't sense exactly how.>

<Fuck it, that's good enough for me.>

He realised Madame Klirin was frowning at him. 'Listen,' said Taro, with what he hoped was a sympathetic smile, 'I don't think we can take your cargo. Sorry.'

'What?' She looked understandably confused.

'It's just … maybe if the captain was here, he might think differently, but like I said, I'm the junior partner, and I really don't wanna make a bad call.'

'But he trusted you to meet me, surely he trusts your judgment … he does know you're here? Or are you acting alone?'

Taro had been in enough shit in his life to read the worst into that question. '*Yes*, Captain Reen knows I'm here; in fact, he's expecting me back at the ship soon. And he trusts my judgment, but I've decided to play it safe. Sorry to screw you around and all, but we've got a rep to maintain.'

'What are you implying here, la?' Medame Klirin said coldly.

Taro cursed his loose tongue. It wasn't like she'd actually said or done anything smoky. Then again, pissing her off – just a bit – might make her let down her guard. 'I ain't implying anything, and I ain't saying you and your people aren't prime and lovely. I've just decided not to take this job.' He made sure he had eye contact when he added, 'We can't risk potentially dangerous or dubious cargo.'

'Fine,' she said, and stood up. Her unspoken response was strong enough that he heard it in Medame Klirin's voice even though her words arrived via Nual: *<Too late for that, arsehole.>*

As she turned to go he began to stand, nerves thrumming. Nual's mental voice froze him in place: *<Stay there, but be ready in case this goes wrong!>*

He read what 'this' was and forced himself to sit back down. Even so, he felt the Angel reflexes kick in: body calm but ready for action, mind alert to danger without being impaired by fear.

Medame Klirin was making her way to the door. Nual, apparently oblivious, grabbed her tray, stood up and turned—

—and ran straight into the other woman. The tray went flying.

Taro heard Nual's embarrassed apology: 'So sorry!'

Medame Klirin tried to step back, and hit a table with her hip. Nual was fussing, trying to brush rice off the woman's top. Taro watched the woman's hands; one grasped the edge of the table she'd fallen against, the other was flailing; she wasn't going for a weapon. Around him, people were looking up, but no one was making a move.

Medame Klirin edged away from Nual slowly, like she was slightly stunned. Finally Nual stepped back. 'I've got the worst off; are you sure you don't want a contribution towards your cleaning bill? That's such a lovely top, la, I'd hate to have ruined it.' She'd even managed to get the local speech patterns down pat, noted Taro admiringly.

6

'No ...' Klirin shook her head, then seemed to remember herself. 'I'm fine. Really. La, I— I should go now.'

Nual stepped aside, and at the same time projected to Taro: *<Stay here for three minutes, then meet me outside, by the upwards walkway.>*

<What are you going to do?>

<Nothing drastic: just call Jarek.>

<Why?>

<To tell him we need to get off this world as soon as possible.>

CHAPTER TWO

Jarek's old partner used to have a saying: 'If a deal sounds too good to be true, that's because it is.' He'd agreed to let his companions meet the contact because they couldn't afford to turn down that much credit without good reason, and though Nual and Taro lacked his years of experience, her unique talents should give them the chance to find out if there *was* a good reason. She'd have been a better negotiator than Taro, but her looks made her too memorable, and she preferred to stay in the background.

The cargo they had arrived here with – dyestuffs and low-volume specialist fabrics for the apparently taste-free Hetarey fashion industry, plus a selection of licensed games, shows and films that local distributors weren't willing to pay premium prices to get beeveed in – hadn't fetched as much as he'd hoped, and nothing available here would turn much profit in the main interstellar markets, so it had been looking like he'd barely cover his costs on this run. The lucrative contract to transport a rich local had been a stroke of much-needed luck; the man was happy to pay starliner prices for no-frills – and no-questions-asked – transport out-of-system. Jarek didn't habitually take passengers, and he really didn't have the space since his solo outfit had tripled in size a couple of months back, but he was unwilling to turn down such a fat fee, not with his creditors snapping at his heels.

Getting paid as much again to ship the mystery box would have been a lucky break too far.

He was overseeing the delivery of the local crafts and overpriced wines he was shipping out when Nual called, and as soon as she signed off he commed 'Sirrah Lamark' to tell him that their departure was being brought forward. Once the cargo was stowed, he went up to the *Heart of Glass*'s bridge, where he divided his attention between pre-flight checks and watching the external cameras.

A man looking uncannily like 'Apian Lamark' was apparently on the run after a bloody coup that brought down a brutal junta on Hetarey's southern continent. According to the local newsnets, the few generals at the top who had escaped the popular uprising had bought their freedom with the blood of their comrades. Still, he didn't have to like the man; he just had to get him offworld. But now Jarek knew the lengths those seeking justice for Apian Lamark's alleged crimes would go to, he had no intention of hanging around on Hetarey any longer than necessary.

His com chimed: it was Taro. 'Where are you?'

'Just coming out of customs.'

'Any sign of our guest?'

'Not yet. How d'you want to play this?'

Jarek saw movement on his cameras. The starport was a shallow bowl cut into the rock, shadow-filled in the early evening sun; two people had just emerged from the passenger departure lounge. He exhaled as they stepped into the light: yes, it was Nual and Taro. 'Get yourselves on board, but leave the 'lock open and be prepared for trouble.'

'How prepared?' asked Taro.

'Just tranq pistols. Let's not go overboard.'

'Got you.'

Nual's peek inside Medame Klirin's mind had uncovered her true affiliation: she was an agent for one of the groups who wanted Lamark dead. They called themselves 'the Hand of Truth' and they'd got hold of a comabox – which they must have disguised somehow, given anyone who travelled the stars knew what one looked like. Their plan was to put their top assassin into stasis inside it, primed to wake up while the ship was on its way out to the beacon, when he would overpower the crew and kill Lamark. If the ship in question hadn't been his, Jarek might have admired their ingenuity.

9

He looked up at movement on his cameras. Someone else was coming out of the passenger lounge: a small man with a big moustache and a ludicrous hat that looked like it was made of fabric rosettes stuck on an upturned bowl. Jarek recognised Apian Lamark from his holo. He moved with the swift care of someone who'd had experience of dodging sniper-fire.

Jarek heard Nual's shout in stereo, coming up from below and over the camera pick-ups. Lamark must have heard the warning too, for he ducked instantly. The shot was silent. It spun him around, and he fell. Then he was up again – he must be wearing body armour under that awful suit.

The second shot came almost at once. Lamark's head jerked backwards; Jarek glimpsed a spurt of red and the man dropped. Presumably the ridiculous head-gear hadn't been armoured; at any rate, it hadn't saved him.

Lamark's body jerked again, and again. Whoever was shooting wanted to be quite sure the target was dead.

Jarek tore himself away from the grisly sight. Well, that was that then.

According to his readouts the airlock had just closed. 'You two all right?' he commed down.

'We're fine,' said Taro, sounding surprisingly calm.

There was more movement outside, people running into the bowl from a side door. Jarek's hands were already moving over the control panel. The new arrivals, dressed in uniforms of some sort, started shooting at the unseen assassin. There were half a dozen of them, and they were good; the fire-fight was over in seconds.

The ship's com chimed. Jarek ignored it.

Two of the guards walked over to where the assassin's body was lying. From the spreading pool of blood it was clear to Jarek that he or she wasn't going to be shooting back. The second pair moved forward to Lamark's body. The remaining pair was heading for Jarek's ship. One of them was waving and tapping his helmet-com, trying to attract Jarek's attention.

He could activate the grav-drive safely even with people around, provided they weren't too close. So far he hadn't broken any laws, but the locals obviously wanted to question them, and that would take time he couldn't spare. He had the next run already lined up back at Perilat, and with this job blown – and any potential profit down the pan – he couldn't afford to screw that up. He'd already obtained permission to depart as soon as they had their passenger on board.

The final telltale on the panel went green.

Ah, fuck it. He pressed the slider, and the ship rose smoothly. The bridge was flooded with sunlight as they rose over the rim of the bowl and the spaceport dropped out of sight.

Jarek finally paid attention to the still-chiming com. As expected, it was the spaceport authority. His hand hovered over the board; he'd have to answer them eventually ...

He turned at a noise from behind. Taro had come up onto the bridge. He looked past Jarek at the purple sky, already darkening as they shot up into orbit. 'Oh,' he said.

'*Oh*, as in?' said Jarek, more harshly than he'd intended.

Taro spread his hands and gave a disarming smile. 'Just, "Oh, so we've left, then,"' he said, then added, 'We'll be downstairs.' He kicked off, using his flight implants to float back down through the hatch.

Jarek took a deep breath and hit *receive* on the com.

'*Heart of Glass*, you must return to the spaceport at once!'

'Sorry, Port Control, we were cleared for departure before that little fracas broke out, and we weren't going to hang around to get shot at.'

'You are material witnesses to a murder. You are required to give statements.'

'I caught some of the action on my cameras, but I'm sure you have your own, far better, surveillance footage.'

'We do: why were two of your associates watching the incident from your ship's airlock?'

Oh hell. 'Were they? In that case, I need to speak to my crew.' He forestalled any further argument by ending the call, then called down to the rec-room, 'Can you get back up here, please? Both of you.'

11

The *Heart of Glass*'s poky bridge felt crowded with all three of them crammed in. When they were settled, Jarek said, 'The locals want to speak to us – you two, mainly – about that little fuck-up down there.' He turned to Nual. 'I heard you shout just before Lamark got shot the first time; was that because you sensed the assassin?' Nual shook her head. 'No, I caught sight of the gun – just a glimpse.'

'Well, at least we can admit that.' As opposed to saying she was one of an apparently long-dead race with mental powers. Not that he ever would say that, given humanity's entirely understandable antipathy towards the Sidhe. 'If all they want is a statement, then maybe they'll let you transmit it while we're on our way out to the beacon. Then again, perhaps the place is rotten to the core and you're being set up to take the blame.'

''cos of us being Angels?' asked Taro.

'Possibly.' He sighed. Travelling with a pair of augmented assassins could be complicated, but Taro and Nual were Jarek's friends, and allies in his crusade against humanity's hidden foe. 'We can't know for sure, though.'

Nual spoke up. 'It's probably not relevant now, but I suspect that the Hand of Truth's original assassin – the one they wanted us to transport for them – wouldn't have tried to kill us, or take the ship. The impression I got was that he or she might have committed suicide once Lamark was dead, that they were willing to die to bring him to justice.'

'Ah. Shame you didn't mention that earlier; I might have still taken the job – at least we'd have been paid!'

'I communicated what I felt to be important at the time.' Nual said, a little frostily.

'No, it's not your fault – if I'd thought it through I could probably have worked that out for myself. The Hand of Truth wouldn't want to break Treaty law by killing freetraders or stealing a shiftship. This is a local matter.' It also occurred to him that even if Nual hadn't found out about the Hand of Truth's plan in advance, she might have sensed the sleeping assassin in their cargo delivery, in which case they could have decided to turn down the cargo then.

And if the assassin in the spaceport had been the Hand of Truth's back-up plan then he might still have got paid for safely transporting Lamark, instead of not getting paid for either job. Ah well, too late now. 'Right,' he concluded, 'I'm going to call the locals back and say you'll both give statements by com. We're far enough out that we're under Traffic Control's jurisdiction now, so— Oh.' He'd been keeping an eye on the sensors; they'd been clear, but now he was showing a contact.

'What is it?' asked Taro.

'Not sure. Possibly an interceptor – in which case we're screwed. I need to make that call.'

The coms light was still on, and the incoming call was indeed from Traffic Control. Jarek spoke over them. 'Hetarey TC, this is the *Heart of Glass*. We're happy to provide the authorities down there with full statements, but we'd rather not have to return dirtside; as I'm sure you understand, we are running on a tight schedule.' He didn't mention the possible pursuit; let them bring that up. Or not, ideally.

'*Heart of Glass*, are you not intending to return?'

'Well, no. As I say, we can—'

'You are unaware of your own change of status, then?

Uh-oh. 'What change of status would that be, TC?'

'After your precipitous departure, we beeveed the Freetraders' Alliance. Would you like to know what they told us?'

Jarek bit back his instinctive response to this latest stupid question, and said, 'Yes. Please.'

'The Alliance's legal department informed us that a repossession order for your ship has just been issued.'

'What? Who from?' Not that this development was such a surprise, under the circumstances.

'The Veryan Syndicate.'

Yeah, it would be that lot; they've got the money and the clout. 'That's bad news for me, obviously, but I can't see how it changes the local situation,' he said as evenly as he could.

'Shall I explain? The claimant organisation has invoked Treaty law against you. Given your recent actions, we will be honouring their request to detain you and take possession of your ship pending arrival of their representative.'

Over my vacuum-frozen corpse you will. 'You don't have to go to any trouble, right?' No doubt the Veryans were paying the locals well for the 'favour' of detaining Jarek. Sadly, it was all perfectly legal.

'Captain Reen, must we point out the interceptor which we recently despatched?' Jarek didn't dignify that with an answer, and the traffic controller continued, 'Were you thinking of doing anything drastic? We hope not: we believe the Veryan rep has alerted both of the systems on transit-paths from Hetarey. They have someone awaiting you at both destinations, whichever one you shift to.'

'The Veryans are certainly being thorough.' He couldn't blame them; shiftships were rare, and any one-ship trading outfit foolish enough to go as deep into the red as he'd fallen could expect a larger rival to make a play for their 'bird.

'Shall I tell them that you'll be returning to Hetarey? And as a gesture of goodwill would you like us to put you and your crew up while we wait for the syndicate representative? That should give you all ample opportunity to submit full statements regarding the incident at the spaceport.'

And quite possibly get shafted for it. 'I'll get back to you,' Jarek said cheerily, and cut the connection. He turned to see Taro and Nual looking meaningfully at each other. 'Er, you got all that, I assume?'

'If we cooperate, what then?' asked Nual.

'Well, if we can come up with enough credit – *somehow* – we could contest the Veryan Syndicate's claim, but that'll involve several months in court on the hub of their choosing, during which time we'll be stuck without a ship.'

'And we got better things to do,' said Taro.

'We certainly have. The mission's well and truly fucked without the *Heart of Glass*.'

'Then there's only one option,' stated Nual.

'Ah. You mean … that.' Jarek looked down for a moment, to indicate the drive column directly below the bridge.

Taro nodded; they'd obviously already discussed this, in their own unique way.

'You're sure?' asked Jarek. 'Last time was pretty hairy.'

Nual said, 'I don't think we have any choice.'

CHAPTER THREE

They came on Midsummer's night.

Kerin found herself suddenly awake, opening her eyes to an irregular white radiance that washed out the lamplight. And there was a strange noise, *peep-peep-peep ...*

She realised what was happening, and looked groggily at the screen on the far side of the room which was the source of the glow, pulsing in time to the insistent alarm. That screen had been dark and silent for three weeks now, ever since her otherworldly husband had gone back to the sky. For a moment she dared to hope that he had returned, but in her heart, she knew otherwise.

She got up and shuffled over to the console. The display meant little to her, though it showed too many words for this to be a simple request for contact, and that made her worry even more. She blinked away the after-images of bright text and walked quickly back across the room to the other bed, narrowly avoiding kicking the chamber-pot sticking out from under it.

'Damaru,' she said urgently, 'wake up please!'

When her son made no response she shook him gently.

He batted at her hand, then opened one eye.

'Damaru, you have to get up. Something is happening to the console.'

He gave an irritated grunt, but began to wriggle free of the covers.

Kerin knew he would do as she asked; however awkward her skytouched child might be when faced with day-to-day tasks, he would never turn down the chance to play with this wonderful new technology.

She went over to the clothes-stand and pulled on the ornate black and silver robe hanging there. She began to work her feet into the specially made shoes with their built-up soles before deciding she did not have the time for that; at this time of the night the guard would be at least as sleepy as she was; he was unlikely to notice such fine details as her height. She fastened the robe, then carefully lifted down the crown-like headdress, wincing as she took the weight of its precious metal and cunningly hidden technology on her injured arm. She settled the headdress on her head and, suitable attired, left the room, pulling the veil across her face as she hurried down the short passage to the cavernous audience chamber. The light-globes studding the lower walls of the great domed hall were at half-brightness; she had similar artefacts in her own room, though she rarely used them – Damaru slept better in natural light, and was less likely to disassemble oil-lamps when he was bored.

In the dim light Kerin could just make out the half-asleep monitor on the far side of the room, leaning against the wall by the bronze doors. She smiled in sympathy as she saw the way his head drooped on his chest, then put her natural self to one side.

'You!' she called out imperiously. 'Fetch Escori Urien, *now*!'

He actually jumped, and Kerin felt amused contrition. 'A— At once, Divinity,' he stammered. He traced the circle over his breast and bowed low before turning to tug open one of the doors.

As soon as the monitor left, Kerin strode up to the throne and reached round to press a button under the armrest. In the blink of an eye, a narrow metal bridge sprang into place across the chasm that divided the rock-hewn chamber in two, separating the mundane far side from the 'divine' space she inhabited.

When she returned to her room Damaru was not sitting in the cunningly designed turning seat in front of the console, but was kneeling beside it. He had pulled off part of the casing and had one hand deep in the console's innards. There was no point in telling him to stop; he had an instinctive, almost mystical, ability to understand and control complex devices, a talent Sais had called 'machine empathy'. He knew what he was doing far better than she.

She breathed, 'Is it a message?', still hoping that it was Sais, here to lend his advice and share his knowledge. The power Kerin had had thrust upon her already weighed heavily.

She was not surprised when Damaru did not answer her. He had more important concerns than listening to his mother. The screen display had changed now: there was still a line of flashing text in the top half, but below that she saw an ever-shifting mass of words and numbers. She looked back at the original message and tried to work out what it said. Urien said she was a quick student, but her duties left her little time to study; in the scant weeks that he had been teaching her to read she had managed to do little more than memorise the letters and recognise her own name. The first letter of this message was an 'R'; the second 'E'; then 'J'. After that … it would be easier if she could get closer and trace the words with a finger, but that risked disturbing Damaru.

He was leaning over the missing panel, his head almost inside the console, muttering to himself. Suddenly he knelt up and stared at the screen. He used his free hand to follow some of the fast-moving patterns and began muttering louder. Then he scowled and looked away. He went back to concentrating on the mess of lights and filaments in the guts of the machine.

Kerin sighed to herself. Though she had tried to explain why Damaru must learn his letters, he showed little interest in such dry study. He had examined the console before, spending several days at the task immediately after Sais left. Damaru had an instinctive love of technology, but he also understood the need to prevent the return of those who had originally put the console in the Tyr. Although there was but this one controlling machine in the whole land, it used the silver thread to speak to the many other devices far above. Hard though it was still to fathom this, Sais had assured them that some of these observed; some allowed communication between the land and the sky; and others were powerful weapons that the world's former rulers had put in place in order to see off unwelcome visitors.

Damaru's initial investigations had been unfocused; in truth, he had most likely been indulging himself, playing, and exploring the device. Whereas now—

Kerin started at the knock on the door, then called, 'Is that you, Urien? Come in.' Not that it could be anyone besides the Escori of Frythil. No one else would dare enter the 'holy' presence.

Urien looked tired, the lines on his thin face etched deeper than ever. He wore his usual priestly robes, and Kerin wondered in passing how late – or early – it was.

'Ah,' he said, on seeing the console lit up. He strode over and Kerin moved to one side. He put his hands on the back of the seat and leant forward to read the text. When he turned to Kerin his expression was one of bitter amusement. 'The main message says: "Rejoice, for your goddess will soon be reborn". Hmm. Rejoice? I doubt that very much.'

'At least they appear not to know of the changes that have occurred here.' Kerin was impressed at how calm she sounded. Now she knew the Sidhe really were back, a cold ball of fear had settled deep inside her.

'For which we should be thankful.' To whom, Urien did not say – after all, their gods had proved false, not loving and divine 'Skymothers' but mortal oppressors. He continued, 'We knew they would return. Sais told us this place is of great value to them.'

'Aye,' said Kerin shortly. The fear was tinged with nausea now as she thought about why the Sidhe cultivated and controlled her world. She shook off the thought. 'Do you have any idea what the rest of the display means?'

'It is mainly numbers, though there are a few words and odd phrases. It changes very fast, as you see, but I will try and make some sense of it … there are words and phrases that keep repeating. See, that one there: "authorisation confirmed". And this … "orbital defence override". '

'I think they are trying to turn off the weapons! The weapons in the sky – Sais said that when the Sidhe come they must – ah – send something – an *override code* – because otherwise the sky-weapons will destroy them.'

'I think you may be right,' said Urien grimly. Then his expression changed. 'Wait! Look—' He pointed to a new message, which was repeated three times. 'Request denied,' Urien read for her.

'Does that mean the Sidhe's attempt to override the weapons has failed?'

'That is what it looks like to me. It appears we may yet see off those who would reclaim our world for themselves.'

Kerin felt a fierce grin pull at her face. Her miraculous sky-touched son was fighting the unseen battle for them, and he was winning. She wanted to throw her arms around him, though she knew better than to interrupt him when he was busy.

The alarm, which Kerin had almost managed to forget, died in mid-*peep*.

Urien was frowning at the screen. The display had changed again: the original message was gone, to be replaced with moving words and numbers.

Damaru snorted; he was angry at having been thwarted.

'What is it?' she whispered urgently.

Urien, still focused on the screen, must have assumed she was speaking to him. 'I think … There is an error. A – a lost connection of some sort.' He sounded unsure.

Desperately she asked her son, 'Damaru, have you still got control? Are the sky-weapons doing your bidding?'

Damaru grunted, obviously annoyed, but said nothing.

Kerin had a sudden, foolish desire to grab his shoulders, but she forced herself to stay calm and silent.

'It keeps repeating the same message,' said Urien, '"Contact lost"; oh wait, there is another message appearing now: "Platform status unknown" – and then the words "All Units", which keep flashing. By the Adversary, I wish I knew what all this meant!'

'Gone.' They both jumped when Damaru spoke. He sounded forlorn.

'What is gone, Damaru?' asked Kerin, trying to keep her voice soft and low. 'Are— Have the visitors gone?' Please let that be so, she hoped silently, please let those evil creatures be dead and destroyed in the vast beyond, so those below may remain free.

'No,' said Damaru.

'They are still coming, then?' asked Urien. 'What is the contact that has been lost?'

Damaru did not appear to hear the Escori. Kerin crouched down next to her child and laid a hand on his arm. 'Please, can you tell us what has happened, Damaru? Have you succeeded, my lovely boy? Have you turned the Sidhe's weapons on them?'

'No,' he said again, 'cannot see the rock throwers!' He sounded peeved.

Kerin said patiently, 'I do not know what these rock throwers are, Damaru. Can you tell us?'

Damaru sighed, as though she were the fool. 'Throwers of rocks. In the sky. To destroy!'

Urien said, 'Kerin, you said Sais compared the sky-weapons to great crossbows: could they perhaps fire rocks instead of quarrels?'

'Aye, I think they could. Is that it, Damaru? Are the rock throwers the sky-weapons?'

'Aye.'

'And you cannot see them any more? What does that mean, precisely?'

'Not in the pattern. Gone.'

Urien said, 'Are you saying you have lost contact? That you can no longer observe or control the weapons?'

Damaru looked up, as though noticing the Escori for the first time. 'Aye,' he said tetchily, then went back to staring into the machine.

'Could that mean they have done their work?' asked Kerin, not wanting to let go of hope.

Damaru shrugged.

'Can you still talk to the watching devices, Damaru?' asked Urien. 'Do you know if there is anyone out there now? Or have the weapons destroyed them?'

'I will look again.' Damaru's already unfocused gaze grew

vaguer; from the way the muscles in his wiry arm were flexing Kerin could imagine his fingers moving deep in the arcane device. Finally he said, 'They still come.'

Kerin felt the cold fear expand to knock at her heart. 'Can—Can you do anything, Damaru?'

'I try to grasp the cutting light,' he announced.

'And what is that, Damaru?'

Damaru gestured vaguely upwards with his free hand, shaking off Kerin in the process. 'Above us, the cutting light on the silver thread!'

Kerin considered asking for further explanation, then thought better of it. 'And can this cutting light destroy the Sidhe?' she asked.

'Aye.' But he did not sound sure.

'I know you can do it,' she said firmly, though she was not.

He wrinkled his nose and sucked in his lips; the expression might have been comical, but Kerin knew it meant he was concentrating as hard as he could.

Kerin drew back. She turned to Urien. 'We should leave him to work.'

Urien nodded tersely. 'Aye.' He was still watching the screen, which appeared to have frozen in place.

Kerin wished she had some idea whether this was a good sign or not. She made herself stand up straight and take a step back, though her legs felt weak and shaky.

If Damaru did not succeed, then the Sidhe would descend the silver thread and enslave her world again. Though she feared them beyond reason, she would not run. She would face them here, in what had been the heart of their power. She would arm herself as best she could, and do everything possible to hurt them before they killed her. She had killed a Sidhe once, and though that memory still haunted her, she hated them enough to do so again. But she must send Damaru away first – if she could persuade him to leave without her.

She realised she was wringing her hands. Cursing her foolishness, she made herself stop, and smoothed them down the side of her robes instead.

22

If Damaru did stay, he could help— No, he must live; though she might fail and die, his life must go on!

Her palms stung; she had been pressing them down repeatedly on her thighs, hard enough to make heat.

The screen went blank, fading all at once to featureless grey. Kerin looked to Urien, his face unclear in the soft lamplight.

'I have no idea what that means,' he murmured.

More time passed, and Kerin forced herself to stay calm and silent. Nothing she could do or say would help now. It was all up to Damaru.

Eventually, Damaru drew his hand out of the device and straightened slowly; he looked exhausted. Kerin reached out to help, but he shrugged her off.

'What has happened, Damaru?' asked Urien.

'All done.' He sounded satisfied, or possibly he was just too tired to care.

'That is good,' said Kerin, responding to his tone, rather than the content. 'What of the Sidhe, Damaru?'

When he turned to her his eyes were still unfocused, but he was smiling his secret, clever smile. 'They burn,' he said.

CHAPTER FOUR

Perhaps, thought Jarek, *shiftspace is hell* – not the Salvatine hell, of eternal and creative punishment, because however much the shift messed with your head during a transit, everything went back to normal as soon as you dropped back into realspace. Physically, the worst he'd ever experienced in the shift had been weird bodily sensations – pins and needles, itchy skin, feelings of emptiness, or bloated guts.

He found himself briefly distracted by this transit's Persistent Illusion. He managed to turn his head away, and found his blurred vision falling on the bridge controls, all safely disabled for the transit, though still sparkling a little, as objects often did in the shift.

No, what he meant by— He caught the thought he'd been chasing: *what he meant by shiftspace being hell* … What he meant was that it made you think about the dead, and thinking about them could make you believe they were there, *with you* in the shift. Which explained why he kept seeing his sister out of the corner of his eye. She looked faintly disapproving, or perhaps disappointed. At least she wasn't trying to talk to him. He risked another look over at her and said, 'I wish you could've forgiven me.' His voice sounded flat and small, like he was talking through a cheap com. The Persistent Illusion gave no sign of having heard him.

It made sense – as much as anything did right now – that he'd see Elarn. After all, they were heading for the place where she'd died. He tried to control his wandering thoughts by recalling the number of transits there should be between the Hetarey and

Tri-Confed systems. He soon gave up: though trying to remember cold facts distracted him from the Illusion, it also reminded him that what they were doing right now (if there is a 'now' here … or a 'here' here— *Stop that and focus, damnit!*) was meant to be impossible. The only other time Taro and Nual had shifted point-to-point it had seriously messed them up, and they'd only missed out a couple of transits that time. The Confederacy of Three was in a whole different sector. He tried to force his thoughts away from the more unpleasant possibilities – *the transit never ends, we come out inside a star, we come out inside-out—* but ended up thinking about the third component of the strange trinity currently propelling them through the un-universe of shiftspace: nameless and mad, *the darkness in the heart*, as Nual had once called it. No, not *it*. Him. And unlike his passengers, that individual was far from unique. *Oh Elarn, if only you'd known just how vile and insidious the Sidhe's influence really is—*

The thought was snatched away, and he found himself staring at the console again. It was no longer sparkling, and suddenly he felt heavy, coherent, *real*.

They were out of the shift.

Jarek twitched and shuddered. He felt the expected wash of exhaustion and its accompanying post-transit headache, but it was no worse than usual. Compared to the first time they'd pulled this stunt it was looking like he'd got off lightly. He smiled to himself; maybe bypassing the rules of interstellar navigation got easier with practice.

Like dying, dreaming …

… like waking, remembering.

The void was gone.

Taro became aware of his body, and of the weight of Nual's body against it. Against *him*. This was *him*: one body; one mind. He was himself again: just himself.

Nual wasn't quite conscious yet, but even though she'd've had a worse time of it, he knew she'd be all right. Without opening his eyes he turned and kissed the top of her head. She was the one who'd forced the ship's transit-kernel to make an impossible leap through shiftspace, though she could do it only by drawing on his strength – which he gave freely, of course.

But it left him so fucking tired. He let himself drift towards sleep.

'Water?'

'Uh …' Taro opened his eyes to see Jarek standing over them, a drinking bulb in his hand. He reached out to take it. 'Thanks.' He took a long pull himself, then pressed it into Nual's hands, sending a silent query her way.

<I can manage, thanks.> Nual's voice was clear in his mind, though her hands were shaking when she lifted the bulb.

'I don't think it was as bad that time,' said Jarek, hopefully. When Taro didn't comment he added, 'How're you two doing?'

Taro thought Jarek didn't look too grim, though he was gripping the back of the ladder up to the bridge for support; Nual had insisted they sat up against the drive column before going into shiftspace, to get as close as possible to the transit-kernel. 'Oh, we're just top prime,' he rasped. 'How's the ship?' The first time they'd done this, Jarek hadn't had time to do a proper shutdown, and they'd paid the price when they came back into realspace. They were learning.

'Everything came up clean.'

'Thank fuck for that. And we're in the Tri-Confed system?'

'That's what the navcomp tells me – as do local Traffic Control.'

Taro managed a weak grin. 'Bet they were surprised to see us.'

'Oh yes.'

'What'd you tell them?'

'I said we came in from Mystil, and had to leave in a bit of a hurry.'

'That's …' Taro searched his memory; though this was his home system, he'd spent his first seventeen years in the mazeways of the Undertow, the slum below Khesh City. He still didn't know very much about the universe outside. He compromised with, 'That's a pretty smoky system, ain't it?'

'Yep, just the kind of place where the rules sometimes get by-passed by reckless traders. Of course, they might want to check my story ... and they'll definitely want to fine us for such a reckless arrival – which is why I need you on the bridge as soon as you can manage it, I'm afraid.'

'Don't suppose I've got time for a caf?' he asked a little plaintively.

'You can have caf, sleep, whatever you want, once you've made contact with——?' Jarek searched for the right word.

'Khesh,' supplied Taro, 'though it's the Minister who'll probably meet us.'

'Right. Khesh.'

'Just give us a moment,' said Taro, and silently asked Nual, <*You're really all right?*>

<*I'm really all right. Go.*>

Taro untangled himself and Jarek stood back as he activated his implants to let him float up the ladder onto the bridge, where he folded himself into the pilot's couch. He took a moment to clear the last remnant of sleep from his head, then looked at Jarek for permission to com out. At his nod, Taro cleared his throat and announced, 'Tri-Confed TC, this is the *Heart of Glass*.'

The image of a female Traffic Control officer appeared on the holoplate in front of him. She looked impatient, and mildly confused. 'Thank you for finally responding, *Heart of Glass*. Are you aware that you do not have sufficient funds to pay the fine for your unscheduled transit?'

'We don't?' Taro favoured her with the best *Who, me?* look he could manage with a shiftspace hangover. 'Then we'd better do something about that.'

'Yes, you had. To whom am I speaking?'

'I'm Taro sanMalia – hang on, I'll append my ID.' He quickly checked it was his real-and-genuine(ish) one before comming it over. 'Could you do me a favour and connect me to Sirrah Emet Krand on Vellern, please,' he added, politely.

'Sirrah Krand?' The officer's expression hardened. 'The High Speaker of the Vellern Assembly?'

'That's the one. He'll clear this up for us.'

'I seriously doubt that.'

'I can see how you might think that, but I can assure you he'll sort this out. I'm asking you to connect us rather than using the comnet and having to, erm, reverse the charges.' Taro sounded like he really didn't want to inconvenience anyone.

'Well, Sirrah sanMalia – and without meaning to be rude – I'd say that the chance of a near-bankrupt adolescent freetrader getting through to one of the most powerful men on Vellern without an appointment or good reason is slightly less than your ship's chances of not getting impounded for non-payment of fines. However, we're having quiet day here, so I'll see what I can do.'

Taro could see she was suppressing a smile. Must be a quiet day there – although if what Jarek had told him was right, they'd probably have to make their own fun out there a lot of the time. Tri-Confed was a high-population system, not just a lone settled world, and their shiftspace beacon was a long way out from the primary. The locals had built a station near the beacon to run their interstellar traffic; he guessed the Traffic Control posting wasn't the most exciting of assignments.

'I'm going to put you on hold while I make the call; please don't cut the connection, as I still need to discuss that fine with Captain Reen.' The image froze.

Taro swivelled round and grinned at Jarek. 'I love it when they call me "Sirrah".'

'That's not what they'll be calling you if this "High Speaker" doesn't want to talk to you.'

'Don't worry, he will.' Taro hoped he sounded confident; though Vellern was no longer his home, he was owed a debt there, a massive debt that couldn't be ignored. Nual was too, of course – and she might've had a better chance of getting through to the people they needed, if she'd had her shit together and not been so screwed up after the shift. After all, she'd been an Angel for the seven years she'd spent on Vellern, one of the Concord's most notorious and valued assassins; he was just a local boy made good who'd only got his Angel implants just before he left the City. But Nual was also

28

known to the Sidhe – hell, they'd been willing to fuck up an entire city to kill her – while Taro had managed to stay below their notice so far.

After what felt like several minutes the image on the holoplate unfroze and flickered to show an elderly man with a high forehead and an expression of frank surprise. 'Back already?' he said. 'I hope you haven't got yourselves into trouble. Or if you have, I hope you haven't brought it with you.'

Taro shook his head. 'No trouble, Sirrah, but we'd like to ask a favour.'

'Really? Well spit it out then.'

'Well, the main favour—' He paused, then said, 'I think it's better if we come and meet you.'

'When you say *me*—?'

'The Minister,' Taro said decisively. 'He'd be the best one.'

'Yes, he would. And he will meet you when you arrive – but you hardly needed to call me out of a briefing session with my senior Consuls to arrange that!'

'No, Sirrah, it's just that we arrived here a bit unexpected-like, and there's fines and questions and shit – stuff—'

'And so you need me to ensure you have a smooth passage in from the beacon, without any unnecessary problems with Traffic Control or Customs? I see.'

'That'd be good, if you don't mind, Sirrah.'

'It can be arranged.'

'And the fine?'

'Good grief, boy! I'm not your father, you know.'

'Well, no – I never had one of them. But it's only credit, ain't it?'

'All right, all right, I will deal with it. Put me through to the young lady who placed the original comcall so I can explain the situation to her.'

Taro smiled to himself: he wouldn't've minded listening in to that particular conversation.

*

Jarek's grand plan was always going to entail a visit to Khesh City, but none of them had expected it to be this soon. When he wasn't asleep, Taro spent most of the two full days it took to get there – Vellern was the system's innermost planet – getting his feelings about his former homeworld sorted in his head.

The cabin he shared with Nual had been stripped down, and it was filled with the luggage of their late, unlamented almost-passenger, but both of them were too tired to care about being surrounded by a dead man's gear. Once they'd slept off the excesses of their shift fatigue, they got their room straight, which took up most of the rest of the journey. That was fine by Taro; if he hadn't been lugging boxes for Nual, he'd have been cleaning the rec-room as it was his turn. This was infinitely preferable.

Jarek kept an eye on local news and com traffic, but he didn't report any problems. Now they were back in the heart of human-space beevee calls were cheaper, and Jarek took advantage of that to talk to media agents and lawyers about a part of their plan that wasn't going to kick in until further down the line – if at all. Taro couldn't see much point, himself, but he wasn't worried about Jarek drawing unwelcome attention – no one who was looking for them could possibly expect them to have turned up in this system. Not that he said anything: it was Jarek's look-out if he wanted to waste his time like that.

Once they were in orbit around Vellern Taro came up to the bridge. The holoplate showed a barren orange dust-ball; only two of the Three Cities were visible from here, tiny specks dotted around the otherwise featureless surface. Taro couldn't tell which one was Khesh.

They would have to leave the ship docked at an orbital platform and take a tourist shuttle down; the Cities were set up to get the tourists in and out again quickly and efficiently, minus as much of their available credit as they could legally extract.

As they waited for final clearance, Nual gave Jarek a last chance to change his mind about coming dirtside. 'It's not a problem; we can ask on your behalf if you'd rather not come down,' she said.

Jarek grinned. 'No, I'm fine leaving *Heart of Glass* here. I went into freetrading to see exotic places, and they don't get much more exotic than this.'

Taro wondered whether 'exotic' meant the crazy politics, or the secret hidden deep inside each of the Three Cities that citizens and visitors alike remained happily oblivious to. Possibly both.

Taro had spent some time preparing for his return to his birth-place. He wanted to make sure he looked the part. He plaited himself a choker of red and black, and wove the same colours into his remaining long dreadlocks. On the shuttle down, the tourists looked at him oddly; Taro was annoyed that more of them mut-tered about *downsiders* than *Angels*. Ignorant coves.

The shuttle took them to a huge domed hall, the only part of the City outside its protective force-bubble, where they queued for one of the dozens of elevators that carried the tourists down the City's central spine onto the massive floating disc itself. It was early evening, and from their transparent car the Streets radiating out from the spine looked like rivers of multi-coloured light.

Taro couldn't get enough of the view. There it was, his home, impressive as ever – just a lot smaller than he remembered it.

When they got to the bottom, they discovered Sirrah Krand had done as he'd promised. Customs didn't give them any shit – though they couldn't hide their amazement at finding Angels – who never normally left the City – coming back to it. The three of them emerged into the crowded transit hall, which was exactly how Taro remembered it, bright with adverts and loud with the cries of hustlers.

Taro led Nual and Jarek to the exit, feeling a strange mix of pride and anxiety. They came out onto a pleasant square over-hung by trees decorated with gently glowing orange and golden light-globes strung through their branches. A queue of pedicabs, adorned with the usual lights and trinkets, waited along one side of the square. No one had been in touch with them, so they'd agreed Taro would lead them to a Street he knew and they would take it from there. They could get a cab, except they'd need two, and it was a nice evening – it was always a nice evening in the City – so there was no reason not to walk, or even fly—

31

Almost automatically, Taro found himself looking up at the heavily-built man strolling towards them. He wore a smart suit, and sported the usual stylish but unnecessary hat on his bald head.

'Good evening,' he said, and Taro felt a faint shiver – of what, he wasn't quite sure – at the familiar sound of that deep, mellow voice.

'Sirrah,' he said. Old habits died hard.

Nual inclined her head a fraction.

Jarek, looking uncomfortable, said, 'I take it you're the Minister.'

'I am.' He gave Jarek a long, hard look, then smiled. People who didn't know better might even call it a friendly, welcoming smile. 'And you must be Elarn Reen's brother, Jarek.'

CHAPTER FIVE

Jarek had met killers before, and he'd met aliens – hell, he *travelled* with one – but his experience with Heads of State was limited. The Minister was all three, and more. Despite his avuncular exterior, he – Jarek decided to think of the Minister as *he*, in the absence of any more suitable term – exuded an air of hidden menace. People really did live or die at his word.

After a moment, he realised the Minister actually expected an answer. 'Er, yes. Pleased to meet you.' He waited to see if the Minister offered his hand, and was relieved when he didn't.

'Your sister was a fool,' said the Minister conversationally, as casually as if he was discussing the nonexistent weather, 'but she didn't deserve to die like that.'

<That's his way of saying he's sorry for your loss.>

Jarek started at Nual's voice in his head; she used mindspeech sparingly with him as she knew he found it disconcerting. 'Thanks,' he said out loud.

'We may as well talk here,' continued the Minister. 'We won't be disturbed.' He steered them to three benches made out of what looked like real wood, set around a planter overflowing with flowers, some of which glowed pallid blue in the dusk. He sat down on the bench at the back. Jarek took one of the side seats, Nual and Taro the other.

The Minister turned to the other two. 'You both look well,' he said. 'Short hair suits you, Nual.'

When no one immediately responded to this unexpected comment, the Minister affected a sigh. 'Small talk,' he said drily. 'I had

33

understood it to be very popular amongst humans.'

'Er—' said Taro, looking between the Minister and Jarek.

'Oh come on, boy!' said the Minister sharply. 'Obviously Captain Reen knows what I am – Nual would never have let him come down here otherwise, would she?'

No one had an answer for that, and the Minister continued, 'To be honest, I am impressed they have already got themselves an ally. You must have loved your sister deeply if you are willing to go to such lengths to avenge her death, Captain Reen.'

'Elarn is one of my reasons for fighting the Sidhe.' He was pleased he managed to avoid tripping over that last word.

The Minister raised an eyebrow, but he didn't ask for clarification, and Jarek reminded himself that whatever else he might be, the 'man' sitting across from him couldn't read their minds.

'So, what brings you back to our fair city in such a tearing hurry?' The Minister addressed the question to Nual.

'We need a beacon,' she said bluntly.

'A beacon? As in a shiftspace beacon?'

'Yes.'

He sounded a little intrigued. 'Now why would you suddenly want such a thing?'

Jarek took over the conversation. 'We – or rather, *I* – found a lost world, one where the inhabitants have no idea the rest of the universe exists. I can't find any record of the place, not in the Freetrader Archives, nor in any of the public Salvatine datastores.'

'Ah,' said the Minister. 'And you think the *females* kept the existence of this world from humanity?' He pronounced the word 'females' like a curse.

'I know they did.' Jarek hoped the Minister wouldn't ask why … Of course, he might already know—

'And presumably this lost world has no beacon?'

'That's right.' Jarek said shortly. It was bad enough knowing the Minister was the head of the City's league of assassins. That he was also a representative – or more accurately, a fragment – of a thousand-year-old male Sidhe consciousness made Jarek feel faintly queasy. Whilst the Khesh City mind could be an incredibly useful ally in their fight, it – *he* – was not someone to be messed around with, or confided in.

'So you wish to plant a beacon there to bring these people into the fold of human-space?' said the Minister, sounding faintly curious.

'Right again.'

'How charmingly idealistic. And it would be massively annoying to the females, of course.' His tone made it obvious which reason he preferred. 'Just what makes you think I might be able to help with this noble mission of yours?'

Jarek swallowed, and said, 'Zepgen.'

'Zepgen. Ah yes, that. What about zepgen?'

Nual took over, and pointing to herself, said, 'You put zepgen in us – in your Angels – to power our gravitics.'

'Why yes, so I do. And how exactly did you come to find that out, then?' Now he was definitely curious.

'A corporation on another world had their suspicions and decided to experiment,' she said.

'On me,' Taro chipped in.

The Minister looked Taro up and down, appraising him. 'You appear to have survived the experience.'

'Yeah, just about – thanks to Jarek,' Taro said, sounding a bit grumpy.

The Minister ignored Taro's little show of pique. 'So, you know that I have access to a small, near-limitless power-source that can be implanted in humans. It also powers all this.' He gestured proprietarily around him at the shadowy trees, the buildings beyond and the distant orange glow of the City's forcedome. 'But beacons ... well, they're a rather different proposition.'

'But they are powered by zepgen.' Jarek resisted the temptation to add, *aren't they?* He was sure he was right, or near enough.

'Well, not exactly. Zepgen is a system for drawing power from ... *elsewhere*. It can only be initiated by a certain type of mind, one capable of reaching outside the universe.' Jarek knew that male Sidhe could do that. 'A beacon is more of a gateway, a door left permanently ajar. That's a much more complex and dangerous artefact.'

'But still something you – your people – do. *Did*. For humanity, to help fight the females.'

'Yes, we did,' the Minister agreed with a slight smile. 'But that was a thousand years ago.'

'Can you still do it?'

The Minister said nothing for several seconds. The trees around the square remained still as a picture. Jarek could hear a faint hum, presumably that of the crowded streets beyond. Finally the Minister said, 'We need to consider this.' Jarek noted the use of *we*, the first time the Minister had used the word. 'I have taken the liberty of booking you into a hotel; just ask any of those burly individuals over there to take you to the Cracked Emerald on Memento Street. Please do not worry about paying for the hotel; as Taro so elegantly put it: "it's only credit".'

At that, Taro chimed in, 'Yeah, actually, we did have another problem that could be solved with credit—'

'I know.' He stood up as he spoke, making it quite clear he had no interest in prolonging the conversation. 'I will be in touch in due course.' And with that, the Minister walked off into the gloom.

'Is he always like that?' asked Jarek.

'Oh no,' replied Taro lightly, 'sometimes he can be pretty fucking irritating.'

'Nual, I don't suppose you—?'

'I can't read him, Jarek, not at all. He is— What we actually interact with is a flesh golem that holds part of Khesh's distributed consciousness.'

'Ah. When you put it like that—' When she put it like that, it was damn creepy. 'Thanks for trying to ask whether he'd loan us enough to stave off the bloody Veryan Syndicate, Taro.'

'Worth a shot.'

'We should probably get going; it'll be dark soon.'

Jarek turned to the rank of cabs, but Taro said, 'We can walk to Memento Street; it ain't far from here.'

'Is that a good idea?' Jarek wasn't sure; the Three Cities had a terrible rep for street crime.

Taro turned and gestured at himself with both hands, inviting

Jarek to take in his clothes. 'City colours,' he said, 'and *who* wears City colours?'

'Ah yes – Angels.'

'S'right. And around here, people know not to mess with us Angels.'

Taro led them along a gently curving street with parkland on one side and buildings on the other. Larger roads radiated off every hundred metres or so, some smart boulevards, gated to keep out the riff-raff, others hosting outdoor parties of varying degrees of wildness. Memento Street, when they found it, fell somewhere between the two extremes.

The crowd on the Street was largely made up of tourists; many of them looked like out-of-system types rich enough to afford to travel on a starliner. A lot had bodyguards with them. The locals were easy to spot; they tended to be compact and dark, though there were also representatives of the other two cultures of the Confederacy of Three. One ethnic group had jewels stuck on – no, *embedded in* – the skin of their hands, while others were pale–skinned, with light brown or blond hair.

Jarek didn't see any other Angels, but he did spot a few down-siders. They were conspicuous, not just because of their height, but due to their dress; they wore ill-fitting, ragged clothes, obviously cast-offs, and they hung around the darker alleyways, begging, hustling or hassling. They moved with the shuffling, careful gait of people in heavier gravity than they were used to. Most of the tourists were avoiding them. He noticed how Taro was enjoying the double-takes as people moved from wary distrust at the first sight of his height and build to what Jarek interpreted as cautious awe at his easy walk and stylish clothes.

Though the full red-and-black of Khesh City was reserved for Angels, a lot of people wore tokens – broaches, armbands, hair ornaments and the like – showing the colours of 'their' City. The paler-skinned types, from Yazil, displayed gold and green, while the jewelled lot from Luorna sported blue and silver.

Nual had told them the other two cities were run in the same way as Khesh, and now Jarek asked if that was what the Minister had meant when he'd said *we*: the other two Cities.

She smiled grimly, and said, 'No, the Concord is far more important than any one human's request, however unexpected.'

'So do the Yazil and Luorna City-minds even know their brother City let a renegade Sidhe hide here?'

'I doubt it,' she said quietly. 'These three males have lived in a ritualised state of near-war for centuries – I don't think they'd know how to begin to trust each other.'

So the *we* in question must have meant the other avatars of Khesh's controlling mind, like the High Speaker, thought Jarek. Which was quite weird enough.

The buildings along Memento Street were low-rise but flashy, a mixture of hotels, restaurants, bars and clubs. Nual said this Street had a historical theme, which was why they were surrounded by unfamiliar cultural references, from the cartoon dogs in suits dancing holographic jigs above their heads to the projected images of women with curvaceous bodies and veiled faces.

Some buildings had damage to their façades, presumably as a result of the upheavals caused by the Sidhe weapon. Jarek suppressed a shudder: Elarn, under the influence of the Sidhe's mental programming, had nearly killed the City, and she had lost her own life in the process. If Taro hadn't been in the right place at the right time, she would have succeeded in destroying Khesh completely.

Despite the name, the Cracked Emerald showed no visible damage. The hotel was all gaudy floral décor and green and red cut-glass, though the rooms were clean and relatively spacious. Jarek was happy to sacrifice taste for comfort, especially when someone else was picking up the tab. After confirming that they could bill the meal to their account, they had a leisurely dinner in the hotel restaurant. Though the food beat ship's rations, Jarek felt it left something to be desired. Nual pointed out caustically that, like the *Heart of Glass*'s own mess, the City was a closed environment, where everything had to be recycled.

Jarek usually tried to sync his body-clock to local time before landing, but because this trip had been unplanned, they'd ended up out of kilter, and the three of them found themselves wide awake just when everyone else was calling it a night. Jarek had no doubt Nual and Taro had pleasant alternatives to sleep, but he was reduced to channel-surfing a wide variety of trash, all that was available on the local holonet. He ended up watching some political channel, which was full of ratings, gossip and predictions of which members of the Assembly might incur the people's disapproval enough to get 'removed' by an Angel. The subtleties were lost on him, and he couldn't help thinking how macabre this set-up was – especially knowing that the whole thing was overseen and quite possibly manipulated by an eccentric, effectively immortal, alien. He was beginning to get the impression the mind at the heart of Khesh City looked upon those living within its bounds as something between wayward pets and a gigantic social experiment.

Finally he gave up and decided to go for a walk. The hotel staff were happy to provide him with a guard – all part of the service, apparently – but he took his gun as well. Better safe than sorry.

The bodyguard, a jovial man of about Jarek's age, asked if he wanted to go anywhere in particular, which Jarek took to mean he'd be happy to recommend bars, brothels and other diversions, but all he really wanted to do was to stretch his legs and get some fresh air, or what passed for fresh air around here. The guard took the hint and shut up, falling into place behind and to one side of his charge.

About a quarter of the bars and clubs were still open, though the Street itself was largely deserted. Jarek decided to meander out rimwards; he doubted he'd actually be able to see over the edge of the floating City, but it gave him somewhere to aim for. Khesh's night-owls were exhibiting various states of inebriation and desperation, but none of them bothered him. For a moment he wondered if he should take the guard's advice after all; this place offered some interesting diversions … unfortunately they were likely to cost credit he didn't have.

Lost in thought, it took Jarek a moment to notice that his guard wasn't behind him any more. He caught movement out of the corner of one eye and spun round just in time to see a woman with a tranq pistol; his guard had just collapsed to the ground. Jarek went for his weapon, but the woman already had him covered.

'Don't,' she said.

Jarek made a show of moving his hands into sight. 'I realise people probably say this to you a lot,' he said as casually as he could, 'but you're making a big mistake.' He studied her covertly; she wore inconspicuous clothes, had light brown skin and was quite young, but she was already hard-eyed. Her gun-hand was unwavering.

'Let us be the judge of that, Sirrah Reen,' she said.

Oh shit, she knew who he was. But who exactly was *she*? The Veryan Syndicate? Surely they hadn't caught up with him already—

'We'd like to ask you a few questions,' she said. She wasn't an offworlder: that accent was local.

Jarek tried to spot the other part of the *we*, but as he started to turn his head, the woman gave a twitch of her gun that was convincing enough to make him keep still and stay focused on her. 'Ask away,' he said. At least while she was talking she wouldn't be shooting.

'Not here; follow me. I'm going to do you the courtesy of assuming you won't try anything stupid.'

He obeyed; he couldn't see any other choice right now. As they moved off he got a brief look at the figure he thought he'd seen out of the corner of his eye: a man, probably another local, with a much larger gun. He was wearing gloves – in fact, Jarek now realised, they both were.

The man fell in behind Jarek, with the woman leading the way. He risked a quick, desperate glance around, but if anyone on the half-empty Street had noticed the unconscious guard and the kidnapping in progress, they weren't doing anything about it. *Shit* – how was he going to negotiate his way out of this when he had fuck-all to bargain with?

She was leading them towards an alleyway. Once they were off the main drag his options would narrow, so he needed to stay calm and think about what assets he'd actually got on him. His com? If he could dial a preset he might get through to Nual or Taro – if they weren't entirely occupied with each other. He couldn't ask for help, but they might overhear what was going on, maybe trace the call … at any rate, it beat waiting to find out what his captors had in store for him. He eased his hand round in front of his body.

When the guard hit him across the back of his knees he was too surprised, too shocked by the sudden pain, to catch himself. He landed hard on the ground.

'Get up.' The man spoke as though Jarek had tripped deliberately. His voice was clipped and efficient.

Jarek found himself staring at the ground – not ground at all, really, because it was completely artificial. Odd shade of grey too. At the same time a tiny panicked voice at the back of his mind was screaming, *Start crawling, just get away before it's too late!*

'I said, "get up".' Now the man sounded bored.

Jarek felt a last twitch go through his arms as he suppressed the suicidal urge to try crawling off. He pushed himself upright, slowly and carefully, a little dizzied by the blood thundering in his ears. His kidnappers watched. He wondered if he could feign injury, but the pain at the back of his knee was already subsiding. These people, whoever they were, knew what they were doing.

'Keep those hands where I can see them,' said the man once Jarek was upright.

He did as he was told, feeling tremors going down to his fingertips. If he was going to do anything, he needed to do it now – but he was out of options … Except that something was nagging at the back of his brain. *Hands, something about hands* … And then he had it: *hands* – or, more importantly, gloves: these people were wearing gloves because they weren't Kheshi: they were from Luorna. The gloves were to hide the implanted jewels that would otherwise identify them! Good, so now he knew who was fucking him over. That was a start.

The light level dropped as they entered the alley. Jarek's eyes were still adjusting, and at first he thought he'd imagined the shadow that crossed the entrance. Then he heard an impact, followed by a strangled gurgle, behind him, and he whirled – *no, you idiot, there's someone pointing a gun at you!* – to see—

Nothing. The mouth of the alley was empty. The man had disappeared into thin air. Jarek pressed himself to the alley wall and looked back at the woman, who appeared to be as surprised as he was.

But she was still pointing her gun at him. 'Throw me your weapon.' Her voice held the beginning of a quaver.

Jarek hesitated; she obviously meant to carry out her plan alone. 'No,' he said after a moment. Possibly a mistake, but the odds had just evened up.

'I'd—'

Her threat was broken off by something dropping down from the darkness, directly behind her. As the kidnapper started to turn, a slender blade emerged from her gut. She fell forward, sliding off the blade with a gasp. She fell, her hands pressed to the wound, and began making painful panting noises deep in her throat. Jarek stared at her in fascination for a moment, then looked up as his numb mind started to register what had just happened.

Behind the wounded woman, the Angel finished flicking the blood off her blade; the implanted weapon disappeared back into her forearm. She was wearing a mimetic cloak, and without the silver of the blade, all Jarek could see clearly was her head. Her pale hair was plaited and coiled, adding to her already impressive height. She wore an expression of fierce disdain, which she now turned on the whimpering woman. 'You'll live,' she spat, then smiled unpleasantly and added in a whisper, 'Long enough to talk, at least.'

She looked up, and Jarek flinched at her gaze. 'Go back to your hotel,' she commanded, 'and stay there.'

Not trusting himself to speak, Jarek nodded, then turned and ran out of the alley.

He managed to avoid tripping over the body of the other kidnapper, which was lying beside the alley entrance. The blow that had cut the man's throat open had been powerful enough to expose his spine.

CHAPTER SIX

On the night she was married, Ifanna am Nantgwyn killed her husband. She had not intended him to die, but like so many events in her short life, her intentions had little bearing on what came to pass.

Her father had claimed the match with Pedrog – fat, ugly, Pedrog, as stolid as his cattle, as cold as his coins – would improve her, though mainly it would improve his own standing and wealth in Nantgwyn. And marrying her off would solve the 'little problem': that's what Da called it, as though her situation were some minor inconvenience visited upon them. Her mother worried that Ifanna was too young to marry, but Da had ignored her, as usual. Maman shut up at once, and that reinforced Ifanna's belief that she knew the real reason. She was coming to believe that Maman had known the truth all along.

Not for the first time, Ifanna considered running away, but there was nowhere to go. So she convinced herself that marriage to Pedrog would not be so bad. In time she was sure she could learn to control him; every day her ability to impose her will on the men around her was growing, after all.

So once the priest had bestowed on the newlyweds the blessings of the Skymothers, and the villagers had drunk themselves into a stupor on spring mead, she let Pedrog lead her to the garlanded bedroom. When he undressed her, then put his fat hands on her, she tried to think of nothing, though his lust turned her stomach. It appeared he believed her a virgin, and he planned to savour this night. She forced herself not to shudder; instead, she made herself go to the place deep inside, where 'she' existed apart from the flesh, and whatever was done to it.

But as he caressed her, his hands felt her belly and he sat up abruptly. 'Damn the man!' he swore, as though Ifanna were not even there. 'Damn him to the Abyss! I *knew* his offer was too sudden!' Then he looked down on her, his eyes full of contempt. 'And what do you say, eh, you little slut?'

Not the truth, that was for sure. 'S— Star-season,' she stammered, 'I came into my womanhood then. A boy at the fair in Plas Morfren, as the sky fell ...'

'Ah, so the child you carry is a gift of Heaven, is it?' Pedrog might just accept that; he was a devout man. But he had been married before, to a wife who had died trying to bring stillborn twins into the world. He frowned. 'T'would be a miracle indeed, that your gut should harden and swell so quickly.'

Ifanna said nothing.

Pedrog grunted. 'You are barely a woman. I am surprised at your Da for putting up with such wantonness outside the holy season!'

She could not help it; she laughed at that, a tight, bitter laugh.

Pedrog, who was not a man known for enduring ridicule, reached down and slapped her face.

No one had hit her for some time; she had thought her burgeoning ability to manipulate men meant she would no longer have to endure such treatment. She was filled with a sudden fury. 'How dare you, you pig!' she shouted. 'You should— You should be with the other pigs – jump out of the window and join your brothers in the filth! Go on, *do* it!'

Subject to a compulsion she barely understood herself, he did precisely what she had ordered him to do, but though the pigsty was indeed below the bedroom window, he landed on the fence, newly repaired with sharp wooden stakes.

Every villager not too drunk to stand was drawn by his screams.

As she looked out of the window at the figures running towards the impaled man, she cursed herself for a fool. She should not have fought back. She could have made being in his house bearable; she might have found some happiness as a wife and a mother, even if it was wife to a sweaty oaf and mother to an Abyss-touched child.

Yet now, because she had let her temper get the better of her, she would be cast into the Abyss herself.

The villagers stood around helplessly as Pedrog died. He went to the Mothers quickly, but sadly for Ifanna, not quietly. His final words, before his breath bubbled away in bloody froth, were, 'The witch has killed me!'

People looked at each other, and at her father; the braver ones looked up at her. Then her Da pointed at her and said, ''Tis true. The girl is skycursed.'

His admission surprised her; his next words hurt her more than anything in a life that had already known much hurt.

'We should kill her, as the Traditions demand!'

But surely Da loved her? He had said so, and whenever he had hurt her, he had been truly sorry – yet now she listened in horror as he told everyone he himself had been under her thrall until this very night, that he had married her off to escape her baleful influence. *How could he turn on her so?*

The villagers lapped up his confession: a wedding and the exposure of an abomination in their midst, all in the same day? What a great tonic in these grim times!

Ifanna let them fetch her down from her wedding bower. Her father, well into his stride now, called on the priest to dispense justice before the sun rose, to fetch ropes and stones and go down to the river at once.

The priest had served in the Reeve's household. He looked to Ifanna's mother, rather than instantly agreeing to her father's demands. Though her choice of husband might have been poor, Maman was still the Reeve's niece. Ifanna, her arms held by men who were careful to stay behind her, blinked back tears and watched her mother's face. So many times she had wanted Maman to intervene, to speak out – or even just to listen. Now, when every eye was upon her, would she dare speak freely?

Finally her mother said, 'My uncle would request a trial, I am sure.' She did not sound sure, but it was enough.

45

The priest ruled that Ifanna was to be taken to Plas Morfren.

Her hands were bound, ready for the walk. The priest would lead her; his blessed status would help him resist her wiles. But the villagers were taking no chances; he would be accompanied by half a dozen volunteers. The priest chose older men over younger, as less likely to be snared by a witch, and sent back those who were still drunk.

Her mother watched the proceedings from the edge of the crowd, her face the colour of ash. Her father had placed himself amongst his cronies, though not all of those he considered friends were eager for his company. Someone had tapped the last barrel of mead, and they drank it, loudly claiming they did so only to ward off dawn's brutal chill.

As Ifanna and her escort were about to leave, her father broke away from his companions and strode up to her, a little unsteadily. Despite everything, Ifanna's heart lifted. She smiled, waiting for him to smile back. His mouth twitched, but then he looked away, though she saw the effort it cost him.

He fixed his gaze firmly on the ground before her feet and began to speak. 'You have become nothing to me,' he stated.

Ifanna was confused. Despite the drink, he spoke like a priest, intoning the words solemnly.

'Whatever was between us before, now it is gone,' he continued. All at once she recognised the words: her father was forever cutting her out of his life, declaring her Abyss-touched. The speech came from the Traditions, which had words for all occasions, even this unthinkable one.

'No—!' She wanted to shout, but she managed only a whisper.

He carried on. 'You are not of my blood, and my hearth will never be your haven.'

She wanted to say, *It is* you *who has wronged* me, *Father!* All that came out was a feeble croak.

Her father raised his voice, hurrying to the end of the declaration: 'I reject you utterly. It is as though we have never met. This I vow in the name of the Five, from now until my soul returns to the Skymothers.'

And he turned away from her, almost falling in his haste.

Ifanna started to reach out to him with her mind, but she did not know whether she would command him to retract his curse, beg him to forgive her or demand he hurt himself as he had hurt her. In her confusion, she was unable to do any of those things.

When she looked at her mother, she saw that she too had turned away.

During the half-day walk through the rice-fields to Plas Morfren, the men kept a careful distance. They viewed her with a mixture of horror, awe and lust; this last she sensed from old Tysul, who was ashamed of himself for such feelings, and quite determined he would never act upon them. She could sense their relief as they handed her over to the guards at the Reeve's manor.

She was taken down to a cell, where she was untied and left alone with her despair.

Despite losing everything, facing a future that held only the prospect of death, it was her father's rejection she felt most keenly. He had made her what she was, and now he had abandoned her. No doubt his friends would believe that her abilities had led him into temptation with her ... she wondered what they would think if they knew he had first touched her long before her curse had become apparent, back when she truly had been a child. Her strange ability had only blossomed this last season or so, and she had started to test the strength of her father's twisted love. To her surprise, the power was not all his; recently, he had come to her only as she allowed. He was the supplicant, and she the mistress. For those few months, she had thought she had found happiness, of a sort.

The cell had a high slit window. The light had gone from it, and Ifanna had cried until no more tears would come, before she heard a sound from outside. She struggled to her feet. Had her father changed his mind and followed her here? But the door did not open. Instead, a panel at the bottom was raised and a tray pushed in. It held a wooden cup of water and a hunk of black bread. Ifanna, suddenly ravenous, fell upon the food, but even before she had finished the nausea hit. She vomited up what she had eaten, barely making it over to the latrine hole in time.

She tried to take comfort from the fact that they had chosen to feed her – but perhaps this apparent soft-heartedness merely indicated that it would take a while for the trial to be organised, and that they wanted her fit and well to face judgment.

Though she managed to keep down some water, she could not face the rest of the bread. She slept badly on the straw pallet, though the other residents of the cell were glad of the company, if the mass of bites on her legs and back the next day were anything to go by.

She was fed again in the morning, a lumpy gruel. She managed two spoonfuls before it came back up.

When, that evening, she returned the tray, she heard her unseen jailer muttering to himself. The next morning the door was un-locked and a woman came in. She had a doughy face marred by a harelip, and was dressed like a merchant's wife.

'Well now, lovey,' said the woman brusquely, 'I am a healer, and I have been sent to find what ails you.'

There was no point lying. 'I am with child,' said Ifanna.

'Ah. I see. Lie down, and let me examine you.'

Ifanna did as she was told.

The woman's hands were cold, but her touch was gentle. When she was done she said, 'You must pray with all your heart, for your child's soul may yet be saved, though yours is surely damned.'

'What do you mean? Oh—!' Suddenly hope dawned, as Ifanna remembered the priest, in capel, telling them that all children en-tered the world as innocents.

'There will be no trial until the babe is born,' the healer said. 'In the meantime, I will ask for blankets and better rations for you.'

The healer was true to her word. For about half a day Ifanna was ecstatic. She was grateful to the healer, to the Skymothers, even to her unseen jailers: she was not going to die! But then reality re-asserted itself: her fate was not averted, merely delayed. The child, though ... The child might live.

For the first time, Ifanna began to think of what was grow-ing inside her as a blessing. Though she herself might be cursed and worthless, she nurtured a life of value. It would be a boy, she decided, and more: he would be a skyfool! She was sure she had heard it said that those boys blessed by Heaven were most often born to skycursed women. Now she thought about it, it struck her as odd that to be touched by the sky was cherished in a boy, but the mark of evil in a girl. She put that blasphemous thought aside and prayed for forgiveness for even considering it. She prayed a lot now, for many things. Alone apart from the bedbugs, with only the passing shadows from the high window to mark the days, she had nothing else to do save think or pray, and the latter gave comfort that the former did not. She did not ask for forgiveness for herself; that would have been too great a presumption. But for her son ...

She dared entertain dreams of *his* fate: how one day he might be found worthy by the Beloved Daughter of Heaven, and sent to take his place as a Consort of the Skymothers. And once he reached Heaven, perhaps he might even intercede on his mother's behalf, and her own soul might be freed from the Abyss where it would otherwise be bound.

From time to time she wondered what was happening back home, but then she decided that she did not want to know. Ifanna felt the love she had for her father curdling slowly to hate as she thought about the unforgivable things he had done. Even Pedrog's death was his fault, for he had forced Ifanna to marry the man, and she prayed that the justice of Heaven should be visited on him. Yet even as she murmured the words she felt guilt, for he had loved her, really he had. And much of the blame was hers ...

As the summer wore on, the cell grew humid, the air close. Flies became her constant daytime companions, and she developed a wrenching cough which, once it became loud and persistent enough to annoy her jailers, was treated with a sticky syrup that came with her morning stew. The cough slowly abated.

Meanwhile her thoughts circled, and her prayers grew longer and more complicated. She spent whole days trying to recall passages from the Traditions. She still cried, often unexpectedly. Sometimes she wished she were dead, and all this discomfort and boredom and uncertainty were ended. But then she remembered

49

her unborn son, and how she must live so that he might come into the world and fulfil his destiny.

One night she awakened in agony, and knew at once it was the baby – but not yet, surely? She had tried to mark the days with fingernail scratches on the slimy rock wall, and she was sure this was too soon. But such sensible thoughts were soon driven from her head by pain. She screamed, grasping her belly, cursing the man who had brought her to this pass, and begging Turiach, the Mother of Mercy, for respite.

As something tore, deep inside, and she howled, she realised that she was no longer alone, and recognised the healer's face. The pain rushed out, and with it came a wet, soft mass.

By the time she had regained her senses, the healer was already busy with a blanket, and Ifanna was too weak to stop her, but she did see one thing. Had it lived, her child would have been a girl.

CHAPTER SEVEN

'No wonder you look like shit,' said Taro. He'd forgiven Jarek for tearing him away from their nice comfy bed-with-full-room-service once Jarek'd explained what'd happened during his early morning stroll. He yawned.

'Thanks,' said Jarek, taking a bite of fried not-meat.

'You're sure they were Luornai?' asked Nual.

'Well, no, not totally – but assuming they were, do you think they were working for their City? The other two Cities do have their own equivalent of Angels, don't they?'

'They weren't Asps – Asps wouldn't have used guns,' she said firmly. 'And sending an Agent of the Concord into a rival City is a provocative move.'

'So they were – what, some sort of runners?'

'Like I used to be, yeah,' muttered Taro. The conversation was stirring up bad memories.

'What do you think they wanted? They were only packing tranq.'

'I suspect they wanted exactly what they said they did,' answered Nual, 'to ask you some questions. I would imagine the other City minds still have no idea what caused the "cityquake" your sister unwittingly unleashed, so when an Angel who was associated with that event returned, they would be sure to take an interest. They can't touch me, or Taro, now he's had the mods, but you ...' She paused, then said quietly, 'Once they'd found out what they could, I imagine they would probably have killed you, rather than allow you to reveal that you had been questioned. Careless tourists turn up dead in back alleys all the time around here.'

Jarek paled. 'I shouldn't have come, should I? You two are under the City's protection – I'm not.'

Nual replied, 'You *are* under the City's protection, just not as directly as we are, and that little incident just proved it: the Minister was obviously keeping an eye out, and he sent an Angel to rescue you. You won't be in any danger, provided you stay in the hotel, or only go out with one of us. Of course, now Luorna has made an overt move, and failed, I don't imagine it'll try again. Such is the nature of the Concord.'

'How about the third City … Yazil, isn't it?'

'The Minister's already pretty pissed off with them,' Taro growled. 'They wouldn't dare.' In his mind's eye he saw the face of the Yazil assassin who'd murdered his line-mother. At least the last memory he had of Scarrion was the fucker's brief expression of surprise just before Taro killed him.

'Ah, now look who it is,' said Jarek.

The Minister was weaving his way between the tables. Those few guests who were paying him any attention smiled at his smart-but-eccentric appearance, currently completed by a silver-headed walking cane. None of them had any idea who he was, of course; the only people who ever met him were the downsiders who worked for him, as Angels or runners. Downsider legend had it that he was immortal, and many of those who lived in the Undertow saw the City itself as some sort of god. For most of his life Taro hadn't given either possibility much thought. Turned out they were both true, in a way.

'Mind if I join you?' the Minister asked when he reached their table.

Jarek pulled up a spare chair. 'Have a seat.'

The Minister sat. 'I believe I might be able to help you,' he said immediately.

'You can get us a beacon?' Jarek's voice was neutral, but Taro could see the eagerness in his eyes.

'Well, I don't happen to have one lying around, no. But I might be able to give you access to the source for them.'

'And where's that?' asked Jarek.

'Before we go any further,' said the Minister, 'I have a question and a proposition for you. Well, two questions, really.'

'Ask away,' said Jarek, guardedly.

'The easy question first: do you have a stasis chamber on your ship, Captain Reen?'

'A comabox? Yeah, I've got one.'

'Splendid. Now my second question is this: if this lost world of yours has no beacon, then there is nothing for your ship's transit-kernel to latch onto, correct? So how exactly *were* you intending to get back there to plant this hypothetical beacon?'

<*You gonna tell him?*> thought Taro to Nual.

<*We have to.*> Out loud she said, 'I am able to navigate Jarek's ship through shiftspace using the technique the female Sidhe employed before the beacons were seeded.'

Taro noted she said *I*, not *we*; she wasn't going to admit to the Minister that she needed his help. He wasn't sure how he felt about that.

'Excellent. That's very impressive for a lone Sidhe, especially one of your tender years.'

'Thank you,' said Nual drily.

'And I assume you know what transit-kernels actually are.' The Minister didn't quite make it a question.

'Oh yes,' said Jarek darkly, 'we know.'

'So you've thought through the implications of bringing— What is the name of the place?'

Jarek hesitated a moment before answering, 'Serenein.'

'—yes, Serenein, into human-space, have you?'

Jarek answered with a question of his own. 'I take it you know what goes on there, then?'

'Let us just say I took an educated guess, which you have now confirmed. And my question still stands.'

'I know there'll be – well, complications, in the long term, but the Sidhe – the females – have manipulated humans without their knowledge for too long. We're going to bring them out into the light, and break their hold on humanity.'

The Minister raised an eyebrow. 'Good luck with that.'

'Don't you *want* us to trash them?' Taro wondered what people would think if they knew that an ancient race they all thought dead and gone was not only still around, but still quietly at war with itself.

'Obviously I would like that very much, but that does not prevent me thinking you might be a little over-ambitious.'

Jarek said, 'You mean you're not convinced that a handful of humans will succeed where the male Sidhe failed?'

'We didn't *fail*,' the Minister said, the faintest trace of anger in his voice. 'We led the rebellion that broke the Sidhe Protectorate and brought humanity out from under the yoke of the females – even if they still, as you say, exert a degree of control from the shadows.'

'But they wiped you out – most of you, anyway.'

'Actually, no, that is not the case. We will perhaps get to that later. First, let us discuss my proposal. Captain Reen, I would like to buy your ship.'

'You'd like to *what*?'

'Buy your ship. The *Heart of Glass*, isn't it?'

'It's not for sale.'

'Really? I was under the impression that it is about to change hands imminently.'

'I'm going to fight that—'

'With what, precisely? Righteous indignation?'

'Wait a moment!' said Taro loudly. 'Why can't you just pay off our debts? Or at least give us a decent loan? It's not like you don't fucking owe us!'

The Minister frowned. 'You are disturbing the other diners, Taro. Please don't. It is true I owe *you,* and Nual, as you so eloquently put it, and whilst I was happy to deal with your immediate problems, I do not owe either the ship on which you travelled here, or its captain, anything.'

'Why would you want a shiftship?' asked Jarek. 'What use is it to you?'

'Let us just say that I am broadening my horizons,' the Minister said expansively. 'And although you might not see it this way, I will in fact be doing you a considerable favour. I am not looking to exert any control over you, Captain Reen; I would act as a silent partner. You will be free to carry on your business without any interference from me.'

'So what would you get out of the deal?' Jarek looked bemused.

The Minister smiled thinly. 'The knowledge that you were continuing the fight. All I ask is that you report any relevant activities to me.'

'Would you expect me to consult you before carrying out any such "activities"? I know we're both fighting the same enemy but, with all due respect, I'm not doing it for you.'

'I understand that. I just wish to be kept fully informed. In return, you will have my financial backing, and that will ensure that earning a living does not distract you from your crusade. I am quite sure you can see the sense in that.'

'And if I can't? What if I refuse to turn over ownership of the *Heart of Glass* to you?'

'Then I shall provide safe passage out of the Tri-Confed system, and you will go with my best wishes for the future.'

'But no beacon.'

'That is correct. This is one of those "all or nothing" deals they talk about, I'm afraid.' When Jarek didn't say anything, the Minister continued, 'Obviously you will need to think about it; I imagine you may wish to discuss my offer amongst yourselves. You will find you have a mailbox number on your com labelled "City information". Use it to let me know your decision.'

After he left they sat in silence. Finally, Nual covered Jarek's hand with her own and said gently, 'Ultimately, it's your choice.'

'I know,' said Jarek. 'Can I trust him?'

Nual smiled. 'I trusted him with my life when I was hiding here.'

Taro said, 'The Minister's a funny old cove, but he won't break his word.'

*

When it came down to it, though it wasn't much of a choice, it still took Jarek several hours to commit to a decision.

The Minister arrived within an hour of Jarek leaving his voice-mail message. They all met in the hotel's otherwise deserted bar – the rest of the guests were apparently spending the afternoon sightseeing. The first part of the meeting was pretty boring, as Jarek and the Minister thrashed out the details of transferring ownership of the *Heart of Glass*. Some of the shit they were discussing sounded a bit smoky, far as Taro could see; it looked like no one would know Khesh owned the ship unless they looked really fucking deep.

He stopped listening after a while. He sipped his drink, his other hand on Nual's knee under the table, thinking about his former life here in Khesh City. He was getting used to being back, but then, this was topside. His real home had been the Undertow, and there were a few people down there he still considered friends.

Finally the deal was done. Jarek sat back, stony-faced.

The Minister cleared his throat. 'Right then, this beacon.'

'So you *can* get us one?' Jarek's tone implied that after what had just happened, he'd better be able to.

'I can arrange for you to get hold of one, though you will have to fetch it yourself,' said the Minister.

'Where from?'

'A system called Aleph – although that will mean nothing to you. You won't have heard of Aleph, because there is no record of anywhere of that name.'

'Another lost world?' asked Jarek, sounding interested.

'Not exactly. Aleph was never ruled by the females. And it is in another galaxy.'

'You're shitting me!' Now he'd signed over his beloved ship to the Minister, Jarek appeared less in awe of him.

'No – well, to be completely accurate, the Aleph system is in one of the smaller satellite galaxies that orbit our own. When the conflict between the male and female Sidhe was at its height, a large number of males fled there. It turned out to be a one-way trip for them, though shiftships can travel to and from the system.'

'That's where the rebellion was coordinated from, wasn't it?'

'Aleph was a major centre of operations, though those of us who remained behind did our part too.'

'And how will these males at Aleph feel about us turning up out of the blue and asking for a beacon?'

'You won't be turning up out of the blue. I have been in contact with Aleph; they are willing to provide a beacon to help you in your fight against the females. However, you must bear in mind that we males have a rather different outlook than our sisters. We are less interventionist – and less unified. The females like nothing more than to band together in dark corners and plot how to manipulate human destiny. We tend to keep our distance, both from humanity and from each other.'

'You're saying there may be factions at Aleph who won't be too pleased to see us?' asked Jarek.

'I would say there is a high risk of that, yes. But given what I know about you, Captain Reen, I suspect that is a risk you would be willing to take to win your beacon.' He turned to Taro and Nual. 'And you two as well, apparently.'

'I already saved your invisible arse,' said Taro. 'Reckon it's time to get really ambitious now.'

Nual just smiled.

'One thing you should probably know about Aleph: the males there are similar to me and my two brothers. Like us, they live through their machines, and interact through their avatars. Right—' The Minister made a show of looking at his com, like he actually needed to check the time. 'I still need to thrash out a few details with my distant brothers, so I will have to leave you for a while. I recommend you take some time to see the sights, Captain Reen. I am confident there will not be any further unpleasantness – though I would still advise against going out alone.' He stood up. 'I'll be in touch.'

As part of the deal, the Minister had taken their cargo from Hetarey off their hands. Taro suspected he'd only done it to indulge them, but whatever the reason, they now had spare credit to their names. Jarek wanted to use some of their new-found wealth to take the

Minister's advice. Taro let Nual act as guide, and they took him to a decent restaurant, then on to an 'exotic cabaret' complete with glitter and grav manipulation. Nual elected to stay sober, so Taro and Jarek kicked back and relaxed – in fact, Jarek acted like a man who didn't know where the next party was coming from. Taro could sympathise: Jarek'd had his head taken apart by the Sidhe, spent months on a lo-tech mud-ball where he'd nearly died, then when he'd finally got away, he'd found that his sister, his one surviving family member, had been murdered. Since then the three of them had been running to keep one step ahead of both creditors and enemies. They sure as shit deserved a bit of fun. The cabaret was heavy on man-on-man action – Jarek was taking advantage of being somewhere without stupid sex-laws – but though he was obviously getting off on the show, he stopped short of taking advantage of the additional services on offer.

The next day Taro and Nual took Jarek to the Gardens, an area of topside that Taro had always loved; they watched an outdoor play, which Taro found pretty boring, and Jarek had a go at tree-walking, which Taro found pretty funny. When the Minister still hadn't called that evening, they ate out again. Thinking he might be in touch later that night, they spent a boring evening in the hotel bar. He didn't call.

The day after, they went for a sightseeing pedicab ride in the morning. Taro had spent his youth not being allowed in *anywhere*; now he had ID that allowed him in everywhere, he insisted they visited the State Quarter, even though there wasn't much to see. Jarek enjoyed the museums, and Taro did a bit of shopping in the kind of boutiques that wouldn't let ordinary downsiders within sniffing distance but were only too happy to serve Angels.

It was late afternoon by the time they got back to the hotel, and Jarek announced he needed some downtime, by himself. Nual, with a smile, agreed to handle any calls that might come in; it didn't take her abilities or Taro's experience to know what his plans for the evening were. Taro was curious, and hung around the hotel lobby until he spotted the cove – he was between Jarek and Taro, age-wise, handsome rather than pretty, and well fed and well-dressed.

If he hadn't been in the profession himself once, Taro might not have clocked him as a joyboy at all. Taro smiled to himself.

When Nual returned from checking the local newsnets he was about to suggest they get an early night too – but then he thought about it, and discovered, somewhat to his shock, that sex wasn't what he wanted right now.

Nual said gently, 'You should go. If you don't, you'll always wish you had.'

'To the Undertow, you mean?' he said aloud.

She nodded. 'Did you want me to come with you?'

'I ... No. I just need to see, for myself.'

'I'll be here when you get back.'

He kicked off as soon as he left the hotel, flying low and slow, enjoying the awed upturned faces and pointing fingers that marked his progress.

The pale disc of the sun was almost level with the rim of the City, and when Taro dropped below the edge, the upside-down shantytown of the Undertow was bathed in orange light. Even the romance of sunset didn't stop him seeing it for the desperate, squalid place it was. A chaotic expanse of tangled nets hung below the maze of hanging vanes, many of which had been cut and pinned over generations to form the narrow ledges of mazeways and boxy, shambolic homespaces. Here and there he could see the damage done by the 'cityquake' – a torn net, an empty loop of rope, a section where a whole mazeway had come free and fallen to the ground, far below.

Well, he was here now. This was unfamiliar territory, and none of the colours fluttering from the dangling ropes of the watertraps meant anything to him. He chose a route close to the edge and began to fly. When he looked upwards he glimpsed the occasional figure, but they were too busy not taking the fall to pay him much attention. Unless you had to cross a net or check for 'trap colours to help you navigate, you kept to the mazeways.

He wondered how the water-trader Fenya was doing – and her lazy, crazy Remembrancer husband; or Arel, who'd been trying to make a new life for herself after Limnel fucked her over: that was a point, who was even in charge of Limnel's troupe now? Of course, there was almost no chance of finding any of them, and even if he did, they knew him as a lineage-less runner, not as an Angel who travelled the stars. It would be too weird, seeing them now. He could probably find the *Exquisite Corpse*, if he put his mind to it; the Undertow's one and only bar was run for the Angels, after all, and it advertised itself with banners meant to be seen from below. But his only friend there was Solo, the place's alien barkeep, and whilst he thought of the gawky winged empath with affection, he/she/it was likely to be too busy to chat at this time of the evening.

He reached the far side of the disc and headed straight back up, without looking back.

The Minister finally called Jarek the next evening, as they were finishing dinner at the hotel – they'd done more tourist stuff in the day, including a visit to the Zoo, but their credit was dwindling, and another restaurant felt like an unnecessary indulgence when the City was picking up the tab at the Cracked Emerald.

'Everything is in place,' said the Minister. 'You are booked on the midnight-twenty shuttle flight. We will rendezvous in the transit hall in two hours.'

Taro packed his few possessions with mixed feelings. When he'd arrived, he'd suspected he'd never call Khesh City home again. Now he knew it. And that felt weird.

They reached the transit hall early, and found a relatively quiet corner while they waited for the elevator queues for the earlier shuttle to subside. The Minister emerged from the crowd a few minutes later. He had a kid of about twelve in tow.

Taro tried not to stare. Children were rare in Khesh City – Vellern wasn't a family destination, and a lot of the citizens who lived and worked here left their youngsters on safer Tri-Confed worlds or habitats.

The boy looked local. He was handsome, in a bland, slightly dazed sort of way. His gaze, openly curious, flicked between the three of them as he approached.

'And who's this, then?' asked Jarek.

'Well, according to his ID, he is the child of a minor Kheshi noble house who you are transporting to a nearby hub-point to complete his out-of-system education.'

'And who is he really?'

'Vy, though that is less a name than a designation. He will get you to Aleph.'

'He'll *what*?' said Jarek. 'I'm not sure I—'

'He's an avatar, ain't he?' Taro interrupted. 'Like you?'

'Not exactly like him, no.' Despite the boy's high, childish voice he sounded serious and grown-up. 'The body you see was created to replace an avatar destroyed in the cityquake; it was still undergoing development. This consciousness is not the one that was originally intended to inhabit it.'

'Not meaning to be rude,' said Jarek, looking a bit queasy, 'but before I let you on my s— before I travel with you, I want to know *exactly* what you are.'

'Precisely what I said: an avatar of Khesh, modified to operate with greater autonomy. And I have within me the beacon address of Aleph, which I will programme into your ship's navigational comp. Then, when we reach Aleph, I will remove it again.'

'My brothers in the Magellanic Cloud are somewhat paranoid,' the Minister said. 'They would never allow a ship with the co-ordinates of their beacon in its comp to remain at large in human-space, for fear the females might get their hands on it.'

Nual said tightly, 'And how do they feel about a female Sidhe visiting them?'

'They have no choice. Although Vy will provide the coordinates, your abilities will be required to persuade the transit-kernel to undertake the journey.' The Minister beamed at her. 'You are hardly the first female to rebel against your race, you know.'

'So you need a female Sidhe to get to or from Aleph?' asked Jarek.

'You do now, yes.' The Minister's smile didn't falter. 'Right then: before you get your shuttle, there are a few things I should tell you.'

CHAPTER EIGHT

As soon as the *Heart of Glass* was safely en route for the Tri-Confed beacon, Jarek gave Vy access to the bridge. The boy – like the Minister, it was better to give him a human designation, Jarek decided – didn't so much programme the comp as *commune* with it. Jarek had already witnessed something similar on Serenein, but it was disconcerting to see a mind like that at work on *his* ship – and it was still *his* ship, whatever the legal documents said. He asked Taro to make him a strong caf so he could keep an eye on Vy while the boy worked. After a couple of hours at the console Vy wandered off, muttering that he was done now. Jarek locked down the ship's controls to stop further tampering, then went to get some rest. He'd got his body-clock in step with Vellern just in time to leave.

He awoke to someone shaking him and for a moment he panicked, until he focused enough to make out Vy. He slapped at the hands on his shoulders and the boy backed off, looking offended.

'What's the goddamn problem?' he rasped at the boy.

'I'm bored,' Vy said, accusingly. 'I want something interesting to do.'

'And I'm trying to sleep,' said Jarek. 'Go bother the others.'

'Taro shouted at me when I went into their cabin.'

I'll bet he did. Jarek was tempted to do the same, but he didn't much like the idea of a bored, immature male Sidhe avatar looking for diversion on his ship. At least the boy had let him sleep for – he glanced at his com – an hour and a quarter. *Great.* 'Fuck's sake!' he groaned. 'All right, I'll sort you a game to play.'

'Yes, do that,' said Vy.

'We humans have a word we use at times like this,' said Jarek, trying to keep his temper. 'It's "please". We also have doors for a reason, which is to allow us some privacy. Have you ever come across either of these concepts?'

'Plea-se,' Vy said, like he was trying the word out.

Jarek sighed and got up.

Vy turned out to be predictably talented at gaming, and voracious in his appetite for new challenges. Good job Jarek had a comprehensive games library, he thought. He had never wanted children – which was fortunate, all things considered – but if he had, then a couple of days trapped on a ship with Khesh's youngest avatar would have been enough to make him seriously reconsider.

Vy ate twice as much as anyone else, and slept half as long. He listened to other people's conversations with a disconcerting intensity before interrupting to ask a question or (as he saw it) correct an error. He also enjoyed juvenile pranks, a particularly dangerous trait in someone so technically accomplished. If Taro hadn't asked about the gurgling sound in the head they might not have discovered Vy's attempts to reverse the settings on the excreta recovery unit until it was too late. In the confined space of the ship the results wouldn't have been at all funny – not to adults, at any rate.

Jarek found himself wondering, more than once, what effect tranq might have on the boy's apparently human body.

He wasn't sure why he had had to bring Vy with them at all, not once he'd provided Aleph's coordinates. The ship was heading to a system full of male Sidhe: surely one of them could just reprogram the navcomp to get them home? It also occurred to him that even with Aleph's coordinates removed from the *Heart of Glass*'s comp, the ship itself was still a liability: once they'd been there, the pattern of Aleph's beacon would be imprinted on the ship's transit-kernel; if the females captured his ship then they could probably force it to shift to Aleph without any intervention from a male. Presumably the Aleph males considered that to be an acceptable risk, whilst having the coordinates actually stored in the comp was not. Or perhaps the Minister was a good enough judge of character to know that Jarek would see the *Heart of Glass* destroyed before he'd let it fall into the hands of his enemies. Then again, maybe the Minister didn't expect them to come back at all – Jarek was pretty certain he hadn't been telling them everything. But whatever the risks, he was committed to this course of action now.

He did try asking Vy why he had to remain on board, but the boy just shrugged, a gesture he'd picked up from Taro and now used almost constantly, much to everyone's irritation.

This time they departed the Tri-Confed system by the book. Jarek took a slow, conservative course out to the beacon, then requested an onward transit to Pior-Terrane, a dual system with good trade links and a transit-path on to Hiliap, the hub where they were contracted to take their passenger.

Nual and Taro got Vy into stasis while Jarek prepped for the shift. Perhaps because they were used to one of Khesh's avatars, the Angels found Vy much easier to deal with than Jarek did. While Nual and Taro viewed the Minister almost like some sort of eccentric uncle, the Minister's casual disregard for human life turned Jarek's stomach, and Vy was part of that same being. But the Minister was an ally – or at least, the enemy of his enemies. Jarek still woke up sweating and terrified from nightmares of his time as a captive of the Sidhe females. And now, in order to fight them, he'd sold his ship to a Sidhe male. He'd have been screwed either way – if he hadn't taken the Minister on as a silent partner, the Veryan Syndicate would have taken every nut and rivet and left him with nothing. At least he had it in writing that the Minister couldn't intervene in his affairs directly.

A gentle ping from the console told him that shutdown was nearly complete and he looked around, a little worried. He'd have expected them to have got Vy settled by now. He had already received authorisation to depart when Nual finally floated up to the bridge.

'That took a while,' said Jarek. 'Everything all right?'

'Vy was scared. He didn't want to go into stasis.' They were down to basic life-support now and her face was hard to read in the dim light.

'But he's the one who insisted we put him in the comabox for the transit!'

'I know.' Nual sounded frustrated; had Vy been human she could have coerced him into obedience.

'Well, we're locked down and we've got our window, so let's get this over with.' As Nual turned to go he added, 'Good luck.' She nodded an acknowledgement.

When she'd gone Jarek tried to settle into his couch. He always got butterflies immediately before a transit; one initiated by some-one else taking control of his ship to propel him into another galaxy made him feel like he had a whole flock of birds circling in his guts.

Then the birds landed all at once and his stomach leapt up his throat. His eyes were filled with the darkness of the void, his ears with the roaring of the universe and he was falling, *falling*—

Gone. Everything. Gone.

Nothing. Something? Someone. Me. Yes!

Pounding, grinding, nauseating. Me. There's ... me. And I ... feel like shit. Like ... the taste of puke. He could sense that, acid and twisted. It was vile, but it was real. He was real. Whoever he was.

It's only shiftspace. I'm in the shift. Not dying.

Not dying: just in the shift.

Keep saying the words, remember you're real. This will pass. *Not dying: just in the shift.*

What if I am dying?

What if I'm already dead and this is Hell?

No. No no nonono. Won't accept that. Won't ... I am someone. Someone, somewhere. There is hope. There is light. Will be light. There is ...

... fading in and out. No. Hold on. *Not dying: just in the shift.*

Remember you exist. Have existed. Will exist. Whoever, what-ever, wherever, there's life. You're alive. Still alive. And ...

Not dying: just in the shift.

Not dying: just ...

Not dying ...
Not.

He woke to the stench of dried vomit, but the memory of the nightmare transit was already fading. He'd never had one that bad – then again, what had he expected? This wasn't a normal transit scheduled via the beevee system and though realspace and shiftspace didn't map directly – two systems within half-a-dozen light-years might be a dozen transits apart – actually transiting to a different galaxy had to be a whole different ballgame.

He prised himself off the floor before opening his eyes, then spent a few moments confirming that the world was still there, and real. Then he brushed himself clean as best he could and laboriously scaled his couch.

Getting the ship's systems back online was always a priority after a shift, but it had never been as important as it was now. Fortunately his body knew what to do, even if his mind was still half in shiftspace.

They'd come out of the shift at quite a lick; the plan, such as it was, was to cancel the velocity and come to a (relative) halt, then wait to be contacted on the channel the Minister had provided them with. But as soon as the ship's systems started to come online again, alarms began going off all over the place. One was the warning every captain making an unscheduled transit dreaded: *proximity alert.*

He stared dumbly at the board, even as his hands tried to coax the in-system drive into life. Sensors were still on minimal, but he gleaned enough from the readouts to know that whatever had tripped them wasn't on a collision course, thank Christos. He had a few minutes' grace, so he spared a glance at the other alarm flashing away on his screen. Electromagnetic energy pulse? From where? *Why?*

The 'where' he spotted almost at once: something was trying to slow-fry his ship from below – 'below' being a relative term. The nav-shields were always the first to come up, and the EM was relatively low-level, so whatever was firing on them wasn't endangering the ship yet. Before it built up enough energy to be an issue, the drive would be back up and they could take evasive action.

He needed to see outside. Given the EM pulse was aimed at the base of the *Heart of Glass*, he decided to risk opening the shutters on the bridge dome while he waited for the more sophisticated systems to wake up. Sometimes the human eyeball was the best sensor.

He briefly wondered how Taro and Nual were doing before deciding that they'd have to wait until he knew the ship was safe.

The shutters retracted to reveal a sky filled with a curtain of shimmering light, coruscating in shades of red and gold and orange. *What the fuck?*

As his eyes adjusted he saw that the light didn't quite fill the sky; there was darkness at its bottom edge – the darkness of space. So some kind of massive, translucent sheet had been hung in front of the stars. Then he spotted a dark spot, just below the centre, which was visibly shrinking as he sped away, arse-first. A tear in the veil. *Uh-oh.* So that would be the rip his ship had made when it tore through the whatever-it-was. He looked away from the beguiling sight to check his heading.

At least the *Heart of Glass* hadn't taken any damage; the curtain must be very low-density. But he'd still damaged it, and that explained why the locals were shooting at him. Except—

—except the EM pulse wasn't coming from the curtain, it was coming from underneath him.

Suddenly he realised what he was seeing: *Holy Christos, it's a lightship!*

And that wasn't a curtain, it was a *sail* – and what he'd originally taken for a weapon was actually the light-pulse being transmitted from a fixed point to fill the sail and propel the ship. Had it not been for Jarek's obsessive interest in space history when he was a boy, he'd have had no idea what he was looking at; no one had used lightsails for thousands of years. But Aleph had existed independent of human-space for millennia ...

He glanced down as another indicator lit up on the board: an incoming message, on the frequency the Minister had called the 'common channel'. Unsurprisingly, his com system didn't recognise the tag, but he could guess who the message was from. He hit receive.

'Enemy! Enemy! Warning: we tell ye, tell ye to consensor! Ye hear us? Ye hear? Aye-okay?' The strident voice had an accent so thick Jarek wasn't sure he was hearing the man's words correctly.

'I'm sorry, I didn't—' he started, but the strange voice cut him off almost at once.

'Query: what sept ye? Tell us wha sept. We tell of ye!'

'I'm sorry,' he tried again, 'I don't understand what you're trying to say. I'm a visitor. I've come to see—' But he hadn't been given a name, he'd just been told to wait until he was contacted. 'Er, I don't suppose you'd like to take me to your leader?'

The man responded with an impressive if incomprehensible string of what sounded like swearing, then cut the connection.

Jarek wondered if First Contact situations always went this well. Hopefully the lightship wasn't armed. He looked out again to check the damage he'd done to the irate local's sail, but the hole was gone, which was impossible ... *unless the sail had mended itself.*

That meant sophisticated nanotech, the sort not found in human-space. Nanofactories were rare, even on those worlds without religious proscriptions against messing with Creation at an atomic level, for they required massive power inputs and were notoriously unpredictable. No religious proscriptions here, though, and the locals had zepgen and the massive intellects of male Sidhe to overcome any technical difficulties. But if they were that advanced, why the hell were they sailing around in lightships?

Another incoming message. Jarek took a deep breath before accepting.

'Greetings: be welcomed!' This voice was friendly and easily comprehensible, if strangely accented. 'Be warmly welcomed to Aleph, Captain Reen.' It was also unmistakably female.

CHAPTER NINE

Kerin was stuck inside the rocky fastness of the Tyr, and so she did not see the fire in the sky. Urien told her later that citizens abroad in the hour before dawn spoke of light silently blossoming overhead, near the Navel of Heaven, then slowly dying away. Though few actually witnessed it, word spread fast and speculation abounded as to the significance of this strange event.

No one save herself, Urien and Damaru knew the truth: that what those below had witnessed was the destruction of the Sidhe ship. And only the three of them knew that the unmoving star high above Dinas Emrys which people called the 'Navel of Heaven' was, in fact, the very non-heavenly structure at the top of the silver thread. Kerin and Damaru had visited that structure, and Kerin's account of her experiences there had convinced Urien of a truth he had already begun to suspect. For everyone else around them, the world above remained the divine realm of the Skymothers.

Urien, ever the pragmatist, used the appearance of the heavenly light to their advantage, and started a rumour that it was a divine vindication of the changes he and Kerin were beginning to make.

Kerin tried not to consider how big a part luck had played in their victory. What if the Sidhe ship had arrived when Damaru were not present? What if this 'cutting light' that he had harnessed had not been something he could turn against their enemies? They knew so little of the technology put here by the Sidhe!

There was one fortunate side-effect of the incident: Damaru grudgingly admitted that he needed to learn his letters; if her son could combine his instinctive understanding of the device with the ability to read the console's display, they would be in a far better position to deal with future crises.

Damaru attempted to renew contact with the 'rock throwers' after the Sidhe vessel had been destroyed, and when the console remained uncooperative, he took it apart, exposing thin smooth tubes of many sizes and colours that made Kerin think of the bloodless guts of some strange beast. He rested and ate only when Kerin insisted. He made occasional odd requests: for blades of skymetal, bone needles, even bowls of burning embers. The monitors did their best to hide any confusion when Kerin conveyed these requests to the guards outside; they knew a skytouched boy shared her room, even if their assumption about his relationship to her was wrong. If their goddess chose to indulge the boy, they would not question – not to her face, at least. Kerin could only hope that Damaru knew what he was doing. The complex workings of the console looked impossible to comprehend, even for a skyfool.

Fortunately, with Midsummer over, the holy calendar was relatively empty: just the Sevenday service in the great square and, the day after that, a blessing to celebrate the birthday of a Consort who had been born in Dinas Emrys, now long gone to his less-than-heavenly fate. Kerin hated speaking at services dedicated to Consorts because she knew what had really happened to them when they had ascended the silver thread. Fortunately the ceremony required only a few ritual responses, delivered from the high balcony where she made most of her formal public appearances.

She had planned to spend some time catching up on her studies, but she found it hard to concentrate while Damaru was fiddling and muttering; at the same time, she did not want to leave him, in case he needed her assistance.

Finally, after four days, Damaru made a sound of disgust deep in his throat and jumped to his feet.

'What is it?' she asked, looking up from her desk.

'Will not work!'

'You are saying you cannot regain control of the rock throwers?'

Damaru grunted.

'Well, you tried, my lovely boy, you tried.' Kerin forced herself to smile. 'And at least we have the cutting light, aye?'

Kerin knew that expression.

'So that does not work either?'

Damaru muttered something in an irritated undertone.

'Damaru! Speak up, please.'

'Not sure. It … fades.' He waved both hands in front of his eyes. 'Cannot see, cannot *see* properly! So cannot fix.'

'Could you see properly if we were up there with the technology?' Kerin pointed upwards. 'Is there anything on the *Setting Sun* that might help us?' Taking the carousel up the silver thread was an option she would not take lightly – witnessing an unscheduled visit to 'Heaven' was likely to have a profound effect on those below. And she was far from enthusiastic about returning to the abandoned Sidhe ship moored to the silver thread, even though the Sidhe who had crewed it were all dead.

'Not sure. Perhaps.' Damaru sounded interested, but that was more his desire to play with technology. She suspected he had no more idea than she did whether a trip into the sky would solve their problems. Of course, Sais might know – but he was not here.

'All right. For now, just put the console back as it was, please.' She almost smiled at herself: that constant mother's plea, asking her child to tidy up. Except Damaru was not a child any more, at least not in body.

Damaru sighed in a put-upon way, then sat down and began to rebuild the console with painstaking care.

As Damaru was putting back what he had taken apart he could probably manage without her. She decided to escape for a while.

She went to a wooden clothes-chest against one wall and dug out skirts, a shirt, a shawl and a headscarf, all clean but plain. The shirt was the one she had worn when she had first arrived in Dinas Emrys, a few weeks and lifetime ago. Her other clothes were not suitable: the upland style of dress would stand out in the city and she wished to walk unnoticed. She completed her disguise with the striped tabard that identified her as a servant of the Tyr.

She explained carefully to Damaru that she needed his help; he

71

made no comment save to *tut* at the interruption, and follow her over to the rich red velvet hanging covering the wall between her bed and Damaru's newer, smaller one. When she drew the hanging back, the rock wall behind looked unusually smooth. A closer inspection revealed faint lines and markings.

Kerin pointed to a slightly darker patch to one side of the hidden door. 'If you please, Damaru,' she said.

He pressed his palm where she had indicated, and the door slid smoothly and silently into the wall, just like the doors Kerin had seen on the *Setting Sun*. 'Thank you,' she said as she slipped through. 'I will not be too long.'

She had learned not to jump when the door closed noiselessly behind her and the light globes on the rock walls lit themselves; unlike the lock on the secret passage, they did not require the touch of a Sidhe to operate. Though Sais had tried to explain, using terms like 'latent expression', 'recessive traits' and 'sub-type mutation', she still did not know how she, an ordinary woman, could have given birth to a child who was, at least as far as the machines of the Tyr were concerned, a Sidhe. She was not convinced Sais understood it himself.

She came to some steps, and descended. At the bottom, the passage turned and at the end she collected the items she had left here previously: a basket with a purse of coins in the bottom and a short, sturdy log. She rolled the log up to the door at the end of the passage, which slid open by itself, and kicked the log into place to hold it open, then went back for her basket. The door was not only hidden by a sacking curtain, far less opulent than the one in her chamber, but it was located behind packed shelves in a rarely-used grain storeroom. As Kerin pulled aside the sack curtain her nose was filled with the burnt odour of malted barley. She paused for a moment, recalling the glow of the hearth in her hut back in Dangwern. Then she put the memory aside. Save for the few happy years with her long-dead husband, her old life was not something she looked back on with fondness.

The scant light from the half-open door was barely enough to see by, and she had to take care crossing the packed storeroom.

She made a mental note to bring a lamp next time; this was only the third time she had used the hidden exit from her room and she was still working out the details. She listened at the wooden door to make sure no one was outside. A lowly kitchen-maid such as she now appeared to be would not normally be permitted in this part of the Tyr; she must procure other disguises if she was going to make a habit of this.

All was silent, so Kerin opened the door, slipped out and pulled it closed behind her. She crept along the passage, taking the third left, then the second right, following the route she had memorised. When she heard voices from up ahead she ducked into a side-turning and pressed herself against the wall. Somewhat to her surprise, the two approaching speakers were female. One was saying, 'The Escori of Frythil? As well as the young Consort, you mean?'

'Aye,' said the other, who sounded older, 'or so I hear.'

''Tis her right, of course.' The younger one laughed delicately, then added, 'But for her Divinity to take all these lovers, after not letting any man grace her bed for so long – one cannot help but wonder what she is thinking!'

They passed the end of the passage and Kerin had a glimpse of revealing white robes, carefully curled and sculpted hair and pale, painted faces: Putain Glan. The older one said, 'Nothing that we should question, that is for sure. You should watch your tongue when you speak of the Beloved Daughter of Heaven!'

'Of course, I meant no disrespect ...'

As the voices died away, the waft of their perfume reached Kerin, and bile rose in her throat. The Putain Glan were allowed to move freely about the Tyr, and Kerin had considered disguising herself as one of them, but even if she knew how to use artifice to hide her plain appearance, she risked any priest she met demanding the use of her body. And had she wished to leave the Tyr, she would have required a sponsor's letter and a brace of monitors to guard her. She had come to her position hoping to put an end to the tradition of holy prostitution, but had already realised that the priests would not give up that privilege easily.

She met no one else until she was in the outer precincts, at which point her basket and air of hurried purpose were enough to avoid unwanted attention. At her chosen exit, she opened the plain wooden door with the key from her purse. It opened onto a quiet street of townhouses, all built with an extra storey on the downslope side to compensate for the steep incline. The buildings leaned towards each other conspiratorially, as though trying to hide the street from the looming bulk of the Tyr.

Kerin wanted some green herbs and fresh fruits; the smell of the herbs would stay with her when she returned to the sterile stone of her rooms, and she could share the fruit with Damaru. The best market for such produce was near the Mint, and she took her time getting there, enjoying the sensation of being under the open sky and taking pleasure in the pretence that she had only the cares of a household and family to concern her, rather than those of a whole world. *How odd,* she thought, *that what was once common drudgery is now a luxury.*

Kerin was glad to find the market was not busy, and that high cloud diluted the summer sun. Coming from the highlands, she was still unaccustomed to both crowds and heat. She shopped slowly, drinking in the sights, smells and sounds of the world she was striving to save. Though the purse hidden in her basket was full of coins, she haggled, purely for the pleasure of such ordinary interaction.

A faint twinge as she leant over to reach for some early strawberries reminded her to find a treatment for her wounded arm. She had already heard one seller of medicines extolling the virtues of his cures to passersby; he claimed he could ease toothache, bad blood and the unpleasant – though rarely fatal – flux that was the latest ailment to sweep the city. No doubt when the winnowing times had held the land in their grip he had claimed to cure the falling fire too. Of course, there was only one cure for that. She doubted even this quack's best remedy would be as effective as the miraculous drugs Sais had procured when her arm had been wounded up on the Sidhe ship. Those healing machines and potions on the *Setting Sun* would be beyond this hedge-doctor's comprehension.

Her route to the medicine-seller took her across the square, towards the speaking-stone. There were several such platforms around the city; Urien called them *playhouses for earnest fools*. Kerin concluded her business quickly, buying a salve whose smell spoke of recent animal origin; as she turned to go, she heard a growing commotion. The current speaker was having some effect on the crowd. Kerin drifted towards the speaking-stone.

It was a man, of course – any woman who tried to take the stand would be shouted off before she could even open her mouth. He looked like a merchant rather than a craftsman, though his clothes did not speak of great wealth. As she got closer, he responded to a shouted comment from his growing audience.

'It is *not* blasphemy! I do not preach against the Mothers – they made us; we are their children. What I say is that the priests, who are mortal men, have lost their way!'

From the crowd a voice shouted, 'They are the servants of the Skymothers. Their steps are guided by Heaven.'

'I once believed that to be true. But something has changed—'

'Aye,' shouted someone else, 'the lights in the sky!'

'I too have seen those nightly apparitions, but I do not presume to understand their meaning. All I say is that we may no longer be able to trust the Tyr to lead us.'

The crowd was becoming restive. Some, it seemed, agreed. Others did not. More shouts were exchanged. The speaker tried to call for calm and was ignored. A moment later he ducked as something was thrown at him. Yellow spattered the wall behind his stand. Nearby, a scuffle broke out.

A helmeted head ploughed through the crowd, intervening between the two men who had come to blows. They quieted at once. In the silence that followed the monitor's intervention someone – Kerin thought it was the man who had first accused the speaker of blasphemy – called out, 'Will you not arrest that man?'

The monitor's response was loud in the now-quiet square. 'I will not. I serve the Mothers first, and the Tyr second. He has a right to speak, though if he is wise he will not say any more.'

The speaker took the hint and climbed down from his stone. The monitor's presence held the crowd in check. Once the focus of the commotion was gone, the crowd relaxed. A few still argued or muttered, but many started to drift away. Kerin turned to two women standing near her, and said, 'What times we live in!' She still cringed inside at treating strangers with easy familiarity, but such behaviour was normal in the city.

'You speak the truth there, mistress,' the older one responded.

'And did I hear aright, that there have been further lights since that most unnerving sight a few nights gone? I have been so busy, and not had call to look outside at night recently ...'

'You did hear aright! My daughter has seen them for herself, have you not, Meri?' said the woman eagerly. Kerin resisted the urge to smile; she had chosen this pair well.

The younger woman turned her hollow-eyed gaze on the currently sleeping child in its sling and said, 'Aye, for this little one keeps me up half the night.'

Kerin made the expected noises of appreciation over the oblivious baby, then added, 'Are these lights you have seen as bright as that first one?'

'Oh no, they are not. But they started only after the great light appeared then faded,' said the girl. Pleased to be seen as a source of authority by older women, she continued, 'They are a little like the Heavenly rain at star-season, save they do not fall to the ground; they merely flash and are gone.'

'They are a mystery and a worry,' said her mother. 'Whatever can such omens mean? We must pray that these uncertain times soon end!'

'Indeed we must,' said Kerin absently, and took her leave before they could ask her to share gossip from the Tyr.

CHAPTER TEN

'Nual! Wake up! Please, you have to wake up—' Taro knew she wasn't dead – he'd know if she died, even if she was on the other side of the galaxy. Or in a different one entirely. But she was *totally* out of it; he could barely sense her in his head. He was still trying to decide whether he should shake her, hug her tighter or crawl off to the medbay when the shakes hit. He raised a hand to his face; his fingers came away crusted with dried blood. It was just a nosebleed; Nual'd had one too.

They needed water. That'd help. He could wash off the blood, and a drink might stop him feeling like he'd sucked all the juices out of his own stomach. He managed to stand up on the third attempt, and, too dizzy to risk flying, crossed the rec-room to the galley in a drunken stagger, bouncing off the furniture. After he'd had a drink and cleaned his face he felt better, and was almost able to walk in a straight line when he returned to Nual with a wet cloth and a bulb of water. She was finally stirring.

<*You all right?*> he thought to her.

<*Will be. Very thirsty.*> She didn't open her eyes when he put the bulb to her lips, but she drained the contents. He washed her face, for she was still too weak to do it herself. He offered to help her to the couch but she assured him she was fine, adding, <*You should go check on Jarek.*>

As he floated up through the hatch he heard Jarek say, 'We'll call back when he's finished. *Heart of Glass* out.'

'Don't know about you,' croaked Taro by way of greeting, 'but I feel pretty much finished already.'

77

Jarek turned, and gave a half-snort, half-laugh. 'No shit? You certainly look like you've been to one party too many.'

'Says the man covered in puke!'

Jarek laughed at that, and Taro joined in, though he wasn't sure what was so funny. They spent a while giggling and pointing at each other like kids who'd been at the burnt mash, but as the hysteria passed, Taro looked around and noticed the view outside.

'What the fuck's that?' he asked, pointing shakily at the red-gold patch of light filling about a quarter of the dome.

'That's a fucking lightsail,' Jarek snorted, then got himself under control and said, 'It's a lightsail. I'll explain later, all right?'

'Yeah, sure.' Taro looked beyond the lightsail, where dozens of lights were zipping or gliding around against the starry backdrop. A few of them were big enough or close enough that he could make out colours, even hints of structure. 'Busy here, ain't it?'

'Oh yes. The woman who just commed us is currently smoothing things out with local Traffic Control.'

'A woman? Thought it was all males?'

'I don't think she's Sidhe; it looks like there might be humans here. She's given us coordinates for our "specially prepared accommodation", whatever that might be, and she'll be in contact again once our passenger has deleted Aleph's coordinates from the ship's comp.'

'You mean Vy? Guess I should go wake him, then.'

'If you don't mind. How's Nual doing?'

'Rough, but getting better.'

Taro went down to the cargo-hold and started the revival cycle on the comabox. When he returned to the rec-room Nual had managed to get herself onto a couch. She sat up groggily when he came in. 'What's happening?' she asked. She was using normal speech so Taro didn't immediately pick up her emotions.

'We've made contact and we're motoring to the rendezvous point,' Taro replied. He thought he knew what was bugging her. Normally Nual travelled under a false ID – since the Sidhe were meant to be long-dead, in human-space no one had any reason to suspect she wasn't just a very hot human woman. But here they knew the truth, and despite the Minister's assertion that there were other female Sidhe rebels out there, Taro still doubted she'd be welcome at Aleph. 'We'll get properly cleaned up, then you should get some rest,' he added gently.

'Good idea,' she said, managing a faint smile.

Taro would've liked to crash out too, but he made do with a bulb of strong caf. By the time he'd got Nual tucked up in their cabin and taken a bulb up to Jarek, the comabox had cycled, and Taro expected Vy to be awake, if not already up. But when he got to the cargo-hold, he found the comabox lid was still down, though the lights were green.

'Wakey-wakey,' he said as he lifted the lid.

The boy lay on the cushioning, panting and wild-eyed. He blinked up at Taro, looking terrified. 'I can't hear myself,' he whispered. 'There's nothing! *Nothing!*'

Taro was confused for a moment, then he realised what was bothering Vy. 'It's all right,' he said, trying to sound comforting, 'you're meant to be here, so you've been given everything you need, right?'

'Everything I need?'

'To do your mission. He – you – *Khesh* wouldn't have sent you out without what you need, would he?' At least, that was what Taro was assuming. 'You'll be fine.'

'I don't— I don't *feel* fine.' He looked harder at Taro. 'You know what it's like, don't you? You and her, you know how it feels.'

'How what—? Oh, you mean how it feels to be part of the City.'

'Yes! Don't you want it to be like that always?'

'Can't say I do, but then, I'm only human. Listen, you got nothing to worry about. It's all going to plan. Here, I'll help you up.'

Vy let Taro support him while he climbed out of the comabox, and kept hold of Taro's hand afterwards. Taro didn't mind: let the boy take whatever comfort he could get. At least Taro knew what he'd lost – well, as far as any human could.

Vy only let go of Taro's hand to climb the ladder up to the bridge, then marched straight over to the comp without a word.

Jarek leaned back and pointedly muttered, 'You're welcome.'

Taro was pleased to see Vy acting a bit more shit-together than when he'd first woken up. 'I guess someone should keep an eye on him,' he said to Jarek.

'Don't worry, I plan to. You can go and get a bit of rest if you like; if he takes as long as last time he'll be at least a couple of hours.'

'Thanks, I will – but listen, he's having some problems.'

'What sort of problems?'

'While he was in the Tri-Confed system he was in contact with Khesh – the mind in the City. He's lost that contact and it's doing his head in.'

'Oh great. And I thought he was difficult before.'

'Yeah … Not sure we can do much about it, though.'

'Well, once he's finished the job he came to do …' Jarek raised his eyebrows meaningfully.

'You're not—?'

'—no, I'm not going to flush the little bastard out of an airlock, tempting though it is. But if you find he's fallen asleep again when you get up, don't panic. That would just be me testing a theory.'

Taro set the alarm on his com; it wasn't fair on Jarek to sleep for too long. Nual didn't stir when he got up.

Jarek was in the rec-room, cleaning up the last of the puke. From the way he moved and the glitter in his eyes, Taro guessed he was currently running on something a bit stronger than caf. Not that Taro blamed him; three hours' sleep had only made him realise how tired he really was. Vy stood by the ents unit with a headset on, hands waving and head dipping, deep in some total immersion game.

'You didn't have to knock him out then?' said Taro, nodding towards Vy.

'No, but I did have to tell him to stop dicking with my comp. Then I suggested he might want to go back into stasis.'

'I'm guessing he wasn't up for that.'

'You could say that. He burst into tears.'

'He's scared he won't wake up.'

'Yeah, that's what I figured. That's why I didn't tranq him. Well, he's distracted for now. We're almost there, so I'm afraid you'll need to wake Nual too.'

Taro went back to the cabin, where he bent over Nual and woke her with a kiss. She came too with a start, then flinched away from his touch.

'Hey! It's all right,' he said gently.

'No...'

Even in the dim cabin light he could see her eyes weren't focused properly.

'It isn't all right. Not all right at all.'

'What's wrong?' Taro felt suddenly cold. 'Have you ... *seen* something? What is it?' he asked breathlessly, 'Is it—? Should we just turn around again?' Part of him wanted to see Aleph; another part was freaked to hell, though that could just be exhaustion combined with the mental backwash from whatever was doing Nual's head in.

'No. Not that I could make another transit right now anyway.' She was calmer now, but she sounded grave. 'What I sensed ... we need to be careful. I mean, more careful than we would be anyway. This flash was about you – or rather, us.'

'What about us?' asked Taro, warily.

'I think – I *believe* – that while we're here, we have to pretend not to be lovers.'

'*What?* Why?'

'Prescience isn't about knowing the next card to be drawn, or what the weather will be like where we're going, Taro. All I get is a certainty that a particular course of action will lead to a bad outcome. In this case ... in this case, I'm pretty certain that to avoid something awful happening we need to hide our feelings for each other.'

'How long for?'

'The immediate future. I know this isn't what you want to hear; it's not what I want either. But if we do not follow my intuition then I believe we're heading for disaster.'

Taro threw his hands up. 'And what's that mean, "heading for disaster"?'

'I don't know! It isn't like these flashes are something I can control.'

Taro felt the edge of her anger before she reined it back. He tried not to be afraid; she loved him, she'd never hurt him intentionally. But the thought of not being able to touch her, to hold her … that did hurt. 'Are you sure? I mean, this prescience shit ain't exactly reliable.'

'You're right,' said Nual quietly, 'it isn't. We cannot know for certain. But are you really willing to take the risk?'

'I dunno. Maybe if you had some idea what'll happen if we *don't* make like we're just good friends …'

Nual shook her head ruefully. 'I wish I did. I'm sorry.'

'You ain't gonna budge on this, are you?'

'No.'

'Shit.' Rather than have a pointless argument he'd end up losing, Taro turned on his heel and walked out.

Vy was still in his game, on a fairly hectic level if all the flailing and lunging was anything to go by. Taro snorted and went up to the bridge.

Now the view through the dome showed a close-up of a pure white sphere, the brightest, cleanest structure Taro had yet seen in space. At first it was impossible to tell how big it was, then he spotted a tiny rectangular pit that he realised was an airlock. That made the sphere at least half a klick across.

'Hope that 'lock's the right size for our ship,' he said by way of greeting.

Jarek turned his couch to face him. 'I think it will be. I reckon the locals made the whole hab especially for us.'

'Fuck really? Well, that was nice of them, weren't it?'

'What's wrong, Taro?'

'Nual, she's— You know how she's seen stuff that might happen a couple of times before? Well, apparently now the universe is telling her we should pretend we're not lovers while we're here.'

'"Here" as in—?'

'I dunno! In there, maybe.' Taro gestured at the sphere.

'I imagine they'll be watching us as soon as we leave the ship; perhaps that's what she's worried about. You've tried asking her, have you?'

''course I have. She don't know either – but she's gonna do it, so I guess I ain't got much choice.'

CHAPTER ELEVEN

The woman who originally greeted them – and who, Jarek noted, had still not introduced herself – commed the *Heart of Glass* again just before the ship docked with the sphere. She explained, a little apologetically, that Jarek and his companions would have to go through decontamination before they could enter the hab. Jarek had expected something like that: Aleph had been isolated from human-space for a very long time. He only hoped they wouldn't pick up any local bugs here. He'd had quite enough of that on Serenein.

Beyond the airlock, a short, plain corridor led straight into the decon-unit. It employed 'wash and flash' tech, like any particularly isolated and paranoid system in human-space: strip naked, get sprayed, get air-dried, put on goggles for a UV sweep, then collect your treated clothes and possessions. Jarek was initially confused not to be put through the usual final step: there was no med-tat reader to scan the invisible tattoo on the inside of his wrist in order to check his internal health. Presumably med-tats were a relatively recent – that is, *human* – innovation.

They met up on the far side of the stark white world of the decon-unit, in a plushly carpeted, tastefully decorated and subtly lit area with several doorways off it. There were no doors, and when Jarek spotted a room with a bed in it, he muttered that he was going to lie down for a bit: exhaustion had overcome stim, and sleep was no longer optional. He didn't bother to undress.

He slept long enough to banish the worst of the shiftspace hang-over.

When he awoke, he suffered a moment of disorientation – *where the hell am I? Oh yes, in another galaxy:* holy shit! – but physically, he felt fine. When he sat up he realised he'd slept through someone coming into his room; there was stuff that didn't belong to him strewn around, and from the look of the rumpled covers, someone had slept on the other side of the massive bed. *What the fuck?* Belatedly, Jarek worked it out: if anyone boarded the *Heart of Glass* and had a look around, they'd quickly spot the fact that the ship had only two cabins. And if he and Taro were going to follow Nual's advice, then not only would they have to make sure no one suspected Taro and Nual were lovers; they'd actually have to give the impression that Taro was *Jarek*'s lover. It was good thinking by Taro, to move into the same room. He wondered how far the boy would take the ruse; the two of them had shared a bed once before, but Jarek had been under no illusions, then or now, about who Taro really wanted.

Between the knowledge that strangers were going over his ship and the cold realisation that they were entirely at the mercy of their hosts, Jarek's initial good mood quickly soured. He got up and went to find the others.

Now he was awake enough to appreciate it, Jarek found himself impressed at their accommodation. The antiseptic stench of the decon-unit had dissipated and he could actually smell how new this place was. Every need was catered for – there was even a swimming pool, complete with artificial waves. The larger rooms, like the pool and the gym – Jarek assumed those devices were meant for exercise rather than torture – had curved floors and ceilings, a reminder that they were built into the inner surface of a sphere. But though he was used to seeing different styles on different worlds, somehow the décor didn't quite match ideas of human norms: furniture designs looked subtly wrong, colour combinations slightly off. The layout was also weird; though there were corridors, rooms often opened straight into other rooms, and none of the rooms had doors, not even the bathrooms.

He found the dining area by following his nose; from the smell of it someone else had eaten in here recently. He was just working out the instructions on the food dispensers – they were marked with a mixture of hard-to-read script and pictograms – when he heard a shriek from nearby.

As he ran towards the shriek, the cry came again, followed by Taro's voice, sounding placatory. He tracked the source of the fuss to a room on the far side of a cushion-filled lounge; the otherwise bare room had been set up as a hologaming cube. It looked like Taro and Vy had been running a game set in a jungle: the room's walls were hidden by the convincing illusion of green and blue foliage, and a soundtrack of hoots, hisses and tuneful whistles was playing under the ongoing argument. When Jarek walked through the holofilled gap, Taro was brandishing a gaming headset at Vy. 'Just keep playing, please? They'll come and find us when they're ready.'

Vy shook his head violently. 'I can't ... can't just ... *It's not enough!* The game ... it's not *enough*.'

'Enough what?' asked Jarek.

Taro turned to him, looking exasperated. 'Wish I fucking knew!'

His com chimed; at the same moment he heard the jaunty tone of Taro's com. Taro looked at Jarek as if to say, *Do you want to get this one?*

Jarek was unsurprised to find that the caller didn't have an ID-tag. He raised his hand and said, 'Yes?'

'Greetings and good day. Query: has sufficient rest been taken?'

Despite the lack of introduction, Jarek was fairly sure he was speaking to the woman who'd originally hailed him. 'Yes, we're feeling a lot better. Thanks for asking.'

'Query: would a face-to-face meeting be convenient at this time?'

'Sounds good to me. Where were you thinking of? We're still finding our way around the place.' Realising he should be a little more diplomatic he added, 'This is a very impressive hab you've created for us.'

'Statement: your compliment is appreciated. Request: kindly return to the lounge behind you. After that, turn left and carry straight on through the next three rooms. That will bring you to a garden area designed to be a pleasant place to meet and talk.'

'Thanks. And does this invitation extend to all of us?'

'Affirmative.'

The detailed instructions were confirmation, if he needed it, that they were under surveillance.

Vy trailed after them, looking close to tears, and they followed the nameless woman's directions and emerged into a garden, which was filled with a mixture of familiar and unfamiliar plants, displayed in a mixture of familiar and unfamiliar ways. Jarek found himself taking a deep breath of the pleasantly scented air. The most obvious path led between a pair of bushes, clipped or force-grown to perfect cubes; they had identical green and white foliage. One bush was covered in pale pink flowers, the other in dark red fruits.

Jarek stopped and squinted up into the bright 'sky'. He could make out a golden glow high overhead; the light was in a spectrum much loved by holodrama makers, said to be that of Sol, the star of Old Earth. Jarek had not yet visited Old Earth, though he planned to get round to it some day, even if the cradle of humanity was more of a destination for tourists than traders. Aleph's own sun was a young, stable dwarf-star, and far redder than Sol. Since the machine-merged Sidhe males were effectively immortal, and had access to limitless energy, it made sense that they'd choose a system with a weak, long-lived star and plenty of loose raw materials.

'We going to this meeting then?' Taro asked, interrupting his reverie.

'Sorry, yes.' He followed Taro between the bushes. Nual, waiting for them on the other side, fell into step next to Jarek, on the opposite side to Taro.

The path led them through further pleasant landscaping, complete with a bubbling stream, to a clearing shaded by golden-leaved trees that emitted a faint but soothing rustle. The 'land' had been built up into shaped banks covered in soft grass, and one of these natural seats was occupied by a small dark woman wearing a black one-piece suit. She stood as they entered the glade. Jarek couldn't tell her age, but she had an open, welcoming face. From the way she checked them over he guessed she wasn't going to miss much.

Before she could speak Vy rushed over to her and gabbled, 'I need to speak to your patron! It's urgent!'

After a momentary loss of composure the woman replied evenly, 'Apologies: your request is not feasible. There is no patron.'

'You're human, aren't you?' asked Vy rudely, thrusting his face up at hers.

<She is human, by the way. I can read her freely.>

Jarek started at Nual's mental observation. For a moment he was illogically worried that even their thoughts were being monitored, but that was rubbish, of course. Only female Sidhe could read minds. The males' talents lay in different areas.

'Assertion: this individual is lingua,' the woman was saying, 'and as such does not answer to any one patron. You are Khesh's avatar, aye-okay?'

'Yes, yes. I need to speak to someone in charge, *now*.'

'Your request is conveyed. However, the situation is complicated. Please allow explanations to be provided, after which all may ask questions freely.' She didn't sound offended at being shouted at by a crazy kid-avatar. Her gaze flicked from Vy to Jarek. 'Query: is the preference for conversing whilst sitting, standing or walking?'

'I'm fine standing if everyone else is,' he said, looking at the other two, who both nodded. Given Vy's unreasonable behaviour, he wanted their hosts to know that the rest of them weren't going to be any trouble.

Vy waved his hands. 'It's *urgent*,' he said, offended that their host dared pay attention to anyone else when he was there.

'Clarification: the relevant parties are now aware of your request,' she replied gently. 'Any response will be passed on at once.'

Her reply satisfied Vy enough to make him back off. He flopped onto the ground and started to pull up grass.

'Sorry,' said Jarek, 'he's been like this since we got here. I'm afraid I didn't catch your name?'

'Clarification and apology: this individual is lingua, and lingua do not generally employ names when fulfilling their function.' Seeing

Jarek's confused expression she continued, 'Further clarification: lingua act as natural speakers, mediating between the patrons – those you call Sidhe males – and as such, lingua speak with one voice, or rather, as a conduit of many voices.' Her smile softened. 'However, lingua – *we* – use names amongst ourselves, and mine is Ain. The choice is yours, whether to use a designation or a name when dealing with this individual.'

'Names are good,' said Jarek carefully. He wondered if she was having to do some mental gymnastics to fit in with his worldview.

Ain went on, 'Statement: this lingua forms the interface between you and the patrons. Please be aware, if you were not already, that your presence is controversial. For this reason it has been decided that only a single lingua should have face-to-face contact with you.'

'So we don't get to meet any of the old males, then?' Taro asked, sounding a little disappointed.

Jarek tried not to wince. Their assigned lingua was their only source of info, and as the males were no doubt listening in, he'd been planning on avoiding that kind of awkward question, at least to begin with.

'Affirmative: you will not meet any patrons.' Was that amusement in her tone, or shock?

'What about avatars? You got them here?' Taro asked.

'Affirmative: most patrons support avatars, but to let any one avatar come here would be seen as favouritism to the patron it represented.'

'Shame.' Taro's tone was sarcastic. He looked down at Vy, still sulking at their feet.

Jarek noted her use of *it* to refer to an avatar. 'You were going to explain the complexities of the situation?' he prompted.

'Clarification follows. Please interrupt if this lingua repeats known facts, or if you require additional information regarding any points raised.

'Know that Aleph has many patrons. The patrons rarely agree, but they have the wisdom not to let their disputes become disruptive to the system at large.'

'When you say "many patrons",' said Jarek, 'how many are we talking about?'

'Clarification: just over twenty thousand hold voting rights in the Consensus. The Consensus is both the place and method of our governance. Any decisions affecting multiple domains must be taken in the Consensus.'

'And a domain is the extent of a given male's influence?' Jarek asked. Twenty thousand non-cooperative Sidhe males living in one system certainly qualified as complicated in his eyes.

'Aye: domains vary greatly in extent and nature. Some patrons live entirely virtually, taking little or no interest in the universe outside. Others support self-sufficient worlds or habitats.'

'And humans live on these worlds? I mean, aside from your people.'

'Affirmative. Humans live in or on approximately one third of the domains. Lingua have no homeworld, unless you count the physical site of the Consensus, where we are birthed.'

Jarek had a sudden suspicion. 'Are you a clone?'

'Affirmative. All lingua are clones.'

Jarek quashed his uneasiness; because of their problems breeding true, most female Sidhe were clones. But Nual said Ain was human. 'How about the humans in the domains: are they clones?'

'Negative: cloning is forbidden save to make lingua.'

'So the understandably-peeved pilot of the lightship I spoke to when we first arrived is an ordinary human?'

'Affirmative.'

'That ship looked like it was heading out-of-system; where was it going?'

'It travels to the nearest star, possibly beyond. I am not party to the intentions of its patron.'

'I thought you – well, the patrons – were stuck in the one system.'

'Affirmative, to an extent. As you now know, journeying here is a more traumatic experience than making a transit within humanity's home galaxy. For the patrons it was worse still. Even you' – for the first time she directly addressed Nual – 'only experienced a fraction of what they endured. When added to their previous transit experience, this was enough to destroy many who made the exodus. Insanity or death took them. Most of the survivors built themselves into constructions too large to enter shiftspace. Even those still relatively unencumbered would never risk repeating the journey. However, the patrons used up much of the matter in this system in building the structures they now rule and inhabit. To procure more, patrons occasionally send ships crewed by humans to nearby stars, where they secure rare resources, returning them via mass-drivers; they may also set up colonies there. Other patrons send human crews out to explore without knowing what they will find. Without shiftspace travel, such missions take many years, and the crew must either pass the time in stasis or else live out several generations.'

'How about the patrons themselves? Do they ever leave?'

'Affirmative. Any patron who feels unable to live within the Consensus may fix a drive to his domain and leave. Some of these remain in contact with the Consensus. Some do not.'

So the inhabitants of Aleph *were* expanding, just very slowly. One thing still puzzled Jarek. 'The lightship we accidentally damaged: it had a hi-tech sail, but why use a lightship at all when you've got zepgen?'

'Request for clarification: the term zepgen is not familiar.'

'Right. It's a power-source.' Jarek hoped he hadn't screwed up by mentioning it.

'Query: does zepgen draw energy into our universe from outside?'

'That's right.'

'Such a device is known to us as a dimension-engine. It is amongst the technologies that are reserved solely for the use of patrons.'

Jarek might have expected the males to be jealous of their tech – which brought him back to their reason for coming here in the first place. 'And how about beacons? I assume you know about them, even if you've never seen one.'

'Beacons are not a subject the lingua have much knowledge of. The patrons have informed this lingua that they are complicated to make, which is why these accommodations have been provided for you. You may have to wait here for several days for the beacon to be completed and brought here.'

'Ah. I hadn't realised that. Not that it's a problem.' Though Jarek wasn't sure Taro would feel that way, given the current situation with Nual.

'While you wait,' Ain went on, 'you may summon this lingua whenever you need, and you may ask whatever you wish. It is a lingua's function to inform; this individual's presence should be viewed as part of the patrons' hospitality.'

'Thanks, that's good to know,' said Jarek. He didn't mention the deal with Khesh. Though the Minister had given them the impression that the Aleph males were providing the beacon as a favour, Jarek doubted it was as simple as that. But for now at least, he wasn't going to question the arrangement.

CHAPTER TWELVE

For the rest of that day, Ifanna lay unmoving on her filthy bed. She was vaguely aware of daylight growing, and of pain receding. The bar of light from the high window moved across the wall; as it crept up onto the ceiling, the healer returned. The woman cleaned up the last of the blood and examined Ifanna again.

'My – the child?' whispered Ifanna, not sure what she was asking.

'Gone to the pyres with a priest's blessing,' said the healer gently.

That was something, at least.

After the healer left, Ifanna wanted to pray, but the words would not come. Instead she waited, empty and numb, for death.

When the door opened the next morning, it was almost a relief.

In the doorway stood the Rhethor of Plas Morfren, a muscular man of middle years who would have looked more like a farmer than a priest without his shaved head and robes. She might have expected the Rhethor himself to come for her, because he was the Reeve's judge and a powerful priest, one who would not easily be turned by her will. She circled her breast, though it felt strange to make the gesture lying down.

'The healer says you are able to stand,' he said, 'so get up.'

He did not call her *chilwar* – child – as a priest should when addressing a lay person, and Ifanna was chilled by this confirmation that, in the eyes of the servants of the Mothers at least, she was already beyond redemption. She stood, though it took some effort.

The Rhethor gestured behind him and men dressed in the

Reeve's livery came in to bind her. There were four of them in all; two held crossbows trained on her while the others hobbled her feet and tied her hands. Ifanna was oddly gratified at still being subject to such careful precautions. She wondered if the fear of her had grown; perhaps her fame had spread as she languished here. While the men checked her bonds, she asked, '*Gwas*, will there be many there?' She called him 'Father', the priestly title of respect: to do otherwise would acknowledge her damned state.

'What do you mean?'

'At— At the trial.' She should have given more thought to this! She determined now that she would retain her dignity to the end, and not beg, or curse.

'You are not to be tried.'

'I—' Would they just kill her, without justice being seen to be done? 'My mother said the Reeve would want a trial!'

'Your mother is dead.'

'Dead?'

'She died some weeks back. She was one of the last victims of the falling fire.'

So Maman had gone to the Skymothers. No doubt she had died without speaking out against Da. Ifanna felt a quick flash of anger at her mother's cowardice. Hard on the heels of that came shame, that she should think so badly of her own dead mother, and grief, for now she would never be reconciled to her. 'And what of me?' she asked faintly.

'You are being given a chance you probably do not deserve,' said the Rhethor. Then, to the men, 'Bring her.'

Ifanna did not resist. Flanked by the guards, she let the Rhethor lead the way out of her cell. Though the corridor outside was as grim as the cell, the sight of a view that stretched beyond three paces nearly made her miss her step. She caught herself and carried on. By the time they came to the turning that led out of the cell-block she had adjusted to this small freedom, and to the possibility of more. '*Gwas!*' she called out to the Rhethor, 'what is to be my fate?'

For a moment she thought he had not heard her, or perhaps had decided to ignore her impudent question. Then he stopped, holding up a hand to stop the guards, and turned to face her. Beyond him Ifanna saw light, a door open to a bright morning. Her eyes drank in the sight.

'Your mother came to see the Reeve while you were awaiting your trial,' he said. 'I do not know what passed between them, but after her death, he asked that I petition the Tyr to have you sent there rather than be tried in Plas Morfren. I believe he did not expect this request to be honoured, but he felt obliged to make it on Mistress Aelwen's behalf.'

'I do not— I am to go to the Tyr? To Dinas Emrys?' She had heard tales of the City of Light, but never met anyone who had seen it for themselves. Yet her mother had travelled to Plas Morfren, no doubt against Da's wishes, in order to petition that Ifanna be sent there. She felt a renewed wash of mingled shame and grief.

'Aye. Once within the Tyr you will be judged by the Beloved Daughter of Heaven.'

'The— The Cariad herself is to hear my case?' Even as Ifanna's hand circled her breast, dread began to descend.

'I too was surprised when the Reeve's request was granted, yet such is the will of Heaven.' The Rhethor's voice was sharp with resentment.

'But—' The Cariad would see into her soul, and be appalled at the corruption there. 'This is not what I want! Let my end be here, please.'

The Rhethor took a step towards her. His face was in shadow, but Ifanna knew the signs of fury in a man. She cringed, tensing for the blow.

He did not strike her, but his voice was low and harsh. 'How dare you question this decision! I would see you drowned for the abomination you are, but others have ruled that this is not to be. Now, you will not speak to me again, do you understand?'

Ifanna nodded, and the Rhethor turned on his heel. Ifanna followed, her heart racing. When they came out into the courtyard she bowed her head under the weight of the open sky, then forced herself to straighten. As she started to look around, something was slipped over her head. She flinched at the pressure across her eyes, until a voice behind her said quietly, 'Steady there, and keep those eyes closed.'

She heard the Rhethor mutter, 'Have you a spare blindfold?'

'Aye, *Gwas*.'

'Then use it to stop her mouth.' As they tied the gag he called, 'I would keep that on her, *chilwar*, lest her words corrupt you.'

Hands grabbed her arms and she was half-dragged, half-pushed forward. More hands lifted her up, and she was laid down ungently on a wooden floor. She heard voices, but could not make out any words, until someone ahead yelled 'Hyup! Hyup!' and the wooden floor began to move. So she was in a cart of some sort, most likely pulled by oxen ...

She spent the rest of the day lying in the bottom of the cart, listening to the steady plod of hooves and the occasional snatches of conversation above her. It took her a while to differentiate the voices, but she had little else to do. She was being accompanied by three people, plus a driver. One was a priest, one a woman; the other appeared to be a guard, possibly the woman's husband. Ifanna did not recognise any of the voices, and nothing they said gave her any further clue as to her fate in Dinas Emrys. She had awakened without hope this morning, believing her situation could not worsen, but she had been wrong: now she was to face Heaven's judgment directly, while she yet lived. The Cariad's fearsome gaze would reveal her every sin; her lies would be uncovered, her small powers of deception and control crushed by the will of the Skymothers' earthly representative. All her secrets would be brought into the light – and those dark secrets were all she had. Of course the Skymothers knew everything already, but the Cariad was here, within Creation, as the living manifestation of their will. Ifanna wondered if her maman had wanted to send her to the Tyr for that very reason. Unable to face bringing the truth into the light herself, she had turned the task over to the gods. Ifanna dismissed the thought as unworthy at best, blasphemous at worst.

Yet the Rhethor had called it 'a chance she did not deserve' – did that mean she might somehow escape death? Or was he talking about a chance to redeem her soul, to not be eternally condemned to the Abyss? That was her deepest hope, and she turned her prayers towards it.

When the cart stopped for the night her gag was removed, though the blindfold and bindings remained. The woman held a cup to her lips and spooned pottage into her mouth, then replaced the gag and led her away from the camp to relieve herself.

Ifanna was told to lie down beside the cart; her hands were tied to one wheel, her feet to the other. They were obviously not taking any chances. As her companions were about to settle for the night the woman said, 'Mothers preserve us! That was a bright one!'

Ifanna had no clue what she was talking about, but the comment provoked uneasy muttering from the others.

The next day she tried to distract herself from brooding by focusing on the sounds from beyond the cart: the *thrum* and *caw* of a paddywader taking wing, and the calls of men splashing through the fields – from the sound of it, harvest had begun.

That evening, after she had been fed and before the gag was replaced, she asked meekly whether she might be allowed to sit up the next day. She received no answer, but in the morning they sat her upright on the floor of the cart, propped up between the end-board and the woman.

It rained that night; the others, asleep under the cart, remained dry while she got soaked.

She had no idea how far it was to the City of Light. From the fifth day on, the sounds around them began to change. Instead of splashes and the sucking of mud she heard the swish of blades cutting crops, and the sounds of unknown animals, quite different from the lowing of water-oxen. The very air began to change; it felt somehow thinner and drier.

The next day was the Sevenday, and she was left tied to the cart while her companions attended a service nearby; the wind brought the sound of chanting to her. She tried to form her own prayers in her head.

She listened intently to the everyday talk of her companions, who were all members of the Reeve's household. The man and woman had volunteered for this job in order to see their son, who was an acolyte in the Tyr, and a source of great pride to them. The driver had coins to trade for luxuries not available elsewhere, so the cart would not return to Plas Morfren empty. And the priest was there to offset Ifanna's evil influence – though he too was looking forward to visiting the holiest place in Creation.

The sight on which the woman had commented that first night occurred again regularly, and Ifanna finally pieced together that they were seeing mysterious lights appearing briefly in the sky, as had happened every night since a single, bright light had appeared around Midsummer. These strange omens were causing great unease.

The road began to improve, something Ifanna, sitting on the hard wooden floor of the cart, was grateful for. They passed other travellers more often now. She wondered if any of them saw her, sitting low in the cart.

She tried not to consider the future, for whenever she did, terror flooded her soul. Given the choice she might take her own life rather than face the Cariad, but there was no more chance of that than there was of making her escape. And if she did kill herself, then her soul would be doubly damned.

CHAPTER THIRTEEN

Taro was happy to leave the talking to Jarek, who asked the lingua about everything, from how their hab was set up to the wheelings and dealings of the Aleph 'patrons' (a good word, thought Taro; from what the lingua said the males were as possessive of 'their' humans as Khesh was). When Jarek's stomach grumbled loudly enough to be heard over the conversation, they moved from the garden to the diner, and carried on talking while they ate. Nual stayed in the background, trying to make like she wasn't there, though Taro knew she'd be listening for lies.

In the garden Vy had been sulky but quiet; when they moved inside he started getting twitchy again. Finally, in one of his freaky outbreaks of formal speech, he asked sniffily how long it was going to take to organise 'a private talk with the powers that be'.

The lingua repeated her promise to tell him as soon as she had any news.

Vy jumped up and started pacing, and Taro, seeing Jarek's imploring look, suggested to the boy that they leave the others to their talk and go explore the hab. He was glad to get away too; being around Nual and not being allowed to touch her was doing his head in.

Vy agreed only after the lingua promised – and repeated her promise – to com Taro immediately she got a response to his request.

The way the lingua had described it, the gardens took up nearly half the hab. The living space comprised a single layer of rooms, in the other half, and inside that was a central core containing the tech that ran the place, plus Ain's living area. They weren't allowed in there, though the core had a passage out to a second airlock; when Jarek had been orbiting the hab, they'd spotted it, looking subtly different in shape and size to a standard airlock. The lingua had told Jarek she was alone in the core, though several patrons had wanted to send in their own avatars. Taro was glad that particular idea had been voted down in their Consensus. He already felt like he was living in a zoo.

The trick with Vy was to keep him distracted, so Taro took him back to the garden and they explored the paths, grottoes and streams (actually just one stream, cleverly looping around and back on itself). The place reminded Taro a bit of the Gardens in Khesh City, except where they were designed for the tourist hordes; this garden had been made specially for the four of them. Some of the plants were pretty weird. The miniature meadow of delicate bell-shaped flowers in purples, pinks and blues was nice enough but he wasn't sure about the clearing next door, full of knee-high mats of dense multi-coloured fibres; they were soft as a bed if you pressed down on them, but if they touched bare skin they set it tingling in a way that was just a little bit freaky – though not unpleasant. Then there was the hammock of living vines strung between two fruit trees that moulded itself around you as you lay in it, and the bush with spiral orange leaves that shivered and retracted if you touched them. Even the grass wasn't quite right: it looked like normal grass, even felt and smelled like it if you picked some, but when you looked closely, every leaf was the same shape and size, and it grew in a regular, repeating pattern.

Vy liked all the new stuff to see and do, but as soon as he'd had a go at something – climbed a tree, swung in the hammock, eaten some fruit, had a dip in a sandy-bottomed pool – he was off again, looking for new experiences. Taro would've liked to hang around in each place a bit longer ... but they weren't here for fun. He couldn't forget that this whole set-up was meant to take their minds off being stuck in a box and spied on. Not that Taro minded the enclosed environment as such; open skies still did his head in, and some deep part of him felt happier inside an artificial world.

What bugged him was that they had to stay here until the 'patrons' let them out.

Still, they were probably safer sealed in the hab than they'd be outside. When Jarek had asked Ain how the males were reacting to having visitors after being isolated for so long she'd admitted there were mixed views: some didn't care, some were curious and some (just a few, she claimed) were hostile to the visit – although, she assured them, all patrons respected the decision to welcome them. Taro hoped they'd keep respecting it.

Other than the core, the lingua hadn't said there was anywhere they couldn't go, so Taro decided to try a little experiment – not only would it entertain Vy for a bit, but it'd be useful to see what they could get away with. He led the way back to a glade they'd passed earlier, and once they were clear of the trees, Taro pointed at the 'sky'. 'So,' he said to Vy, 'what d'you reckon's up there then?'

Vy looked up, shading his eyes. 'Fusion ball,' he said.

Taro noted this useful piece of info, then said, 'No, I mean on the walls – the ones that separate this half of the sphere from the core.'

Vy shrugged. 'Dunno.'

'How about I go find out?'

'If you like.'

Taro kicked off and hovered about ten metres up, checking out the view. It was certainly pretty, but he didn't spot anything new or unexpected. Vy was staring up at him; at least he'd got the boy's attention. Knowing the 'sun' really could burn him made him cautious, but he wasn't interested in that. Instead he flew across to the blue-painted wall that divided the gardens from the forbidden half of the sphere. Close to, it was just that: a wall, with no markings or openings or anything else of interest. He'd expected that, but he gave it a good once-over anyway, just in case. He was half-expecting a call from the lingua, telling him to stop arsing around, but his com stayed silent, so it looked like a certain amount of arsing around was allowed. He took one last look at the gardens – which were a pretty freaky sight, not so much *below* him as wrapped *around* him – then he flew back down.

'Did you find anything?' asked Vy as he landed.

'Nice view, but other than that, fuck-all.'

Vy looked up again, as though expecting Taro to be proved wrong at any moment. Then he looked down and asked wistfully, 'Can you really remember nothing from the Heart of the City?'

Taro answered cautiously, 'Nothing I could put into words.'

Vy knew he and Nual were pretending not to be lovers, so talking about that here might not be so clever. Their experience of – temporarily – taking over from Khesh's consciousness was one of the things that'd brought them together. 'Look Vy,' Taro tried, 'I know you're not happy, but maybe if you told me what the problem is—'

'You *know* what it is!' the boy cried. 'I'm *alone*. I can't— It's just *me*. You can't imagine what that's like!'

'No,' said Taro evenly, 'I can't. And I'm sorry.' Watchers be damned, Taro wanted to know what was really going on. 'I know it's shitty being cut off from the rest of your consciousness, but that wasn't what I meant. Something else's eating you.'

Vy shrugged, and Taro recognised the gesture; he wondered if people found it as irritating when he did it.

'You wanted a private chat with the locals, didn't you? Why?'

Vy shrugged again.

'I thought we were friends,' Taro said, sounding hurt. 'Friends tell each other what's bothering them.'

'Can't tell you,' he said sulkily.

''course you can, if you want too. I won't tell. Even if you just gave me some idea—'

'I *can't* tell you, all right?' Vy shouted, and with that, he stormed off.

Taro hesitated, then followed. He found Vy standing in front of a tree, banging his fists into the gnarled wood. Taro called his name gently, and when Vy turned Taro saw he was crying, and there were spots of blood on his knuckles where he'd been hitting the tree.

Taro raised his arms, and Vy rushed into them. Taro hugged him, patting his head and letting him cry until he was done. Finally

Vy pulled back and said, 'I want to go play some games now.' He turned, expecting Taro to follow.

Perhaps this was what having a younger brother would be like, thought Taro as he trailed along after Vy. *You want to slap him, but you end up helping and protecting the little fucker, even if he doesn't notice.*

They'd only been gaming for a few minutes – Vy was beating Taro as usual – when Taro's stomach cramped. He'd had a snack with Jarek earlier, but it was ages since he'd had a proper meal. The fact that Vy had gone so long without food was further proof, if Taro needed it, that something was fucking up the boy beyond just being apart from Khesh.

He persuaded Vy that they needed to eat, then commed Jarek. Nual was already in the diner with Jarek when he got there. Between them they prepared dinner from an odd mix of foods – Taro didn't recognise any of them, but they all tasted better than ship's rations. While they ate they chatted about nothing in particular, conscious that every word was being overheard. Jarek did tell them he'd gone back to the *Heart of Glass*, and it looked 'just like we left it', which was good.

Taro spent most of the meal trying not to look at Nual, though she didn't seem to have any trouble ignoring him. He found himself getting irritated, and that made him annoyed at himself for being unreasonable. He caught her eye and thought at her, *<Are you angry with me?>*

<Of course not.> She managed to reply without apparently paying any attention to him. *<But we need to keep up the pretence.>*

<If you say so,> he thought back grumpily, and went back to his meal.

Vy returned to the gaming room once they'd eaten. Taro sighed and followed him, though he was pretty tired. At least Vy was losing interest in 'amusing' practical jokes – although he had tipped Taro out of a hammock earlier. But then he'd actually apologised; Taro got the impression the boy was growing up.

After a couple more hours of gaming, Taro needed to crash out.

Vy looked at him earnestly and said, 'I will try to hold myself together. But it's so hard. I need your help. Please.'

'All right,' said Taro, 'but I gotta sleep, even if you don't.'

'Most of these games run in minimal mode. We can take headsets to your room, then you can sleep when you have to. I just ... I don't want to be alone.'

'I understand – better not use my room, though; we don't want to keep Jarek up all night. There's a nice-looking bedroom a few rooms back; why don't we take the gaming gear in there?'

They found when they left the gaming room that the lights outside had dimmed; Taro guessed the others had already turned in, so Ain, or whoever controlled the hab, had decided it was 'night'.

They played together until Taro really couldn't keep his eyes open. 'I really can't stay awake any longer, Vy,' he said, and yawned.

Vy nodded uneasily, saying nothing, and Taro wondered how long the boy could manage without sleep. The *Heart of Glass*'s medbay had a prime selection of drugs to keep a normal human up and active but he had no idea what they'd do to Vy.

As he lay down he had another thought: when did Ain sleep? If she adjusted her night to fit in with theirs, then perhaps night-time might be the right time to have a bit more of a poke around. They obviously didn't mind, or they'd have got Ain to bawl him out for flying up the wall in the garden. Tomorrow he'd get his shimmercloak from the ship so's he could creep around without being seen. Maybe he'd see if he could find one of the doors into the core. But not tonight.

'You must awake now!'

Taro started at the voice. As he opened his eyes, he realised it wasn't Vy, but the lingua Ain. She was leaning over him, gesturing urgently. 'It is vital that you get up and come with me. Now.'

'Wh— Why?' he croaked. It was still dark, but he thought he saw another figure behind her. Vy?

'You are in danger!' the lingua whispered.

'Danger? Y'said we're safe here,' he mumbled, panic cutting through his confusion.

'The situation has changed. Time is short. We must hurry.'

'The others—'

'Gone ahead to your ship. Come on, please!'

Taro sat up and began to struggle off the bed. Good job he'd been too tired to undress properly. When he looked round for his jacket he noticed Vy staring back at him from the doorway. He turned to Ain. 'Why didn't you just com me?'

'Coms are down. All will be explained in due course. First, escape.'

No coms? That sounded serious. As he followed the lingua out, Taro checked the com on the back of his hand. She was right, no network. *What the fuck was going on?* Should he try and contact Nual? He needed to sit still and concentrate to get in touch mentally when they were apart; stumbling through dim, unfamiliar rooms while his heart was going like the slug-autopistol from last night's game wasn't going to make it easy. And if Ain was right, she was already on the *Heart of Glass*. It made sense that the others had gone ahead; their rooms were nearer the 'lock.

Taro didn't complain when Ain upped the pace. The sooner they were all together on the ship and safely out of here, the better. Then Ain could explain what the fuck was happening.

Even before they reached the airlock Taro felt uneasy – more uneasy than just being woken up and told to run away in the middle of the night made him feel. But he was still too befuddled by sleep and panic to work out what the problem was. It was only as they stepped into the 'lock that he realised what was bothering him: his com should have worked even if the local net was down, because it was routed through the *Heart of Glass*. He was turning to say that to Ain when the inner 'lock door opened.

'Hey wait!' he started, 'this ain't—'

CHAPTER FOURTEEN

Nual woke suddenly to the hot aftertaste of ginger and foreboding. Even as she gulped against the burning in her throat, the sensation faded. She tried to hold onto it, repulsed yet desperate; that taste always accompanied a prescient flash, a packet of possibilities from time not yet experienced. She *needed* this—

But it was gone. And so was sleep.

She couldn't relax here. She had been brought up to despise the males of her kind, but though she might no longer feel that mindless hatred – these days she was an enemy of the Sidhe females herself – she was still deeply uncomfortable. All her life she had believed the males were dead. Finding out about Khesh and his two City-state brothers was one thing; discovering that thousands of independent males were living in their own system was something else entirely ...

Yet it took a female Sidhe to navigate here – or at least, it did *now*. When had that changed – and why? If only she could have read the Minister ... but some combination of the males' natural resistance to female powers and the nature of their avatars left the Minister, and Vy, blank spaces in her mental landscape.

She was sure of one thing: she was the first female to come to Aleph for centuries: millennia, even. The thought chilled her.

She had taken on the fight against her sisters knowing it would be hard. Sometimes the sheer scale of what she and her companions were facing paralysed her. Better to have stayed in the mazeways of Khesh City, safely in hiding; better yet never to have rebelled, never to have made herself an enemy of her own people.

But there was no going back.

Jarek had been born for this fight. He was a natural crusader, impulsive and brave. But he did not always consider the consequences of his actions. She wondered if it had occurred to him that the lost world whose cause he had taken up so vigorously existed only because it was of use to the females. They had set Serenein up, kept its location secret, and maintained its rigid theocratic society. Jarek did not seem much inclined to consider what was going to happen when he denied them that asset. And had he considered how Serenein might fit into the males' schemes? The Aleph males must have suspected the existence of such a world, but the females would have gone to great lengths to hide it from them. Serenein was probably the only place in the universe where male Sidhe still existed in the flesh, albeit in a mentally neutered form … and now someone who knew where it was had come to Aleph. Nual shuddered, imagining the machinations going on even now amongst their hosts.

As for Taro, she was glad he was bonding with Vy, even if she detected an element of denial in his actions. Being in love with Taro didn't stop her finding him irritating. However, his current frustration with her was understandable; the prescient flash that had convinced her they should act coolly towards each other had been no more than a strong intuition, with that tell-tale sensation of spicy heat at the back of her throat. The problem was that she had so few experiences to compare it to. The flashes had started only a couple of months ago and they were notoriously vague, as Taro had been quick to point out.

She remembered a story that had circulated amongst the unity when she was growing up, about a seer who had tried to use her sight to avoid a terrible outcome. In the end she had inadvertently caused the disaster herself. Nual shuddered again. No doubt human cultures, where prescience was a legend rather than a rare talent, had plenty of tales like that.

She had not told Taro everything she had sensed about the future; she had said nothing of the deepest and darkest of all her insights, the one that might yet affect the whole of human-space.

If it became more than an unhelpful foreboding she would share it, but for now it remained, along with certain details of her past, nobody's business but her own.

She tried to steer her thoughts onto a more positive track. They could be grateful for one thing: as far as she could tell without an invasive scan, the lingua was exactly what she appeared to be. Ain was nervous, but that was only to be expected: she was dealing with someone she thought of as the enemy, and with outsiders whose mere presence could disrupt her entire world. She had not lied, or withheld any information relating to Jarek's questions, and she felt no personal animosity towards any of them. She really did want to keep the peace and see the visitors happy and safe, just as she claimed – well, actually, she mainly wanted to see them safely gone, but in the meantime, she wanted to minimise the disruption they brought.

Had her talents not been needed to navigate the ship, Nual would never have come to Aleph. And had Taro's support not been necessary to make the transit, she would have asked him to stay behind. But they were committed to this course; to reclaim a world previously controlled by the Sidhe would be a major blow against the hidden empire.

Lying here brooding was not going to achieve anything. She sat up. The lights remained dim, even when she requested them to brighten. It looked like they didn't respond to voice commands, though she hadn't seen any manual controls either. She experienced a sudden pique at having her day controlled like this. It was like being back on the mothership, she thought grimly. As she dressed in the semi-dark she decided that burning off a bit of nervous energy might help. She considered the gym, but didn't much fancy trying to work out alien exercise equipment in the dark. The pool was out too; she was not a good swimmer at the best of times. Finally she settled on a gentle jog through the gardens; though the 'sun' was switched off to simulate night, the paths were well marked by coloured lights.

The garden was silent, and ghostly in the semi-dark. After one lap of the perimeter she augmented her body's reactions to the exercise, inducing it to produce a higher-than-usual level of mood-positive chemicals while ramping back on adrenalin-based changes that would put her more on edge. She ran another three circuits, by which time sweat trickled down her back, and her breathing was harsh in her ears.

Through exhaustion or distraction, Nual left the gardens by the wrong exit, and found herself in a dining room she thought she recognised. Sure she was near the right area, she carried on, through three more rooms, until she came to a door – a *closed* door, which did not open when she approached and had no obvious lock. In a habitat with no doors ... ?

Despite her earlier assumption Nual was no longer so sure she had been to this section of the hab before, and it wasn't long before she admitted to herself that she was lost. Perhaps she should have asked Ain for a floor-plan.

She reached a dead end, and turned around, picking a slightly different route back. This was getting ridiculous; the hab wasn't *that* big. If only the lights would come back on, she would be fine. Surely it must be 'day' by now!

She didn't spot the broken door immediately, as it was half-hidden by draped curtains, but as she got closer she saw the opening in a wall. It looked too small to be a proper door, but when she went up to it, curious, she saw that it *was* a doorway, and a sliding door had been jammed half-open by what had once been a chair and was now a partially flattened tangle of metal tubes. When she peered through, she saw a very different view: a utilitarian corridor, with more closed doors off it. This had to be the way into the core.

For a moment she considered calling Jarek, then decided that she wanted to have a quick look around by herself first. She reached for the half-crushed chair and gave it an experimental tweak. It was jammed tight; the door was not going to close on it. Even so, she decided to fly rather than climb through. She kicked off, then hesitated. She had best check for other sentiences nearby, just in case. Not that she expected anyone; the lingua was probably still asleep—

There was someone behind her.

She spun round in the air—

—to find Ain, standing on the far side of the room, emanating surprise. Nual curtailed her urge to dominate the lingua and dive straight into her head for answers. Instead she made herself say out loud, 'What is going on here?'

'Apologies. A— A problem has occurred.'

'So I see. What sort of problem?'

'There is little data. Power distribution has been affected in some places, though life-support is functioning correctly. Many other systems are unavailable.'

Nual could sense that the lingua was scared, trying hard to hold herself together. 'What are you doing about it?'

'There— Apologies, but there is little this individual *can* do. There are no coms, internal or external; however, the missing surveillance feed will have been noted, and the G— someone should arrive soon to aid us. Please be assured that you are safe and secure here.'

The word she'd tried to avoid saying was *Gatekeeper* – and she was far from sure they were safe. Nual decided not to press the point. 'We should wake the others.'

'Affirmative. That is what this individual was about to do.'

'I may be able to save you a journey.' Nual raised her hand and activated her com. The call took a moment to connect, which was odd. Despite her concern for Taro, she made herself com Jarek first. His initial sleepy irritation evaporated when she explained the situation. Nual suggested he tell Taro, but Jarek said Taro wasn't with him; he had last been seen in Vy's company. 'I think we'd all feel a lot safer back on board the *Heart of Glass*,' he added.

Nual sensed Ain's dismay at the suggestion, but she ignored it. 'I agree,' she said. 'I will call Taro for you, and meet you there.'

But when she tried to com Taro, she got through to the *Heart of Glass*'s voicemail: either he was not answering his com or he was out of range.

Forcing herself to stay calm, Nual said to Ain, 'There is a

problem with Taro's com. We will have to go and get him. Do you know where he is?'

'The room where he and Vy chose to rest is not far off.'

Ain led Nual through vaguely familiar rooms until they came to the closed door Nual had found earlier. The lingua radiated concern and confusion. 'This is not right.'

'You don't say.' Nual extended her senses, feeling for presences beyond the closed door, but there was *nothing*.

She concentrated harder: even a sleeping presence should register, and Taro's most certainly would, but she couldn't sense anything.

The lingua opened her mouth to speak, but Nual cut across her. 'There is no one in there.'

Ain was smart enough not to question Nual's assertion. 'Opening the door will not be possible until the power returns fully. A failsafe must have been tripped.'

'Then let us go and meet up with Captain Reen.' Though Nual kept her tone unconcerned, worry gnawed at her. *Where was Taro?* She attempted to mentally contact him as they made their way through the hab, but without success.

They were halfway to the ship when the lights came back on. Nual felt Ain's relief.

'It appears at least some of the systems have reset,' said the lingua, 'This individual will return to the core to check those which still require intervention or repair.'

'Yes, do that. Unless Captain Reen objects, I'll head back to the area where Vy and Taro were last seen, in case the door has opened again.'

Jarek agreed they needed to find Taro and Vy, but he also pointed out that the problem with Taro's com might be originating at the ship – and he wanted to look over the *Heart of Glass* anyway. 'The situation is getting a bit too hot for comfort,' he muttered, meaning: we might have to run away, even without our beacon.

Nual made her way back to the door, but it was still closed, so she began to retrace her steps, this time examining the doorways she passed through. Now she looked closely, she could see about a quarter of them had recesses which might hide sliding doors.

Her com chirped. It was Ain: the internal com system must be up.

'Urgent request for face-to-face meeting,' said the lingua. Even through the com's tiny speaker Nual could hear the strain in her voice.

'What is it?'

'This news must be given in person. Please, come to the garden; the glade where— where we spoke yesterday.'

Nual resisted the urge to run or fly; she needed to stay calm. Jarek was waiting for her by the bushes where they had met up on their first foray into the garden.

'This doesn't sound good,' said Jarek tersely.

Nual did not trust herself to comment. Instead she asked, 'Is the ship all right?'

'Far as I can tell. I'll want to check the logs again when Ain's told us ... whatever it is she called us here to tell us.'

They continued towards the glade in uneasy silence.

The lingua stood where she had before, under the gold-leafed tree, her mind giving off waves of distress.

'I am so sorry,' said Ain.

'What is it?' asked Jarek.

'An accident has occurred. Vy and Taro are both dead. There was nothing that could be done.'

Nual could sense the lingua truly believed that Taro and Vy were dead. But Nual knew it wasn't true. She would have felt Taro die.

Wouldn't she?

CHAPTER FIFTEEN

Although she had become accustomed to a world defined by sound and smell, Ifanna felt the lack of sight keenly when the ox-cart finally reached Dinas Emrys. She would have loved to see the great buildings and crowded thoroughfares the others were oohing and ahhing over. Instead, her impressions of the City of Light were limited to smell and sound: a cacophony of noise, with traders crying their wares, beggars pleading for alms, shoppers haggling, the creaking of many carts, dogs barking, pack animals braying, and the smells of sweat, incense, ordure and fresh bread, mingled with a dozen others she could not identify.

After a while their route steepened; the oxen pulled harder, snorting with effort, and Ifanna felt herself begin to slide towards the back of the cart. As she scrabbled for the backboard, a firm hand came down on her shoulder, holding her fast.

It was said that the massive rock spire of the Tyr rose straight up from the very centre of the city, and the slender silver thread of the Edefyn Arian issued from deep within the heart of that spire. She imagined this unseen wonder now, towering over them, bridging the gap between Creation and the Heavenly realm. Suddenly she was glad of the blindfold; such a sacred vision might be more than her sin-washed soul could bear.

At last the cart stopped. Her feet were unbound and her female companion helped her stand. Someone picked up the rope that trailed from her hands and led her forward. Ahead she could hear someone speaking – it was too far away to hear what was said clearly, but she could make out the voice of the priest. He seemed to be having a minor disagreement with someone whose voice she did not recognise.

After some time the priest came back. 'There will be a slight delay,' he announced.

Her guard replied, 'Is there a problem, *Gwas*?'

'Hopefully not. But we should put her back on the cart for now.'

As they did so, Ifanna wondered what would happen if there really was a problem, and she was not to go to the Cariad after all. She could not see them taking her all the way back to Plas Morfren.

Finally someone called the priest over; there was more quiet discussion, and she was led forward. She felt the rope being passed to another pair of hands and a voice she did not recognise told her to start walking.

As she did so the sounds around her changed and the air became cooler. She must have entered the Tyr. She could feel the smooth, chill rock through her thin sandals, and the light that seeped in at the edge of her blindfold was white and cold.

The fear returned; she was surrounded by strangers – worse, by *priests* – and she suddenly wished for the company of the party from Plas Morfren, even though they had treated her as little better than baggage.

They turned a couple of corners, then stopped, and someone touched her head. Ifanna flinched away before realising that her blindfold was being removed.

She blinked; though the light was not bright, it took a moment for her eyes to focus. She was standing in a passage cut into rock, at the bottom of a set of steps. The strange white light came from globes set in niches in the walls. Her escort consisted of two priests of Mantoliawn, and four monitors. She had seen monitors before, accompanying the tithe-wagon when it visited Nantgwyn, but these men were far more impressive, with feathers in their helmets and midnight-blue-stained armour that shone with oil. The priests' yellow robes were heavily embroidered and ornamented with metal fragments. One of the priests turned to her and said,

'Your blindfold was removed to allow you to negotiate the steps. Remain next to me until I instruct you otherwise.'

Ifanna was still gagged. She nodded to show her understanding, and followed her escort up more stairs and along further passages. They passed other priests and monitors, and some men wearing striped tabards. She saw only one woman, in the distance. Everyone they encountered took great care to ignore her.

They stopped outside a wooden door, and the monitors unbound her hands. The air was cold on her raw wrists. The priest who had first spoken said, 'Inside this room you will find the means to cleanse and prepare yourself, and suitable clothing for your audience with the Beloved Daughter of Heaven. Someone will return for you in due course.'

The room, which had no other exits, contained a steaming bath, a chair with a soft cream-coloured towel on it and a table loaded with bottles, tubs and pots. For several moments Ifanna just stared at this unlikely outbreak of luxury. Though she knew what a bath was, she had never used one; she had only ever washed in the river, or with a cloth. Yet here she was being offered the chance – no, *ordered* – to take a bath. She snatched off the gag, then rushed over and knelt by the bath. The water was milky, and soft perfume rose with the steam. When she dipped her hand in the water it stung the sores on her wrist, but she did not care.

She stood, stripped off and climbed in. *For now,* she decided as she ran her hands through her hair, teasing out tangles and filth, *I am an animal. I live from moment to moment. And this moment is good.*

She would have liked to stay in the bath longer, but the water was growing scummy and cold, and the priest was bound to return soon. Reluctantly, she got out. Underneath the towel she found a white robe of unusually fine fabric, somewhat short, and lacking in sleeves; there was no under-tunic, and no scarf for her head. She dried, dressed, and combed out her hair. As well as the containers she had seen before, the table held a polished metal disc with a long handle: a mirror, another luxury she had heard of but never seen. She lifted the mirror and stared at the unfamiliar face it showed.

It was far clearer than the occasional reflections she had glimpsed in water. She put the mirror down and examined the containers. They held cosmetics, such as she had seen rich women wear during star-season in Plas Morfren; Ifanna smelled them, and dipped her finger in the pots, but she had no idea how to apply them, so in the end she put them down again.

She did not consider trying the door; even if she had dared, she had heard the priest lock it. She did consider praying, before deciding that it would not be appropriate, given she was merely an animal now. She would live as best she could until death came and made an end of her. She sat on the chair to wait.

After a while, the door opened and a priest beckoned her out. She emerged to find a far larger group than her original escort – which included, she suddenly saw, a girl of her own age, dressed as she was. She smiled at the girl, and received a tight smile in response. The other girl had used the little pots: her pale skin contrasted sharply with eyelids that sparkled deep green and lips as red as ripe fruit.

The priests and monitors were conferring, and not watching their charges closely. The other girl muttered, 'What kind of fool are you then, peasant?'

Ifanna, who had been hoping for an ally, was taken aback. 'One with a civil tongue in my head,' she hissed back. Her response shocked the girl into silence, and Ifanna took the opportunity to ask, 'Why do you call me a fool anyway?'

'Your face. 'Tis plain as a baby's.'

'And yours is as painted as— as—'

'A whore's? Of course it is!' The girl's tone was contemptuous, but Ifanna sensed the fear beneath it. Before she could ask what the girl meant, the priest in charge looked up and bellowed, 'Silence, you two!'

Ifanna made to move away, but the girl looked into her eyes, and to her surprise, Ifanna heard her voice, though her lips did not move: <*You really do know nothing!*>

Ifanna tried to hide her astonishment.

The girl spoke silently again, <*By the Five! You were not even aware we* could *do this, were you?*>

By *this* she presumably meant the silent speech. Ifanna tried to form her thoughts into words. <*No, I was not. Am I to blame for my ignorance?*>

<*No. You should enjoy it while you can.*>

<*Or you could tell me why I am such a fool for not painting my face.*>

<*You have no idea what awaits us, do you?*>

<*I know we are to be judged.*> Ifanna was glad she had not had to admit that out loud. Her carefully won calm was ebbing away.

<*Aye, and if we are found worthy in body and mind we will become Putain Glan.*>

<*And what is that?*> Out of the corner of her eye Ifanna saw a guard coming over.

<*Holy whores, for the use of the Tyr priests.*>

Ifanna was too shocked to respond.

<*Better that than dead, peasant-girl! They say that the Cariad will make serving the priests our deepest pleasure.*>

The guard walked between them, and the contact was lost. Ifanna was unable to re-establish their strange communication as they were led forward in single file.

Now the procession was accompanied by much chanting and wafting of incense bowls, but Ifanna was barely aware of the ceremony attending their progress down the corridor. Could she become one of these holy whores? The thought of strangers using her body sickened her – yet the girl had said the Beloved Daughter of Heaven would ensure she took pleasure in being so used. Obviously the Cariad was quite capable of reshaping hearts and souls, for she was a goddess … yet Ifanna had sensed doubt beneath the girl's brave scorn.

They stopped before a pair of massive doors which shone like the sun on water. Ifanna had not known so much metal existed in the whole of Creation!

The doors opened silently. Not that Ifanna could hear much over the pounding of her heart.

Beyond was a strange and wondrous room: a dome, cut into the rock, large enough to fit the whole of the Reeve's manor into. The space was lit by the same cold lights she had seen elsewhere in the Tyr – or rather, half-lit, for the far side of the room remained in darkness. Then, even as she strained to see through it, the darkness was dispelled by a golden light, like a sudden and miraculous dawn.

The light revealed five men in ornate robes. They must be the Escorai: the most powerful men in Creation. Each one was dressed in the colour of his goddess: red for Carunwyd, orange for Medelwyr, green for Frythil, blue for Turiach and yellow for Mantoliawn. They were ranged about a throne, and on it sat the Cariad herself, resplendent in black and silver, her face hidden from unworthy mortal eyes by a shining veil.

Even as she circled her breast and fell to her knees, Ifanna found herself wondering what that veil hid. Was the Cariad truly so beautiful that a glimpse of her face would strike the unworthy blind? She caught the thought, suddenly terrified the Cariad might sense it. She looked down, and noticed the line on the floor, separating her party from the divine one. The room was divided by a chasm: did it lead to the Abyss itself? Ifanna's head swam; had she not already been kneeling, she might have fallen. She dug her nails into her palms, determined not to show weakness.

The Escori of Mantoliawn, Mother of Justice, spoke up. 'You stand before us today to receive judgment.'

Then the Escori of Medelwyr added, 'None but the Cariad can reveal the will of the Weaver.'

'You are tainted, but you are not yet beyond the healing power of salvation.' This from the Escori of Turiach, Mother of Mercy.

'For your bodies may yet be given a sacred purpose,' added the red-robed Escori of Carunwyd.

The words gave Ifanna a small glimmer of hope; she was in the hands of the Skymothers. All was not lost. Though the darkness in her soul would be exposed, the Weaver might yet have plans for her! She could find a place in the Mothers' designs, if their

Daughter would only accept her – and change her, to make what she must do bearable.

'You will now hear the charges laid against you both,' said the Escori of Frythil, speaking for the first time. 'Hylwen Tremglas. You used your skycursed powers to drive two boys to fight over you, until one killed his erstwhile friend for your pleasure. You enchanted another young man to steal and lie to indulge your whims, thus bringing about the death of a jewel-merchant.'

Ifanna stole a glance at her companion – Hylwen – and saw that the other girl was still as a rock, her face set. Even with the cosmetics she looked too young to have caused such mayhem.

'Ifanna am Nantgwyn.' Ifanna flinched to hear the Escori of the Mother of Secrets speak her name. 'You are known to have killed the man to whom you were wed; no doubt other unholy acts have gone unrecorded.'

The Cariad would reveal her every secret. She shuddered, and realised that next to her, Hylwen was beginning to tremble, her shoulders quivering and her fingertips twitching.

'The Cariad will look into your hearts, and you will each be treated as you deserve.' The green-robed Escori's voice was heavy with contempt, leaving no doubt as to what fate he believed they merited. But it was not up to him.

In the silence that followed, Ifanna felt utterly, unreservedly penitent. Yet she also wanted the Beloved Daughter to know that she could still be of use, that if she willed it, to serve as a Putain Glan would be a fate she would welcome gladly. *I want to live*, she thought, *I will do anything to live.*

The room was utterly silent. Her knees ached from kneeling on the rough floor, and the air was chill on her damp hair.

And she sensed ... *nothing*.

She began to panic: had her presumption counted against her? She should not have assumed she had any right to life: she had *no* rights. She was *nothing*. She opened her heart to the Cariad, trying not to think, merely to be ready to receive judgment – whatever that judgment may be.

But she did not hear the voice of Heaven – and when even a

lowly witch could speak in Ifanna's head, why did the Cariad remain silent? She tried to think directly to the woman on the throne, as Hylwen had shown her – it might be a blasphemous act, but this empty silence was unbearable. <*Please, oh Divine One, judge me as you will!*>

There was no response.

Finally the Cariad spoke. 'Hear now my judgment, for it is the will of Heaven.' Her voice was soft, almost gentle, though it filled the room. 'You shall not be made into Putain Glan.'

Hylwen whimpered, but Ifanna made herself stay calm. Death was her rightful lot; she had been foolish to ever think otherwise.

'Instead, you will be taken from this place and escorted to the edge of the marshlands to the south of the city.' They mean to drown us after all, thought Ifanna, feeling suddenly cheated; some twisted part of her had hoped to die by the Cariad's own hand, as though that might redeem her soul. The Cariad continued, 'There, you will be given bread and fresh water, enough for five days, and be set loose. You will never return to Dinas Emrys.'

Around her, Ifanna sensed confusion.

'Such is my will and decree. This is the will of Heaven. The girls are to be sent into exile.'

She was not to be killed, nor yet given over to the priests for their pleasure. She would live.

CHAPTER SIXTEEN

'What happened?' asked Jarek sharply. 'You say there was an accident: what sort of accident?' He managed not to look at Nual as he spoke. *Christos, Taro*, he thought, *don't you* dare *have got yourself killed, you stupid,* stupid *boy.*

Ain looked away for a moment, 'Clarification,' she said quietly. 'Perhaps "accident" is not entirely accurate.'

'Explain!' snapped Nual.

'This hab is very new; parts of it are still being ... consolidated. It is possible an error occurred.'

'What do you mean "an error occurred"? What sort of error?'

'This individual cannot—'

'You do not believe this accident was due to a fault in the hab's fabric at all, do you?' interrupted Nual.

'No,' said Ain miserably. 'This lingua suspects it may have been matter-eaters.'

'Matter-eaters? What the fuck are *matter-eaters*?' Jarek didn't try to curb his emotions: the lingua already believed Taro was more than a friend to him.

'They are ... You have a word—' The lingua mastered herself. 'This – I believe you call this technology a *nanite plague*? All that is known currently is that something ate through the outer shell of the hab before local failsafes neutralised the effect.'

'Is there any danger now?' asked Nual coldly.

'No. The affected area has been isolated and the nanites deactivated.'

'And what about the problems with the lights and the coms?'

'When the nanite plague began, some of the hab's internal systems experienced a— the—' She stopped, then started again, 'I believe your word is datastrike – this lingua is sorry for all this and for, for failure to act, and now to communicate properly!'

'It's all right,' said Jarek, gently. It wasn't the lingua's fault.

'It would have been quick,' continued the lingua, 'when they died. Very little suffering.'

'Let us be clear about what has happened here,' growled Nual. 'At the same time as a datastrike affected the hab's internal systems, nanites penetrated the hull in the area where Vy and Taro just happened to be, and it depressurised. Is that correct?'

'Aye, exactly. The closed door you found saved the rest of the hab.'

'Assuming this was not some internal problem with the hab – and the timing of the datastrike implies it wasn't – then how did this nanite plague get here? Because you said we were safe!' Jarek had never heard Nual so angry. For the lingua's sake he hoped Ain wasn't going to dissemble.

'Apologies … this lingua truly believed the hab *was* safe! The exclusion zone was not violated: as far as can be ascertained no one approached the hab. Perhaps a micro-missile, too small for the hab's sensors to detect or – or something planted beforehand, like the worm must have been …' The lingua's voice trailed off. She had obviously only just begun to consider the full implications of the attack for herself. It had to be an inside job.

She recovered herself a little and said, 'All this lingua knows has now been imparted. Whatever else is discovered will also be shared.'

'Who might have done this?' asked Nual.

'Currently there is no way of knowing. A number of patrons oppose your presence, but such an act … There will be consequences.'

Right now Jarek didn't care about *consequences*, he cared about the life of his friend. And the longer the conversation went on, the more he began to believe that Taro really was dead. He found himself demanding, 'I want to see Taro's body. Vy's too.'

'Aye-okay, of course. This will happen as soon as external coms are restored and a retrieval mission can be organised.'

'Make it a priority,' said Nual fiercely, 'and keep us informed.' With that she swept off, leaving Jarek and the lingua standing in awkward silence.

Ain said, 'This lingua should return to the core to oversee the repairs.'

'Good idea.'

'This individual again conveys sympathies. Your loss grieves th— grieves me.'

'Please, just go.'

After Ain left, Jarek sat down on the ground. If he'd had the strength he might have gone after Nual, because she'd be feeling even worse than him, however well she hid it. He decided that for the sake of his sanity he was going to assume Taro wasn't dead. When Ain produced the body ... well, he'd cross that bridge when he came to it.

Even aside from the possible loss of Taro and Vy, they were in big trouble: *someone* had sabotaged their 'safe' haven. Jarek cursed his ignorance. He'd been thinking of the Aleph males as a single group who were broadly sympathetic to his cause, and that had been an enormous mistake. Not all of his enemies' enemies were his friends.

He wondered if he'd always been so reckless. Perhaps he wouldn't have let himself get into a situation like this, back before the Sidhe violated his mind and took away his memories. He still wasn't sure he'd got all those memories back, but he did know he'd never been one to respect authority, and he believed he'd always been a bit crazy. But looking at the way old friends had treated him since he returned from Serenein, he suspected he'd become more extreme in his passions and less careful in his decisions. He couldn't know for sure, of course; that was a question for philosophers. Or possibly for Nual, if he ever dared ask her to probe him to find out the truth ...

The realistic garden included realistic morning dew, and it was seeping into his clothes. He stood slowly and then, his mind made up, took the quickest route to the airlock.

Before he reached the *Heart of Glass* Ain commed him. 'This lingua earnestly hopes that you are not planning to leave.' She sounded concerned, rather than angry.

'No, I'm, not.' Tempting though it was, he had no idea what he'd end up running into if they bugged out now. 'I'm going to my ship, as I told you I was. But just as a matter of interest, what would happen if I did undock? Would I be shot down?'

'Of course not!' Ain sounded shocked. 'I told you yesterday, space weapons are not permitted.'

She was right; she'd said that any patron who owned weapons capable of intruding into another's domain would be jumped on by the ruling Consensus. She hadn't said anything about localised comp viruses or nanite plagues, he noted. 'Tell that to whoever killed Taro and Vy,' he said, and cut the connection. There: he'd said it, admitted Taro might really be dead.

Back on the ship, he went over the logs in detail, as much to distract himself as because he expected to find anything. Whoever had checked his comp must have either had access to serious anti-surveillance tech, or free access to the ship's systems: the airlock camera didn't show anyone coming aboard, and the bridge logs claimed the ship had been locked down and empty since they'd arrived. He went deeper, trying to unravel exactly what had happened on his ship while it had been at the mercy of their hosts.

At last he found the hack that had looped the surveillance feed, though he had no idea how he could recover the missing eighty minutes' footage. He'd be willing to bet his visitor was a Sidhe male's avatar.

The sensor log didn't flag up anything suspicious, though that might just be because it had been tampered with too. Though he was no expert – he had the comp and coms knowhow to run his ship – he spent a while reviewing the sensor feed anyway, checking for suspicious movements. The delivery system might not have been visible from here, as the nanite attack occurred on the far side of the hab, but he left the system on full sensitivity, just in case.

Still feeling paranoid, he checked the com system – and was surprised to find a problem. According to the log, the ship's coms had gone offline some time during the night, and come back only when Nual had commed him to wake him up. But the ship's system was completely independent – so *no way* did it just happen to randomly fail at *exactly* the same time that the shit hit the fan on the hab. So what had happened, Jarek wondered: had the males hacked into his ship remotely? He thought that unlikely, given the *Heart of Glass*'s old-fashioned design. Why would they even need to, when they could easily have boarded the ship and planted a timed glitch into his coms system, synced to the datastrike on the hab's comp and the nanite plague inception.

So it was beginning to look like whichever male had checked the ship's navcomp to make sure Aleph's coordinates had been removed was almost certainly also the one responsible for the attack on the hab – and for killing Taro and Vy.

Should he tell Ain about his suspicions? Maybe later – but Nual needed to know now. He decided not to ask her to come to him; given the recent violation of his ship's systems, the *Heart of Glass* didn't feel like such a safe space right now. Instead he suggested they meet in the garden; he had a wilfully naïve idea that the hab's surveillance might not be as close there.

He found her sitting on an ornamental bench, looking pensive. She stood as he approached and opened her arms, her face full of sympathy. For a moment he was confused, then he remembered: *he* was meant to be the one in pain, *she* the one offering comfort.

As she hugged him, he projected silent sympathy, and her response hit him like a stim-hit laden with despair. Tears flooded his eyes as her anguish spilled over into his mind. He didn't fight it, or stop her using him to express her grief.

When the worst of the emotional backwash had passed she thought to him, *<I am sorry. I had to let it out somehow.>*

<It's all right, I understand,> he responded. *<Is he really dead, then?>*

<I don't know!> Her mental cry made him flinch, and he pulled away. Nual's eyes were damp, but her expression remained

125

impassive. *<I have not felt his death, but I cannot make contact. Perhaps he is too far away, or unconscious.>*

<Let's assume the best for now. I do have a lead of sorts ...>

Nual, still outwardly calm, steered him to the seat, where she sat next to him, holding his hand while he sniffed out loud and spoke in silence, communicating his discoveries so far.

Finally he said out loud, 'I'm moving back to the ship, Nual. Ain isn't happy about it, but that's tough.'

'A very sensible move,' she said, letting go of his hand. 'I think I may join you shortly.'

Back on the *Heart of Glass*, Jarek dug out his portable bug-sweeper kit – most freetraders carried one on board, to reassure not-entirely-reputable potential customers looking to trade not-entirely-legal cargo that though they might be meeting in not-exactly-secure places, whatever was said would nonetheless be entirely confidential.

He'd checked the bridge and was halfway through the rec-room when his com beeped – not an incoming call, but an alarm: his sensors had picked up something anomalous. He raced back up the ladder, but when he checked the console, he could at first see nothing obvious. He wound back the log, getting it to project a composite image into the holocube, but it took him a moment to work out what he was seeing. It looked like one of the ships lurking at the edge of the exclusion zone, on the far side of the hab, was on the move. It appeared to be heading this way.

He commed Ain. 'Listen, are the hab's external sensors up and running?'

'They have not been a priority,' she started. 'This lingua has been trying to fix the external com system in order to request your companions' remains. Allow me to check now ... Aye-okay, the system has reset, so passive detection is functioning.'

'Then would you mind checking what's going on at—' Jarek paused, unsure whether his coordinate system would mean anything to the Alephan; finally he settled on, '—just inside the exclusion zone on the far side of the hab from my ship.'

'Wait a moment, please …'

Jarek wasn't sure how long she considered a moment to be, but it felt like at least a minute had passed before he called, 'Ain?' unable to stand the wait any longer, 'Ain, is there a problem?'

Her voice was very small when she finally replied, 'Aye. There certainly is.'

CHAPTER SEVENTEEN

Someone was shouting at him. *Fuck's sakes, why couldn't they just let him sleep?* Who was it anyway? Didn't sound like Nual ...

Suddenly he remembered the last thing that'd happened. Dazed and panicky, he recalled seeing darkness beyond the airlock instead of the *Heart of Glass*, then the darkness stung his head—

—and now someone was making this awful racket ... He opened his eyes to find himself in a bright, white room, lying on a squishy floor. The only obvious feature was a line of close-set grey bars across the centre of the room. Someone was prowling and gesturing on the far side of the bars, talking double-speed: 'Come on, come on, wake up! Are you dead? You're not dead, are you? Hello? Hello? I can see you moving!'

Ah, so that was who was making all the noise.

Taro sighed. 'Shit and blood, Vy,' he croaked, 'just pack it in, will you? No, I ain't dead. And I ain't *deaf* either.'

Merciful silence. Then Vy said in a voice of hungry confusion, 'Vy? You say ... Vy. *I'm* Vy, yes?'

'Yes, you're Vy. And I'm Taro. And we're in the shit. Now shut the fuck up and let me think.' Taro levered himself to a sitting position as Vy stopped pacing and sat down, then began to grizzle like a baby.

Taro tried his com. No signal. *Well, there's a surprise.* He looked around. The room was the size of a large hotel room, with no visible exits or windows. Vy was in a cage that filled half the room; there was a bed, a table and what had to be a crapper in with him.

128

Taro wondered why he didn't have his own cage. And where the hell were the others?

Maybe Nual and Jarek were in the next room? He tried to empty his mind and contact Nual, but he couldn't feel anything. He'd try again later, ideally when Vy was asleep and he could concentrate properly.

Ah yes, Vy.

Taro guessed that whatever had knocked him out had got Vy too, and being unconscious had fucked the boy up, just like he'd said it would. It looked like the lingua had tricked them, though he was surprised; he'd have expected Nual to spot if she'd been lying to them. Had Ain been working for someone, but somehow managed to hide it? But who – and how?

Vy's grizzling was getting louder, building into a hopeless keen. 'Vy!' shouted Taro, and when the avatar shut up, added, 'I'm gonna regret asking this, but what can you remember?'

'Nothing!' Vy's answer was a forlorn howl.

'That ain't helpful, and it ain't true, 'cos you can obviously remember some stuff: you know I'm a friend, and you can remember how to speak. Right?'

Vy stopped looking completely forsaken and looked at Taro.

'Good. Now, what happened before you got put to sleep?'

'I—' Vy screwed up his face in concentration. 'I followed you. Then there was darkness, and it hurt.'

'That's right, and it's good that you remember. So when you woke up, was everything just like it is now?'

'No. You were lying down and you had your eyes closed. I thought you were dead.'

'But everything else was—'

'Taro sanMalia!' he shouted.

Taro jumped. 'What?'

'That's your name.'

'Yeah, it is, but—'

'I remembered!' Vy sounded massively relieved.

'That's pure blade, Vy. I bet everything else'll come back if you give it a chance.' *Hopefully.*

'Were there others? Someone else, with us?'

'There were,' said Taro slowly. 'Have you seen them since we got knocked out?'

'No, no. I— What're their names?'

'Nual and Jarek.'

Vy mouthed the names to himself, then whispered, 'I don't know what I've lost. Everything slips away. Yes, slips away … I mustn't let it. Mustn't, mustn't—'

'No,' said Taro, 'you mustn't. You gotta stay focused. I'll help you—'

'Not enough.' Vy held up his hands and looked at them like he was seeing them for the first time. 'Need to hold it together until … until—'

'Until what, Vy? *Until what?*'

'Can't say!'

'Can't, or won't?' Taro was wary of tipping Vy further over the edge, but he needed to know what was really going on.

Vy stepped back from the bars, looking miserable.

Taro got to his feet – he was still woozy, but everything appeared to be in working order – and walked over to the bars. 'C'mon, Vy, *please*. We're in enough trouble as it is. If there's something you know and I don't, you really need to be telling me.'

Sulkily: 'Said I can't.'

'Please?'

'Really can't. Not—'

'This is a gun.'

Taro spun round. A figure stood on the far side of the room in a doorway that hadn't been there a few moments ago. It was a man, well, sort of – it looked like someone who'd been filed down to the skin, no hair, no nails, or whatever, then painted gold. It wasn't wearing any clothes, but it didn't have anything to hide. It was holding a spiky little white thing that might well be a gun. 'Kindly do not misbehave,' it said, 'or I will use the weapon.' Its voice was almost toneless, with less of a weird accent than Ain had.

'Haven't got any plans to misbehave,' said Taro as evenly as he could.

'Good. I would like to speak with you.'

'Speak away, friend.'

'Only you.'

'Not sure I—'

'I wish to speak to you alone.' The voice held a faint hint of impatience. The figure gestured dismissingly at the cage. 'Without that.'

'Whatever you say,' said Taro. *You're the one with the weapon.* 'Your place or mine?'

'You will come with me.'

'Yours, then.'

Taro spared a glance for Vy. The avatar's face was twisted into an expression Taro found hard to read through the bars. Horror? Hatred? Taro murmured, 'Don't worry, Vy. I'll be back.'

The figure (*another avatar?*) stepped aside to let Taro leave the room, keeping a safe distance. Not that he was going to try anything yet: he wanted to know what was going down before making any sort of move.

They walked into another white room, slightly bigger, and with a non-squishy floor. As well as the door they'd come through, the room had two open doorways, on opposite walls. The golden figure gestured at the remaining wall. 'You may sit there,' it said.

Taro made out a thin line of shadow on the white surface. As he walked closer, he realised it was a cube, jutting out of the wall, made of the same white stuff as the room. *Don't think much of your decorator*, he thought as he sat down. Like the bit of floor he'd awakened on, the seat was soft. He noticed that the entrance to his room had disappeared again.

The golden man stood to one side, still holding the gun. He waited until Taro was seated, then said, 'It is important that we are friends.'

Taro bit back his instinctive retort – *Like fuck, you shiny gold arsehole* – and said carefully, 'Fine by me.'

'Good. I imagine you have questions.'

'Just a few.'

'Please, ask away.'

Where to start? With the obvious one. 'Where are my other two friends?'

'Other?' asked the figure, almost echoing Vy's earlier question, then, 'I assume you are referring to Captain Reen and the Sidhe Nual?'

'Yeah, them.' *'Cos if you've harmed Nual I'll peel off your pretty gold skin and shove it down your ugly black throat.*

'They are, as far as we are aware, alive and well.'

Even as he felt himself relax a fraction Taro noted the *we*. 'They're not here, then?'

'That is correct.'

'Are they still at the hab?'

'I believe so.'

'And where exactly is *here*?'

'Although you may ask any question you wish, some will not be answered at this time.'

Oh yeah, definitely *an avatar with an attitude like that.* 'I'll try another one then: where's Ain?'

'We do not know to whom you refer.'

'The lingua. The one on the hab.' *Who sold us out to you, apparently ...*

'She is also still there, as far as we know.'

'Is she working for you?'

'No. She is lingua, and is loyal only to the Consensus. Your confusion arises from a logical but incorrect assumption. The individual who took you from the hab was not lingua. It was a custom-made simulacrum.'

'You mean another avatar, like you?'

'That is correct.' The avatar sounded pleased that Taro had worked it out.

'And whose avatar are you, then?' Taro wasn't sure if that was the right way to put it, but he reckoned the avatar would correct him if not.

It replied with a question of its own. 'Would you find it easier to use only the singular first pronoun along with a name in our dealings to give the impression that you are addressing a wholly independent entity rather than a semi-autonomous agent?'

'Sure,' said Taro, who wasn't.

'That is acceptable. In that case, I can be referred to as Device.'

'Pleased to meet you, Device,' Taro lied. He decided not to bother introducing himself. He guessed they already knew who he was. 'So whose … who d'you represent?'

'My patron is known as the Gatekeeper. The shiftspace beacon you arrived at lies in his domain.'

'Were those coves in the lightship his people, then?'

'I think you misunderstand how closely settled even the out-system portion of Aleph is. The Gatekeeper's domain is not large; by the time your ship encountered the lightship, you had moved into neutral space.'

'Right.'

'Of course, in some ways the Gatekeeper has access to the largest domain of all, for he is keeper of the beacon. Although he has no populace of his own he takes a great interest in human-space. He designed the hab you and your companions were housed in.'

Which explained why the place looked like a lifestyle beevee made by an exec with a shitload of credit and no sense of style. 'Is that unusual, him being into human-space?'

'Indeed it is. It has resulted in the Gatekeeper being held in low esteem by some of the other patrons – at least until your arrival. Now the knowledge he has gained from human-space is proving invaluable!'

'There's a lot of factions here, ain't there?'

'There are many septs, with many alliances within and between them. However you should not let such things concern you. I will keep you safe and comfortable.'

Taro didn't point out that being snatched from his lover and his friend and put in a white box with a loony avatar wasn't his idea of safe or comfortable. Instead he made himself smile and say, 'That's good to know.' Device seemed to be buying it, so Taro decided to risk asking, 'How about Vy? He ain't doing too well.'

'No, it would not be. I will be observing its disintegration with interest.' The avatar sounded almost eager.

133

'You're not going to help him? He's really suffering in there.'

'Indeed it is, although it is more tenacious than I expected.'

Taro felt his anger rising; Vy wasn't an 'it', Vy was a thinking being, a lot like Device himself! But he couldn't afford to piss off his captor, so instead he changed the subject. 'Won't the Gatekeeper get into trouble with the other patrons for kidnapping me and Vy?'

'That is a perceptive question, but the answer is no; removal of Khesh's avatar was sanctioned by the Consensus. Your presence is an unexpected bonus.'

Not as far as Taro was concerned, it wasn't. 'You're saying the males planned to kidnap Vy all along?'

'That is correct. Normally, creating fully sentient simulacrum of lingua is prohibited, with punishments commensurate with those for mounting weapons on a ship or invading another's domain, but the Gatekeeper was given permission by the Consensus.'

'Why go to all that trouble? What did you want Vy for?'

'Those are also questions I am not going to answer.'

Taro clenched his fists, fighting the urge to rip the smug fucker apart. He had to stay calm and find out all he could.

The avatar continued, 'For the moment we must be careful, but when things are calmer I will provide somewhere much more spacious and interesting for you. I saw you fly in the hab – we were not aware that humans had access to that technology. I will make sure you have space to fly. Also, I will make you a simulacrum of Captain Reen. It may lack certain mental capabilities, but I can reproduce his physical details – I could enhance any, if you would like me to.'

'I'm not sure I understand,' said Taro, horribly afraid he did.

'Taking Khesh's avatar was planned in advance. The Consensus' command was that it be removed from the hab and that the remaining visitors be convinced that it had died. As you can see, I have not killed it. That would be a waste: it will be far more interesting to observe its disintegration now it is cut off from its patron. It is a process rarely witnessed, and I intend to record and analyse every stage.'

'And where do I fit in?' Taro flashed on the idea of himself as next in the cage after poor Vy had died.

'You were not part of the original plan, but you insisted on keeping company with the avatar, making its removal far more complicated. In a situation like that many patrons would just have killed you; you are hardly essential, whatever emotional strength you may lend to your captain. Fortunately for you, the Gatekeeper saw your value.'

'My value? As what?'

'As a source of information! The Gatekeeper is fascinated by human-space, but has had to exist on the few titbits that are beeveed in via our beacon. Yet here you are, a living being from mainstream human culture. You know so much of interest! The Gatekeeper looks forward to discussing your life and experiences in great detail.'

'So he's just going to keep me in a box for the rest of my life? Ain't he worried my friends'll try and find me?'

'Oh no. As far as your friends are concerned, you died when the avatar did. Bodies will be provided, sympathies expressed, et cetera. But do not worry, you will not be imprisoned in a box. Your living area will be spacious and luxurious, and you will even be able to explore some of the Gatekeeper's domain, provided you be-have yourself. You will want for nothing. Your life will be long, safe and happy.'

CHAPTER EIGHTEEN

Unseen hands lifted Ifanna to her feet. She did not resist. She noticed in passing that the other side of the rocky chamber was dark again. She had a brief glimpse of Hylwen's shocked expression as the monitors led the two of them from the room.

Ifanna was shoved into another room, this one bare of any amenities, and the door was locked behind her. She felt disconnected, as light as an empty vessel. She held on to the one, impossible, truth: she was not to die – nor was she to endure the lesser fate that Hylwen had spoken of; instead, she was to be freed. This was *totally* unexpected – but the Cariad had not acted as *anyone* expected. Of course, she was a goddess and she could do as she wished, but Ifanna could not shake the feeling that her ruling had amazed everyone.

As time passed she realised what the sensation of lightness was. It was hope.

The door opened, and two monitors returned. She did not want to be bound and gagged again, but she knew better than to resist; at least they left the blindfold off, and only tied her hands. They took her out to Hylwen, who walked next to her, and they were surrounded by a cordon of monitors, with a priest at their head.

The escort led them out of the Tyr, but this time, instead of the stern reverence she'd sensed on the way to the audience with the Cariad, the guards' chilly demeanour hid a deep unease. And Hylwen was afraid, despite their reprieve. Ifanna tried to get her attention, and after a while Hylwen looked over at her.

Ifanna spoke silently, *<We are to live, Hylwen! We should rejoice and be thankful, should we not?>*

<If it is true ...>

<Why should it not be? It is the will of the Cariad!>

<That is not the Cariad!>

Ifanna did not answer at once, for she had been trying to avoid that very conclusion. Surely she should have felt the goddess look into her heart? Yet she had sensed nothing. *<Is there another Cariad, a true one?>* A foolish question perhaps, but the alternative was unthinkable.

<I do not know. I do know that something is wrong. It started even before the lights came.>

<I have not seen those lights.> Knowing Hylwen was likely to remind her of her ignorance, Ifanna added. *<I was imprisoned for many weeks before being brought here.>*

<Some say they indicate the displeasure of the Skymothers. Others say that Consorts intervene for us. My father's business supplies the Tyr's cured meats, so he has many priestly contacts, yet the priests do not know any more than we do. Back at Sul Esgyniad, most, perhaps all, of the Escorai were replaced in a single night! And since then, there have been many changes and strange decrees ...>

<That may be so, yet surely it does not alter our situation. The Escorai must obey the Cariad, and she has said we are to be freed.> Ifanna refused to lose hope so soon after rediscovering it.

<We are skycursed! It is an offence against the Mothers that we should live to employ our powers.>

<Perhaps that was true before, but might there not be exceptions? Perhaps these changes you speak of indicate that Heaven has become more merciful.> Such thoughts were close to blasphemy, yet Ifanna found they came easily to her now.

<Oh, there is change, all right, but not for the better. As far back as last year there were strange rumours ...>

<Such as?> Hylwen obviously wanted Ifanna to have to ask.

<A distant cousin of mine became Putain Glan three years ago. Last year she ran away. Such a thing should not be possible: everyone knows

when the Cariad bends a witch to the service of the priests, her will is broken.>

<What happened to her?>

<I heard that she was hunted down and killed! I believe they will kill us too, whatever was said to our faces by the woman who sat on the Cariad's throne. They will take us outside the city as they were ordered, but then the monitors will murder us. Out there, no one will be any the wiser. And we will be dead.>

<You cannot know this!>

<I cannot be sure, no. But I do not want to take the risk: do you?>

Ifanna wanted to believe the Cariad's promise, to grasp hope with both hands. Yet Hylwen spoke sense. And her encounter with the Cariad had not gone at all as she had expected. *<Could we not try to find out?>*

<From the monitors, you mean?>

<Aye. I can sense moods, and sometimes intentions.>

<I rarely manage to read the intentions of strangers,> admitted Hylwen.

<Then let me see if I can find out anything.> Ifanna concentrated on the nearest guard, who held the end of the rope binding her hands. Certainly he was not happy; that much she could tell by looking at his face. To find out more, she needed to get closer, ideally to make eye contact. But that would be neither simple nor wise. She abandoned her plan, and looked back at Hylwen. *<I am not sure. They might expect us to try and use our powers like this; perhaps only the priest knows the truth.>*

<Aye, and he is the one who will give the fatal order when the time is right!>

They came to a door which the priest unlocked. Outside, night had fallen, though the darkness was partially dispelled by unearthly glowing globes like those in the Tyr, these ones set on high poles to cast pools of white radiance around them. The houses here were as grand as any in Plas Morfren. Ifanna shivered in the chill night air. She half expected the guards to blindfold her now there were no more steps to descend, but they did not, and she soon found that there were steps and slopes to negotiate out here too.

138

Her bare arm touched Hylwen's as they descended a narrow stairway, and Ifanna felt the spark of contact. *<Hylwen?>* she thought.

<Aye.>

<What are you planning?>

<We must distract them, then run away.>

Ifanna noted the use of 'we'. *<But they have crossbows!>*

<Use your eyes, Ifanna; only two of them carry their weapons cocked.>

Trying not to feel foolishly gratified that Hylwen had finally decided to use her name, Ifanna thought back, *<But they can still kill us.>*

<Not if we command them not to. You would not be here if you were not able to influence men. The priest may resist us, but by the time he sees what is happening, we will be gone.>

She made it sound so simple. Yet she only had Hylwen's word for it that they were in danger. *<And if I refuse to be part of your plan?>*

<Then you are a fool.>

Ifanna had not meant that: she was asking whether Hylwen would go ahead without her anyway. She suspected not: the other girl needed her help. Ifanna's offence at Hylwen's manner was replaced by a warm glow of conspiracy. She had an ally, and they were going to fight back. *<If we are to do this, when should we act?>*

<We will wait until we are in the lower city. I am familiar with the route they will most likely take; it goes through an area of narrow alleys. Once we are away, it will be easy for us to lose them in the side-streets.>

Ifanna did not have the advantage of Hylwen's knowledge of the city; wherever she ended up, she would be in unfamiliar territory. *<All right.>* She could trust Hylwen, if only because she needed Ifanna for the plan to work.

Ifanna took stock of their opposition. One guard walked beside the priest at the front, carrying a lantern to light the path where the white globes were sparse. She and Hylwen each had two guards walking alongside them. She looked at the two with her: one was loosely holding the rope around her hands; the other, immediately behind him, carried a loaded crossbow, though he held the weapon pointed down. Two more guards brought up the rear. The odds were not good, but Ifanna had already made her choice. She kept close enough to Hylwen for them to stay in contact.

As they silently refined their plan the streets became narrower and the globes less frequent, until the lights shone only at the intersections of major routes. The few people they met silently stepped aside for the party to pass, though some, openly curious, looked at them.

The streets were flatter and less well-surfaced here, the houses meaner. Hylwen silently warned her they were approaching the junction she deemed best for them to make their escape, then spoke in Ifanna's head: <*Now!*>

Both girls stopped dead and turned. Ifanna caught the eye of the armed monitor, then thought, with all the force of lust and compulsion she could muster: <*Shoot this man and you may have me!*>

She saw him begin to raise his crossbow; his companion, in his surprise, relaxed his grip on the rope. She grabbed her end of it and yanked it out of his hand. The guard with the crossbow hesitated, and someone shouted an alarm. Ifanna looked around, desperately trying to spot her escape route; Hylwen had picked this spot precisely to allow the two of them to take opposite alleys, thus splitting the guards. The dark path to freedom lay just beyond the armed monitor.

Someone tried to grab her from behind and she ducked, just as she heard the twang of a crossbow, and a scream. So Hylwen had succeeded. Her own guard still looked confused, standing there with his weapon only half raised, and the guard who had held her rope was going for his knife.

She heard another crossbow shot, and this time the scream was female. Though Hylwen's cry chilled her heart, Ifanna was already pushing through the gap between the two distracted monitors. She shoved the crossbow aside, which the monitor had not expected; he kept hold of his weapon, but took half a step back as he did so. Ifanna felt the weapon discharge and the bolt skittered across the cobbles. A heartbeat later, something tore her tunic, pricking her flank.

She dodged into the alley, her heart pounding, and heard more shouts – something about a rooftop? – but her only concern now was to escape. The lightness she had felt after the Cariad's judgment was back, and she expected to float free of the ground at any moment – either that, or be brought down by a crossbow bolt in her back.

She skidded down a side-turning. From behind she could hear the sound of running feet, only one man, but that was enough; she needed to lose him. But her hands were still bound in front of her, and though she held the loose end of the rope bunched in her fists, still this slowed her down. She could never outrun her pursuer, so she would have to lose him. In the dark she ran straight past one alley, and when she spotted another one ahead, she took it, only to find it was a dead end, with a high wooden fence at the far end.

Ifanna looked around in panic. She could hear the monitor close behind; if she retraced her steps, he would surely spot her. There was a large barrel, standing halfway down, and she crouched down and slid behind it, pressing back into the gap against the wall. The wood felt slimy, and her nose was filled with the stink of stagnant water, but it was better than standing in the open, waiting to be caught. She prayed to the Weaver that she would remain unseen.

The slap of boots grew louder, accompanied by the creak of oiled leather and a man's heavy breathing.

Ifanna held her own breath. The monitor carried on past the end of the alley. She allowed herself to exhale, but made herself stay where she was, though she could feel the beginnings of pain, and a wetness she did not want to consider, just below her ribs.

She started to scan the walls, looking for anything that might help her, and saw something she had missed before: faint light, coming from what might just be a side-turning, a gap in the wall of this apparently blind alley.

She stood, and took a step forward, but she had dropped the end of the rope, which tangled around her ankles, and she fell hard onto the cobbles.

For a moment she lay there, her raw wrists stinging and her head throbbing where she had banged it. *She had to get up, to keep going.* She tried to move, willing strength into her arms, but light danced in her eyes. She tried to blink the illusion away.

It was no illusion. There was light coming from ahead of her: a lantern. She looked up to see a priest and a monitor.

She had tried so hard, only to fail at the last! She might have screamed her frustration, had her mouth not still been gagged.

But wait a moment: these did not look like her escort; they wore dark cloaks, and neither of them were out of breath.

The monitor addressed the priest. 'Give me the lantern; I will speak to them.'

Ifanna stared at the pair, wondering if striking her head had addled her senses. The priest handed the light to his companion, then bent down to help her up. His gentleness surprised her.

Ifanna had no strength to resist. She let him lead her down the side-alley.

The priest whispered, 'You are safe now.'

Safe? she thought. *In what way is this safe?*

People were talking, somewhere nearby, and like everything else that had happened since she hit her head, the words made little sense. After a while, the voices stopped. The priest was still holding her arm.

The monitor came back a few moments later. 'I told them I saw nothing,' he said, 'so they should not come back this way. Still, we should not tarry.'

CHAPTER NINETEEN

Jarek found himself muttering under his breath, *Hurry up, hurry up, hurry up!* He wasn't sure whether he was haranguing the ship, which was slowly coming to life, or Nual, who was even now flying through the corridors of the hab towards him.

He spotted movement on a monitor; Nual was in the airlock at last. On the vid feed he saw her reach out to close the door. Jarek activated internal coms and said, 'Hold on! Ain's on her way.'

'Do we have time to wait for her?' Nual looked over her shoulder.

'If I get a green board before she shows up, I'll rethink, but I don't want to abandon her if I can avoid it.'

'Wait, she's coming.' A few moments later the lingua arrived in the 'lock, flushed and breathless. Nual closed the door behind her. Now all they needed was the ship to show a state of readiness ... and ...

Yes! Jarek hissed in triumph as the console flashed. *Time to get the fuck out of here.*

He undocked, and they headed away at max acceleration.

He'd set up a full sensor feed to the holocube while he was waiting for the *Heart of Glass*'s flight systems to warm up. Once they were speeding away there wasn't much else for him to do other than stare at it, willing something to happen – or nothing, preferably.

Because the approaching mass was on the far side of the hab, he didn't see it hit. The impact showed as a faint tremor in the image, following by a spray of debris exploding out – no: *two* sprays, one behind and one in front. Then the side of the hab nearest them deformed and burst as a blunt spike thrust out from the ruined structure. Whatever it was, it had skewered the entire hab.

'*Holy Christos!*' breathed Jarek. He heard someone behind him, and turned to see Nual rise up through the hatch. 'Get Ain,' he said. 'We need to talk to her.'

The lingua's usual calm expression had been replaced by blank shock by the time she arrived on the bridge.

Nual followed, hovering silently behind her.

Jarek turned to Ain and asked 'So what the fuck just happened?'

'Th— It was a ship, a mining barge, according to the core's sensors. There are many ships observing the hab from the exclusion zone radius. They are not allowed to make contact or approach, but people wanted to see the visitors – you – even from a distance.'

'And this ship just broke away from the other watchers and rammed the hab?'

'Aye-okay. That is what appears to have happened.'

'Why didn't someone do something?'

'No one expected anything like this! There would be no time to react. Besides, what could they do? No doubt the other ships tried to send a warning, but the hab's external coms are – were – inoperative. It was lucky you saw the attack.'

It was down to paranoia more than luck, but what mattered was that he *had* seen it. 'Wait,' he said, 'this mining barge – did it have a crew on board?'

'I would imagine the ship came from a lo-tech domain, probably an out-system scavenger colony—'

'How many people, Ain?'

'That sort of ship generally requires a minimum crew of eight,' she whispered, 'but unless they had the opportunity to let some of the workers disembark – which is unlikely – then there were probably between seventy and eighty people on board.'

'Shit! What the hell was the captain thinking? No one could've survived an impact like that!'

'Clarification: Captain Reen, you do not yet grasp the full relationship between a patron and his populace.'

'Call me Jarek, for fuck's sake, Ain – I just saved your goddamn life! So what you're saying is that they trashed the hab, wiping themselves out in the process, just because their patron *told* them to?'

'Aye-okay. Many patrons are as gods to their populaces. The patron may have assured those aboard the mining barge that they would receive their reward in the afterlife in return for their sacrifice. Or he might have said he would kill their loved ones back in his domain if they did not obey without question.'

'Talk about the old carrot and stick!' Jarek said. 'And you don't know which particular patron ordered the ship to fly into the hab?'

'This lingua – *I* – do not.'

'But you have your suspicions,' Nual said, her voice a husky murmur; she concluded, more forcefully, 'Which you will share with us now.'

Ain looked taken aback, then said, 'Of course. Though I cannot be sure, evidence suggests that the patron responsible for the suicide attack is a member of the Sons of the Silent Age, or possibly a smaller but closely allied sept. Of all the septs based in this region, they are the most strongly isolationist, and they maintain a tight control over their populaces.'

'How many males are there in this Silent Age sept?' asked Jarek.

'Allegiances shift, and are not always revealed until called upon in the Consensus, but that sept is a large one, with a core membership of fifty or sixty.'

'So at least fifty Sidhe males want us dead badly enough to sacrifice their people and seriously piss off the Consensus. Great.' Oddly, Jarek found he was more angry than afraid: he was angry at himself for being too trusting, and angry at the local males who treated their human charges with such contempt – though perhaps it wasn't so different from the Three Cities, with their democracy by assassination …

145

He found his eye drawn back to the cube, where the image of the ruined hab was just starting to lose definition as the *Heart of Glass* sped away. It was no longer venting debris, and the nose of the ramming ship had emerged through the section where the hab's airlock had once been. 'Except that we weren't the real target, were we?' he said, half to himself. 'They were trying to destroy this ship – trashing the hab, and us, was secondary. They probably blindsided the *Heart of Glass* because we had working sensors, while the hab's were still flaky after the datastrike. Coming in from the far side didn't matter because they used a vessel hefty enough to punch right through the hab and into my ship. And if I hadn't been on board and watching out, that's exactly what would have happened. *Christos!*'

Nual said drily, 'It appears that at least one of your septs will do pretty much anything to stop a ship with Aleph's location in its comp returning to human-space; I think they may have overestimated the number of rebel Sidhe females who would be willing to navigate such a ship.'

'Of course they have,' said Ain with surprising fire in her voice. 'They will always assume the worst of you, because you are female.'

For a moment Jarek wondered whether Nual, still holding in her grief and anger, would do something unfortunate, but she just said tightly, 'Believe me, the distrust is mutual. However, I am trying to overcome my natural instincts.'

Jarek changed the subject back to their immediate problem. 'So what do you recommend, Ain? Run away and hide behind a quiet moon until all the fuss dies down?'

Despite his sarcastic tone Ain took him at his word. 'There are no quiet moons. Every solid body here is a heavily populated domain. No, your safest course would be to rise up out of the ecliptic. There are far fewer domains up there, and they mostly belong to introvert patrons who will ignore you unless you enter their territory.'

'But once we're out of the high traffic areas we'll be easier to spot.'

'Affirmative. But a potential enemy will not be able to do anything about it unless they break cover to pursue you, which they should think twice about. Even if they do try and give chase, most of our ships are designed to cross small distances in a crowded system; please correct t— my assumption if it is wrong, but was your ship not made to travel long distances quickly, to get between planets and their beacons? If so, you should easily outrun anything sent after you.'

'True: that's something. So, back to my original question: what the fuck do we do now?'

'We could go to the Consensus and demand an Extraordinary Session—'

'Ah, right, so we'll unleash the full force of Alephan bureaucracy on the bastards who just tried to murder us, will we?'

'Please, hear me out! The Consensus is the site as well as the mode of government. There is a large habitat in a close polar orbit around the sun – known to lingua as the Egg – and all important decisions are made in the Star Chamber at its heart. The Consensus hab is also the site of the beacon manufactory. And, most importantly for you – for *us* – it is the only truly neutral inhabited territory in the system: any patron who launched an attack on the Egg would be condemned to shiftdeath.'

'Shiftdeath?'

'It is the ultimate sanction, not used for many centuries. A group of patrons force the condemned patron into shiftspace, permanently.'

'Nice. Okay, so it sounds like we need to head for this Egg of yours. I'll need some coordinates.'

Ain looked uncomfortable. 'Navigation and logistics data was stored in the— in my ship.'

'And where's your ship?'

'It— When I was chosen to liaise with you, it was built into the core of the habitat intended to receive you.'

'Ah. Guess we won't be using that then. And I don't suppose you can remember much without your ship's comp?'

'I am sorry. I am not used to operating without access to my comp. If there had been time to download the data— But there was not ...' She looked distraught.

'It's all right, that wouldn't have been my priority either.' Jarek thought for a moment. 'Can we com the Consensus to get directions, once we're a bit closer? Or were the Consensus' com frequencies and encryption algorithms all in your ship's comp too?'

'They were,' said Ain, her voice small.

'It's not your fault. I'd be lost without the *Heart of Glass*. We could broadcast a wide-beam request for aid, but that would confirm our location to our enemies. I guess the only option we've got is to run away and hope to shake off any pursuers, then swing back in towards the primary and hope we can locate the Egg.'

'I wish I could be of more use,' said Ain miserably.

'No, you've done everything you could. If you don't mind, you can check over the data I've gathered so far from this system. You'll know more than I do even without your comp.'

'Of course; please tell me what I can do to help.'

'I'll be in my cabin,' said Nual out loud. When Jarek glanced at her she added silently, *<I'm going to try and contact Taro again.>*

'Sure,' said Jarek, 'see you later.'

He chatted to Ain for a while longer, keeping half an eye on the sensors, and once he'd concluded that if anyone was coming after them, they weren't doing it quickly enough to make their intentions obvious, he discussed the ship's course with Ain.

They had to make sure they headed out of the disc on the correct side, Ain said. She had been on secondment to the out-system sector nearest Aleph's beacon and was not entirely sure where the Egg currently was in its orbit, but she had an idea it was passing through the disc of the ecliptic about now. That was good news, because they wouldn't have to go right through the disc and out the other side if they got it wrong; though if the Egg was just one domain amongst many, they might have trouble spotting it.

By the time Jarek had chosen a course, the lingua's attempt to maintain a calm and equable façade was failing, and when her voice broke as she let slip that the ship at the heart of the now-destroyed hab had been her home for the last few years, Jarek took pity on her and suggested they take a break.

CHAPTER TWENTY

After their little chat, Device told Taro to go back into the cell 'for the moment'. Just as he turned to leave, he asked, 'How is my idiolect?'

'Your idiot-what?'

'My speech patterns and vocabulary, Taro. Would it pass for human? I have studied linguistic drift in human-space, but I find slang and casual speech do not come naturally, and I have had only a reduced dataset – until now.'

'You sound great, Device. Very convincing,' he said as casually as he could. *And I'm not your fucking dataset.*

Back in the cell, Taro turned and squinted at the near-invisible outline in the white wall. A handle would be too much to hope for. The door probably only opened on Device's command.

Vy was sitting on the floor of his cage, rocking slowly backwards and forwards. He looked up when Taro came over, then went back to muttering. At least the little sod had stopped shouting.

Taro sat down against a wall to think.

He wasn't going to live his life out as some crazy Sidhe's pet, never seeing Nual or Jarek again. When it came to it, he'd fight Device, whatever the consequences.

He did have one advantage: he was pretty sure Device didn't know about the blades implanted along the length of both his fore-arms. If the whole flight thing had been a surprise, that implied the Minister hadn't actually mentioned Angel implants. Maybe he'd left it out because he didn't totally trust the locals himself? Good call that, given how the bastards were treating his avatar. And the males here were probably used to humans bending over whenever the 'patrons' told them to. He could use that attitude; Device had already given away some prime info by telling him about the Gatekeeper and admitting that the locals wanted Vy out the picture – even if the bastard wouldn't say why.

He decided to try and contact Nual; maybe she could come and get him out of— Well, wherever this was. And even if she couldn't help him right now, he had to let her know he was alive, and warn her that, despite what Ain said, the locals *were* out to shaft them.

The problem was, the few times they'd managed to mindspeak long-range, Nual had always made the first move. All he could do was make sure he was ready for her when she tried to enter his mind, and that meant being lightly asleep, or in a trance – and he was crap at entering the trance state. She'd tried to teach him a couple of times, but no matter how hard he tried to totally empty his mind, some thought always ended up trickling back into it, even if it was only the thought that it was really fucking difficult to totally empty your mind.

That left sleep. He was tired enough, but he sure-as-shit wasn't relaxed … He lay down anyway, and closed his eyes. The soft floor was quite comfy, and the room was warm, almost too warm. He sighed, and imagined himself sinking into the floor. A sudden thought made him tense up: what if the floor swallowed him? Nah, that was dumb. He just had to chill, let it all go. He tried counting breaths, and as he did so, he remembered the sound of Nual's voice – *Breathe out for longer than you breathe in* – and that made him relax more, which was good. Idle thoughts intruded; he let them. He wasn't making himself go into a trance, just trying to sleep.

There! He thought he felt her presence, but it was so faint …

He wanted to reel himself in on the slender connection, but the more he tried to focus, the more it slipped away from him; he just wasn't strong enough to hold onto it. *Keep relaxing, that's the way.* The link strengthened: she must have picked up on it. He'd be fine now, because she'd made contact. Or not … this wasn't like before. It was so faint, and there was some sort of background 'noise'.

What was that? No, don't get distracted: he had to stay relaxed and focused if he was going to have any chance of—

'Don't!'

Taro snapped back into full consciousness. He blinked and sat up.

'Don't leave me!'

Taro sighed. 'Vy, you stupid little fucker, I'm not going anywhere. I'm just—' *I'm just resisting the urge to throttle you!* 'I'm just trying to get some rest, all right?'

'I need you,' whined Vy, holding his arms out. 'There's no one else.'

'Looks like you're right,' muttered Taro. Had he imagined the contact, dreaming Nual up out of desperation? 'All right, how about I come over there for a while?' He got up and walked over to the bars. He had no idea what they were made of, but they looked too thick for his blades to cut.

Vy reached out through the cage and Taro gave the boy an ungainly hug. Vy quieted down at his touch; perhaps if he could get him to settle he'd leave Taro in peace to try and sleep again, though he'd find it a lot easier to relax if he wasn't so hungry and thirsty. Maybe he should have asked Device for something to eat when they'd had their little chat, but it hadn't occurred to him then. The thought gave Taro an idea.

He began to whisper to Vy, hoping that whatever Device was using to spy on them wouldn't pick up his words. By the time he was reasonably sure Vy understood what he was on about he realised that, on top of everything else, he needed a piss.

He untangled himself from the boy's grasp. 'Hey,' he shouted into the air, 'Device, can you hear me, friend?' That last word tasted sour, and he carried on quickly, 'I don't wanna be rude, but we could really use something to keep us going – food and water, y'know? Also, I need to— I need to use the facilities. Only problem is, there're in Vy's bit. Don't suppose you could help me out here?'

There was no response.

Vy sat down and hugged his knees.

After a while Taro tried calling out again, 'Hallo?' but still there was nothing.

Vy began to mutter distractedly to himself.

Looks like he's about to go off again, Taro thought. *And if I don't do something soon, I'm gonna piss myself.*

He unclenched his thighs and staggered over to a corner. If this didn't get their host's attention, nothing would.

'Sorry 'bout this,' he said to the air in general as he fumbled with his belt, 'but I can't wait no longer.'

Even as he let out a long relieved breath he noticed how the liquid was absorbed by the floor. Freaky. He was glad to get himself sealed back up again.

He picked a different bit of floor to sit down on, one with a good view of the door.

He hadn't been waiting long when Device came in. The avatar had the gun in one hand and a tray in the other. Taro got up slowly. 'I thought you'd forgotten us,' he said, making like he was hurt, but glad to see the avatar.

'My apologies,' said Device with what probably passed for sincerity where he'd been made. 'I heard your request; it took a while to synthesise sustenance suitable for the human metabolism.'

'That's all right,' said Taro. He tried not to look at the door, which stayed open even after the avatar had stepped into the room. His plan might just work. 'That for us?' He nodded at the tray.

'Yes, it is.' Device held out the tray, and Taro walked up and took it, slow and easy-like. As he put it down on the floor he said, 'I've been thinking about what you said, about how we should be friends? Reckon you're right.'

'That is good. Please, consume food and water now.'

Taro didn't need to be told twice, though sitting down in front of his enemy made his shoulder-blades prickle. The water was flat and warm, and the 'suitable' food made the recycled gloop they usually ate on Jarek's ship taste nice. He'd had worse, and he'd have had no trouble finishing the meal, but he made himself stop when he'd eaten half, then sat back and said, 'You really don't need that gun, you know.'

'For now I think I will keep it. Please, finish the meal. Or is it not suitable?' Vy had been getting more restless while Taro ate, and Device had to raise his voice to be heard above his moans.

'No, it's pure blade' – *if you like eating shit* – 'but I thought the rest was for Vy.'

'That was not the intention.'

In his cage, Vy made a kind of strangled begging noise.

'He's in a really bad way,' said Taro.

'I know. Fascinating, is it not?'

'Yeah, but if you don't feed him, his body'll give up before his mind goes. Won't that be less interesting?'

Device thought for a moment. 'A valid point. He does suffer the limitations of a humanoid body. You may give him some water.'

Taro took the cup, which was made of the same grey stuff as the bars, and offered it to Vy. He tried to keep eye-contact with the boy, willing him to remember what he'd told him to do.

Vy edged up to the bars, one hand outstretched. Then he hurled himself away with a screech. *That's the way*, thought Taro, even as he jumped at the sudden outburst.

'It does not appear to want the water,' observed Device.

'No, no, he's just freaked. Listen, I know him pretty well. Let me take the tray in there, and I'll get him to eat and drink.'

'I do not think that would be wise.'

'If I don't, he's gonna fade real fast, I'm sure of it.'

'Your concern for the broken avatar is intriguing.'

'Yeah, well, that's what you keep me around for, ain't it? To show you how humans tick. You said I'd get what I wanted if I behave, and what I want is to help Vy.'

'Even though your effort will only prolong what you perceive as its suffering?'

'Yeah, well, maybe I want to help him *because* he's so fucked. We humans are funny like that.'

'All right, take the tray inside. See if you can convince it to take sustenance.'

Taro bent to pick up the tray. When he straightened, a section of the bars had gone. Device had moved away and was standing well back, his gun trained on the opening.

'I'm coming in, Vy,' said Taro. 'Just stay calm, right? That's it, calm, and ... *whoa!*'

As he drew level with the opening, Taro jerked back, flinging the tray over his shoulder, just as Vy rushed forward.

Taro flew up and back, tensing against a possible shot in the back, and was barely clear of the cage door when Vy hurtled out of it, his arms flailing.

Something crackled like distant lightning, but whatever it was, it missed him. He flipped and turned in midair, poised to dive down from above, but Vy had flung himself at Device, forcing the avatar back towards the door. The Angel combat mods were fully online now, and Taro had plenty of time to adjust his plan accordingly. He landed just as the grappling figures staggered into the central room.

The crackling sound came again, and for a moment the two avatars froze. Then Vy sagged.

Taro's body wanted to obey its programming, but his mind was too busy being furious and fearful for Vy, and getting ready to die if that was the only way out. He ran through the cell door with an incoherent cry just as Vy slid to the floor. Then the mods took control again, squashing his brief moment of passion.

He let the Angel conditioning take over. There wasn't time to take flight, but with a simple step and twist he was coming at Device from an angle the avatar wasn't expecting.

The gun discharged again, and missed again.

Device moved his hand, ready to shoot once more, but he was too slow: Taro batted the gun away. Device was no faster than an ordinary human, he noted coolly.

The movement carried on, smooth as a dance: back arm round in an arc, turn using the opponent as a pivot point, and stop.

As the gun clattered to the floor Taro came to rest, looking down on Device from one side. The hand he'd disarmed him with was hooked around the back of the avatar's neck; his other arm was drawn back, piston-like, and pointed at Device's chest. The tip of his fully extended blade rested on the point where the heart would be in a human.

Taro heard himself draw breath, and the world began to settle around him.

In a voice of infuriating calm Device said, 'You have disrupted my investigations. This is not acceptable behaviour.' At the same moment, all the doors closed silently.

The original plan had been to take Device hostage and demand he let them go. Taro now saw that the avatar wasn't going to give in to threats. Plus, the fucker had just shot Vy.

'Fuck you an' your "acceptable behaviour"!' spat Taro, and stabbed Device.

The blade caught on Device's 'skin' for a moment before breaking through. Between the unexpected resistance and his adrenalin-fuelled anger Taro misjudged the attack and the blade only stopped when his open palm slammed up against the avatar's chest.

For a moment nothing happened. Then the avatar twitched and made a faint noise, somewhere between a buzz and a whisper. He felt the weight of the body as it went limp.

He stepped back quickly. The avatar slid off his blade. Its body jerked once when it hit the ground, then lay still.

Taro stared at it. *Was it dead? How would he know?* Thick clear fluid was leaking from the wound. He prodded the avatar with his foot. If it was faking, then it was doing a top prime job. Before he could think better of it, he stabbed the fallen avatar again, through the head. That'd take the smug expression off its stupid golden face. This time the fluid that seeped out was dark as old blood.

There'd be a price to pay for the calm of the fight; he needed to act before the crash hit. He went over to Vy.

Khesh's avatar lay sprawled on his back, body still and eyes glassy. When Taro bent down he saw the boy's chest rising and falling; he wasn't dead. Thank fuck for that.

As he got up, he saw all three doorways were back: the doors must have opened when the avatar kicked it. He went over and picked up Device's gun, which had odd protrusions and a tiny opening in a chunky barrel. Taro pointed the gun at the wall and tried squeezing what might be the trigger. Nothing happened. He examined it more closely, if carefully, tried again, and finally gave up. It probably only worked for the avatar. He'd just have to trust to his blades if he met anyone.

He picked the leftmost exit and went through it cautiously. The room looked like some sort of bedroom, with a person-sized platform against one wall and something that might be a table against another. There were no exits.

He went back to the room with the two avatars in and took the only unexplored doorway through to a room with a huge holoscreen across one wall. Or maybe it was just art. It showed dozens of multicoloured traces and dots, some of them projecting out towards him, several of them moving. There was also another cube-chair-thing. But no exits. Killing Device, getting Vy shot – it had all been for nothing, Taro thought; even though the internal doors were open, there was no way out of here!

He was shaking; he could feel the fight draining from his body, taking his energy with it, but he wouldn't expect the shakes to hit just yet. No, wait: *he* wasn't shaking; the *floor* was. In fact, the whole fucking room was. A high, ear-itching hum started, coming from all around.

Some of the lights on the wall began flashing more urgently. Taro stared at them, hoping the horrible suspicion he was starting to have was wrong. He was used to human tech, where you always knew where you were because of comforting hums and faint vibrations. Jarek had once told him that those little noises and movements weren't really necessary; engineers only put them in 'cos passengers demanded it—

The hum ramped up a full-blown whine and the shaking became a violent shuddering. He almost fell over the chair, saving himself only by activating his flight implants.

He wasn't in a prison building, or on a station. He was on a ship. A fucking hi-tech incomprehensible spaceship. And he'd just killed the only person who could fly it.

They were so screwed.

CHAPTER TWENTY-ONE

'There were two of them. *Two*, Urien!'

'I know; that was not the plan.' The old Escori sounded peeved.

Kerin was beyond peeved. She had expected Urien to come and berate her, but by the time he finally arrived, Damaru was already asleep and Kerin had been through anger to panic and back to anger. 'Then how did it happen? Who was this Ifanna am Nantgwyn anyway?'

'I believe there was – *ahem* – an administrative error.'

'A *what*?'

'The other Escorai and I were unaware that another girl had been put forward until she arrived here, at which point we had no choice but to proceed with both penitents.'

'How can that be? You always tell me the Tyr runs on respect and records.'

'To be honest, Kerin, right now I have no idea.' In an emotional shift typical of him, Urien went from annoyed to resigned. 'May I sit?' he added.

Kerin wondered, a little spitefully, if such mood swerves were deliberate, to disconcert opponents. She nodded, and he picked up the wooden chair from her desk and brought it over to the console. Kerin looked across at Damaru, who was sleeping on, oblivious. She felt something uncurl, then tighten within her breast.

Urien sat down and Kerin swivelled her own seat to face him. He sighed and said, 'I suspect that I failed to spot the problem with the second girl because I am concentrating on the big picture, on keeping order as we implement the changes we need to bring our world into the light. But there being two witches should not have changed our arrangement. Do not forget what these women are, Kerin: effectively they are Sidhe, the very enemy we seek to defend against.'

'No, they are not – trust me, Urien, I have met *real* Sidhe. These girls may have the ability to play upon men's hearts, but their powers are nothing compared to the creatures I encountered.'

'Nonetheless, they are dangerous; Hylwen's record proves that.'

'I know – and I know that by judging a penitent – even if she was found unworthy – I was helping fight the rumours that the Cariad would abolish the Putain Glan. But I *will* see an end to that vile practice one day, Urien, I swear it.'

Urien sighed. 'I suppose we should be grateful you did not decide to recruit them after all. Even some of the Putain Glan conditioned by Lillwen have proven problematic, and you do not have her witch talents.'

'Indeed I do not.' Kerin spared a thought for the skycursed woman who had worn the Cariad's robes before Kerin took on the role; Lillwen had been a temporary puppet put in place by the old Escorai to await the 'rebirth' of the 'true' Cariad. 'Actually, I did consider putting the girls to sleep on the carousel.'

'I could not have stopped you doing that, of course,' said Urien stiffly.

What Urien saw as a misguided act of charity on Kerin's part had used up five of the sixty-four places on the great wheel of coma-boxes that periodically transported the skyfools to 'heaven'. She was not sure how long the now-ownerless slaves from the Sidhe ship above them would remain asleep on the carousel, but when the festival of Sul Esgyniad came around next year, people would expect at least a couple of 'worthy' boys to be chosen, and Kerin would have no choice other than to put them to sleep on the wheel as well.

'Had I done so, I would only postpone the problem, not solve it,' said Kerin. 'You are quite correct in that.' She still had no idea what to do with the skyfools now the Sidhe were – hopefully! –

no longer going to collect them, so she could not afford to fill the carousel without good reason. She continued, 'If it had just been the one girl we discussed, I would have had her cast into the chasm as we agreed; it could be argued that she deserved it. But to have to condemn two girls, when the other had committed only one crime – and for all we knew that could have been hearsay – I am sorry, Urien: I could not do it.' She could still see the expression of terrified despair on the Fenland girl's sallow face. 'And if she was to be spared, then I saw no reason why the other girl should not be given a second chance too.'

'Your mother was skycursed, was she not?'

Kerin started. 'Aye – how did you know that?'

'I did not for sure, until you just confirmed it; my sources of information do not extend as far as mountain villages no one in the City of Light has ever heard of,' he said wryly. 'But a family that produces a boy with Damaru's talents is likely also to produce women with talents; theirs as dangerous as his are valuable. I should have considered the possibility earlier. I assume your mother was killed?'

'She was.' Kerin would never forget watching from the reeds as her fellow villagers cast her mother into the mere.

'I am sorry for that. But it does not change the fact that these two girls had to die – not just because of what they were, but because of what they *knew*. Lillwen could demonstrate some power, as they would expect the Cariad to do, but those girls would have sensed no such power from you, Kerin, which means they now know you are mortal, ordinary – not a goddess. And that is why they had to die, regardless of your public ruling.'

'What have you done, Urien?' asked Kerin uncertainly.

'What you would not.' Urien bowed his head for a moment, and the lamplight fell on the text from the Traditions that had been tattooed onto his head at his initiation. In the season since the Sidhe had tried to retake Serenein, Kerin had advanced in her studies enough to read the words: *Knowledge makes foolish men arrogant and wise men humble.* The Traditions had nothing to say on what knowledge did for women, presumably because they were

159

not allowed it. He looked up again and said, 'Do you really want to know the details?'

'I – tell me the essence of it.'

'It took a little time to arrange – hence my delay in coming to see you. I had to hire men who would have no compunction about shooting witches, and who had the skill to make sure they could kill the girls cleanly and safely from a distance. I also had to ensure that whichever priest accompanied the girls would not go out of his way to save them when my trap was sprung.'

'That sounds ... risky.' Criticising Urien stopped her having to think about the dead girls.

'The men I chose know their business; the girls would most likely never have realised the assassins were there before they met their end.'

'That was not what I meant,' Kerin said, adding, 'well, not just what I meant, anyway.'

Urien's tone was mild. 'I think you know me well enough to be sure that none of those involved in this incident will ever have the faintest idea who really initiated it.' Urien often went abroad dressed as a priest of a different rank and order; people saw the robes, not the man.

Kerin was pretty sure his other personas cultivated contacts of their own; she found herself envying him his many lives. 'Then there is nothing else to say, is there?' she sighed. 'I am sure you have other business to attend to.' Kerin had taken on the mantle of the Cariad determined to reveal the truth to her people, but so far most of her efforts had been bent towards ensuring that it remained hidden.

'Always. Kerin—' He paused, then changed his mind about whatever he had meant to say. 'Nothing. Sleep well.'

'Good night, Urien.'

When sleep would not come, Kerin resorted to taking a herbal draught to bring oblivion. It was a crutch she found herself relying on all too often these days.

CHAPTER TWENTY-TWO

'And this is caf?' asked Ain, staring dubiously into the mug.

'It is,' said Jarek, 'and you're the first person I've had on board my ship who doesn't like it.'

'I am sorry. But that leaves more for you!'

She smiled nervously and Jarek realised she was trying to make a joke. He wondered if she'd ever attempted anything as radical as humour before. Talking to the lingua by himself was making Jarek uncomfortable, not because Nual wasn't there to check Ain wasn't lying – it was obvious she'd been at least as fucked over as they had by the destruction of the hab; he was happy to consider her an ally, at least for the duration of the current crisis. He just wasn't sure what to say to her, now the natural distance they'd been maintaining had broken down in the face of their common plight.

There was one thing he was curious about which seemed harmless enough. 'You know,' he said, 'your speech has changed a lot since you first commed me.'

'Language modification is a fundamental ability for lingua. Many patrons use their own dialects or languages. If a lingua works with a given patron for a long period she is expected to modify her speech accordingly. Learning a new language takes a little longer, but when I spend a while with anyone who speaks a variation of Arc, I automatically mimic their accent, tonality and lexicon. To talk like them, as you'd say.'

'Right. And what's "Arc"?'

'Apologies: I should have explained that. "Arc" is short for "Archaic", which is the diplomatic and trade language of Aleph, based on the common tongue of human-space at the time of the Exodus.'

That explained why Ain's original speech had reminded him a little of the way people spoke on Serenein, though the lack of change there was because the Cariads had kept the place hermetically sealed and in a state of arrested development. 'Good job human language hasn't evolved too much then.'

'Indeed it is. I imagine that's due to your own need to keep a common language for your— your beamed virtuals, isn't it? Your communications network.'

'That's right. We call it beevee. Do the patrons communicate much with human-space?'

'Most have no interest, but I believe periodic updates are exchanged with those males who remain there.'

'Any idea how many old males there are in human-space?' He only knew of Khesh and his brother City-minds in the Tri-Confed system, but he'd bet there were more out there somewhere.

'Apologies: that isn't data the patrons feel the need to share.'

'Shame. They don't keep you very well informed, do they?'

'Lingua do not expect them to, beyond what is required to fulfil our function. Though we don't worship the patrons, we do acknowledge their superiority. They tell us what we need to know, and we accept that. Although I suspect I might have been chosen as your liaison because I've been out-system for so long, and so I know very little of any recent developments at the Consensus. An ignorant mind cannot give away secrets ...'

'... and they knew Nual would read you.' Another thought struck Jarek. 'Ain, do you know which male boarded my ship to remove Aleph's coordinates from the comp?'

'It would have been an avatar of the Gatekeeper; he considers himself the unofficial custodian of the shiftspace beacon, and the main authority on human-space. He has taken a very active part in your visit.'

'I assume he's not one of these Silent Agers?'

'No, he is aligned with Shining Iron Face, one of the septs actively in favour of contact with human-space.'

'And do you trust him?'

'I both trust and distrust all patrons; this paradox defines the lingua. However ... it appears likely that the Gatekeeper may have deceived you.'

'Well, somebody certainly tampered with my ship's com system to ensure it was offline during last night's little fuck-up, and he's the one male who's definitely had an avatar on my ship.'

'This is true. Also, it appears that the nanite plague did not arrive via an external delivery system but was on a timed release, and that implies that the patron who designed the hab must have known about the attack, even if he didn't actually initiate it himself. That would be the Gatekeeper again. The final log entry before things went wrong was an encrypted coms burst, which the hab's comp automatically accepted: I suspect that was the trigger. It also shut down the coms, though perhaps that was more of a side-effect. While the surveillance feed remained down, the Silent Agers took advantage to launch their own improvised attack.'

'And they want us dead. What do you think the Gatekeeper wants?'

'I'm afraid I have no idea.'

'I did wonder if someone here might try to steal my ship, given they don't have the means to get back to human-space. They don't, do they?'

Ain said, 'I do not believe so – but even if they did, they would be able only to send representatives. An avatar out of contact with its patron becomes unstable.'

Just like Vy had. Jarek also suspected the males might not approve of human shiftships, given the nature of the transit-kernels that powered them. 'So they're happy to carry on living out here, while humanity's still being secretly fucked over by the females.'

'They have no choice.'

'I guess not. To be honest, given how many of them there are, I was a bit surprised they just upped sticks and ran. What little info we have from that far back suggests the males were killed off slowly, over many generations.' He didn't feel the need to add that Nual had been told the same thing by her people, before she rebelled.

'What to do you mean?' asked Ain.

'Twenty thousand males – more originally, before some of them died getting to Aleph – would have been a force to be reckoned with, so why didn't they stay and fight?'

'Do you not know about the A-S Plague?'

'The A-S—? No, I don't. What is it?'

'It isn't something the patrons talk about much, but it's the reason they came here in the first place. The females created a viral agent that targeted Sidhe males.'

'Aha. And what did this virus do?' Jarek knew all about the Sidhe's tailored pathogens; he'd nearly died from one on Serenein.

'The A-S Plague was double-tasked. Firstly, it damaged the males' ability to freeshift – until then, the free males had expanded beyond the systems held by the females and returned to launch attacks on the females' territory. Once infected, they could no longer strike out for new star-systems; they could only use previously established transit-paths. Encoded males were more resilient to the virus than those who remained in the flesh, but it still eroded – and in some cases completely destroyed – their ability to transit.'

Jarek suspected that the Three Cities had succumbed to this virus; it would explain why they'd stayed behind. He wondered how it felt for natural starfarers like that to be stuck in one place. 'And the second effect?'

'The second part of the virus affected only non-encoded males, but it infected all of them, and it spread very quickly. It reduced the intellect of any infected male to that of a self-absorbed child.'

Or as they called them on Serenein, skyfools, thought Jarek.

Her expression dark, Ain concluded, 'And that's why they called it the Anti-Sentience Plague.'

'So the males ran away to avoid getting infected, and now they can't go back?'

'Even if they could, they wouldn't want to. The A-S virus is harmless to humans or female Sidhe, but they can carry it, and it is likely the pathogen is still live and endemic in human-space.'

Hence the extra-thorough decon they'd been through on arrival. 'Nasty,' Jarek muttered. *And typical of the Sidhe.*

'Do you mind if I rest now? I think the last few hours are beginning to catch up with me.'

Jarek realised she looked exhausted, and said quickly, 'Of course. You can have my cabin.'

'If you are sure this will not inconvenience you?'

'Not at all,' he told her with a smile. 'I'm quite used to sleeping on the bridge. Give me a few minutes to tidy things up in there and the room's all yours.'

No one tried to com them while Jarek napped on his control couch, though he suspected plenty of locals were watching his ship pull away from the densely populated disc. He dreamt about Serenein again: this time he was arguing with Kerin, who was trying to persuade him to give her people Angel implants so they could fly to Heaven and find out the truth for themselves. His months on her world remained startlingly vivid, often flooding up from his subconscious when he relaxed, while his life before was veiled by a strange haziness. Serenein was where he'd got his stolen memory back, and he suspected the place would always haunt him.

He had combined Ain's info with his own to plot the best course. They needed to come back down into the main planetary disc at a steep angle, but not so precipitous that they couldn't make adjustments once they'd located the Egg. The ship was just about to start its programmed descent when Nual came up onto the bridge.

'Any luck?' he asked, thankful he didn't need to spell out his question. It was painful enough without having to actually ask, *Is Taro still alive?*

She gave him a wan smile. 'He isn't dead. I think I made contact, but it was fleeting – it might be due to distance, or maybe interference. This is a very crowded system.'

'But you're sure he's out there somewhere?'

'Yes. He is definitely alive.'

'That's something. Your premonition—?' Jarek wasn't sure what he was asking.

'I believe that lying about our relationship saved Taro's life. If those who kidnapped Taro had known of our link, then they

165

would not just have *claimed* he was dead. They would have actually killed him to avoid their deception being uncovered.'

'If he *were* dead, what would you do?' he asked, curious. There was no point mincing words with Nual.

'Not go on some foolish quest for vengeance, if that's what you're worried about. I would try to force the shift back to human-space without him. Assuming you would be willing to risk it.'

'Well, let's hope it doesn't come to that, shall we?' He checked the board; the ship had turned and they were now heading back in. 'Right, we've got about ten hours before we're back in the high-population area. Assuming we get that far in one piece, we need to decide what we're going to say to the Consensus.'

'I think we need to speak to Ain about that,' Nual said after a moment.

'She's opened up to me a lot recently,' Jarek said. 'I'd say we can afford to be honest with her.'

'That won't stop me reading her.'

'I'd expect nothing less.'

Jarek stayed on the bridge, watching the busy lights of the ecliptic begin to fill the monitors. After the comp had registered a couple of attempts to ping them, he called the others.

Ain sat next to Jarek on the folding stool he had used when he was training Taro to fly the ship. Nual waited silently at the back.

As they dropped towards the inner system, there were more pings, and some com calls; Jarek ignored them all. Right now he was more worried about physical interception. As space got more crowded, they'd have to slow down to manoeuvre around the local domains, each of which had a fixed radius of space they claimed as their own. Ain told them about the temporary corridors of neutral space created when orbital mechanics brought two domains too close together; it was Jarek's job to make sure they stuck to these corridors.

'Any sign of the Egg yet?' he asked Ain.

Ain was monitoring the holocube. 'I'm not sure. I am finding your tech a little confusing,' she admitted.

'That's all right,' said Jarek, trying not to get annoyed, 'just tell me what you think you're seeing, and I'll tell you what I've got on my readouts …'

For the next couple of hours they deciphered the congested sensor readings together. The best tactic for picking out something in a polar orbit was to stand off a little and watch how everything moved, as they were mainly seeing domains in flat orbits round the sun, or ships under power. Even so, by the time he was sure they were closing in on their destination, four ships of various sizes and configurations were following them at a discreet distance and the coms board was lit solid. If only he could work out which messages – if any – came directly from the Consensus, he could answer them—

—he nearly missed the hazard warning. The debris cloud between the *Heart of Glass* and the Egg initially showed only as a tell-tale in one corner of the screen, but Jarek reached for the nav-shield controls as soon as the alarm went off. A moment later the holocube and screens flickered. Out of the corner of his eye he saw Ain open her mouth in surprise, but he raised his free hand and she stayed quiet.

The ship gave a series of faint jolts.

The jolts stopped. The readouts stabilised.

They were through.

'We just flew into a debris-cloud,' he said, a little breathlessly. 'It was all small stuff, but that would have been enough to hole the hull of a ship with inadequate shielding going too fast – which we weren't, obviously. Looking at it, I'd guess someone dumped it there very recently, and I think we can assume it was specifically intended to do us some damage.'

'The Consensus will not be pleased,' Ain said shakily.

'I should bloody well hope not.' He made another check on local space. 'Right, I'm going to broadcast a wide-frequency hail. We're near enough that everyone must have worked out where we're heading by now, but I prefer to ask for permission to dock before I get too close—'

—especially since the Consensus' habitat had the best weapons in the system, according to Ain – just in case any males were crazy enough to try and break the rules.

His hail was answered at once, and a female voice very similar to Ain's directed him to the main docking ring.

'Almost there,' he announced. 'Time to get a proper look at our destination.'

The vector plot in the cube was replaced by their first detailed image of the Egg. From behind him he heard Nual draw a sharp breath.

'Yeah,' he said over his shoulder to her, 'it is, isn't it? We probably should have seen that one coming.'

CHAPTER TWENTY-THREE

Taro stared at the wall display. It had to be some sort of console – maybe it even controlled the ship – but he was fucked if he knew how it worked. There weren't any screens, or sliders, or any of the shit he was used to, just the lights and traces covering the wall. And the shaking and humming were getting worse by the moment. He had to do something, but he had no idea what—

A large red light near the top of the display expanded and brightened, then began to blink slowly and compellingly. Taro stared at it, mesmerised. *Something pretty to look at while I wait to die* ...

Was he imagining it, or was the shuddering easing off? Yep, things had definitely begun to calm down. That had to be a good thing.

He looked away from the hypnotic light. The rest of the display didn't look so frantic now, and the hum had died away. When he decided to risk standing on it, the floor just felt a bit unstable, though that could be him. Whatever the problem was, it looked like it'd sorted itself out – so maybe he wasn't going to die after all.

He went back to check on Vy. The damaged avatar was still alive, but out of it. He sat down next to him and put a hand on the boy's shoulder. Was that another shudder? It felt kind of distant. His eyes began to close, and he felt himself falling forward ...

He caught himself just before he hit the floor. *Damn fucking adrenalin comedown.* He stayed where he was, collapsed beside the prone avatar, willing himself to stay alert, but nothing was happening, and nothing was boring, and boredom made him sleepy.

He should try and get up, fly, go check the place out – but what was there to check out? They weren't dead, and the ship hadn't crashed. So, no immediate threat. And it'd be a lot easier to work out what to do next once he'd got some rest ...

He woke up sprawled across the floor, with no idea how long he'd been asleep. It didn't feel like long enough, and now he was thirsty again. Something smelled a bit odd, though that could be him. He levered himself into a sitting position and looked down on Vy. The boy's open eyes tracked him, and his mouth twitched.

'Hey,' murmured Taro, 'how y'doing there?'

'I'm dying,' said Vy calmly.

'Nah, you'll be fine.' Taro put all the conviction he could muster into his voice. 'I'm gonna have a look around, see if I can find us a drink. You'll feel better once you've had a drink.'

Vy's mouth turned up into a dreamy smile, but he didn't say anything.

Taro got up. He took a look at what'd been their cell from the doorway. The door was still open – or rather, missing – but he didn't trust the fucking thing not to close again if he went inside. Anyway, the water and food from the tray was spilled all over the floor, and the mush, whatever it was, had dried to a nasty crust, which might explain the smell.

Next he tried the room he'd decided to call Device's cabin. Device had talked about sorting human food, so maybe he'd done that in here – but none of the nodules, lumps and rough portions of wall responded to Taro's touch. He wondered about moving Vy in here, onto the bed-thing, but when he touched the platform it wasn't soft like the cell floor had been.

He started at a noise from outside and called, 'Vy? You feeling better?' He walked over to the doorway.

Vy was still lying on the floor. There were three other people in the room with him. They were even taller than Taro, and aside from some off-white things on their arms and ankles, they were naked. They all carried thin, white-tipped poles that looked suspiciously like weapons. Their skin was dark, or possibly just really

170

dirty, and they had long tangled red-brown hair, with more stuff plaited into it. One was bending down over Device's body. The other two stood next to Vy: one was leaning on his pole – yeah, those were definitely spears – and the other was just about to use his to prod Vy.

'Hey!' yelled Taro, 'what the fuck d'you think you're doing?'

The three men started, then stared at Taro with odd, narrow-eyed expressions, like they were surprised, but couldn't see him properly. The one about to poke Vy took a shaky step back. His companion put out an arm to steady him.

The third one said something like, 'Gloo tsah mahin!' in a high, piping voice. All three started backing off, their eyes still screwed up. They moved clumsily, keeping their spears on the floor in front of them, almost like they were using them to push themselves back-wards.

'Listen, I could actually use some help here,' said Taro, looking between them.

The one who'd spoken said something else incomprehensible. He sounded scared, though it was hard to be sure with that funny voice.

When they reached the door to the bridge the front two had a brief comedy moment trying to work out who was going through first. The winner had to bend over to get through, and he held onto the edge of the door like he expected to fall.

'You don't have to leave,' said Taro. 'We can talk about this.' Assuming he could get them to understand. He pointed to his chest. 'Friend,' he said slowly and emphatically.

They weren't having any of it. The second one went through the door, eyes wide in his dark – no, it really was filthy – face as he backed away. Taro picked up Device's useless gun, pointed it at the door and said firmly, 'Wait right there, you.' The remaining visitor looked scared, but he didn't hang around either.

Taro ran up to Vy and asked, 'Did they hurt you?'

'No,' said Vy, who looked surprisingly content.

'Good! Right, I'm going after these weird-looking fuckers. You, er, just stay there.'

'I'm not going anywhere.'

Their brief chat had given the intruders time to get across the probably-bridge. As Taro came in the first one was just making his exit – through a door that most certainly hadn't been there earlier. Taro decided against trying to stop them. They appeared more scared of him than he was of them, but they outnumbered him, and he wasn't at his best right now.

He waited until they'd made their way outside, then counted to ten and went over to the door. He peered through cautiously, wary of possible attack. It was very dark out there, the sky black, and star-filled.

And it looked like he'd been wrong: the ship *had* landed – or possibly crashed, though the ship's tech had done a good job of cushioning the impact. But whether it had landed or crashed, the ship had trashed the immediate area; it was sitting in the centre of a shallow crater. The place smelled funny, sort of like a mixture of farts and incense. That was the smell he'd noticed when he'd first woken up.

Taro spotted movement and watched the three locals disappearing at a fast trot into a tunnel in the side of the crater, their feet kicking up puffs of dust.

He had another look around the landing site, but he could see only the one tunnel. There were no other signs of life in the crater. He peered at the ground, two metres down, then stepped into the air and floated down slowly. His flight implants automatically adjusted to the local gravity, but he'd grown up in a low-grav environment – he realised that was why the locals had been having so much trouble on the ship. And the lack of light here wasn't too much of a problem for him; the Undertow had also been a twilight world. He shivered as he thought of the parallels between his old home and this place; Khesh City was, after all, just another male Sidhe's domain, even if no one who lived there knew it.

He decided against landing and instead flew towards the tunnel, checking behind him to make sure he was alone before he stuck his head in the perfectly circular opening. The inside surface had been sealed with something that glistened faintly in the starlight. For a

172

moment he considered going in, then decided against it; he didn't want to leave Vy alone and undefended.

Instead, he flew up towards the lip of the crater. The sky up there looked a bit fuzzy, and as he got closer he started to feel odd: his hair began to stand on end and nausea stirred in his guts. He stopped and hovered, thinking. He'd felt that before – there was a forceshield across the top of the crater. Some sort of automatic defence to stop the air leaking out? Whatever the reason, he wasn't going any nearer.

Before he went back inside the ship he examined the hull around the outside of the door, but there was no sign of any controls, inside or out. Well, looked like the door would be staying open for now. Device had obviously been controlling the ship directly with his mind. Jarek had told him about human ships that used neural-interface tech, though Jarek didn't hold with them himself; he was leery of implants, probably due to his religious upbringing. Taro would happily get the neurolink mods given the chance, but they weren't cheap. Device's ship was the most hi-tech ship Taro had ever seen – in fact, all of Aleph's tech was beyond anything Taro had come across in his admittedly limited travels. Jarek'd had a theory about that: he'd reckoned the female Sidhe secretly put the knackers on human progress, to make sure humanity didn't get too advanced and hard to control. Taro preferred the less paranoid explanation: that humans just weren't as smart as male Sidhe.

Even if Device controlled most of the ship from his head, there was still the display wall. A lot of the lights and traces had gone out and those that were still lit weren't moving much. That made sense: the ship would have powered down after its emergency landing. A human ship would have also sent out a distress call, but given how the males around here hated each other, he couldn't rely on that.

Taro had another go at working the wall out. He put out a hand towards an orange bar, ready to snatch it back; his hand passed through the light. He tried again, this time flying up to touch a pale mauve blob that was gently bouncing around near ceiling height. The blob stopped, pulsed twice in an annoyed sort of way, then carried on bouncing. He looked around, but nothing appeared to have changed. He tried touching a few more random lights; his hand went through them and they either remained unchanged or throbbed or twitched, then went back to doing whatever they'd been doing before.

He decided he'd better check out the rest of the ship, just to make sure he hadn't accidentally activated something by fiddling with the wall. He couldn't see any changes.

Vy was asleep when he got back. Taro, concerned about the avatar, especially with his talk of dying, crouched down and shook him gently awake.

Vy's eyes opened at once. 'Did you find water?' he asked.

'No, sorry.'

'There were people here, weren't there?'

'There were, but they're gone now. Not sure if they'll be back. You sound better.'

'Not so crazy, you mean?'

'Yeah. Not so crazy.'

'I've consolidated my remaining functions. Many of my irrelevant memories have been purged, but I will remain lucid within the necessary parameters for the remaining time I have.'

'Right.' Taro wasn't sure he liked the sound of that. 'Are you strong enough to stand up yet? You can't be very comfy lying on the floor.'

'This is as good a place as any for me to be.'

'Yeah, but it's making my neck ache looking down at you. Tell you what, why don't I help you over there to the wall and you can sit up.'

Getting Vy to the wall turned out to be harder than Taro had expected. The avatar was as light as a human child, but the body already felt like dead meat. Vy kept smiling vaguely while Taro manhandled him until he was sitting up with his back against the wall.

After that, Taro tried to drag Device's body away so they wouldn't have to look at it, but it was too heavy, and he quickly gave up.

When he turned back, Vy had slid to one side and was bracing himself on one arm. His head was lolling over, like some life-sized boneless doll. 'I have devoted some functionality to the physical task of keeping the body upright,' he said primly.

'Good,' said Taro slowly.

'You have to live, Taro.'

'Yeah, well, that's the plan.' Or perhaps more the intention: to have a plan he'd need to have some idea of where the fuck they were and how the fuck they'd get back to the others. Especially Nual. Shit and blood, he'd been trying not to think about Nual. He shook his head to dispel the pain.

'No, you really do,' said Vy, possibly mistaking the gesture. He no longer sounded anything like the mad, petulant kid he'd been. 'Because I can't. Won't. I acknowledge that now. Hence my choice to reprioritise. I will die, whatever happens.'

'That's bollocks, Vy – you'll be fine. I won't let anyone hurt you, and I'll get us both home.' *Somehow.*

'This body no longer functions. And my mind ... I now acknowledge that my original mission cannot succeed as planned.'

'Your original mission? The one you couldn't tell me about?'

'Yes.'

'And— So does that mean you're willing to tell me about it now? I mean, I wanna know, but only if you're sure you want to tell me.'

'I'm sure,' said Vy firmly. 'I will explain everything. And then you must kill me.'

CHAPTER TWENTY-FOUR

Ifanna let the two men hurry her away down the alley. She heard distant shouts, and wondered vaguely if Hylwen was dead. Her own pain was worse now, but she was still gagged and could not tell anyone. She thought suddenly about hunters in the village, who tracked wounded wild pigs by the trail of blood the animals left in the mud. She slowed and grunted, inclining her head to indicate with her eyes what the problem was.

The priest stopped, his companion following suit a moment later, and in the light of the single lantern their expressions of confusion looked like to turn to hostility if she gave them any excuse. Ifanna bent her head harder, and finally the priest looked down.

'Mother of Mercy! She is wounded!' He looked to his companion. 'Siarl, there is blood. Can you see how serious it is?'

He took the lantern, and the monitor crouched down next to her. Ifanna felt a strange sensation; the priest had sounded almost *concerned*. Concerned for *her*. She got her first good look at her saviour as he watched the monitor tend to her. He was an older man, a little jowly and sunken-eyed. His shaved scalp was wrinkled above his ears.

She drew in a sharp breath. She could feel the cut clearly now, and the monitor's fingers probing it.

The pain receded a little and the monitor – Siarl – straightened. ''Tis not deep. Olwenna could dress it—'

'No, I will not ask that of you. There will be medicines at the house, will there not?'

176

'Aye, there should be.' The monitor did not sound sure. Ifanna sensed that this venture made him uneasy.

'Then we should not change our plan.' He addressed Ifanna. 'Can you walk—? Oh, I am a fool! *Chilwar*, you are still gagged. Here.' He reached up, then said sternly but not unkindly, 'If I remove this, you will not cry out, will you?'

Ifanna shook her head vigorously. He had called her *chilwar*, as though she were not damned.

He undid the gag. Ifanna said meekly, 'Thank you, *Gwas*.'

'Let me unbind your hands, too, *chilwar*.'

His companion said, 'Maelgyn, I think we would do better to wait until we are at the house.'

'I suppose so.' To Ifanna he said, 'Does your wound pain you much?'

'Hardly at all, *Gwas*.' She did not want to disappoint or annoy the priest when he was treating her so well. 'I drew your attention to it because I was worried that I might bleed on the ground and they might— I mean—' She did not want to continue that thought, did not want to remind these men that they had just gone against the will of Heaven – or the command of their superiors, at least.

Siarl gave her a look tinged with admiration. 'A wise thought, Ifanna, but there is not enough blood to track us by.'

They knew who she was!

'Then we do not need to worry,' the priest said, his voice belying his words. 'Let us carry on.'

Surprise had overcome her natural reticence. 'Wait,' said Ifanna, instantly regretting speaking out when she saw the priest's thin-lipped expression. But he did not command her to be silent, so she carried on, her voice tremulous. 'Please, Master Siarl, how is it you know my name?'

Gwas Maelgyn answered for his companion, whose uneasiness was growing, and was now tinged by embarrassment. 'Actually, *chilwar*, he is *Captain* Siarl.' He spoke lightly, as though to a child. 'And as for how he knows your name: all will be explained later.'

'Of course, *Gwas*. I did not mean to question.'

The priest kept hold of her arm when they set off again, though more to steer than to restrain. Despite her assertion that she could walk unaided, Ifanna soon began to feel lightheaded. The wound in her side was a constant, draining ache, and her feet dragged. She stumbled, and the priest caught her.

'You are not all right, are you?'

'I am sorry, *Gwas*—'

'Hush. Let me help.' He put an arm around her, supporting her. She could not remember the last time anyone had showed such concern. And this man was a *priest*!

As they carried on, and Ifanna became more tired and lightheaded, *Gwas* Maelgyn let her lean into him, for which she was deeply grateful.

Finally they stopped in an unlit alley, outside a two-storey house with a small yard. The yard had clay pots in it, but the plants in them were long dead. The windows of the house were shuttered, and the lamplight illuminated a blue circle painted on the closed door. Ifanna tensed.

'There is nothing to fear,' said *Gwas* Maelgyn softly.

But all Ifanna could think was that these two men who had rescued her from death and treated her well now wished to take her to a shuttered house – a *plague house*! – where she would be at their mercy. When she looked at the monitor, she was alarmed to see him reaching for the dagger on his belt.

'Please, Captain Siarl!' she cried out, reinforcing her words with raw compulsion, 'do not hurt me!'

The monitor captain hesitated as the priest said, 'Trust me, Ifanna, you will be safe here. But if we are to help you then you must not – *must not* – employ the curse that brought you to this sorry pass. Not *ever*. Do you understand?'

'I understand.' She released her hold on the monitor's will.

Captain Siarl looked at her fearfully. He knew what she had tried to do, and he was not happy.

Ifanna stared at her feet. 'I am sorry. I should not ...'

'No matter,' said the priest with false heartiness. 'I understand your worry, *chilwar*; this house was indeed touched by the falling fire. The young family who lived here went to the Mothers during the winnowing times. It has been shut up ever since, while distant relatives bicker over who will inherit the place. You can stay here safely without fear of being found.'

The monitor held out his dagger again, and now she saw he intended to use it to get them in. He slipped it into the gap between the door and frame, and raised the latch slowly. She heard a click, and the door opened a crack. He went in first, then called softly and Ifanna and the priest followed. They came into a kitchen. The air smelled stale, and there was a faint tang to it that made Ifanna wonder how long the bodies of the previous occupants had lain here before being discovered.

Captain Siarl put the lantern on the table and started looking through cupboards.

When the priest asked, 'May I borrow your knife?' Ifanna tried not to react. She wanted to believe that she was safe, but this was all so unexpected, after her months of confinement.

The monitor handed his blade over and as he continued searching the cupboards, the priest started to cut her bonds, grasping her wrists with one hand and sawing at the rope with the other. He had dark stains on his long fingers, which she identified, after a moment, as ink.

Captain Siarl came back with a candle, which he lit from the lantern and put in the pot on the table. 'Can you manage, Maelgyn?' he asked.

'I almost have it,' the priest replied, 'though more light would make my job easier.'

'I do not think that would be wise, in a house that is meant to be abandoned.'

'A valid point ... ah, there we are.'

Ifanna's bonds fell away. Now her hands were free she wondered if she should circle her breast to show respect for the priest, but the thought seemed irrelevant. Instead she leant on the table. She was not sure how much longer she would be able to stand up.

'Ah, I am sorry, *chilwar*. Sit down if you need to.'

Ifanna was happy to obey, and while Captain Siarl continued searching the kitchen, the priest appeared content to watch Ifanna

179

in silence. She found his scrutiny both disconcerting and flattering.

The captain found what he was looking for and came back to the table. 'I should look at that wound,' he said, and knelt next to Ifanna.

She eased her chair back, scraping it on the flagstones and drawing a sharp look from the priest. The monitor's blunt-fingered touch was all business, with none of the healer's gentleness, and Ifanna had to force herself not to cry out or flinch.

After a while he said gruffly, 'I will need to lift your tunic up to dress the wound.'

'I will hold it out of the way,' said Ifanna. She was no happier about having to expose her nakedness than the monitor was at seeing it. Though she could not see his eyes, from the touch of his fingers she knew how uncomfortable he felt at being so close to a witch. He was only prepared to do this because of his friend the priest, and any lustful thoughts that dared enter his mind as he touched her were quashed ruthlessly.

The priest sat and watched. His expression was soft, full of sympathy.

Ifanna opened her mouth, closed it again, and then decided she would speak, if only to distract herself from the discomfort of both body and mind. '*Gwas*,' she said, 'I am grateful to you – to both of you, Captain Siarl – for what you have done for me this night. But – and forgive me for asking this – why did you save me?'

'Have you not noticed our looks, *chilwar?*'

'Your— Your *looks, Gwas?*'

'Aye. Captain Siarl and I are Fenlanders, like you. We too come from the Terraced Marshes.'

It was too dim in the kitchen for her to really distinguish their features, but now the priest mentioned it, Ifanna realised most of the people she had seen in here had lighter skin, and faces of a subtly different shape to hers. This priest and monitor looked normal to her eyes. 'I do see, *Gwas*.' But such a tenuous link was not enough, surely, to make them disobey the Cariad's ruling?

'In fact,' continued the priest, 'we are from Plas Morfren.'

'Plas Morfren?' The sound of that familiar name was balm to Ifanna's ears.

'Aye, *chilwar*: Siarl and I grew up there, and we have been friends all our lives.'

Captain Siarl grunted his assent from near Ifanna's waist.

Gwas Maelgyn continued, 'You come from Nantgwyn, I believe, and that village falls under the jurisdiction of the Reeve of Plas Morfren.'

'Aye,' said Ifanna, 'I do.' Or rather, did: she could not imagine ever returning to her birthplace.

The priest sat back, satisfied he had made his reasons clear, though Ifanna was unsure why coming from the same region was enough to make these two strangers take such risks on her behalf.

Captain Siarl stood. 'There,' he said tersely, 'as I thought, the wound was not deep. If you do not exert yourself or interfere with the bindings you will be fine.'

The priest looked over at his friend. 'You should probably get back to Olwenna.'

'Aye; she knows my shift finished some time ago, and will no doubt be cursing my men for luring me to the tavern.'

'And I must return to the Tyr.'

'What about me, *Gwas*?' asked Ifanna.

'You will be safe here,' said *Gwas* Maelgyn. 'I will come back tomorrow morning.'

'Tomorrow?' echoed Ifanna. She glanced over at the door, which had a latch but no lock. 'How— How do you know I will still be here?' She shrank inside even as she asked the question.

'I do not know for sure,' said the priest mildly. 'But we Fen-landers are a sensible, practical people. Given the choice between wandering friendless in a city where you are hated and hunted, and remaining hidden and letting your allies help you, I would expect you to show the wisdom we are renowned for.'

Ifanna had no answer for that, and hearing the gentle reprimand in his voice, she could not bring herself to ask anything else. Instead she followed them to the door, circling her breast as she bade them farewell, and put the latch down behind them.

CHAPTER TWENTY-FIVE

'A Sidhe mothership?' said Ain. 'I had no idea.'

Jarek, busy lining up the *Heart of Glass* for the complicated docking manoeuvre, let Nual answer. 'There was a legend about a mothership captured by the males,' she said. 'I assumed the story was propaganda, meant to promote hatred of our wicked brothers. It appears I was wrong.'

The other Sidhe mothership Jarek had seen had reminded him of a great bronze egg. This ship looked bigger than that one, and it had been heavily built over and modified, although he could see the egg-shaped structure was still there, under all the platforms, gantries and additional modules.

He turned his attention to getting into position for the multi-purpose clamping mechanism which took the place of normal docking bays. He winced at the faint shudder as it locked in place. This set-up would be a bastard if they had to make a quick getaway.

'Right,' he said, 'we're here, so we may as well get this over with.'

'No one will interfere with your ship,' said Ain, almost as though she could read minds.

'Yeah, well, no offence, Ain, but no one was meant to interfere with us on the hab that got remodelled by that mining barge.'

'That was out-system, in a hastily built structure arbitrarily assigned as neutral territory,' she said. '*This* is the Consensus. I can request that the Arbiter posts guards to your assigned umbilical, but I should warn you that such a request would not only break protocol, it would imply distrust.'

'No need to *imply* distrust, Ain,' Jarek said. 'I've yet to find a reason to *trust* the patrons – any of them.'

He followed the others into the airlock, which was only just big enough for three people, and made sure he double-checked the tell-tales before opening the outer door. They stepped into a short transparent tube, and Nual gave a sudden gasp as she caught sight of the slice of star-filled sky above them.

Jarek was more concerned with the *Heart of Glass*'s airlock. When he turned to look at it he was pleased to see that the alien docking umbilical had aligned perfectly with his 'lock and a flashing red light beside the now-closed door confirmed that his ship was in full lockdown mode; in theory, only someone with both a ship-linked com and a retinal scan registered on the *Heart of Glass*'s comp should be able to open that door again.

He wished Ain hadn't insisted both he and Nual had to accompany her onto the Egg. More of the males' so-called *protocol*, apparently. The patrons had demanded that Nual appear before them in person, and Jarek was there because, despite the well-distributed footage from the hab, Ain said some of them continued to believe he was in Nual's thrall. Showing his face in person was the only way to challenge that – and it also meant that he and Nual would most likely be split up.

None of this was ideal, but their only hope of getting out of here alive was to cooperate fully with the rulers of this crazy system.

The airlock at the end of the tube opened into a featureless grey corridor, and a silvery humanoid was awaiting them there. It raised a pair of slender wands and took a step towards Nual.

Jarek forced himself not to react; Ain had warned them they would be scanned on their arrival. The avatar ran the wands over the three of them quickly and efficiently, working in silence. When it had finished, it stepped back and addressed Nual: 'Warning: any attempt to use your implanted weaponry will be severely punished.' Then it turned and strode off.

Ain took charge, leading them through one identical corridor after another, pausing at junctions to receive further directions from the Consensus' comnet. Since using the *Heart of Glass*'s coms would have been seen as another sign of distrust, Jarek and Nual had also been linked in. No doubt all their calls would be monitored.

They passed some lingua, who acknowledged them with a quick, open-handed tap on their lips that Jarek thought was rather like blowing a kiss. They wore the standard lingua uniform, a simple black overall, with no adornment or personalisation. The first avatar they passed, another dull silver figure like the one that'd scanned them, ignored them; when Jarek glanced after it Ain said, 'That is an avatar of the Arbiter. He administers the Consensus; he has no voting rights, but the Egg is his personal domain.' From the almost fond way she spoke, Jarek got the impression Ain viewed this Arbiter as some sort of mentor, or even a father-figure, much as Taro had apparently once done with the Minister.

The next person they met was a slightly older-looking lingua, who smiled warmly when she saw Ain, and after a formal greeting to Jarek and Nual, kissed Ain on the lips before continuing on her way.

Both Jarek and Nual were taken aback when a large dog with shaggy purplish fur came loping along the corridor. When it saw them it stopped and sat back on its haunches. They all gave it as wide a berth as they could, but as Nual passed it, the dog spoke. The voice came from its chest, while its mouth moved in what looked worryingly like a growl: 'Ah, the beautiful enemy. Somehow I thought you would be taller.'

Nual ignored it and kept walking, looking straight ahead. When they were out of earshot Jarek said, 'I assume that was an avatar.'

Ain said, 'You are correct. That was an autonomous avatar, answering to a moderately high-ranking halo patron who aligns himself with the Moonlit Glory – they are isolationist, but not violently so.'

'Have the alignments and sept groupings changed much since you were last here?' asked Nual.

'I am not yet sure,' Ain admitted. 'I will study them at length as soon as the opportunity arises. Normally change comes slowly to the Consensus, but these are eventful times: we are about to have the second Extraordinary Session in as many weeks.'

Ordinary humans were not usually permitted in the Consensus, so he and Nual had been allocated rooms intended for lingua, on the same corridor, but not adjacent. Jarek looked around, unimpressed. His room smelled stale, and looked like it hadn't been used for some time. The basic furnishings reinforced his first impression, that this was a sterile, inhospitable place.

Ain told them to use the open com channel to request refreshments. 'You will be unlikely to be able to procure anything particularly exciting, I'm afraid,' she added as she left them to find her own quarters.

'I'm fine for now,' said Jarek. 'How long do you think they'll keep us waiting before they speak to us?'

'It should not be too long,' Ain said. 'Any delay at this stage will be due to last-minute power-brokering behind the scenes.'

Another less-than-reassuring thought. Alone in his room, Jarek's paranoia redoubled, and he got up to check the door; it opened when he approached, which was a relief. He resisted the urge to pace and instead sat on the hard chair until, bored and uncomfortable, he tried lying on the bed. He'd almost managed to relax enough to close his eyes when his com chirped.

'We have been summoned,' Ain said.

'Right. Guess we'd better go then.'

It was a short walk, and this time they didn't encounter anyone on the way. Ain led them to a dimly lit circular room. She looked at them both and asked if they were ready.

Jarek glanced at Nual and then nodded at Ain while Nual murmured her assent.

The room darkened further until they were surrounded by darkness, and the floor began to move, which did nothing for Jarek's nerves. Slowly, pinpricks of light appeared around them.

When Ain had referred to the heart of the Consensus as the Star Chamber, Jarek hadn't realised she meant it this literally. Their platform was rising into the centre of a projection of Aleph, positioned where the system's sun would be in reality. Jarek had no idea how big the Chamber was, but the illusion of being surrounded by infinite space was certainly convincing. They looked out across a disc of coloured lights, with a few scattered dots above and below.

One particularly bright light, close enough that Jarek had to blink to focus on it, flashed three times, and a voice said, 'Consensus in Session. Date as per register. Single item agenda: request from the visiting human-space delegation.' The voice was dry, efficient and even-toned: the very essence of impartiality. 'The following septs register vetoing objections to the presence of a Sidhe female in the Consensus. They waive all voting rights for this session ...' The Arbiter listed some two dozen names, then added, 'A further sixty-seven septs make formal complaint, but do not employ right of veto. Their names are recorded in the annotations.'

Jarek reminded himself that as a percentage of the total number of septs in the Aleph system, ninety or so wasn't that many.

Several lights around the projection started flashing. Jarek looked down and noticed his com was also going off silently; with the screen still furled and nothing in here to project against all he could see was tiny text speeding across the display, far too fast to read.

Ain, noticing the direction of his gaze, whispered, 'Having the Arbiter speak aloud is partly a way of reinforcing decisions, and partly a concession to what they perceive as human frailty. Most of the action is going on in the background.'

The Arbiter spoke again. 'All comments are noted. One valid query is chosen. Recognise Last-Cloud-of-Fire, rep:Chaos in Motion.'

The frantic flashing stopped, except for one light above them, in the halo beyond the main mass of the ecliptic. When the voice spoke up it sounded tetchy, although the voices were as much an illusion as the celestial bodies apparently filling the chamber. 'Statement: This female is the first we have seen for a thousand years. She claims to be a rebel. Query: What evidence is presented for this claim?'

'Clarification: we assume you do not wish the female to be granted speaking rights?' asked the Arbiter drily.

'Negative! We wish to ascertain the reason for her presence and agenda.'

'Clarification: that is what this session is for. We remind you – and any others who might have *forgotten* – of the resolution reached at our last meeting, to whit: although we have not been openly at war with the females for a millennium, we view their attempt to deploy a mindbomb against one of our brothers in human-space as an end to our truce with them.'

The cold declaration chilled Jarek's soul. But it was personal too. *That's my sister you're talking about there, God rest her.*

The Arbiter continued, 'Clarification of previously stated protocol: anyone wishing a private audience with the female can request one. We will grant limited access to non-hostile sept representatives according to a randomised selection routine. If your patron's location precludes real-time contact and he does not grant his avatars full autonomy, we suggest allying yourself with a trusted in-system sept. In your *own* time, not that of the Consensus.' Jarek decided he must have imagined the small sound of annoyance that followed the Arbiter's comment. A few more lights flashed, before dying down again.

'Now, lingua,' continued the Arbiter, 'state your case.'

Jarek expected Ain to be nervous. The patrons had no advance warning of the business a lingua brought to the Consensus, and the requests Ain was about to make were likely to cause a degree of upset. But as she started, she sounded calm and confident. This was, she had told them, what she was born to do.

'Honoured patrons, this lingua has three points to raise. First, this lingua wishes to formally register complaints of abuses that require investigation, specifically, the assaults upon the habitat created to house the visitors, and a more recent attempt to disable their ship.'

'We are aware of these incidents. The formal complaint on behalf of your charges is noted,' said the Arbiter.

More lights flashed, and after a moment or two the Arbiter said, 'Ruling: as several septs wish to comment, we will choose a representative speaker for the isolationist cause. Recognise Indiroth, rep:The Grave and the Constant.'

The male had a pleasant, youthful-sounding voice; 'his' celestial body was near the representation of the Consensus, though lower on the ecliptic. 'Statement: the intruders disrupt the pattern of our home. They must be eliminated, especially the female. Any attempts made by any sept to achieve this should not be taken personally.'

Just how the hell do you expect us to take it? Jarek bit his tongue; Ain had warned them to stay silent unless directly questioned by the Arbiter.

'Query: is this an admission of responsibility by your sept?' asked the Arbiter drily.

'Negative. We merely wish to point out how disruptive the outsider presence is, and how its removal cannot come soon enough.'

'Noted. Lingua, you may continue.'

'Thank you, Arbiter. The second point is in regard to the beacon requested by and promised to the visitors. The sooner they have this item, the sooner they will leave. Given the attempts on the visitors' lives while they were out-system, this individual felt it was logical to bring them to the location of the item they came here seeking. This way, they may wait in safety, and can take the beacon as soon as it is ready.' For the first time, Ain's voice faltered. 'This lingua realises that in facilitating this she may have passed on information not intended for the visitors' ears, specifically, the location of the source of beacons. If the Consensus disagrees with this lingua's decision she will accept chastisement.'

Jarek had no idea how seriously Ain might be punished for taking them into her confidence, but he was relieved to see relatively few flashes going off. The Arbiter said, 'Ruling: no immediate irreconcilable objections have been raised to your decision. However, we have also informed the Council of Lingua, and they may wish to question your actions. Was there a request associated with this statement?'

'Affirmative: to ask whether the beacon is ready yet.'

188

'No,' said the Arbiter shortly. 'The visitors will be informed when it is. Proceed to your final point.'

This was the tricky one. The last time he'd been in a situation like this, sworn to silence while someone who – hopefully! – knew what she was doing put his case for him, Jarek had been up against ignorant peasants, not god-like male Sidhe. And his life was not the only one in danger. He stole a look at Nual; she appeared composed, gazing out with interest at the entrancing illusion surrounding them.

Ain said, 'Patrons, the visitors were told that the first "accident" on the habitat resulted in the death of the third member of Captain Reen's crew. However, there is reason to believe that Taro sanMalia is not dead.'

Now lights lit up, lots of them, all over. The Arbiter himself raised the obvious question. 'Query: what evidence have you for this assertion?'

They'd discussed this: how to make their case without directly accusing the Consensus of lying, especially as it looked like the Gatekeeper had acted with their knowledge, if not their actual permission. Ain had confirmed Jarek's suspicion that making such an accusation would be dangerous, if not downright fatal: the Consensus' power relied on being seen to be open and impartial – even when it wasn't. Jarek clenched his fists. *Let's hope they'd made the right decision.*

'Honoured patrons,' Ain said calmly, 'this lingua can convey only what has been told to her. The Sidhe Nual knows that Taro sanMalia is alive.'

'We hardly need remind you,' said the Arbiter, 'of the one thing we all agree on: the word of a Sidhe female is worthless. And we are all aware that the female can make you think whatever she wants you to think.'

'This lingua agrees: she cannot be entirely sure that coercion has not been employed. However, this lingua is as sure as it is possible to be that she acts and speaks freely. Taro sanMalia is alive. And the Sidhe Nual requests that he be returned to the visitors' ship before it departs.'

189

'Query: why?' asked the Arbiter.

'He is her lover,' said Ain.

'We have had no indication of such a relationship until now.'

'That is because the Sidhe Nual had a premonition. It convinced her to hide her feelings.'

The Chamber was silent unless someone had been given the floor to speak, so it was hard to tell, but Jarek could have sworn Ain's comment actually shut them up, at least for a couple of seconds. Then a crazy ripple of lights filled the darkness.

The Arbiter appeared to be ignoring the furore erupting around him. 'And she admits perpetrating this deception because of her "premonition"?'

'She does. She has a high regard for her own intuition. She did not see how hiding this fact would make any difference.'

Aside from saving Taro's life, thought Jarek.

'Precognition is extraordinarily rare.' The Arbiter almost sounded like he was talking to himself now. 'Her duplicity reinforces the general opinion the Consensus holds of her kind. Whether it constitutes an insult, or an unexpected honesty that could be seen as verification of her apparent wish to eschew her sisters, is an interesting question – fascinating, even.

'Lingua, do you have anything to add to your statement?'

'No, Arbiter.'

'Then your part is done. The Consensus will consider your request regarding the human boy. It is likely that your charges will be subject to questioning. Until then you will remain in your rooms.'

CHAPTER TWENTY-SIX

Taro wished he had some way to clean the blood off his hands, but there was no water, no cloth, nothing at all useful in this stupid white, soulless fucking ship. In the end he used Vy's clothes – it wasn't like the poor bastard needed them any more. Despite the calm that filled his head whenever he used his blades, he felt sick to the depths of his stomach, because this wasn't combat. This was butchery.

Having done what Vy wanted, now he couldn't stop crying. Pathetic. Pointless tears kept flowing while the avatar's body cooled behind him. After a while he crawled onto the bridge so he wouldn't have to look at what he'd done.

Thanks to what he'd found out from Vy it was more vital than ever that he spoke to Nual. She had to know what he'd discovered. And he had a mission of his own now.

He sat on the floor, head tilted back against the wall, waiting for the sobbing and shaking to stop, trying to think of some way out of the shit he'd managed to get himself into. Perhaps he should have another look at the control wall, or maybe go outside and see what—

'Haallooo!'

He stood up as the high-pitched cry came again. 'Who is it?' he called back.

The strange voice shouted something incomprehensible.

Wary of a trap, he sidled up to the door, squeezing his eyes shut to encourage his night-vision. When he peered outside he saw six locals, armed with spears, flanking a hunched-up old cove with bonus white ornaments and a really wild hairdo.

'Er, yes?' said Taro.

'Be welcome!' said Big Hair expansively.

Taro hadn't found the first lot of locals particularly welcoming. 'Thanks,' he said cautiously. 'And hello to you too.'

'Offer: we have gifts.'

One of Big Hair's mates held something small up in his two hands to demonstrate.

'Light of earth. Gift. Then talk.' Big Hair had a gappy accent, but he spoke slowly and carefully.

Taro wasn't convinced, but he needed all the help he could get. 'Sounds good to me.'

Big Hair put a palm out and down, then raised his hand and pointed to the ship. 'Talk there?'

'How about I stay on the ship and you lot stay down there?'

Big Hair looked confused and Taro repeated his offer more slowly, with hand gestures.

'Offer: gifts, then talk. There.' Big Hair sounded pretty certain about coming up.

Whilst Taro didn't want anyone to see the state of things in the other room, neither did he want to leave the safety of the ship. Better to meet the locals here, where the ship's gravity would slow them down if things turned nasty.

'You'd better come up then,' he said. He pointed at the pair of spear-men nearest Big Hair. 'Just you and those two, right?'

There was some muttering, then Big Hair and the guards Taro had picked out came forward. Taro stepped back to give them room to climb onto the ship, which they did with some difficulty, the two guards hauling Big Hair up between them.

As well as spears, the guards carried long sacks slung crosswise across their bodies. From the look of it, whatever was in the sacks was pretty heavy. As they stood blinking in the bright light, Big Hair turned to one of the guards, who gave him the round, flattish container he'd been waving around earlier. Big Hair unscrewed the top to reveal a bowl of luminous green-yellow goo. 'Receive gift: light of earth,' he said with relish, and held out the bowl.

'Very nice,' said Taro, smiling carefully. 'Why don't you just put it over there' – he pointed to the corner of the room – 'and I'll find somewhere for it later.'

Big Hair wobbled his head like his neck was stiff. Combined with the screwed-up eyes the effect was pretty funny, though Taro made sure he didn't laugh. Big Hair said, 'Gift for now. To eat.'

'You want me to eat that sh— stuff?'

'Light of earth. To eat. Hosp-i-table.'

Taro *was* pretty hungry, and he didn't want to piss the visitors off. 'That's good, but how about you eat some, then I eat. Right?' He backed up his words with exaggerated hand gestures. He didn't want to get poisoned, either.

Big Hair looked offended and Taro tensed, ready to defend himself if he'd fucked up.

Then Big Hair did a slightly different head-wobble and said, 'Honour to eat first.' He dipped a hand into the gloop and licked the stuff off his fingers like it was the best thing he'd ever tasted. Then he held the bowl out to Taro.

'Thanks,' said Taro. As he closed the distance between them, he kept a wary eye on the guards. His nose was filled with the stink of unwashed bodies, and he could make out their weapons and ornaments more clearly now. The spears were tipped with bone and the ornaments were made from it too ... or rather, from the look of the wrinkled, scabby skin at the edge of them, *grown* from bone – human bone. Taro wasn't too freaked – his most valued possession was a flute made from his birth-mother's arm-bone – but it appeared that, like the Undertow, this was a place where nothing, not even a human body, went to waste.

He took the bowl, and thanked them. When they looked at him expectantly he scooped up an experimental fingerful of goo and put it in his mouth. It tasted chill and bitter, but it would fill the hole in his belly and soothe his dry throat. They continued to squint meaningfully at him so he carried on eating, wiping his finger round the bowl when he'd done and giving a small belch.

He put the bowl on the floor. 'That was *delicious*. Sorry, I ain't got nothing to offer you in return.'

'Offer: we have rock,' said Big Hair, with what sounded like pride in his voice. 'Good rock. Gift of rock, then more talk.'

'Great,' said Taro, wondering what they were on about.

Big Hair half turned to the others and muttered at them, still watching Taro from the corner of his eye. The two guards began rummaging in their sacks. Big Hair stepped back and stood aloof, a half-smile on his face.

Taro decided to take advantage of the pause. 'Er, listen,' he said, 'what I really need is to find others like me.'

'Query: others like me?'

'No, others like ... *people*, with ships – like this one. And people who—' *People who aren't freakishly tall and covered in shit and scabs.* 'I need to find outsiders. Visitors.'

'Visitors,' said Big Hair enthusiastically. 'Good!'

'So are there any here? Could you take me to them?'

'Visitors,' said Big Hair again. 'Statement: we have rock. Good rock. See?' He stepped back and the guards straightened. They each held several lumps of rock in their cupped hands. Taro had no idea what the rocks were, though they did have a faint sheen to them.

Big Hair said, 'Offer: we find more. Father's father's father find more. We save. We wait.'

'Good for you. Are they for me, then?' They appeared to be expecting him to actually check out the rocks.

He obliged, picking up a particularly shiny rock, hefting it in his hand, nodding sagely all the while. The effort of holding the rocks was beginning to tell on the visitors; the guard's arms were twitching and one man dropped one of his rocks. 'Listen, you can put them down now.'

'Query: good enough?'

'They're great – like you say, *good* rocks.' Taro pointed to the floor. 'Go on, put them down.'

With some relief, the guards did so, dropping several in the process.

'Thanks again,' said Taro. 'Now, about these visitors?'

Big Hair looked puzzled, then he pointed to Taro triumphantly. 'Visitor,' he said.

An unpleasant realisation began to dawn. 'You're saying there's just me?' said Taro.

'Aye,' said Big Hair again. 'Come for rock.'

'Ah.'

'Offer: we go now, go see.'

'Go where and see what?'

'Offer: see rock. More good rock. To trade.'

'Right, think we've got ourselves a bit tied up here. I ain't here to trade – sorry, but that's not it at all. I've crashed. I need *help*.'

Big Hair narrowed his eyes even more, and repeated, 'Query: come see rock?' He sounded confused.

Even if he went to look at their precious rock, they'd soon work out Taro wasn't here to buy it. And then things were likely to turn nasty. 'Right,' he said in a businesslike tone, 'tell you what, I need to, er, do some tests on the good rock you brought me. See just how good it really is, y'know? I'll come and check out the rest of your rock later. *Later*. All right?'

'Query: later?' said Big Hair dubiously.

'Yes. See rock, but not now. Now, I need to do … tests. And stuff. Alone. So, how about you go? Please?'

The guards exchanged glances. But Big Hair said only, 'Later,' and did the head wobble thing. Then they turned, leaving their rock samples, and laboriously made their way back out.

'Thanks again for the "light of earth",' Taro called after them. 'And the rocks.'

Other than getting him a meal of sorts, making contact with the locals hadn't left him much better off. In fact, it might even be worse: given how important this rock-trading thing obviously was, they were gonna be pretty pissed off with him once they realised that wasn't going to happen.

He had another look around the ship, just in case some sort of random miracle had occurred, but the only change was that the carnage in the central room was starting to smell. He briefly considered trying to contact Nual again, before deciding that he was way too jumpy.

So, his choices were to wait here with two dead avatars, both of whom he'd killed, until the locals came back – probably in a less 'hosp-i-table' mood – or to go and look for some way off this crazy world. Not much of a choice, really.

'Fuck it!' he said, and strode back to the exit. He checked that the crater was deserted, then stepped out of the airlock. He flew across the crater to the mouth of the tunnel, and landed, then listened hard. He heard nothing, so he went in.

Away from the starlight, the smooth walls gave off a faint yellow glow, just enough to stop him walking into them, though not enough to give him much idea of what was further down the passage. That was fine; he wasn't going to let a bit of alien darkness freak him. When the tunnel forked he hesitated, then plumped for the left path. After a while he reached a T-junction, with the right-hand tunnel going down, and the left-hand one sloping up at a fairly steep angle. Dim light came from the right-hand passage; red, this time, unlike the walls. Interesting: he'd go that way. The ground evened out as the tunnel widened, and then began to curve. He passed a side-tunnel, but the glow was still coming from straight ahead, and it was getting brighter.

He heard a sound and stopped, listening carefully. There it was again: a long, murmuring hiss, then another sound, further off – a voice? He thought so, though he caught only a few incomprehensible words. The first sound came again as he crept carefully down the tunnel, all the while trying to work out what it was he was hearing. There was a definite pattern to it: *hiss* ... pause ... *hiss*.

What was that? It sounded like ... breathing. *Shit.* Something was taking vast, slow breaths, just up ahead. He swallowed, and pulled his hand away from the wall. Was it his imagination, or did it feel faintly sticky?

Whatever-it-was gave a snuffling, pained moan, and a quiver of fear thrummed through him, until the Angel mods dampened it down.

He carried on. He'd gone about a dozen steps when two locals stepped out from a side-turning further down the passage. They looked even thinner than the ones he'd meet earlier, and they weren't carrying spears. Taro stopped and held out his hands in what he hoped was a friendly gesture, but the pair gave high fluting cries, then turned and ran.

Taro almost did the same. But he made himself pause, letting his Angel instincts overrule his natural ones. Now wasn't the time to panic. A few moments to get calm again, then he'd carry on. He'd come this far, even if he hadn't found anything useful yet, so he may as well—

The gaggle of locals who emerged from the side-turning *were* carrying spears. And they were coming right for him, moving in an ungainly lope that covered the ground surprisingly quickly.

Now was the time to panic.

As he turned, he considered taking to the air, but he'd only end up flying into one of the twilit tunnel walls. Instead he ran. He regretted his decision at once: in this gravity his body didn't react like he expected it to. But he did know how to move in low-g; he'd grown up doing it. The trick was to push off from each step carefully, like he was taking a leap across a netted gap. He found his rhythm after a few more steps.

He looked for the turning he'd come down earlier. Was it the first or the second one? Second, it was the second ... which was good, because he'd just passed the first one.

His pursuers weren't making any noise, which was worse, if anything. He fought the urge to look back, to see if they were gaining on him.

When he reached his turn, he failed to compensate fully for the lack of gravity. He skidded and clipped the wall, yelping at the sudden pain in his shoulder. Though he had no idea what was happening behind him, there was no one ahead, and right now that was what mattered. He passed a side passage and felt a moment of doubt, until he managed to make out the faint white circular glow up ahead: yes, that was the way out!

He wasn't far off when he saw a shadow cross the mouth of the tunnel. With only a split second to decide what to do, he kicked off, hands straight out ahead of him, blades still sheathed – they'd be more of a liability than a help in this confined space. As Taro shot out of the entrance, he knocked the figure flying, but he ignored

the fallen local, instead speeding across the crater and into the airlock—

—to see half a dozen men with spears, standing around on the
ship's bridge. One of them was holding what was left of Vy's head,
while Big Hair examined it. He turned when Taro arrived, as
did his companions. Taro assessed the situation and decided they
weren't a serious threat; he'd pit hi-tech blades against bone spear-
tips any day, especially as he had the added advantage of flight, and
they had the added disadvantage of higher gravity than they were
used to. If he stayed in the airlock, there wasn't room for more than
a couple at a time. Though he'd have to watch his back and would
most likely take a few minor wounds, he could win this fight . . .

. . . *but he'd had enough of killing*.

'Right,' he said slowly and clearly, addressing Big Hair, who was
clearly the man in charge, 'is there anything at all I can say at this
point that'll stop your mates just rushing me?'

Big Hair glanced at Vy's severed head. He sounded almost apologetic when he said, 'Not trade. Not visitor. Enemy.' He called out
something to his men in their own language that sounded rather
like an order.

Taro muttered, 'Yeah, thought not.' He looked over his shoulder,
scanning the crater for the cove he'd knocked over on the way
through.

It was dark out there – not just night-dark, he suddenly realised,
but—

He looked up.

Something huge was hovering above the crater, blotting out the
stars.

Taro kicked back from the airlock to avoid the incoming spear-
men, then glanced at the ground again, where he now spotted the
man he'd crashed into earlier. He'd climbed to his feet and was also
looking up. *So there really is a ship up there*, Taro thought thank-
fully.

His eye was drawn to movement overhead; a large square box
had detached itself from the dark underside of the ship. It dropped
straight down through the forceshield, barely slowing, though

ripples of energy spread out from the contact point. As it got closer he could see that it was plain and grey, with slightly softened edges.

As the man below scarpered into the tunnel, Taro wondered if he should run too. He was a bit short on escape routes, though ...

The box drew level with him as he hovered a few metres from the airlock, and an opening appeared on the side nearest him, revealing a woman, dressed in a hooded one-piece black suit. Her face was covered in something hard and clear.

She held out a hand to him. 'Query: are you alone?' she said.

'You mean aside from the gang of angry locals over there trying to kill me?' asked Taro, pointing back at the ship.

'Clarification: are you the only survivor from this crashed vessel?'

'Yeah, I am.'

An odd expression passed over her face, but she didn't say anything.

'Not meaning to be rude, but who the fuck are you?' asked Taro.

'Answer: we are here to rescue you.'

CHAPTER TWENTY-SEVEN

The priest and the monitor had taken the lantern with them, leaving Ifanna the candle. She picked it up carefully, shielding the flame with her hand, and went to explore the plague-house.

Save for the faint odour, and an indefinable sense of emptiness, there was nothing to indicate that the former occupants were now dead. She found honey and lentils and rice in the kitchen cupboards, and in the parlour embroidered cushions were scattered over the worn wooden seats. But in the hallway, the flowers in the house-hold shrine had shrivelled, and the corn was covered in mould. A blue votive candle, no doubt bought when the first family member fell ill, had been burnt down to a stub. Ifanna shivered and looked away.

Upstairs, she found a small room containing storage chests and a rack stuffed with rolls of leather. Below the rack were some half-finished shoes: apparently the husband had been a cobbler. Ifanna breathed in the familiar scent of the leather. The bed in the main room was still made up, covered in a throw decorated with what Ifanna was beginning to recognise as the wife's embroidery. Ifanna hesitated at the thought of sleeping in a bed whose last occupants had come to such an unpleasant end, before deciding that they had no further use for it and she most certainly did.

It was only after she had lain down that she saw the empty wooden crib on its stand in one corner. Tears sprang to her eyes and this time she let them fall. She was still crying into the soft pillows when she fell asleep.

*

For a moment she had no idea how she came to be waking up in a large, comfortable bed, not on the ground or in her cell. Then she remembered that this was a house of the dead; she found the thought reassured her, for she felt as though she too had died – though the twin aches in her head and bandaged side reminded her that she had not quite managed to escape the flesh. But she had escaped her fate; she was free.

She sat up, wary of her wound, and started to think about her circumstances. She could take what supplies she wished from this house and simply walk away. A ghost stealing from other ghosts was no sin. But *Gwas* Maelgyn and Captain Siarl had helped her when no others would, and they trusted her not to flee. It would be wrong to betray that trust.

She jumped as someone started knocking on the door. Was it the priest? Or guards from the Tyr, come to take her to the fate she had foolishly believed she could avoid? For a moment she wondered if she should pretend she was not here, but she swiftly realised that if it was monitors, they might just burst in and search the house, and if it was *Gwas* Maelgyn, he might go away again. She jumped up – and almost fell over, her head was spinning so badly. Carefully she made her way into the back room, where she peered through a crack in the shutters, trying to see into the yard.

The lone caller had a bald head covered in tattooed writing: a priest; she could not be sure it was *Gwas* Maelgyn, but she could not imagine who else it might be. She hurried down the stairs, hanging onto the rail for balance, and unlatched the door.

Gwas Maelgyn's wary expression dissolved into a smile on seeing her. He looked younger in the daylight. 'At last,' he said, though he did not sound angry, just relieved. 'You hit your head last night, did you not, *chilwar*?'

'Aye, *Gwas*, I did,' she said, stepping to one side to let him in.

'One of my fellows who serves the Mother of Mercy said that those who have sustained such a blow should not be permitted to sleep until they have recovered their senses, for there is a risk they might not awaken. When you did not answer the door, I was concerned.'

Warmth battled caution; the latter won. 'You ... you told the *Gwas* I am here?' She closed and latched the door.

'Of course not! No, *chilwar*, only Captain Siarl and I know you are still in the city.'

'What is being said about me? About what happened, I mean.'

'All that is known is that you and the other witch attempted to overcome your guards; she was killed, and you managed to escape – where to, none can say.'

Ifanna offered up a small prayer for Hylwen; though she had not liked the girl, Ifanna would most likely be dead now without her help.

'Ifanna.' The priest's expression was hard to read in the dim light of the shuttered room. 'What happened last night, before I found you? Why did you and the other skycursed girl decide to run away?'

'I ...' What should she say? She could not lie to a priest, yet the truth would reveal her doubts.

'You may tell me after you have eaten, if you prefer.' His voice was gentle.

'Aye, if you please, *Gwas*.' How considerate of him, she thought.

'I have fresh bread, cheese and apples.' He held up a small sack.

Ifanna sat at the kitchen table, the priest opposite her. The food tasted wonderful, maybe because it was a long time since she had eaten such pleasant fare, or perhaps because it was the first meal of her new life. She realised, belatedly, that she should share, but *Gwas* Maelgyn waved the offer away, apparently content to sit opposite her in silence. Ifanna had watched men eat, and she had eaten with them, but she had never before been watched, and such intimate regard stirred up complex feelings. She pushed them down again: he was a *priest*, and if he chose to observe her, who was she to question?

'So,' he said, when she had finished, 'what happened to make you flee last night?'

Ifanna thought she had worked out a way to avoid anything he might find blasphemous, but when she opened her mouth, she started coughing. 'Please,' she croaked, '*Gwas* … may I have some water?'

'Oh, of course – I should have thought of that.' He looked around, but soon realised there was none in the kitchen. As Ifanna continued coughing, he found a jug and said, 'I suppose I must fetch some. I believe there is a pump at the end of this alley …'

He left the door ajar as he went out and Ifanna stared at the thin sliver of light, trying not to worry, though he took a long time. When he did return, the front of his robe was wet.

She thanked him hoarsely, and drank her fill until her throat was soothed and she could speak again. She wiped her lips, then asked, before she lost her nerve, '*Gwas*, before I answer you, may I ask something? You said that you intervened to save me because I came from the Fenlands …' His presence in that alley had not been a coincidence; he and Captain Siarl had most probably followed the escort party. Not that she would mention that. 'Forgive me, *Gwas*, but I imagine you risked – still risk – the disapproval of your superiors for what you have done. I am not sure I understand why you would take so great a risk merely because I come from a place you know of.'

The priest looked down at the table. 'It is a fair question, *chilwar*. Although I was born in Plas Morfren, I lived in Nantgwyn for a while. After I completed my training at the Tyr I returned to the Terraced Marshes. The old Rhethor at Plas Morfren was ailing, and I had hoped, given I had studied the Traditions in the Tyr itself, that I might be considered as his replacement when he went to the Mothers. Alas, it was not to be – but I wished to serve as best I could, so I took the job of village priest when it came up, even though I had many more qualifications than were required for such a role. I was not in Nantgwyn long, for I found village life did not suit me, but it was nonetheless a part of my life I have since had great cause to reflect on.'

'So you did what you did because I came from Nantgwyn, and you once lived there?' Ifanna had no idea her tiny village had once been home to a Tyr-trained priest.

'Aye, *chilwar*.'

She looked at him, and he continued, 'Still not enough to explain my actions?' He sighed. 'You are right, of course. You are a very perceptive girl, Ifanna. There was more to it than that; I made mistakes while I was in Nantgwyn, and it is those mistakes for which I am now trying to atone.'

'What sort of mistakes, *Gwas*?' She could not stop herself asking, though she knew she should not.

He waved a hand dismissively, as though it was nothing, though Ifanna was sure that could not be the case. 'I fell out with a man of that village. His name was Esryn.'

Ifanna felt her heart grow cold. 'Esryn?'

'Aye.' He looked up, and his eyes were troubled. 'Your father, I believe.'

'You believe correctly, *Gwas*.' Ifanna could manage only a whisper. She entertained a brief, ridiculous fantasy that Da was somehow behind everything that had happened, and that he would burst through the door at any moment, a scowl on his face and his belt in his hand ...

'I would not see that wrong perpetuated,' said Maelgyn, 'so I followed you when you left the Tyr. I had no clear plan, but I could not let you die.'

'I— *Thank* you, *Gwas*,' she said, not only for saving her, but for his honesty, for answering her question honestly.

'I have no desire to revisit the events that caused our feud,' said Maelgyn firmly.

'Of course, *Gwas*, it is between you and— It is your business.' *My father has disowned me,* thought Ifanna, *and though he does not know it, I have disowned him. He is gone from my life forever.*

More gently *Gwas* Maelgyn added, 'And I think you understand the need to atone for past mistakes.'

'Aye, *Gwas*.' Ifanna sat with her eyes downcast, listening to the distant sounds of the city going about its business.

'*Chilwar?*' said the priest, 'you were about to explain what happened last night.'

'It was not my idea, *Gwas*,' she started, aware that she sounded like she was making excuses, even if she was telling the truth.

'Hylwen – the other girl who was judged – convinced me that we should run away, because we were going to be killed.'

'Why would she believe such a thing, *chilwar*?'

'I— I am not sure, *Gwas*. She said that there were problems … in the Tyr, that is.'

To Ifanna's surprise, the priest laughed, a bitter, barking laugh with very little humour in it. When he did not say anything else, Ifanna continued tremulously, 'Is this something to do with the lights in the sky, *Gwas*? Are they portents of evil?'

'Portents of evil? An interesting question, *chilwar*. Such matters are being debated even now in the halls of the Tyr.' He lowered his voice, and she had to bend near to hear him say, 'They are portents of change, that is for sure. Whether it is change for the better, who can say? Still, we must not gainsay Heaven, must we, even if it appears to be at war with itself.'

'No *Gwas*,' said Ifanna obediently, aware that he was voicing concerns he would surely never dare speak openly in the Tyr. Such blasphemy, from the mouth of a priest, should probably have appalled her, but instead, his trust delighted her.

'Yet surely it was not the fear of living in such dark times that made you and Hylwen act as you did?'

'No, *Gwas*. She said— She told me that the Putain Glan— they do not—' She was stammering in her embarrassment, and at last she managed, 'Hylwen claimed to know someone who failed as a Putain Glan, and was killed for it.'

'Really?' The priest sounded intrigued. 'Do you know the woman's name?'

'I do not, *Gwas*.'

'No matter; I can find out. So, *chilwar*,' he continued, 'you made your impetuous bid for freedom on the strength of a tale told by another witch?' He did not quite make it sound like an accusation, but she recognised the tone of his voice: slightly incredulous, like when her father exposed what he saw as the foolishness of women.

Ifanna, disappointed to hear him speak so when she was coming to admire him, was quick to defend herself: 'No, *Gwas*, Hylwen's tale reinforced my own doubts!'

He frowned. 'Your own doubts, *chilwar*? What doubts are these?'

Ifanna cursed her thoughtless words, but now there was no way out. Priests could sense lies. But she found she wanted him to know, and in a rush she said, 'The Cariad, *Gwas*, when she examined me, I felt nothing, and I did not understand – I *cannot* understand – how that could be if she is truly the Beloved Daughter of Heaven! But if she is not, then her judgment is nothing, and the will of men alone holds sway, and men hate us and will kill us, and so I thought I was to die, and that is why I ran.' She got to the end of her breath and stopped, not daring to move.

Gwas Maelgyn said slowly, 'So, Ifanna, you are saying that you felt *nothing at all* when the Cariad looked into your heart?'

Ifanna breathed out. He was not going to damn her for her blasphemy. 'Aye, *Gwas*,' she said firmly, though a small voice in the back of her mind was telling her she must surely be bringing down Heaven's wrath upon herself.

He moved to stand up and Ifanna shrank back. He held up a hand, saying, 'Do not fear, *chilwar*; you have done right in telling me this. But now I need to go back to the Tyr. I will return, when I can. You must stay here, Ifanna.'

She smiled. 'Aye, *Gwas*.' As though she had anywhere else to go.

CHAPTER TWENTY-EIGHT

According to Jarek's body-clock, it was the middle of the night, and he was certainly tired enough to sleep, despite the less-than-sumptuous accommodation. But first he checked out the sanitary facilities. If the males were monitoring the room, they'd have an entertaining view of him puzzling how to work the alien toilet, followed by the no doubt highly amusing expression of relief on his face when he finally did.

When he was done, he walked up to the door, curious to see if it still opened. It did, so he turned around and walked straight back to the bed. No point antagonising their hosts for no reason.

He checked his comlog to see if he could review the full proceedings from the Consensus session, but the mass of flashing data hadn't been saved anywhere that he could access. He wasn't really surprised.

He lay down on the uncomfortable bed and commed Nual.

'Jarek? I'm a little busy.' She sounded stressed.

'Sorry – I just wanted to check you're all right.'

'I am, but I have a visitor. I'll com you later.'

'Sure,' he murmured, 'we'll talk later.' Presumably her 'visitor' was one of the males who had petitioned to see 'the beautiful enemy' in the flesh. He felt a pang of concern, then quashed it; Nual could look after herself – and even if she couldn't, it wasn't like he could do much to help. Given he was pretty much surplus to requirements right now, he might as well get some rest.

He'd just lain down when the door opened – they *really* weren't big on privacy around here! – and a silver avatar came in.

'We wish to ask you some questions out of the presence of the Sidhe,' it said by way of a greeting.

'Sure,' said Jarek, 'pull up a chair.'

'I will stand. Query: Have you had sex with the female Sidhe?'

Jarek forced himself not to react. 'Er, no, I haven't,' he said after a moment. 'She's not my type.'

'Query: how long have you known the female?'

He thought about it, then said, 'About seven years. Most of that time she was in hiding from her people – from the females, I should say. She and Taro have been travelling with me for a couple of months.'

'Query: do you consider yourself a rebel?'

'Against the Sidhe? Yes I do,' he said, feeling himself get a little heated. 'And before you ask why, they killed my sister, and nearly broke my mind.'

'I see. And do you trust her?'

'Trust Nual? Yes, I trust her with my life.'

'Has she displayed prescient abilities in your presence?'

He paused, and then said, 'That's a tricky question: sometimes she's said things no human could know, but whether that's prescience or just being a Sidhe I really couldn't say. I do know that it's not a controllable ability, and she hasn't had it long.' He decided not to mention how Nual's ability had awoken; they thought badly enough of her already. He didn't think finding out she had fucked an enemy to death in order to access his shielded mind would improve their opinion. It might be seen as proof that she was every bit the monster she feared she was. He didn't believe she was a monster; to Jarek, Nual would always be the frightened child he had rescued.

'Do you have anything further to add?' asked the avatar.

'Nope,' he said shortly.

'Then you may rest. We may wish to ask additional questions later.'

Jarek waited until the avatar had left before muttering, 'I can hardly wait.'

*

By the time she admitted her eighteenth visitor, Nual had begun to see a pattern emerging. So far, four of the avatars had wanted to berate, taunt or bait her; in three cases, this involved an abusive, ranting monologue listing the failings of the female Sidhe; in the fourth a confrontational question-and-answer session where everything she said was treated as a lie.

Nine of the males' representatives asked rational questions about how she came to be here, and engaged in degrees of reasoned discussion.

The remainder viewed her as a curiosity, an exhibit in a zoo or museum: one asked her to act like it wasn't there – easier said than done – while another observed her while she walked around the room.

Several of them asked, in different ways, how Nual felt about them, and to each she answered honestly: they made her uncomfortable, but she felt no personal animosity towards the males of her race. Most of them appeared satisfied with this answer.

No avatar approached closer than two metres; this was probably a condition of being allowed to be alone with her. They were also time-limited; each avatar spent no more than six minutes in her presence.

She did her best to cooperate, and to keep her temper, even when the more unreasonable males tried to provoke her. Any hint of what might be seen as negative behaviour would justify their contempt for her, and quite possibly lead to punishment, perhaps even death.

Exhaustion began to creep up; her voice became ragged and her responses slower. She wondered, in the brief gap between the twenty-third and twenty-fourth visitors, whether they were trying to wear her down, but she decided probably not; it was more likely the males did not know – or did not care – that she was flagging. Whilst in conversation with the twenty-sixth male, a realistically humanoid avatar who wanted to know what 'lies' her sisters had told her about the Protectorate years, her voice dried up completely.

The next time the door opened it was Ain, carrying a tray, and

Nual gratefully drank the water and ate some of the sludgy food the lingua brought her. Then she asked if Ain knew how many more visitors she was to have.

'There will be no more for now. You will be allowed a short rest, after which you will be called back into session.'

'Into the Star Chamber?'

'Affirmative.'

'With Jarek?'

'No, just you. He is resting. Kindly be ready in one hour.'

Nual sighed. She'd feel much more comfortable if she was able to communicate with Jarek without going through the Consensus com system. She had never before tried to mind-speak with Jarek when she was in a different room; though he was a friend and she could pick out his mind in a crowd of strangers, she didn't have the deep link she shared with Taro. Perhaps she should give it a try.

She stretched out on the bed and put herself into a light trance before searching through the presences around her for the one she knew. The few minds she touched were all lingua; none tasted familiar. She sighed and brought herself out of the trance, then raised her com and left Jarek a message. Her arm felt so heavy ...

She set the alarm for forty minutes, let her wrist drop onto her chest and closed her eyes.

Even though she had put the alarm on its loudest setting, it took a few moments for her to wake up. She rolled off the bed with a groan and went to splash cold water on her face.

Ain arrived with more refreshments shortly afterwards. Nual accepted the drink, but she left the food; the thought of the upcoming Consensus session was making her feel nauseous.

She scanned Ain's surface thoughts while the lingua walked beside her back to the Star Chamber, but Ain knew nothing more than she was saying. Nual would have been amazed to discover otherwise.

As the speaking platform rose up into the ersatz sky, Nual tried hard not to think of this as a trial.

The Arbiter opened the session, then said, 'Lingua, your independent testimony has been considered. It reflects well upon the

Sidhe female. A vote has been taken. She will be granted limited speaking rights.'

Ain said, 'Thank you, honoured patrons.' Then she turned to Nual and said, 'Please speak only in response to the patrons' questions.'

A little impatiently, Nual nodded to show her understanding.

'Statement: the lingua will leave now,' said the Arbiter.

Nual picked up Ain's confusion – the lingua had not expected this – but she obeyed without hesitation, stepping back into the darkness. There was a slight vibration in the platform, then she felt Ain's presence recede.

'Query: you call yourself Nual,' said the Arbiter. 'Where did you get that name?'

Female Sidhe in the unity did not use names, so this question was not a great surprise – in fact, one of her visitors had already asked it. It looked like the avatar had not shared her answer. That was not the males' way.

'Jarek named me.' She was damned if she was going to call them 'honoured patrons'.

'Query: how did you meet Captain Reen?'

No one had asked her that before, and she hesitated, deciding how much she should reveal.

Into her silence the Arbiter said archly, 'Observation: he has affirmed that you have not had sex with him.'

Though the remark was calculated to infuriate, Nual found a smile pulling at the tense muscles of her face. 'No,' she said succinctly, 'I have not.'

'Conclusion: he must hate the Sidhe females a great deal.'

'Yes,' she said, her tone deliberately echoing that of her first answer, 'he does.'

'*Repeated* query: How did you meet him?'

'He ... He helped me – rescued me.'

'Clarification is required: you say he *rescued* you?' The Arbiter's tone was heavy with disbelief. 'From what or whom?'

Nual knew she would have to tell them the truth. Although the patrons' avatars lacked any active abilities– they could no more sniff out deception than they could open a route into shiftspace – in her current frazzled state she doubted she could come up with a plausible lie, especially as she had no idea what Jarek had already said. And if they discovered any attempt to deceive them, they would most likely kill her.

'I grew up amongst my own kind,' she began, 'on a mothership.'

'Query: how many motherships are there in human-space these days?' The Arbiter's tone was conversational.

'Six,' she said after a moment's hesitation. Were they gathering information to help when they restarted the millennia-old feud between the Sidhe sexes?

'A satisfactory answer,' said the Arbiter – though whether he considered it so because he was pleased with her cooperative attitude or with the news that the female Sidhe's powerbase was so limited she could not say. 'Request: continue your account.'

'When I was on the cusp of adulthood – sixteen or seventeen years old by human reckoning – I began to question certain things—'

'Observation: dissent is not permitted in the unity,' interrupted the Arbiter.

'No, it is not. I was punished. Excluded.'

'Observation: that must have been traumatic.' There was no trace of sympathy in the Arbiter's voice.

'It was.' She waved his comment away. 'An incident occurred while the ship was in shiftspace. I— It disrupted the unity.'

'Request for clarification: what sort of incident?'

'I was excluded from the unity, so all I can be sure of is that something damaged the minds of those who were in communion at that time.' Entirely true, as far as it went.

Several lights flickered around the chamber. The Arbiter ignored them and continued, 'Query: what part in this did Captain Reen play?'

Nual smiled. 'He found me on the mothership. He got me out.'

'Observation: why would he do that? Humans hate Sidhe.'

'I called him to me.'

'Observation: most fascinating.'

Nual refused to let the Arbiter goad her. 'Initially I exerted some control, but I am not like my sisters. I did *not* impose my will on him. He *chose* to rescue me.'

'Observation: how very noble of him.'

'You may believe me or not as you choose. Nonetheless, he and I share the same cause.'

'Addendum: along with your human lover.'

'Yes.'

'Observation: the lover who initially appeared to be sleeping with Captain Reen.'

Nual hesitated. The Arbiter had not said it was a question.

Eventually the Arbiter said drily, 'We await your next statement with interest.'

'My next statement on what subject?' she said with all the innocence she could muster.

'Observation,' said the Arbiter slowly. 'Do not make the mistake of forgetting how many sentiences observing and listening to this exchange wish you dead. Fortunately, theirs are not the only voices here and our – *my* – wish is to take the least disruptive course. However, I cannot stop you if you choose to condemn yourself.'

Nual swallowed. 'You are asking why Taro and I pretended not to be lovers? For the reason the lingua told you: I had a premonition.'

'Observation: that is a very rare ability.'

'It is. In my limited experience it is also unreliable.'

'Observation: and yet you acted on it.'

'I did. I decided I had nothing to lose.' Even if it had annoyed Taro ... Nual experienced a sudden pang, remembering how hurt he had been.

Some of the lights had gone out; others lit up. Nual guessed there were thousands of simultaneous conversations going on around her. She wished there was a railing, or some other support to hold on to, but all she had to keep her upright was her willpower.

Finally the Arbiter said, 'Query: tell us of your relationship with Khesh.'

Nual was a little taken aback at the abrupt change of direction,

213

but she determined not to let it show. She said calmly, 'Khesh discovered I was Sidhe soon after I arrived in his City. He decided to offer me shelter to spite my sisters.'

'Query: do you trust him?'

'Yes,' she said, adding, 'to an extent.'

'Request clarification.'

'I doubt Khesh is entirely honest with me, but I also believe he would not sell me out.' She had meant specifically to the females, but she was beginning to wonder if they were not the only ones she should be worrying about. Just what bargain had the Minister struck with the Aleph males in return for a beacon? Not her life, surely – without her, Jarek's ship could not return to human-space.

There was another pause, then the Arbiter said, 'Ruling: your testimony so far is deemed acceptable.'

Nual tried not to let her relief show.

'I will now allow more detailed questions on the matters you have touched upon.'

Nual was not sure if she was supposed to respond. After a moment she nodded her assent.

'First, recognise Ipsis, rep:No Strange Delight.' The corresponding light was on the edge of the halo, almost directly below her pseudo-stellar viewpoint.

'Request for information: we would know more of the shiftspace incident. You must have seen its effects. If a human was able to board the mothership and remove you from it, one presumes these effects had disabled the other Sidhe.'

'They had,' Nual said succinctly, though she realised she would not be able to get away without a fuller answer. Naturally they would be interested in anything that might damage the female Sidhe.

'Query: how, precisely?'

'It drove them mad. They turned on each other.'

'Query: how did they react to the human?'

'They ignored Captain Reen. He defended me.'

'Query: when you left, were some of these insane females still alive?'

'Some – not many, I think.'

'Query: what happened to the mothership after you left?'

'Its transit-kernel was dead, so I would assume it is still in the realspace location where I last saw it.'

'You say this madness descended on the unity in shiftspace. Query: have you any idea of its nature?'

'I had been excluded. I was outside the unity,' she repeated.

The Arbiter said, 'That is not what was asked.'

Nual decided to share more of what she knew with the males – they were her people, after all, despite the millennia of estrangement, and if the threat was as serious as she believed, then she – no, *everyone* – would need their help. Not to mention not wanting to give them an excuse to kill her for failing to cooperate. 'I do not know what the presence was,' she said, 'but I believe it was not native to our reality. I think it came from a different universe and it used shiftspace as a connecting medium.'

The original questioner said, 'Query: why do you believe this, if it did not touch you?'

'It— it did touch me, briefly. But it passed through, and left no trace.'

'Query: why were you unaffected when everyone else was driven mad?'

'I am not sure.' Again, not strictly a lie. She hurried on, trying to steer them onto a course of her choosing, 'I did not witness the process directly. I had barricaded myself in my cell and withdrawn my mind behind my shields. I heard screams, and even through my shields I could sense this otherverse entity, spreading madness and destruction. It went on for some days; the effect was just beginning to abate when the entity forced the ship back into the shift. That broke the transit-kernel, and also gave me a chance to contact Captain Reen.'

'Request for clarification: you called to him from shiftspace?'

'Yes.'

There was another, longer, pause, then the Arbiter said, 'Observation: that is another highly unusual talent. Query: do you know what makes you so special, Nual?'

215

'No,' she said, 'I do not – and given the fate of those who might know, and my opposition to the rest of my race, I can see no easy way to find out.'

'Query: do you believe everyone on the mothership where you were spawned is dead?' said the Arbiter.

'I hope they are, given what happened to them.'

'We have many requests for further information on your encounter with this – what did you call it? An "otherverse entity"? – so let us go over your experiences on the mothership in more detail ...'

CHAPTER TWENTY-NINE

Given the choice between a pitched battle with the locals and a ride with an unknown rescuer, Taro decided Option Two was the way to go. 'Why didn't you say?' he said to the woman. 'I'll be right over.'

He flew across the gap to the boxy shuttle, glancing back once to see a hairy head poking out from the airlock of Device's ship. Big Hair looked understandably pissed off.

'So long, sucker,' muttered Taro as the woman stepped back to let him into the shuttle. Close up he realised she was actually wearing a black hi-tech v-suit.

On the far side of the shuttle's small cabin was a youth, also suited up, lying back in a comfy seat which reminded Taro of Jarek's command couch on the *Heart of Glass*. Taro guessed he was the pilot, and given the lack of visible controls and the fact that the boy's eyes were closed, he guessed he was flying the shuttle on neurolink. Unless it was another fucking avatar. Out of the corner of his eye Taro saw the opening he'd come through disappear, to be replaced by a featureless wall.

'Nice suits,' said Taro a little nervously. 'Do I get one?'

'Negative.'

'Er, why not?'

'Clarification: there is a high risk you picked up an infection on CN-361.'

Great, just what he needed! 'So that's what it's called? Catchy name, that: CN-361 – beats "Dingy Shithole", I suppose.' He knew he was prattling; the woman was watching him like he was a specimen, and he'd had enough of that recently. 'Er, who did you say you were again?'

'Answer: I am Six-Zhian-Silver. My companion is Nine-Etrinak-Mercury.'

'Prime names you coves've got.'

'Request: please clarify your last statement.'

'Your names, they're a bit longer than I'm used to.'

'Suggestion: feel free to use the familial versions: Zhian and Trin.'

The pilot raised a hand in greeting, though he kept his eyes shut.

Taro relaxed a bit at the casual gesture. 'I'm Taro sanMalia.'

'Statement: we know this.'

'Yeah, 'course you do. Sorry, I'm a bit fried.' There must be shit-loads of questions he should be asking right now, if only he could think of them. He settled for the most obvious one: 'I'm guessing there's more of you — not just two people in a shuttle, I mean.'

'Query: was that a question?'

'Er, yeah.'

'Answer: a total of fifty-three free humans inhabit the vessel we are returning to.'

'Oh, right — free humans: so that means you ain't got a patron?' He wondered if he'd been picked up by some sort of rebels.

'Negative. Clarification: we have a patron.'

'But he don't mind you wandering around rescuing waifs and strays?'

'Answer: our patron allows us to travel the system and act with considerable autonomy.' She sounded proud of this.

'Good for him,' muttered Taro. He wondered about asking the patron's name, but just keeping up a conversation with these people was a serious fucking effort right now. Besides, he doubted the name'd mean anything to him.

'Statement for visitor: we are here,' announced Trin.

'Here?' echoed Taro.

Zhian turned, so Taro did too. The doorway was back, only now it opened directly into an airlock. 'That was quick,' he said, to cover his confusion. Round here they obviously didn't go in for ships that made any noise.

'Is chill,' said the pilot. He wasn't much older than Taro.

Zhian said brusquely, 'Request: kindly follow me,' and Taro did as he was asked. He noticed that Trin stayed where he was. The airlock led into an ordinary-looking corridor. They passed one door, which didn't open, and another, which did, to reveal a room-sized medbay. Zhian gestured for Taro to go in first, and after a moment's hesitation he obeyed. It wasn't like he had much choice.

She said, 'Request: kindly remove your soiled garments and lie down on this couch.'

'On a first date? What makes you think I'm that sorta boy?' Taro joked, nervously.

'Clarification: you may keep your undergarments on.'

A strip-search would be inconvenient, but Taro didn't mind losing the filthy tunic and leggings. He undressed and lay down. Zhian waved a handheld doodad over him, checked some readouts, and then said, 'Warning: you will now experience slight pain.'

'What the—? Hey!' he cried as something stung his arm, but it faded almost at once and a pleasant, heavy feeling began to spread through his body. He should probably be trying to fight it, 'cos he didn't know shit about this Zhian and her ship, and everyone around here had some sort of fucking agenda ... but it felt good just being somewhere where no one was trying to kill, kidnap or shout at him. He realised his eyes were closing and twitched, trying to stay awake.

A hand touched his arm gently. 'Clarification of current situation: your body requires medical attention, fluids and rest. These we will provide.'

He tried to think of a smart comeback, but sleeping was a lot easier than speaking.

Taro felt much better when he awakened – and he even knew where he was, sort of: on a ship, having just been rescued by humans. There was something about the rescue, the way Zhian had reacted ...

No, it was gone.

He opened his eyes: he was in the same medbay, but this time he was by himself. He flexed his arms experimentally—

—and stopped. The med-tat on the inside of his wrist was livid purple.

'Er, Zhian?' he called. 'You there?'

He sat up without too much difficulty. He didn't *feel* ill, just a bit lightheaded, and, now he thought about it, distinctly hollow-bellied. He was swinging his legs off the couch when the door opened and Zhian came in. She was wearing a shapeless shipboard one-piece in a forgettable shade of beige.

Taro held up his wrist and pointed to the tattoo with his other hand, 'You might wanna put your sexy suit back on, and I don't just mean 'cos it looks better.'

Zhian frowned. She had a chunky face, not really pretty, but trustworthy-looking. 'Query: does that mark indicate pathogens in your system?'

'Pather—? Yeah, says if I'm ill.'

'Clarification: you are not ill any more,' she said carefully.

'Then why's my tat showing?'

'Supposition: your medical implant is still reacting to the infection you picked up on CN-361. However, be assured that your bodily systems, with our help, will shortly be experiencing flawless functionality.'

'Flawless functionality? Bring it on.' At least she was answering his questions, sort of. 'How long have I been asleep?' From the way his stomach was grumbling it had to be a while.

'Answer: it was necessary to induce sleep lasting somewhat longer than a normal rest period in order to facilitate your recovery. I have only awakened you now in order to give you news that you will wish to hear.'

'I will?' He wasn't so sure.

'Aye-okay. You are to be returned to your companions.'

'My— I am?'

'Clarification: we are en route to the Consensus, where you will be reunited with the rest of your crew.'

The relief was so intense it was almost physical: an unwinding sensation deep inside. His face broke into a smile. 'That's pure blade – just what I wanted to hear.'

Zhian's answering smile looked genuine to Taro.

'Er, listen,' he continued, 'I don't suppose I could maybe com them?' Quite aside from being desperate to hear Nual's voice, there was something he needed to warn her about.

'Clarification request: you wish to use our com system?'

'Yeah – unless we're nearly there.'

'Negative. Apology: such activity is not feasible at this time.'

Whatever that meant – but then, it probably wouldn't have been a secure link anyway, and what he needed to tell Nual wasn't something he wanted anyone else – certainly not a male – to overhear. 'I'll leave it for now then. Don't want to be any trouble. D'you know how long before we get to this Consensus place?'

'Answer: this is a fast ship and we will reach the Consensus habitat in a matter of hours.' She sounded pleased with herself.

'Prime. Any chance of something to eat before then? And some clean clothes maybe?'

'Aye-okay. Request: kindly wait here for the moment.'

As she vanished back down the corridor, Taro eased himself off the couch. The floor was chilly, and he jiggled from foot to foot while he was waiting. He hugged himself as though trying to keep warm, using the excuse to check the fold in his underpants where he'd hidden a certain tiny item. Yep, it was still there. His med-tat had already faded back into near-invisibility, which was a relief.

Zhian returned with his clothes, cleaned and folded. 'Nice ship you've got here,' he said as he dressed. 'You the captain?'

'Negative. Clarification: our command structure does not have that rank. However, I hold a position of authority. Request: kindly follow me to where sustenance will be provided.'

She led him out of the medbay and he looked around him with interest. The ship was halfway between Device's cold perfection and Jarek's random homeliness. A little way along the corridor they passed a couple of 'free humans', both wearing unflattering suits like Zhian's. These people had no sense of style, Taro thought. Still, they nodded politely as he passed.

Zhian led him to the canteen, where several crew members were eating. They nodded too, and Taro nodded back. He reckoned these coves were a bit freaked, but trying hard not to show it.

The food came from wall dispensers but was surprisingly good: some sort of chewy vegetable, fresh crispy leaves, and a tasty pale meat Taro decided not to think too closely about. Once he'd crammed enough down his throat to remind himself what his stomach was for, he looked over at Zhian, who was nursing a sweet-smelling hot drink.

'I ain't thanked you yet,' he said.

'Request for clarification: thanked me for what?'

'For rescuing me.'

'Statement: you are welcome,' said Zhian gravely.

'So, d'you just happen to be passing when you noticed someone'd made a hole in the surface of CN— Uh … CN-361?'

'Negative. Clarification: we responded to the downed ship's distress message.'

'Oh, so it did put out a mayday … I wasn't sure.'

'Clarification: if an avatar's ship has to make an emergency landing in another patron's domain it automatically broadcasts a brief distress call, then goes into open-minimal mode to await assistance.'

Which might explain the mysteriously opening doors … Taro really wanted to know what she knew about the Gatekeeper and his plans, but decided it might be wiser not to mention anything for now. Instead he said, 'Good job you turned up when you did: the locals had just worked out that I didn't want to buy their rock.' When Zhian didn't look confused at his statement he continued, 'What's the deal with that place, anyway?'

'Answer: CN-361 is a semi-neutral domain, which is why your ship was permitted to land. However, it has a bankrupt populace.'

'A *what*?' There was no way that sounded good …

'Answer: a bankrupt populace is one that has lost contact with both their patron and the outside world.'

Taro was interested to see Zhian's hands tighten slightly on her mug as she spoke. He got the impression she was finding talking to him stressful, despite the friendly face. Nual would know the truth, of course … He felt a sudden pang, sharp as the physical hunger he'd just sated. He told himself he'd see her soon.

'I thought patrons cared for their people.' Taro tried not to make it sound like a criticism.

'Response: most do.' She sounded offended. Then she smiled a little, and asked, 'Query: do you require clarification on this matter?'

'Yeah, I'd like to know whatever you can tell me.' Ideally without all the stupid 'query' 'answer' shit, though he knew better than to say that.

'Clarification: on rare occasions a domain's populace may fail and fall. This is one such occasion. CN-361's patron turned over his assigned planetoid to his populace. It contained rare elements which he wished mined by lo-tech methods. The humans in question were modified accordingly and provided with bio-engineered animals capable of aiding the mining process and filling critical gaps in the world's limited ecosystem.'

Taro remembered the huge, slow breaths he'd overheard in the dark tunnels.

'Their society was structured to exploit the resources of their planetoid. Eventually, these resources were exhausted. By this time the patron had also changed focus.' Zhian's mouth kinked. 'As a result, the humans on CN-361 were left isolated and untended.'

Taro thought of the filthy, hopeless bastards scraping a living and breeding new and interesting diseases, living for the day when someone would come back to trade for their shiny rocks. Except no one ever would. *Poor fuckers.* 'That ain't the way we do things in human-space,' he said.

'Negative,' said Zhian coldly. 'Clarification: we are not in human-space. The patron would have been within his rights to kill the bankrupt populace and reseed his domain, but he chose instead to let them live.'

If you called that living … Taro took the hint and dropped the subject. He decided to ask a question that'd been bugging him – Zhian might refuse to answer, but even that would tell him something. 'Talking of patrons,' he said, 'I was wondering if there's an avatar on this ship. You said you don't have a captain – is that 'cos there's an avatar in charge?' And possibly in charge of every ship, though the angry lightsail cove who'd commed them when they first arrived hadn't sounded much like an avatar.

'Negative,' said Zhian. 'Clarification: we are free humans.'

'So you don't let avatars on your ship?'

'Answer: we sometimes transport avatars from our own or allied septs. However, our main function is as traders between open domains with differing resources.'

'Does your patron know you've got me on board?'

'Affirmative.' Her tone told him how stupid she thought *that* question was.

Taro hoped her patron wasn't one of the Gatekeeper's mates. 'And you just happened to be passing when you picked up the distress call, that right?'

'Request for clarification: please rephrase your query.'

'Did your patron tell you to pick me up, or did you do it 'cos you wanted to?'

'Response: naturally our decisions are those we are certain our patron would endorse.'

So much for being 'free'– and so much for clearly answering questions!

Zhian continued, 'Apologies: I have other duties to attend to now. I will leave you alone for a while. You are free to do as you wish; I will notify you when we are close enough to the Consensus for secure communication.'

'Sure. Thanks.'

Zhian was already getting up. Taro got the impression she was glad the conversation was over.

CHAPTER THIRTY

'Where is she now?' asked Kerin.

'I have no idea,' replied Urien wearily.

Kerin tried not to feel any pleasure at discovering that Urien's plan had failed. She hoped the girl had run as far and as fast as she could, and that she was already on her way to start a new life. 'Well, that is that, then.'

'So we must hope,' muttered Urien.

'What do you mean?'

'Nothing that should concern you, Kerin.'

How she hated it when he gave the impression of doing her a favour by not keeping her informed. Kerin had no choice but to trust Urien, for he was her only link to the complex hierarchical world of the Tyr, but the previous evening's events had shaken that trust. He had not seen the cursed girls as lives destroyed, just as another problem to be solved.

'As you wish,' she said coldly. Then, on impulse, she added, 'Urien, may I ask you something?'

'Of course.' His tone belied his words. He would far rather she never asked questions, just listened, and did as he suggested – which only strengthened her resolve further.

'What really happened to Lillwen?' Kerin had only briefly met the woman who had previously masqueraded as the Cariad. Lillwen had been a figurehead only, controlled by the old Escorai, all of whom were now dead. And the Escorai themselves had been acting out the roles assigned to them by the last Sidhe Cariad. Sais had told her how the Sidhe left compulsions within a person's mind; he had called it 'programming'. In the case of the conditioned Escorai, the 'programming' ensured that order was maintained if a Cariad died in office – always a risk, because the Sidhe left Serenein to its own devices for years on end, while they waited for its strange harvest to mature.

'What do you mean?' Urien asked, sounding weary.

'You said that when Lillwen recovered from her mistreatment she was given money and set free. Is that really what happened? After all, she was a witch too.'

'She was, but she was no threat. Her experiences had left her too damaged. As far as I know, she left Dinas Emrys in search of her daughter.'

Not for the first time, Kerin wished she had the priestly ability to know when she was being lied to. 'I hope she found her,' she said, bitterly.

'Kerin, rulers cannot afford to think or behave as ordinary people. They must weigh up what will be gained and what will be lost with every choice they make.'

'And what happens if we are too busy making those choices and we lose sight of what we strive to achieve?'

'That is an excellent question. I wish I had an answer for you.' Typical Urien: at once calmly accepting and faintly disapproving.

After he had left, Kerin wondered, not for the first time, if Urien only put up with her because she was the mother of the one person able to operate all the Sidhe technology.

She made an appearance at the Senneth that morning, sitting in on a ruling to allow non-priests to use skymetal. The Senneth was made up of merchants, guildmasters and representatives from the provinces and the law passed easily once she had given it her personal blessing.

As her palanquin was borne back through the sweltering streets afterwards, she found herself musing on the relationship between greed and fear. Those holding secular power were only too eager to embrace a change that brought them profit, provided they were first reassured that said change would not also bring Heavenly retribution. What had been true in her village was equally true here: understanding and manipulating the balance of greed and fear lay at the heart of effective leadership.

She disembarked and returned to her rooms alone, dispensing with the formality attendant on any public appearance. She was grateful that the previous Cariad had been used to wandering the halls of the Tyr by herself. The Sidhe Cariads had obviously valued their privacy.

Despite her lack of talent, she sensed a certain unease in the priests she passed. It might be the unpopularity of her ruling on the use of skymetal, which further eroded priestly privilege, or it might be that this particular law had required a change to the Traditions themselves, although Urien had assured her there was precedent for that. Cariads had often made small modifications to the accepted rule of 'Heaven' before now. What was different was the pace of reform. Naturally, some people were not happy.

Damaru was playing with the wooden puzzle she had bought for him on her last incognito foray into the city. He had solved it within minutes of being given it, but he still continued to rearrange the pieces. She persuaded him to activate the console, and he obeyed with relatively good grace, then went back to his puzzle. Since he had established that he could not regain control of the technology above, the console held little interest for him.

Though it took a Sidhe's touch to wake it, once it was active the console could be worked by anyone. Kerin called up an image from one of the recording devices high above the world. She steered the image down a long valley between two mountainous ridges, then brought it into focus. A cluster of huts sprang into view: the village where she had lived for most of her life. Although spying on her old life stirred up feelings of guilt, relief and regret, it also lifted her spirits; though she had no desire to return to Dangwern, she was both reassured and vindicated to see that life went on there without her.

The scene was viewed as if from the eyes of a hawk, distant yet clear. Today Kerin could make out two familiar figures striding down from the huts to the stock pens on the valley floor. She recognised Arthen by his confident gait and Fychan by his eye-patch when he glanced upwards. They paused and conferred at the stockade, where the yearlings were munching contentedly on summer hay. She wondered if the chieftain and his son were choosing which bullocks to overwinter for next year's drove, and which to slaughter for food when the weather turned. Since his return to the village Fychan often shadowed his father; Kerin hoped the boy's experiences on the last drove might have turned him from the feckless youth he had been and set him on the path to becoming as good a chieftain as his now-dead brother would have been.

She watched as they made their choices, then switched focus to the women who were washing clothes down by the stream, but though the images brought her comfort, she knew they were really just a sop. She needed a reality she could hear and touch. It would also be useful to get a better feel for the true mood of the priests.

She turned off the console, got changed, then took her secret route from the Cariad's room, stopping to collect the pile of clean linen she had hidden ready for her next trip, a passport to parts of the Tyr forbidden to the kitchen servants. Servants, being invisible, often overheard interesting conversations.

The console held a storehouse of knowledge on the Tyr and city, and she often enjoyed calling up maps and records, many of them created by the previous Cariads – notes on politics, feuds and scandals, recorded to allow their successor to seamlessly continue the reign as one 'eternal' goddess. It was clear the Sidhe who ruled here had taken considerable pleasure in observing and nurturing the intrigues of the Tyr.

Tonight her route took her near places where the priests met – the eating hall, the shrines and scriptoriums, even the quarters of the Putain Glan – but she heard nothing of interest, other than that people thought the mysterious lights in the sky were becoming less frequent of late. No point mentioning this to Urien; he would already know.

After a while her burden of linen began to weigh on her injured arm. The wound had healed cleanly, but the Sidhe weapon had destroyed some of the muscle, leaving that arm weak. Sais had told her that the miraculous devices on the *Setting Sun* could have made her as good as new, if only they had had the chance. He also told her most of the diseases and ailments habitually endured by the people of Serenein were virtually unknown in the wider universe – humans elsewhere believed health and long life were everyone's right. Yet her people were denied these things.

But it was worse even than that: every generation the Sidhe returned to spread the falling fire. What people believed to be a visitation from Heaven, sent to root out the sinful, was in truth a careful strategy intended to control the population and increase the number of skyfools. And her people believed that worthy skyfools went to Heaven, to become the Skymother's consorts – instead, their real fate was very different: they were driven mad and bound into the ships that travelled between worlds.

Once she had come to understand those two facts – what the people of Serenein were denied, and what was taken from them – Kerin had had no choice but to fight the Sidhe.

As she made her way back towards her rooms, one question kept running through her head: what did she have to trade for the security and comfort of her world?

Her husband – for so Sais was, in fact, if not in flesh or feeling – was a trader; he would have considered such things. Though she had known him for less than a season, she believed him to be a good man, and that he truly cared for her people. Yet the more time she spent in the Tyr, the more suspicious she became of others' motives.

She could not help thinking that her world had only one thing of value: the means to open up the paths between the stars. But that asset was no crop or mineral; it was the living souls of their children, boys like her own son, Damaru.

So here was the big question: was that cost too high to ensure the future for those who remained?

When she had first taken the Cariad's throne, she would have said it was, without question. But now—

'Oof!' The air left Kerin's lungs as she ran into something solid and her burden went flying.

229

Strong hands caught her before she could fall. 'Mistress! I am sorry.'

'I—' She looked around. A monitor had hold of her arm, and the linen was strewn across the floor. 'No,' she said, 'the fault is mine. I did not see you when I turned the corner there.'

'No matter. Shall I help you with that?' He bent down to start collecting up the fallen items.

The man looked vaguely familiar. 'Aye, thank you,' she murmured, reminding herself to behave like a menial afraid of getting into trouble for her carelessness. As she picked up a bed sheet and started to fold it, she realised where she had seen this man before. That day she had heard someone speak against the Tyr he had been in the square; it was he who had defended the speaker's right to voice his fears. This might be a contact worth cultivating.

'Master— I mean, Captain,' she said spotting the two wavy lines tooled into the leather armouring his right shoulder, 'I must apologise. I was distracted.'

'Do not worry.'

'Oh, oh but I do – that is why I was not looking where I was going.' She heard the tremulous note in her voice, and wondered if anyone could possibly be fooled by such terrible acting. But he was smiling at her, so she continued, 'I am newly come to the Tyr, you know.'

'Ah, I see. I know myself how much there is to learn – and how intimidating it can all be.'

'You are from the provinces too, then?' She had thought as much.

'I am, though I have been here many years.' He passed her a blanket. 'I am sure you will get used to the ways of the Tyr.'

'Oh, aye, I am sure I will. Except …' She ducked her head, and said shyly, 'Forgive me for speaking out of turn, but it appears to me that all is not well here.'

'In what way?' The monitor's tone was guarded.

'I cannot be sure, having nothing to compare against. But I feel a certain unease – people tell me changes are being made, not necessarily for the better – not that I would presume to know,' she added hurriedly. 'And I have prayed for guidance. Please do not laugh, but I did not see you just now because I was praying to Mantoliawn – she is the Mother who rules my birth – to show me if my fears are justified.' Mantoliawn's order was the one headed by the most awkward of Urien's chosen Escorai; it seemed an obvious choice for a dissenter.

'I would never mock such a pious admission,' he said seriously. 'Time spent speaking to the Mothers is never wasted.' He seemed to reach a decision. 'As for your fears . . . you are not alone in them.'

'I am not sure whether to be relieved or alarmed to hear that,' Kerin said with all the meek uncertainty she could muster.

He was silent as he reached for the last few blankets to pass them to her. Then he said, 'May I ask your name, Mistress?'

Kerin's heart leapt – the monitor trusted her – then sank as she realised what his request would mean. When she had first decided she would walk the Tyr incognito, she had asked Urien whether she should lay claim to some other life – a kitchen worker, maybe, so she could spin a believable tale if she were challenged. But Urien had pointed out that the priests' meticulous record-keeping would make that difficult; at the very least, some poor hearth-mistress would be asked to explain the non-appearance of one of the workers for whom pay was being drawn. Still, she had chosen her alias, and she could hardly refuse to answer the monitor's question. 'Gwellys am Penfrid,' she said, head bowed.

'Of which hearth and shift?'

'I report to the housekeeper at the west kitchen. My shift is day, second. And who are you, if you do not mind me asking?'

'I am Siarl am Nantgwyn, Sub-Captain of the Sixth Cohort of the Third Watch. You are working very late, mistress.'

'I am, aye.' Kerin cursed her incorrect guess; she had not realised the time. But at least she had his name in return. 'I am pleased to make your acquaintance, Captain Siarl.'

As he handed her the final blanket Captain Siarl's gaze lingered on her hand. Kerin saw the tiny widening of his eyes; hers was not the hand of a woman who washed many sheets.

He stood and said, 'I will wish you a good evening then, mistress.'

'Aye. Good evening to you too, Captain.' She made herself pick up the pile of linen; if nothing else it should hide the sour expression on her face from anyone she passed. She had tried to play Urien's game, and found she had little talent for it.

CHAPTER THIRTY-ONE

Nual found Ain waiting for her when she finally emerged from the Star Chamber. She'd been questioned for what felt like hours; only her Sidhe abilities were keeping her on her feet now.

The males had accepted her statement that she had been touched but not corrupted by the otherverse entity; when it came to a force that could damage female Sidhe, they cared less about causes than results. Nual had no idea whether they truly understood the danger the alien presence posed.

They had wanted to know more about her prescient flashes; she could not say whether the lack of concrete information she had so far gained pleased or disappointed them.

'You will find refreshments in your room,' said the lingua as she gestured for Nual to follow her. 'However, be aware that more avatars wish to talk to you.'

Nual's heart sank: why couldn't they just let her rest? 'Aren't they busy debating' – she caught herself before saying *my fate*, and instead concluded – 'what I said?'

'The sept leaders are; those visitors who are scheduled to see you are mainly lesser representatives.'

'That makes me feel so much better,' she growled.

When she reached her room she ate the food, drank the water that had been provided, and looked longingly at the bed. She tried to com Jarek, but he wasn't answering; no doubt he was still asleep, the lucky man.

A few minutes later the first visitor walked in – without

knocking, of course. They never did. Nual sighed and composed her face into a smile.

By the tenth visitor she was drawing on her deepest reserves of energy, regulating the balance of mood-affecting neurotransmitters to keep herself calm and friendly. She disliked making such drastic adjustments to her body chemistry: there was always a price to pay when one cheated nature. She only hoped she could put off what Taro would call 'the crash' long enough for the males to tire of pestering her.

Because she was so strung-out, she did not initially notice anything odd about the twelfth avatar. Unlike the others, it remained standing by the door, hands behind its back. Perhaps it planned to harangue her from across the room like some stern parent. She tried to suppress the exasperated sigh she felt building.

She was taken by surprise when it brought out a small pistol from behind its back. Although she tensed, ready to attack, exhaustion slowed her reactions. Before she could move, the avatar shot her.

Jarek woke from a deep dreamless sleep to find three messages on his com. Two were from Nual. The first, left not long after he'd crashed out, apologised for having been so abrupt – she said a lot of males wanted to talk to her. Her voice was ragged but calm in the second, received just half an hour ago; she said she had just returned from the Star Chamber, and more visitors were due soon; she would com him as soon as she was allowed some time to herself.

The other message, which had arrived just after Nual's first one, was delivered in the Arbiter's neutral tone: 'Captain Reen, we are pleased to inform you that both of your requests have been granted by the Consensus. Work on the beacon has been stepped up, and it will be ready for you within one standard day. Your missing crew-member has also been located, and will be returned to you in a similar time-frame.'

Finally, their luck was changing. He wondered if the males had bothered to tell Nual. She didn't answer her com, so he tried Ain.

'How may this lingua be of help?'

'Oh hi,' he said, 'I expected you to be with Nual.'

'Clarification: the lingua assigned to the Sidhe is currently rest-ing,' replied the voice at the other end of the com. 'This individual has been temporarily allocated to serve you. Query: did you require anything?'

'Right.' They really did all sound the same. 'Food would be good.'

'Offer: some will be brought to you.'

'And I don't suppose you know what caf is?'

'Negative. This lingua apologises.'

The lingua who brought the meal was distant and efficient, and the food was every bit as tasteless as Ain had warned, but he fin-ished it all.

After he'd eaten, he went up to the door again. This time, it didn't open. He commed the lingua again. 'I can't get out of my room,' he said, as evenly as he could.

'Offer: a lingua will bring you anything you require,' she said.

'I'm sure you will, but that's not the point.'

'Explanation: you were instructed to remain in your assigned quarters.' The lingua managed to make it sound reasonable, like the males were doing him a favour.

'Yes, and that's fine: I've no problem with staying here. I'd just rather not be locked in.' He didn't add that the door had opened when he'd tried it earlier. The lingua could check that for herself.

'Conclusion: this lingua conveys your request,' she said.

He thanked her, and started pacing again. He forced himself to sit down again, but he couldn't settle. He'd just resumed his pacing when the same lingua – at least, he *thought* it was the same lingua – commed back to tell him his door was now open; she offered no explanation as to why it had been locked.

More male Sidhe mind-games, Jarek thought as he checked the door really was unlocked. This time when he commed Nual, he got through to the local messaging service. He didn't leave a mes-sage.

All he could do was wait. He wondered what lingua did for

entertainment round here. Probably memorised lists of sept alliances.

Checking his com for the umpteenth time he calculated that Nual had been alone with the males for the best part of ten hours now. Sidhe stamina or not, she must be exhausted. He commed again, putting the call through on *discreet* in case she'd crashed out without telling him. This time when the call failed the display came up *Unknown Recipient*.

Trying to ignore the sinking feeling in his gut he commed again, in case he'd done something wrong, or there was some temporary glitch in the Consensus' com system, but he got the same result: *Unknown Recipient*.

Jarek swallowed hard, then jumped up and ran over to the door. He half-expected it not to open, but it did, and he ran down the empty corridor to Nual's room, the eleventh door on the left. None of the lingua's rooms had call buttons, buzzers or visible locks, and the door wouldn't open. He knocked, in case the door was jammed or locked from inside, but there was no response. He banged hard and shouted Nual's name, to no avail.

He commed Ain, and got the replacement lingua. 'Where's Nual?' he asked brusquely.

'Answer: that query is not valid,' replied the lingua.

'What do you mean, "not valid"?' He could feel himself about to lose his temper and he reined it in. Whatever was going on here, he had to remain calm.

'Kindly refer to your primary assigned lingua.'

'Well, yes – that's who I was trying to call!'

'Clarification: that individual is currently resting.'

'Then why did you—? Is there anyone else I can talk to?'

'Response: a request is being placed.'

'Yeah. Good.' Jarek cut the connection rather than swear at the lingua. Still muttering, he carried on up the corridor. Ain's room was just round the next corner, third door along, he thought.

The third room along was empty; his heart sank, but he tried the next one and felt a wash of relief when he found Ain there, asleep on the bed. When he called her name she opened her eyes and looked at him in bleary surprise.

'Where is she?' he said, more harshly than he intended.

'S— Sorry, wh—' Ain struggled to sit up, rubbed her eyes, then said more firmly, 'Who?'

'Nual, of course!' he said, and rushed over to her. As Ain cowered away from him, Jarek caught himself up short.

'I believe she is in her room,' Ain said quickly.

'Then why can't I get in?'

'I am not sure. Perhaps because she has visitors?'

'And what's wrong with her com?'

'Her com? I have no idea.'

Now he thought about it, there was no reason why she would; she'd obviously been asleep. As he looked at her, Ain's expression began to change.

'What is it?' he hissed. 'What are they saying to you?'

'Statement: you should leave now,' said Ain, her voiced quavering.

'Not until you tell me what's going on.'

'A— Answer: there is nothing "going on". All is well.'

'Then where's Nual?'

Quietly, but with a certain self-assurance, Ain said, 'This individual does not know anyone of that name.'

'Oh, come on!' Was this really Ain? Yes, he was certain it was: she knew him, and she'd been using the informal speech patterns she'd learned from them, at least until a few seconds ago. 'Ain, this is me, *Jarek*. Your friend – or so I thought.'

Ain said nothing. It was hard to tell in the low light, but Jarek thought she was looking at him with pity.

'Request: kindly do not harass the lingua.'

Jarek turned to see one of the silver avatars standing in the doorway. 'I wouldn't have to, if you told me what was going on,' he snapped. Behind him, he heard Ain moving hurriedly.

'Leave the lingua to her rest. I will talk to you.'

Trying to ignore the impression that he was being told off, Jarek strode out of Ain's room. A last glance back showed her standing, respectful and blank-faced, by her bed.

He turned to the avatar, which immediately said, 'Query: did you not receive the message giving you the good news?'

'What good news is that?' Jarek regretted his sharp retort; this was an avatar of the Arbiter, and being sarcastic wasn't going to help. More equably he said, 'I did get the message about you granting our requests for the beacon and the return of my missing crew-member.'

'Observation: this is good.'

'Yeah, it is. Only thing is, I appear to have lost my *other* crew-member.'

Neither the avatar's face nor its voice were particularly expressive, so for a moment Jarek wasn't sure he'd heard it correctly when it asked, 'Request for clarification: *which* other crew-member?'

'Nual, the Sidhe: remember?'

'Statement: I have no record of any such individual.'

'Now, come on.' Jarek fought to keep his voice even. 'She arrived with me, she came to the first hearing at the Star Chamber, and then she went back in alone. She's left two messages on my com since I've been here!'

The avatar just stared at him, saying nothing.

Jarek stabbed at his com to call up Nual's last message, but there was no record of it, or of the one before.

'Christos!' he shouted, 'what the *fuck* is going on here?'

The avatar said, 'Statement: we have granted your requests. I would expect you to be grateful to us.'

Jarek wondered if that was a threat. He chose his words carefully. 'I'm grateful for the beacon, and I'm grateful that Taro's on his way back. But I have also lost a member of my crew. Please, just tell me what's happened to her!'

'Statement: we do not know to whom you refer.'

'I already told— This isn't getting us anywhere.' He had an idea; it might not be a smart move but it beat this absurd, circular conversation. 'Tell you what, why don't I check she's not waiting for me on my ship? That all right with you?'

'Affirmative: if you wish.'

Jarek had expected argument, possibly even forceful opposition. The avatar's calm acceptance threw him, but into his moment of confusion another thought arrived. 'You *know* I had a Sidhe female with me, because I could never have got here without her! Hell, there's a good chance I can't get back without her!'

'Observation: your problems are not our concern; we are keeping our promises.'

'So you say. Except now you're pretending someone who arrived with me doesn't exist!'

'Statement:' said the Arbiter's avatar firmly, 'what the Consensus decides is true *is* true. This is not negotiable.'

'Fuck that!' muttered Jarek, no longer caring if he offended the impassive avatar. 'If you want me I'll be on my ship.'

The avatar said nothing as he stalked off.

The *Heart of Glass* was exactly as he'd left it, at least, as far as he could tell. He started waking up the locked-down systems and disconnected his personal com from the Consensus' system, hesitating for a moment before linking back into the *Heart of Glass*'s private com. The males must have hacked the inbox he'd been allocated on the Consensus comnet in order to delete Nual's messages, but the com itself should be safe enough. He used the ship's com to try and contact Nual again, but she still showed as unavailable, which meant her com was either turned off, out of range or broken – all of which were better than not ever having existed, like the goddamned Consensus comnet claimed, but not much help when it came to finding her.

What the fuck were the males playing at? He began to prep the ship for departure: if they had a problem with that, then they could contact him and ask him nicely what he was up to.

When he'd completed a full systems-check and they still hadn't called, he sighed and sat back on his couch. He wasn't going to just leave, not without his crew or the beacon. But he was going to be ready to get the hell out at a moment's notice.

CHAPTER THIRTY-TWO

Taro took Zhian at her word, even if only half the doors actually opened for him. The crew members he met were polite and helpful, though not exactly friendly. He couldn't find anything that looked like the bridge. He did find what was probably a rec-room, with devices that might be for exercise or gaming, but there wasn't anyone around to show him how any of it worked. He also found a communal washroom, currently empty, and decided to have a shower. He unwrapped the chip he'd taken from Vy and, after a moment's hesitation, put it in his mouth. He'd promised he'd keep it on him at all times, and he meant to keep that promise. Given where he'd found it, he knew it wouldn't suffer from a few minutes in his mouth.

Once clean again, he spat the chip onto his hand and examined the fingernail-sized golden square. 'So that's you,' he murmured to himself.

Taro had put Vy's bizarre request to kill him down to the avatar being fucked up after so long out of contact with the Minister – or rather, with Khesh. But Vy had insisted: 'I will die soon anyway. If you kill me now, while we're alone, then my death will have a purpose. My mission could still succeed.'

Taro, cradling the boy's head in his lap, had asked, 'So what is this secret mission then?'

'What do you know about beacons?'

Taro had no idea how that was relevant, but he decided to humour the dying avatar. 'They transmit beevee, and let ships find their way out of shiftspace.'

He thought he could detect the faintest touch of contempt when Vy commented, 'Is that *all* you know?'

'Well, yeah,' Taro told him, 'I spent most of my life under a floating city, didn't I? You might even remember the place.' But Jarek had said something else about beacons; what was it? *Oh yeah!* 'Do they— Do the beacons contain males, or something? You know, like the transit-kernels in shiftships do ... are.'

Vy said, 'In a manner of speaking ... There is a male component in every beacon – each beacon is tied to a particular male Sidhe mind. Part of that mind is backed up into the beacon.'

Taro had tried to visualise what Vy was saying. 'Backed up? What, like with a comp?'

'Rather more than that, Taro. Beacons contain fragments of male Sidhe consciousness. They may remain inert, non-sentient, but they can be awakened and used to host the full, active mind of a male if necessary.'

'What do you mean, "if necessary"?' Taro had struggled to understand what Vy was saying. 'Ain't *you* a fragment of male consciousness?'

'I am. And I carry the ability to pass on a copy of myself—'

'—to a beacon. Shit, that's it, ain't it? You're part of Khesh, a bit of his mind, and he wants you to put yourself in the beacon, the one we're here to get. *That*'s the secret plan, ain't it?'

'It is my purpose, Taro, my reason for living. After coming so close to death in the mindbomb incident I – Khesh – re-evaluated my decision to limit myself to the Tri-Confed system. I asked the Aleph males if mine could be the consciousness chosen to imprint on the new beacon, which you would then take to Serenein. Choosing me would save conflict between those septs who might otherwise wish to be linked to the beacon. It was also in keeping with the Alephan policy of non-intervention in human-space. They agreed. I was led to believe that on arrival at Aleph I would be taken directly to the location where the beacon is being constructed. But they broke their promise. The Aleph males – or a dominant faction within them – have decided they want possession of the Serenein

241

beacon after all – no doubt they have already chosen one of their own to imprint on it.'

'The bastards! So if you die now, here, you can't get to the beacon. I'm sorry, Vy.' And he really was – but none of that explained why he wanted Taro to kill him.

The boy had managed a grin. 'I may yet be able to imprint successfully, even if they have already downloaded their choice of consciousness into the beacon. But I need your help.'

'You've got it. Only …' Taro had looked around the stark cabin of Device's ship, the white monotony broken only by the body of the Gatekeeper's avatar. '… I'm not sure what I can do for you just now.'

'I have already said: you have to kill me.' Taro had picked up some of the old impatience in Vy's voice; then, more evenly, the avatar had explained, 'We avatars are flesh-machine hybrids – mainly flesh, in my case – but the seat of my consciousness is technology, specifically, a small chip buried deep in my brainstem. I need you to remove that chip.'

And that meant removing the avatar's head, Taro had guessed, which would leave Vy as he knew him well and truly dead.

And that, Taro suddenly realised as he recalled the conversation, was what Zhian had been pleased about – *that* was what'd been nagging him! When she'd first turned up, she'd asked if there were any other survivors, and when he'd said there weren't, she'd been *relieved*. He'd be willing to bet she'd known Vy was with him; she was glad to find the alien avatar was dead – so did that mean she knew about Vy's real mission? But she hadn't searched him for the chip … Now he thought about it, she probably didn't know shit about beacons and downloaded consciousnesses – why should she, unless her patron thought she needed to know? He'd probably just told her to make sure Khesh's avatar didn't get off CN-Dingy Shithole alive.

He had another worrying thought: why had Zhian only told him he was going to be reunited with Nual and Jarek after he'd been on board her ship for the best part of a day?

There was all sorts of smoky shit going on behind the scenes here, and all he could do was keep his eyes and ears open and act like he trusted his rescuers ... until and unless it looked like they were about to fuck him over.

His musings were interrupted by the sound of someone coming into the bathing area. 'Nearly done!' he called, palming the chip again. The man and woman who came into the steamy room didn't act the least bit embarrassed, and they were as polite as everyone else around here.

After he'd dried and dressed, he returned the chip to its hiding place, then made his way back to the canteen. The food dispensers didn't appear to need any sort of cred or ID; the only problem was there wasn't an obvious way to select what you wanted to eat.

Behind him a voice said, 'Greetings, Taro.'

When he turned, he recognised the pilot from the shuttle. 'Oh, hi, Trin,' he said. 'Any chance you could sort me a drink and maybe some food?'

'Okay-aye.'

Trin was happy to help – and to chat. Taro suspected there weren't many people of their age on the ship. But he was still wary, and if Taro strayed into difficult territory – questions about their sept, their tech, or their relationships with patrons – he smiled fixedly and said Taro would have to ask Zhian. And there were deeper differences: when Taro commented on the way patrons could order their 'populace' to do anything, up to and including topping themselves, Trin looked taken aback and said, 'Statement: most never would practise such cruelty.'

Taro knew he should let it drop, but he hated the idea of being owned and controlled like that, even if your particular owner happened to be one of the reasonable ones. 'Yeah, I'm sure your patron – whoever he is – is nice enough. You still have to do what he tells you, though!'

'Okay-aye. Assertion: this is how our lives are, we would not want it any other way.' Trin paused, then asked, 'Query: how is it you manage to live without such certainty?'

'What d'you mean?'

'Clarification: we know where we stand. We know that in return

243

for our loyalty, our patron will protect and defend us. Supposition: to be without that, without someone greater than you to look up to, must surely make you feel a bit ... lost.'

Before Taro could work out what to say to that, Trin's face took on an odd, vacant expression. Then his gaze focused and he said, 'Interrupt, high priority: Zhian wishes to speak to you.'

'Er, right. Where?' Taro decided he had to get himself one of them invisible com implants.

'Clarification: she is on her way here.'

When Zhian arrived a few minutes later Trin stood, waved farewell to Taro and walked off. Out of the corner of his eye, Taro saw the handful of other people in the room just happening to choose that moment to leave as well. Definitely smoky.

He looked at Zhian. Judging by her expression, Taro guessed that whatever she had to say wasn't gonna brighten his day.

She stopped next to his seat and said, 'Statement: I have news of your lover.'

'My lover.' Taro's mind raced. Did they know about him and Nual? But they'd been so careful! 'Who would that be?' he said, fighting to keep his tone even.

'Statement: we have been made aware of your relationship to the Sidhe female.' She didn't sound too happy about it.

'Her name is Nual,' said Taro slowly, 'and if something's happened to her I want to know, right now.'

'Statement: she has been disappeared.'

'What d'you mean, "been disappeared"? How can someone *be* disappeared?' He could feel his stomach start to contract.

'Clarification: perhaps a more appropriate term would be kidnapped.'

'Shit and blood!' That couldn't be right – he was on his way to her; they were supposed to be together again, soon. 'Do you know where she is?' he asked desperately. If Zhian was telling him this, then perhaps she wasn't his enemy.

'Answer: she is still within the Consensus structure.'

'So, what're you – *we* – gonna do about it?'

'Statement: be aware that her disappearance was sanctioned—'

'What the fuck's that mean? Sanctioned by wh—? Oh. You're saying the males agreed to this, and you're prepared to go against them?' That didn't sound likely: even the so-called 'free humans' jumped when their patron told them to.

'Clarification: we have been informed that a majority in the Consensus recently approved the abduction of your lover.'

'But not your patron, right?'

'Assertion: our patron would never act directly against the Consensus. No sane patron would.'

Not when they can get expendable humans to do their dirty work for them. 'So he's going to turn a blind eye while we go in and get her out?'

'Statement: my crew's actions cannot be seen to reflect badly on our patron.'

'I thought your stupid talk was meant to stop people misinterpreting each other, Zhian. Just tell me what the fuck's going on here.'

Zhian paled; he probably shouldn't have snapped.

'Sorry, sorry, it's just—' He stopped, took a deep breath and said, more calmly, 'So: what's the plan? You do have a plan, don't you?'

'Statement: we have been instructed to put you in a position to rescue the Sidhe female.'

'You seem pretty certain I'm going to just agree to—' Taro searched for a polite way to say it, gave up, and concluded, 'to jump straight into the shit.'

Zhian said frostily, 'Statement: she is a female Sidhe, and you are her lover.'

'Yeah,' said Taro, 'you got me there.'

'Statement: we understand that her com is no longer active. However, we believe that you may have other, less orthodox means of getting in contact. Query: are you willing to employ them now?'

'Whatever it takes.' The ship was steaming in towards the Consensus; maybe he was close enough to pick up Nual's mental signature. 'I'll need somewhere quiet.'

'Query: would the medbay be suitable?'

'Should be.' Taro considered asking for drugs to get him into a more receptive state, then decided against it. Zhian was helping him because her patron's agenda currently fitted with his; that didn't mean he trusted her. He needed to stay sharp.

Even with the lights dimmed and Zhian's assurance that he wouldn't be disturbed it took Taro a while to get into anything like a trance.

Eventually he managed to achieve something resembling a calm and receptive state, but that was all it remained: a trance, of sorts. There was no hint of contact with Nual.

He mustn't panic. Their long-distance communion only worked if they were both asleep or in a trance at the same time.

Zhian came back in as he was sitting up, but she stayed by the door. 'Statement: I shall take you to the area of our ship analogous to a "bridge",' she said. Before, she'd been wary; now she was treating him like he might explode if she spooked him. He guessed that was 'cos he was a Sidhe's lover – even if the Sidhe was a female Sidhe, the enemy – and that made him something more-than-human in her eyes.

His guess was confirmed by the reactions of the crew-members they passed. No more polite nods; now they looked awestruck. *Guess I'd act like that too*, he thought, *if someone had slept with one of my gods. Or devils.*

The bridge had no obvious controls, just couches. Two of them were occupied by semi-comatose people.

As they came in one of them, a man, opened his eyes and sat up. He didn't introduce himself, but watched them intensely. Taro looked between the man and Zhian. 'So,' he said uneasily, 'what's the plan?'

'Statement: we will set up conditions that allow you to find and rescue Nual,' said the man, as if he'd been part of the conversation from the beginning – and maybe he had been, given the way their tech worked.

'From the Consensus? How big's the place anyway?'

'Answer: it is approximately twenty-two klicks across.'

'So even if you manage to get me in there, how'm I gonna find her?'

The man said, 'Answer: our patron has told us precisely where your lover is to be found.'

'Then let's go get her.'

CHAPTER THIRTY-THREE

Back in the bedroom, Ifanna used the chamber-pot, washed her hands and face, then searched the chests in the bedroom for more appropriate clothing than the barely decent tunic she was wearing. The woman who had once lived here was shorter and fatter than she; the skirt Ifanna chose ended some way above her ankles and the shirt needed a lot of tucking in. Ifanna looked for some perfume to disguise the musty odour of the clothes, but the only thing she found were a few old incense cones in a carved wooden box on the dresser, and their scent was all but gone.

She did wonder about lighting one anyway; it had been a long time since she had sent any offering save prayer up to the Mothers – and even prayers came hard now. The Mothers must know that she had gone against the decree of their Daughter, yet they had not punished her – so did that mean the Cariad was indeed false, and Ifanna had been right to disobey her? The priest's reaction to her admission implied he already suspected as much ...

But the Cariad was Creation's link to Heaven, at once the pinnacle of earthly order and the will of the Skymothers made flesh. Without her, everything would fall apart ... and that was what appeared to be happening – unless there was some higher purpose at work? What if the Cariad had *chosen* not to manifest her power in order that Ifanna *should* doubt, and, because of her doubt, run away? Yet why would she do that? Ifanna's thoughts were tying themselves into knots; no wonder such questions were left to the priests. She put the carved box back.

She wandered the house for a while, trailing her hands over the possessions of the recently dead and peering through cracks in the shutters at the world outside. This should have been enough after being so long confined in her squalid cell, but Ifanna wanted more – besides, she had used all the water: she should fetch more. She peered through the crack in the shutter again to check no one was outside then picked up the jug and lifted the latch on the back door.

The yard, and the alley beyond, were empty. She looked around: the houses across the way were shuttered, or else showed open but empty windows. She could hear a mother scolding an errant child, and slightly off-key singing from another house further down the row. She spent a while examining the ordinariness of the world outside: the houses, with their red-brick walls and roofs of small blue tiles, the lines of bright washing, and the potted plants that enlivened the yards.

She was about to venture out when the door directly opposite opened; she stepped back hurriedly, pulling the door closed behind her. She must not be seen! And even that brief exposure to the sky had set her heart racing; she put the reaction down to being too used to having roof above her, rather than fear of the naked gaze of the Skymothers.

She returned to the parlour and sat down in the most comfortable chair. She was still thirsty, but while she had been imprisoned she had learned to put aside physical discomfort, taking refuge in memories and daydreams. Now she let her wandering mind alight on *Gwas* Maelgyn. She did not think of him as a priest – priests were cold, distant figures who preached and disapproved. Maelgyn treated her with care and consideration, and he listened to her. All he demanded was her honesty. And he had risked much for her. The thought that anyone should act so on her behalf was intoxicating.

Ifanna wondered how she could ever repay him ... He was not so bad-looking; she had been unfair to think him ugly at their first meeting – a bald head covered in tattooed text was never flattering. And she thought he was attracted to her ... He was a priest, and her powers would not work on him, which meant that if he *did* respond to her, it would not be because she had entrapped him. Such love would be something genuine; something precious. This was a man who might love her for herself.

And, said a small wicked voice deep inside, seducing a priest who is immune to the witches' curse would be a great achievement! Her father had hated her, even as he loved her. With Maelgyn, things would be different—

The sound of someone at the door set her heart racing, until she recognised the pattern of knocks – two slow, and four fast, the same sequence Maelgyn had used that morning. As she jumped up to let him in, she was surprised to find the house dimmer than she remembered. She had dreamt the whole day away.

Maelgyn wore a cloak, though the evening was not cold. He presented one to Ifanna, saying, 'Put this on, *chilwar*. There is someone who wishes to meet you.'

'To meet *me*?' She wanted to protest: *surely no one knows I am here, save you and your friend.* But she stayed silent.

'Aye, and their time is precious, so we should be going.'

'Of course, *Gwas*.' As she put the cloak on, she looked out of the half-open door, which showed a clear summer evening drawing towards night. *Gwas* Maelgyn raised his hood, and indicated she should do the same. She was glad to have her head covered.

Maelgyn pulled the door closed, but did not try and re-latch it; she took comfort in that, for it implied they would be coming back.

When they reached the water-pump, Ifanna asked if she might take a drink; Maelgyn agreed, though he appeared somewhat impatient. As Ifanna straightened after slaking her thirst, curiosity overcame caution and she asked, '*Gwas*, this person we are to meet, is it Captain Siarl?'

'No.' He set off again, and Ifanna fell into step beside him.

'I see,' she said, though she did not.

'Siarl and I have had a falling out,' he added in a low voice.

'Over ... over me, *Gwas*?' She had to ask.

Maelgyn made a small noise of annoyance, though when he spoke his voice was soft. 'Amongst other things: Siarl is a devout man, Ifanna, but not overly imaginative.'

Whatever that meant. They came onto a wide, crowded, thoroughfare. Ifanna, momentarily confounded by such hustle and bustle, found her eye drawn to the divine globes of light, high on their poles. Only a few were lit, but as she watched, another one sparked into life. She drew a quick breath, amazed and obscurely reassured to witness such a miracle.

When she looked at *Gwas* Maelgyn to share her wonder, she could not at first see him, but before her momentary fear sparked into panic she spotted him; he had just drawn ahead a little. As he stopped and looked around for her, a man with a tray of fresh loaves on his head almost ran into him. The simple disguise obviously worked, for no one would dare curse a priest way the baker did. She hurried to rejoin him.

'You had best take my arm to stop us getting separated, *chilwar*,' he said.

The thoroughfare widened further, and open-fronted shops, like those she had seen in Plas Morfren, were doing a brisk trade.

Beside her, *Gwas* Maelgyn grunted in disapproval. 'Look at that, *chilwar*!' he said, pointing at a shop which appeared to be selling medicines: powders were displayed on wooden plates, while baskets overflowed with dried herbs, roots and bark. 'Oh, if I were not hiding my calling I would go over there now and take them to task!'

'I am not sure what you are showing me, *Gwas*.'

'There, by that tray of yellow bark! Those bundles of coloured sticks.'

'What are they, *Gwas*?' Priests might claim that no remedy beat prayer, but Ifanna did not know of any medicines the Traditions specifically banned.

'What they *are* does not matter; it is what they are used for that is my concern: they are the tools of divination!'

Like Maelgyn, Ifanna was appalled – and to see them sold openly? That was surely inviting Heavenly retribution: only the Cariad could indicate divine will! But she was a fraud …

Maelgyn led her down a smaller street off the main road, and she realised they were heading uphill towards the dark shape of the

Tyr. As she looked up at it, she glimpsed a momentary flash high overhead. Was that one of the portentous lights? She looked more carefully, hoping to see another, but instead she saw a star she did not know, near where she thought she had seen the flash. 'Is that the Navel of Heaven?' she murmured.

Gwas Maelgyn glanced up briefly. 'Aye,' he said, sounding troubled.

Ifanna bowed her head again, nervous under Heaven's gaze. As they took another side-street she wondered if the *Gwas* was taking her to the Tyr by some roundabout route. 'What rank do you hold in the Tyr, *Gwas*?' she asked.

'I am of the fourth tier,' he replied.

'And that is a high rank, is it, *Gwas*?' She knew little of the priestly hierarchy, but surely someone as wise as he was important.

'Aye, it is – quite high.' He paused. 'Though not as high as I would have achieved had I come from a rich city family.'

'What do you mean, *Gwas*?'

'There is a bias against Fenlanders here, and against those of humble birth. I have been thwarted in my career, denied promotion on the grounds of my origin.' His tone was bitter.

Ifanna said sincerely, 'I am sorry to hear that, *Gwas*.'

'It is not your problem.' He sounded tired.

'And you serve the Mother of Justice first amongst the Five?' Ifanna had noticed the yellow trim on his robes.

'Indeed I do. We who honour Mantoliawn above all others are the life-blood of the Tyr, *chilwar*. We are also the most fortunate of all the branches of the priesthood: our Escori, Garnon, is the noblest and truest priest in the land.' His voice swelled with pride.

'He was at my judging, though he said very little.' She barely remembered the man; he was just one of five voices who condemned her.

'And which Escori spoke most, I wonder?'

Ifanna was not sure if the question was one she was meant to answer, but she searched her memory anyway. 'I think it was the Escori of Frythil.'

'Hah! Of course it was.'

'Why do you say that, *Gwas*?'

'This spring, there was a coup in the Tyr. Only two Escorai survived it, and one of those subsequently went mad and took his own life. The sole survivor was Urien, Escori of Frythil. Some say he initiated the coup, though how a man who serves the Cariad could act so without her sanction ... One thing is certain: he wields more power than he should.'

Ifanna knew so little of the Tyr priests and their ways. 'But your Escori, he is ... He is good?'

'Garnon is a man I admire greatly.' Again, this was spoken with pride. Then, unexpectedly, Maelgyn laughed. 'But you need not take my word for it.'

Ifanna was still trying to work out what he meant when he pointed ahead. Their alley crossed another, and on the corner was a house with light pouring from most of the windows. Sounds of merriment came from within. As they approached, Ifanna identified the building as a tavern. There was a wooden sign hanging at the corner, showing some sort of animal's head.

Gwas Maelgyn led her to a door at one side of the main entrance and knocked, the same sequence he had used with her. The man who opened the door was not in uniform, but he did carry a crossbow. He lowered the weapon when he saw them and made the circle, though he did his best to avoid looking at Ifanna as he admitted them. He remained below while she and *Gwas* Maelgyn went up a flight of stairs.

The stairs came up to a short landing, then a large room with chairs and tables pushed to the side. It was lit by a single lamp on a table at the far side. A man in dark clothing sat by the lamp; his head was uncovered, and Ifanna could see he was a priest. He was flanked by two men with crossbows, standing loosely to attention.

Gwas Maelgyn circled his breast, at the same time bowing his head, and Ifanna did the same.

'*Gwas*,' said Maelgyn, 'I have brought the girl, as you asked.' His voice was low and earnest.

'Have her approach.' The priest's tone was casual, almost

uninterested. Ifanna looked to *Gwas* Maelgyn, who motioned her forward.

She obeyed, though her knees kept trying to knock together. This man was old, she saw, with deep lines around his thin-lipped mouth. He watched her walk towards him with eyes that missed nothing. The monitors watched her too, their weapons half-raised. 'Has he told you who I am?' he asked while Ifanna was still a few steps away.

'He has not, *Gwas*,' she said, stopping. 'But— But I would guess that you are Garnon, Escori of Mantoliawn.'

She heard *Gwas* Maelgyn's sharp breath at her impudence, though she had not intended to be rude.

He did not confirm her guess but said mildly, 'And you are the witch who claims the Cariad is a fake.'

Ifanna forced herself not to panic.

'Well?' The Escori's gaze bored into Ifanna's soul.

'I told *Gwas* Maelgyn what I experienced,' she said carefully.

'And that was what, precisely?'

Neither lies nor evasion would serve her now. 'When the Cariad said she would look into my heart, I felt nothing at all.'

'Not even the silent voice that witches are said to employ to beguile their victims?'

Ifanna had no idea any man, let alone a priest, knew of that trick. 'No,' she said, determined not to let her surprise show, 'not even that.'

'So, would you say that, as far as you could tell, the woman who sits upon the throne of the Cariad is mortal, ordinary and not possessed of even a witch's abilities?'

'I would say she is nobody of note.' For a moment Ifanna wondered if the Mothers would strike her down; she had just denied the divinity of the highest power in the land to the face of the second highest!

But they did not. And the Escori merely smiled.

CHAPTER THIRTY-FOUR

Jarek was expecting the message, when it finally came, to be from the Consensus, so he was amazed and delighted when he heard a familiar voice.

'Hi there!' Taro sounded unfeasibly cheerful.

'It's good to hear from you,' said Jarek warmly.

'Yeah, and soon you'll see me too. My friends here tell me this ship'll be at the Consensus in less than three hours.'

'That's great news,' said Jarek, straining his ears: Taro's voice sounded a bit odd, like he was forcing himself to come across as carefree and happy. Was he under duress?

'Listen, apparently the patrons don't want my friends to land on the Consensus hab, so we'll meet you in orbit, all right?' continued Taro chattily.

'Sure, no problem.' He'd prefer that himself – but what about Nual? Not that he'd any intention of mentioning her on an open com channel.

'The locals want to see what we're up to, though, so you gotta stay in orbit around the – whaddya call it, the Egg?'

'That's what the lingua call it, yes.'

'Yeah. So listen, I'll send you some coordinates then, shall I?'

'If you like.' What the hell was Taro playing at?

'Here they come. I'll be in touch again when we're closer. Bye for now.'

'Bye, Taro.' As he signed off he received the data-package. The encryption was basic, and he opened it to discover coordinates given in human-space notation, just as Taro had said. But he hadn't needed a coded databurst for such a small snippet of info; Taro could just have given it verbally. Unless ...?

Sure enough, at the very end was another set of coordinates, along with an exact time and one word: *tight-beam*.

Jarek smiled. Sometimes the boy surprised him.

He made one last attempt to persuade the Consensus to hand Nual over, and when they continued to deny all knowledge of her, he asked, with his voice full of not-entirely-feigned pique, for immediate permission to undock. They granted it without comment or complaint.

At precisely the moment Taro had specified he made sure the *Heart of Glass* was in precisely the position he had specified, and got ready to receive the tight-beam communication, which would be invisible, and untraceable by any third party unless they were in precisely the right position to physically intercept the transmission.

Taro sounded a lot less self-assured when he greeted Jarek this time. 'This is gonna have to be quick,' he started, and went on to explain the plan. Jarek had to resist the urge to call him crazy; he wasn't crazy, just in love. And getting Nual back wasn't just about keeping Taro happy. Still, Jarek felt obliged to point out that they were being used by whichever sept Taro's friends owed their allegiance to, and Taro didn't bother to argue. They both knew they didn't have much choice. Taro also told him that Vy was dead. Jarek wasn't sure how he felt about that.

He had some tricky flying to do if he was to make the rendezvous whilst at the same time ensuring the *Heart of Glass*'s final position looked like chance, not design. Jarek rolled his shoulders, cracked his knuckles and gave his full attention to the controls. 'Right,' he said to himself, 'time to make this look easy.'

Space made you feel naked – though Taro wasn't naked, of course: the v-suit Zhian had provided was so thin he could feel his clothes through it. The struts and braces of a lifter-harness encased his limbs like the skeleton of an extra suit, running from the nape of his neck to the soles of his feet. Even though it was currently powered down, he liked having the additional layer between his flesh and the void.

He'd have liked an actual spacecraft around him even more, but he couldn't argue with Zhian's logic: quite aside from needing the shuttle as a decoy to (apparently) carry him back to the *Heart of Glass*, he had to stay out of sight as he crossed the klick or so between her ship to the Egg, and even a powered-up lifter-harness would leave a detectable signature. Angel mods, on the other hand, left him all but invisible, unless someone trained sensors with hi-mag visuals or ultra-sensitive grav pick-up on his exact location.

He spent nearly an hour clinging to an external holdfast on the hull while Zhian's ship closed the distance to the Consensus. As it adjusted course, his view of the massive habitat swung first to the left, then the right, then the middle, all the time getting closer. So that was – or had been – a Sidhe mothership. He remembered Vy's words: 'Back when the rebellion against the Protectorate was kicking off, the free males caught themselves a Sidhe ship: the biggest mothership of all. They kept it, sort of like a trophy, and turned it into one of their habs. No point wasting it.' *Or its crew...* No wonder they called it the Egg.

The view below him rolled, and the calm, sexless voice of the suit's com said, 'Prepare to disembark.' He unclipped his tether-line. The two ships would only be positioned over the right area of the hab for a few seconds.

Setting this up had required some brain-aching calculations – carried out by Zhian's patron and transmitted tight-beam to her, then on to Jarek – followed by some snazzy flying by both Jarek and Zhian's people. So far, Taro had just been along for the ride. Now it was up to him.

A loud double chime sounded in Taro's ear: on the far side of Zhian's ship the shuttle would be undocking and heading towards the *Heart of Glass*.

He flexed his legs and leapt into space, flinching as he broke free of the cover provided by the ship. If he'd felt exposed clinging to the outside of a spaceship, flying through open space made his balls positively shrivel – and that was with the Angel mods working full-out to stop him panicking and keep his innards at a constant gravity!

He focused on the view below. He was already close enough to the hab that its curve was barely visible. Most of the surface was covered in tech-crap – dishes, aerials, and less identifiable lumps and nodules.

Movement drew his eye. Directly below him, a squat tower was swivelling. *Shit and blood, what was it?* Sensor? *Gun?* His mods damped down his fear, but didn't have any useful tactical suggestions.

The tower swivelled further, then stopped.

Nothing happened.

He let go a massive sigh; the hot puff of breath whooshed disconcertingly through the tiny gap between his mask and the skin of his face before the suit absorbed and diffused it. Whatever that thing was, it wasn't a gun, thank fuck.

In his ear the suit-com instructed him to move a little to his left, and for the next few minutes his attention was focused on course adjustments, while trying to keep an eye on the cluttered surface looming up to meet him.

He blinked as the view went dark; the hab had rotated out of sunlight. He was aiming for a maintenance airlock, slightly recessed in an otherwise clear section of hull. It all looked the same from up here in the dark, and he couldn't risk turning on his light, so it was a good job the suit knew where it was going.

When he was ten metres away he cut his speed, and made an ungainly landing a little way from the 'lock. He looked around, and spotted something moving, off to his left. Whatever it was, it was coming this way. He wasn't going to panic; it was most likely a maintenance bot ...

Yes, that was it: just a bot, trundling unhurriedly across the hab's surface. It was quite a big fucker, though, and definitely heading towards him. What should he do? There was nowhere to hide, and if he powered up the harness to use the extra strength to defend himself, that'd blow his cover for sure. And if he flew off, that'd expose him too. *Fuck.*

He settled for staying very still, while being prepared to jump instantly if he had to. The bot, looking like a rolling pile of animated junk, trundled closer, until it was near enough for him to see that it was a flat cylinder about a metre across, with tracks on the bottom, and a variety of arms, manipulators, sensors and antennae sprouting out of the top. It looked like a pretty lo-tech machine compared to the slick and seamless tech Zhian's people were so proud of.

It didn't look like the bot had noticed him yet. How smart were these things anyway? The worst-case scenario was that it was like an avatar, an extension of a male Sidhe mind, and if that was the case, he was well and truly fucked. But he knew from his experience with Khesh that even a male built into a massive structure could spread himself only so thin; maintenance bots would usually be well below the threshold of its consciousness. Unless something happened to alert it, of course …

The bot was only a couple of metres away now. It drew level with him … and carried on, oblivious. It was just heading for the airlock. He hadn't got in its way, so it'd ignored him. As the lock opened and the bot drove in, its tracks reorienting to tip it over the lip, Taro's suit spoke again, sounding almost impatient: 'Stage two should now have commenced.'

'All right, all right, gimme a moment here!' Taro touched the controls on the back of his gauntlet, hastily jury-rigged for a user without neurolink implants, and he felt the lifter-harness's embrace tighten. It constricted his body, but it also enhanced it, giving him strength far beyond that of an ordinary human. His feet dragged slightly as the harness compensated for the hab's lower grav by sticking him to the deck.

He edged up to the airlock. As he'd expected, there were no controls; only bots used it, and they just had to query the hab-mind when they wanted to come in. He'd just have to make his own entrance. He thumbed the controls to activate the harness's cutting torch and the visor darkened automatically until the blue-white tip became the only bright point in a world of deep shadows.

After a last check around to make sure he wasn't going to be disturbed, he began tracing a wide C-shape into the door; it reminded him of the cut fences round the edge of Khesh City: for non-Angels, they were the only way up from the Undertow into the wider world.

Once he'd cut his entrance, he had another look around, then used his harness-enhanced fist to punch the jaggedly cut section in: to a low-intel bot the damage would appear accidental.

He realised he'd forgotten something when his hand started tingling painfully – the moment he'd breached the door, a forceshield had sprung up to preserve the atmosphere inside. He told his suit to activate its own minimal shield – like the one he'd just put his hand through it was designed as an emergency response to a breach, but it would let him pass through the airlock's field without injury. Then he shook his hand to get some feeling back into it, held his breath and jumped into the hole. He felt the forceshield as a thin line of cold rushing up his body. The rebreather pack on his back caught the edge of the hole for a moment, and his heart tripped – then the pack slid free, the cold line was gone and he was in.

He activated his suit-lights, sending shadows chasing around the inside of the airlock. No doubt silent alarms would be going off, warning of the hull breach, and bots would be heading this way, quite possibly including the one that had passed him earlier. So, no time to hang around. He remembered to switch off the suit's forceshield – it was an emergency feature with limited duration, and he'd need it again later. He also turned off the lifter-harness; not knowing his own strength in here could be a bad thing.

He stopped just short of the inner airlock, hoping Zhian was right; she'd said most of the hab's inside doors worked on sensors – assuming the hull breach hadn't overridden them. After what felt like several seconds, the door opened, and he heaved a sigh of relief: no way did he have time to cut his way through every door he came to. He didn't fancy encountering any of the bots in this confined space, even though the circular ducting was wide enough to get past them; quite aside from all those scary bits sticking out of the fuckers, he couldn't afford to be spotted. He needed the hab-mind to stick with the most likely explanation for the air-lock problem: that it was an accident, not the result of some crazy human trying to break in.

His suit directed him down smaller, less well-used passages intended for the more delicate bots that looked after the hab's internal systems. He wondered if the big vacuum-hardened bot he'd seen outside was one of the original ones, from way back when the hab was actually a Sidhe ship ... but he decided it probably wasn't the *actual* machine, given this place had been here for thousands of years; most likely it was the same design though. The hab-mind probably didn't need the out-of-sight tech to look all prime and sexy: it just needed to work.

He kept to the centre of the tunnel, flying slow and careful, until he came to his goal. It wasn't much to look at; just a recess in the wall. He flipped up a panel to reveal a line of three holes, then unsealed the hardened cache on the back of his forearm and took out a dataspike. Of course, the unknown patron could've given the 'spike to a bot and reprogrammed it to come to this particular over-ride node – hell, a male Sidhe could've inserted the command-code straight into the Egg's systems without all this fucking about ... But that would be traceable; a lone human crawling through the ducts like a virus in the massive body of the hab wasn't something anyone would expect – or, hopefully, spot.

He had a bit of trouble getting the short, fat 'spike in, but on his third attempt he managed it. Now that the code it contained was loose in the hab's systems, the crap would be heading towards the whirly-thing, and nothing he could do would stop it.

CHAPTER THIRTY-FIVE

Jarek hesitated, his hand stretched out over the console. If this went wrong, then even if Taro got Nual out safely, they might not have a ship to come back to. Normally an incoming vessel would dock with the *Heart of Glass* using the main airlock, but the Alephan ship's airlock didn't mesh with his human-space tech, and the local humans didn't have an all-purpose docking-tube like those on the Consensus. Instead, he had to open the *Heart of Glass*'s massive cargo-hold doors, usually used for loading only when the ship was inside a station, and let the Alephans physically fly their shuttle inside. He'd have to repeat the manoeuvre twice more for other incomers, assuming all went to plan. The last time would be the killer.

His external vid-feed showed the approach of a plain, rectangular vessel with rounded edges, the smooth grey surface relieved only by a small cluster of instruments on the top at the front end.

A synthesised, asexual voice came over the com: 'Permission to board requested.'

Jarek checked, yet again, that the ship's forceshields were at max, then keyed the control to open the doors. 'Permission granted,' he said out loud.

The shuttle took its time. The moment it had finally settled on the floor of the hold Jarek closed the doors and switched to internal cameras.

Then he allowed himself to breathe again.

The Alephan shuttle sat quietly in his cargo-hold, looking for all the world like actual cargo.

Jarek sprang out of his couch and headed down off the bridge and through into the hold. As he approached the shuttle, a door opened in one end and a homely-looking woman in a one-piece emerged, followed by a youth about Taro's age.

'Welcome aboard,' said Jarek.

'Thank you,' said the woman. 'Query: are you monitoring the Consensus in order to respond when they ask about the delay?'

'Oh yes. Soon as they call, I'll tell them all about those minor technical difficulties we're having due to incompatible tech, and how I'll be running a few minutes behind schedule as a result.'

There were no technical difficulties, of course – not that the Consensus would be able to tell, now the doors were closed – but the manufactured delay would buy Taro the time he needed.

Jarek didn't particularly like having visitors on his ship, though he'd had to get used to it in recent times. These people were risking a lot to help him and his crew. 'Would you like a look around,' he asked, 'then maybe I can offer you some refreshments?'

'Thank you,' said the woman.

The boy asked, 'Query: do you have caf?'

'Caf? Yes, I do. Is that what you'd like?'

'Okay-aye. Statement: Taro has told me of it and I wish to try some.'

'Yeah, why not?' At least making a round of drinks might distract him, and stop him worrying about the part of the plan he had no control over.

Now the hack was in place Taro really was up against the clock. As soon as the light on the end of the dataspike flashed amber he pulled it out and stashed it carefully. Whilst he didn't much care if the males fought amongst themselves, he didn't want to get Zhian's people into trouble. They might have their own agenda, but they'd kept their word, and he wouldn't leave anything to implicate them, not even an empty dataspike.

As he followed the new instructions from his suit-com his thoughts returned to his final conversation with Vy. He'd still been digesting the revelation about males being able to download into beacons, and he'd asked, 'So if you do manage to imprint on the beacon, then you'll be linked back to Khesh – to the City – all the time, even if the beacon's at Serenein, right? That means you've got some sort of opening into shiftspace active, permanently like.' Jarek had described beacons as doors left ajar, to allow ships from the realspace universe to escape from shiftspace; he hadn't thought much about it at the time, but if beacons contained downloaded male consciousnesses— He looked down at Vy. 'Won't that fuck you up? It certainly don't do transit-kernels much good. I'd've thought being inside tech that's always open to shiftspace would leave you well screwed!'

Vy had smiled. 'Not *me*.' There was something knowing, something nasty, about that smile. 'The imprinted male in a beacon isn't the one holding open the door to the void. The males thought it was fitting when they came up with the idea – nicely symmetrical. They were completing the pattern, *and* paying them back.'

He giggled, and Taro'd had to resist the urge to shake him. Instead he'd said, 'Fuck's sake, Vy, tell me what you're on about!'

'Don't you see? It's the females – for millennia they'd stayed sane in shiftspace by travelling in unity, using us to blaze the trail. We came up with a way to turn the tables on the bitches – and into the bargain we gave humans a way of steering shiftships for themselves, without females.'

Taro felt sick. 'I really hope you ain't saying what I think you're saying.'

'Depends what you think I'm saying,' Vy countered, mimicking Taro's accent, 'don't it?'

'Shiftships have a male at their heart, so beacons—'

'—have an insane female mind bound into them, yep. It's ironic, really.'

'*Oh shitting fuck!*'

'Language, Taro. Back when everything was kicking off, the males caught themselves the mother of motherships. They killed some of the crew, and put the rest on ice. Later, they used those females to build the beacons.'

So when Zhian had told Taro Nual had been put in stasis and

stashed next to the beacon manufactory, he hadn't been surprised, though he didn't think it meant anything to Zhian. All that mattered to her was doing what her patron wanted, and luckily for him, that happened to be for Taro to get his lover out. But it made horrible sense: the males of Aleph had used up one of their captured females to make the new beacon. Some of them were bound to be furious at the waste; this way they got a replacement.

Now his suit was directing him back up to the surface of the Egg; progress through the ducts was too slow, and he needed to be in the right place at the right time. When he reached the exit airlock, he was relieved to find it was on a sensor; you only needed to ask the hab-mind for permission to enter, not to leave.

He'd turned off his suit-light but it turned out he wouldn't have needed it; he emerged into bright sunlight, reflecting off the pale surfaces all around. His visor instantly dimmed the blinding glare. He had five and a half minutes to reach his target. He knew roughly where to head even without the suit-com's help: towards the fat disc of the *Heart of Glass,* hovering just above the surface of the hab. Looked like Zhian's shuttle had come and gone safely; so as far as the males knew, Taro was now back on board Jarek's ship.

Zhian had assured him that the software package he'd just delivered would run interference on the local sensors and surface weaponry, but the tight timescale meant the patron who'd come up with the hack had had to concentrate on the main mission, so the countermeasures might take a while to cut in, and when they did, they might not be entirely reliable. Best walk, not fly, for now.

Fortunately there were access paths between the clumps of tech, wide enough for a human. Bizarrely, a lot of the clumps looked very similar, each some variation on box, dish and aerial ... of course, this was the hab's *coms equipment*. Why'd they need so much, though? As he edged round a massive dish Taro answered his own question: because each sept would have their own, transmitting their own code to whichever part of Aleph that sept was based in ... this huge fucker would be broadcasting to out-system, he'd bet.

There was a patch of open space beyond the dish and as he looked up, Taro saw movement on the far side of the *Heart of Glass*: a large orange cube, rising slowly from the surface of the hab towards the ship. The beacon.

Taro suppressed a shudder, then crossed the open area and headed into a gully. The top of the force-cage containing the beacon was drawing level with the bottom of Jarek's ship. He had to hurry. Movement caught his eye: a small gawky-looking bot was working at the base of one of the aerial arrays, its manipulator arms deep inside an open access panel. It blocked his current path, and he didn't have time for a diversion. Taro followed his instincts and kicked off, ready to leap over the bot.

His Angel implants included the ability to compensate for variable gravity. Taro hadn't realised that his suit, even without the lifter-harness active, was keeping him stuck to the hab's surface. The Angel mods didn't allow for that. He tore free, but his flight was erratic, and too low, and his trailing foot clipped the top of the bot.

As he landed, the bot's arms whipped back out of the access panel and it took off diagonally, heading straight for him.

Shit and blood, this little fucker could fly!

He turned, feeling time slow as his mods assessed the situation and worked out his best course of action. A single thrusting cut across the sensor apparatus would blind it, then a follow up to sever— No, if he used his blades he'd breach his v-suit. Even with the emergency forceshield, it was too risky.

His hesitation gave the bot time to close and Taro had to duck and roll as it sailed over his head. Something silver shot past his face, so close that if there'd been any atmosphere he'd have felt the near miss. He suspected Consensus maintenance bots weren't always this unfriendly; presumably they were on alert, thanks to the package he'd just delivered.

He came up into a crouch, and touched a couple of buttons on the back of his gauntlet. If his harness wanted him stuck here, who was he to argue with the tech?

The bot had turned and was coming back in for another pass.

Taro forced himself to ignore the subliminal instructions his Angel mods were giving him and straightened. The bot was coming straight for him. He overrode the urge to weave and slash, stood his ground, drew back both arms and bunched his fists. When the bot arrived, he jerked his head back to avoid its attack, at the same time punching out with all his – and the lifter-harness' – might.

The contact jarred his entire upper body, but the harness, holding fast to the deck below, soaked up the force of a blow that would otherwise have knocked him flying, not to mention probably breaking his arms.

The bot sailed back, moving absurdly fast in the airless, lo-grav environment. It hit the base of an aerial tower along the gully. The aerial wobbled for a moment, then settled at a slight angle. A broken manipulator arm floated slowly off into space.

Taro waited, in case the bot was still active, but all was still. His suit chose that moment to helpfully inform him that he was now running twenty-nine seconds behind schedule.

Fuck it. Well, they *definitely* knew he was here now. He disengaged the harness and kicked off again, more carefully this time. He began to fly low and fast, weaving between obstacles, scanning for bots heading his way or weapons drawing a bead on him. His suit squawked, trying to keep him on course now he was no longer at ground level. Ahead he could see Jarek's ship beginning to move off slowly; he hoped it was moving slowly enough.

The airlock opened while he was still a dozen metres away. All pretence at stealth gone, he arrowed in, reaching the 'lock just as the comabox began to float sedately out. He wrapped his arms around it, wondering for a moment if he should be able to sense Nual inside – but no, she'd still be unconscious.

The suit increased his strength and let him offset the comabox's momentum, but it didn't extend his reach. Not even his long arms would fit around the box and he swiftly realised he needed to push it, not grasp. As he slid down to the end, he said, 'Suit, can you give me directions to the ship I'm looking at right now, and can you keep doing it even when I can't see it?'

'Conditional affirmative: using inertial guidance I can direct you to a rendezvous; however due to the difficulty of precise vector matching and occlusion of the target by your burden there will be a significant margin of error, even assuming the ship does not significantly change its course or speed.'

'How significant a margin of error're we talking about?'

'Five to ten per cent.'

That didn't sound like too much. 'Fine. Do it.' He got himself under the comabox and began to push it up and away into space, towards the *Heart of Glass*. He used everything his mods and the suit could give him to go as fast as he could. It was time to find out if the virus he'd just planted really had taken out the hab's guns.

CHAPTER THIRTY-SIX

'What precisely were you *expecting* me to do about it?' asked Urien. 'Invite him to take tea with me and share his concerns?'

They were alone; Damaru had gone out after suffering Kerin to paint his forehead with the mark of a skyfool in order that he could walk unmolested wherever he wished. Kerin was glad he was not here to witness this argument. 'Of course not!' she said, 'but I thought you would just have him watched, and perhaps get one of your people to try and draw him out later.'

'And that is *precisely* what I did: when you told me about Captain Siarl this morning, I had someone observe his movements for the rest of the day. As soon as he got off duty he went to an unoccupied house in the lower city. He obviously expected someone to be there, for he knocked and then waited for some time. My informant tells me he called out to someone within at one point, but my man was not close enough to hear what he said. No one answered, and eventually Captain Siarl left. Such activity is suspicious in itself, but it also transpires that he comes from the same town as the girl who unexpectedly turned up for judgment earlier this week.'

'Do you think she could be at that house?'

'It is entirely possible, and when I have a moment, I will send someone to find out. I decided that the combination of my investigations into Captain Siarl, and your own report of his actions in the market-place and of his attitude last night – not to mention the fact that we have now aroused his suspicions – meant we had no choice but to detain him. Had we left him at liberty, he would have warned his associates.'

269

'If he has any! And even if you are right, and we need to stop Captain Siarl spreading dissent and alerting any allies he *might* have, would it not be sufficient merely to put him in prison?'

'There is no other way, Kerin. Truly, I wish there were. I did try questioning him when I initially had him arrested, but he professes to know nothing. I know he lied when he told me that, but being able to sense a lie is not the same as being able to sniff out the full truth, and we need to know the truth, for if there is organised opposition, we *must* counteract it before the situation gets out of hand. If we do not nip dissent in the bud now, then I fear that the day when we will not need such measures may never come. So, if you will excuse me—'

'You are going there now? To the dungeons?'

'That is so. I cannot trust anyone else to hear Siarl's confession—'

'*Confession!*'

'It is a term used with some irony, but it is nonetheless accurate.'

Kerin suddenly realised that true evil was not something huge and imposing, something that could be fought like a mythical beast; it was small and insidious, and it came in many guises. She wondered how many people who had been accused of doing evil would ever have chosen that label for themselves. Perhaps even the Sidhe believed they did right.

'Wait,' she said, suddenly resolved, 'I will come with you. I wish to witness this man's torture.'

'Kerin, truly, I do not think that would be a good idea.'

'I put us on this path. I must know what it truly means to commit to it.' She barked a short, bitter laugh. 'Besides, as you so like to remind me, fear is a vital tool in controlling people; if this hapless monitor is confronted with someone he believes to be his goddess, might he not confess more freely, and quickly?'

'Perhaps,' Urien conceded. 'If I did not know better I would say you also wished to save this man, who may be a traitor, from undue pain.' Amazement warred with dark amusement in his voice.

'Perhaps I do. I met him, Urien; my words condemned him, and I must face up to the price we are paying to bring our people into the light. If I cannot accept the consequences of our – of *my* – actions, or worse, if I pretend there are no consequences, then I have no right to impose my wishes on people. Besides, I know you think me soft. This will harden me. Urien, you cannot dissuade me.'

The Escori of Frythil led the way through rarely used corridors that wound ever downwards. Those few people they met, priests and servants alike, reacted with the usual awe. As they passed near the acolytes' hall, the distant singing of young voices, sweet and pure, brought unasked-for tears to Kerin's eyes; she blinked them back.

The deeper they went, the fewer light-globes there were. They reached the top of a rough staircase cut into the stone; the light from below had the dim and inconstant quality of lamplight. Kerin shivered and thought of the canto of the Traditions that described the Abyss as a bottomless pit of undying flame. They descended carefully to a passage lit by guttering oil lamps hanging from the ceiling. The passage was lined with heavy wooden doors: some were barred shut, some opened into narrow cells. The air was dank, and stank of unwashed bodies, excrement and fear. The floor was slick. Kerin heard groans, and in one case muffled sobbing, coming from behind the closed doors.

The passage turned and divided. Urien led her to the right, towards an arch, through which was a larger room. He bade her wait just up the corridor. 'Your presence will be more effective if used as a last resort,' he whispered.

'Do not think to keep me out now! I will see what havoc I have caused,' she hissed.

'I do not doubt it, but I would appreciate being permitted to conduct this inquiry in my own way.'

She gave in, muttering, 'As you wish.'

Urien carried on up the corridor, and turned through the archway. His voice carried clearly back to Kerin. 'So, Captain Siarl, now that you have had both opportunity and incentive to rethink your answers, I will ask you again: are you part of any organised movement to oppose the current order?'

For a moment there was no sound. Then a man's ragged voice ground out a single word: 'No.'

'Captain Siarl, as with the last time I asked you that, your answer almost has the ring of truth.' Urien sounded genuinely regretful at having to push for answers. 'But "almost" is not enough. Let us move on to the second question, then: do you know of any such movement?'

Another pause, and the same answer, this time barked out: 'No!'

'Please, Captain Siarl, understand this: I *will* have the truth. Once I have it, no further injuries will be visited on you, and your wounds will be treated. You may even hope to see your family again one day. *But only if you share everything you know.*'

'Will not ... betray ...'

The strain in the man's voice chilled Kerin's soul. She realised she had been breathing shallowly through her mouth, to guard against the stench of men brought low; it was making her light-headed, and now she made herself breathe more deeply through her nose, despite the smell.

'Betray who, Captain Siarl?' Urien's voice was all reason and sympathy.

Siarl muttered something.

'I did not quite hear that.' Now Urien sounded as stern as a schoolmaster.

More muttering.

'Your friend?' said Urien, 'and who would that be?'

Silence, save for harsh breathing. 'As I have explained before,' said Urien slowly, 'to refuse to answer a question is to invite pain.'

Kerin heard a sharp click, and then an animal scream. She flinched, her heart beating faster in response.

'Not – betray – a friend, even – even friend who betrays ...' The monitor's response was breathless, as though every word escaped against his will.

Kerin waited, breathless herself, but he did not finish his sentence.

Urien said, 'We need a name, *chilwar*; that may be enough to end this, you know. Just a name.'

'Have – no – name ...' The man sounded resigned to his fate.

'Perhaps we will come back to that later. Let me ask you something less difficult. Why did you visit the lower city earlier this evening?'

'What ... visit?'

'Please, Captain, we are past the time for games. I know you did, for you were seen. What I wish to know is *why*.'

'Will – say – nothing – more – on that.' Though every word was ground out, Kerin could hear the resolve in the captain's voice.

'I think that would be a mistake.'

More silence. Kerin braced herself – but apparently that had not been considered an unanswered question, to be punished with pain, for Urien continued, 'What will you tell us, then? I leave the next topic up to you.'

'Nothing ... nothing at all ...' This time the voice had a sing-song quality to it.

Urien came out into the corridor a few moments later. His face was pale and sweat-sheened, almost as though he were the one being tortured. He walked up to Kerin, and muttered, 'I believe this man will die before he tells me anything of use.'

'Do you want me to come in?' Despite her earlier brave words, as she listened to the proceedings, Kerin had come to hope it would not be necessary to see the full truth for herself.

'I fear we are out of other options. However, it is your choice ...'

'I will come in. I said I would, and I will.'

Urien nodded gravely. 'I will call you, then,' he said, and went back into the room. Kerin heard him say, 'Captain Siarl? Can you hear me? If you will not speak to me, perhaps there is one whom you will trust with the truth.' More loudly, he added, 'Divinity, would it please you to enter now?'

Kerin took a deep breath of the foetid air and walked slowly through the archway.

Her first impression was how cluttered the room was. Devices of unknown function lined the walls and hung from the ceiling. In the centre of the room stood a large wooden frame, like a bed with no mattress. On one side of the frame was a great wheel and some smaller cogs, to turn the frame to any angle. A naked man was strapped to the frame, his hands pinioned above his head. His feet were contained in a wooden box with a handle on the side. The frame was currently inclined at a shallow angle facing the door. Urien, standing at its foot, turned to Kerin as she entered and swept back in a bow, making the circle as he straightened.

The third man in the room also made a deep obeisance. He was a rangy, stolid-faced youth whose large ears protruded from long, straggly hair. He stared at her with an expression of horrified awe, grunting softly as his hand repeatedly circled his breast. Urien had told her that the inquirers, themselves prisoners of suitable temperament whose own death sentences had been commuted, had their tongues removed when they were put to work in the dungeons.

Kerin made herself approach the bound figure. *Siarl, his name is Siarl*, she reminded herself. At first she could not focus beyond the stained wooden box encasing his feet. The stains were the same colour as those in the indentation in the stone floor below the frame. She looked up abruptly. One of Siarl's arms was marked with long, dark streaks and a lacework of thinner trickles ran down into his armpit. The other arm was unmarked. There were a dozen or so raw spots on his chest that looked like burns. When she saw what had been done to his groin it took all her willpower not to look away.

Urien remained half-turned to her, to maintain the illusion of respect while he addressed the prisoner. 'Captain, you are honoured. The Beloved Daughter of Heaven has chosen to hear your confession in person.'

Siarl stared at her: one of his eyes was bloodshot and puffy; the other looked unnaturally wide and bright in contrast. She saw the agony in his face, and the effort of not giving voice to his pain.

'Div— Divinity!' His right hand twitched in its manacle. Despite everything, he was trying to make the circle. 'Divinity, I – I tried to be worthy! Of you. Of the … Mothers. My faith is strong – beyond – all this.'

'Then speak your confession, *chilwar*,' said Urien gently.

'Unburden your soul,' Kerin said, as imperiously as she could manage, grateful for the hidden technology in her headdress that smoothed her words, even, if she wished, amplified them. The Sidhe had been careful to ensure that the Cariad's voice remained constant throughout the ages.

Siarl stared at her. His gaze made her feel naked, despite her veil. He continued to stare, his damaged eye watering copiously. Finally, his mouth twitched. He made a strange noise, deep in his throat. For a moment Kerin could not place it. Then he did it again, and this time she realised: he was laughing. The laughter had a raw edge to it, and it ended in a word, growled out long and slow: 'Impostor.'

Kerin had no doubt he meant her. Siarl had drawn breath again, and the laughter restarted, but quickly turned to sobbing.

She looked at Urien, who was watching Siarl with an expression on his face Kerin initially took for distaste, until she saw it was more like disgust, though not, she suspected, for the poor man disintegrating before them.

Captain Siarl began to mutter, and Urien leaned closer. Despite herself, Kerin tried to hear what he was saying. He was praying to Turiach, beseeching the Mother of Mercy to give him succour in his time of need; it was a prayer she knew well, and to hear it in these circumstances made her feel sick.

Suddenly Siarl said, quite clearly, '—should never have gone there—'

She wondered if Urien would try and follow up the unexpectedly coherent phrase, but he said nothing; looking back at Siarl's rolling eyes and twitching mouth, Kerin suspected they would get very little sense from him now.

Siarl continued, his chest heaving and his voice louder, as though fired by some hidden reservoir of manic strength, 'Had to try and warn her … not innocent, but better she goes, just goes … He damns himself, he always has ... knew as soon I saw her, it was those eyes, Aelwen's eyes ...'

Kerin turned her head a fraction to look at Urien; if the name Aelwen meant anything to him he gave no sign of it. She smelled urine, and saw the fresh tears on Siarl's cheeks. Everything was running from him: liquid, words, sanity ...

'—would not listen ... he never would, when it was about her ... says it is not true, but anyone can see ... he can be a foolish, stubborn man, always was, always ... Olwenna will scold me for being so late!' This last was delivered loudly, and in a tone of great affront.

'Olwenna. Your wife,' Urien said to the raving man, answering Kerin's unspoken question; she was, after all, supposed to be all-knowing.

Kerin could bear it no more. She turned and stumbled round the corner, almost tripping over her heels, and into the first empty cell she found. There she ripped off her headdress and bent over, bracing herself against the wall with her other hand as hot vomit rushed up her throat. She kept retching until her guts were aching, weeping so hard she could not see straight. Her legs tried to give out, but some stupid, practical impulse would not let her fall; *what if the Cariad were seen abroad with her clothes covered in filth and puke?* Instead she put both hands against the wall and focused on the feel of the rough stone digging into her palms. She thought she could still hear Siarl's unhinged ranting.

By the time she had regained control of herself, there was only silence.

CHAPTER THIRTY-SEVEN

'I've got you on sensors,' said Jarek. 'Well, when I say you …'

'Just the box – yeah, I know. I'm right behind it, pushing. Best way to move it.' Taro sounded out of breath.

'I don't want to worry you, but we're drawing a lot of attention.' The coms board was a solid block of colour, and he was the lucky recipient of several active sensor sweeps – though no weapons were locked on them yet – at least, none the *Heart of Glass*'s comp recognised.

'No shit. You think they know something's up?'

'Reckon they do.' He checked the readouts again. 'Uh, your heading's off.'

'I know. Fucking thing's a pig to drive. Hang on …'

'Yeah, that's better. Right, I'll bring the ship about so you're lined up with the cargo-hold.'

Once he'd repositioned the *Heart of Glass*, Jarek opened the com again. 'You're on course for intercept in fifty-five seconds. Soon as you're a bit closer I'll open the doors. You ready?'

'As I'll ever be. How hard … can it be?'

'That's the spirit. Just like spitting into a moving bucket.'

'Yeah, and I'm the spit.'

'At this speed it's— *Shit!*'

'What is it?'

'I think they're firing up a mass-driver.'

'And that's bad, is it?'

'Potentially – but we stick with the plan, all right?'

'Sure. Am I still heading for the hold doors?'

'You're heading for the doors. More or less.'

'In that case don't change course and don't speed up.'

'You've got it.'

'Here we go ...'

Taro'd've thought the lack of grav would've made it easier to move the comabox, but no such luck. He only had to give it a gentle shove and it was off like greased shit. Any time his aim wasn't spot-on, he ended up having to re-adjust its course immediately. It was like juggling jelly.

He was going at a fair old lick, but as the *Heart of Glass* loomed larger he realised this wasn't necessarily a good thing: quite aside from the comabox being harder to steer the faster it went, Nual, inside the box, wasn't in for a soft landing when they got there. Given it was too big to hold, the only way to slow the comabox down was to get in front of it and use his body as a brake, but when he flew round and tried that, the bastard thing just pushed him back. For a moment he panicked, until he worked out that he needed to actively fly, opposing the box's momentum with the power from his implants.

That worked. The only problem now was that he was facing the wrong way.

'Taro! Quick! – you need to go left about twenty degrees.'

'Whose fucking left, Jarek?' Taro twisted his head to look behind at the *Heart of Glass*, oriented himself, and shimmied to his right. Just in time, he flew up and away from the box, which sailed neatly in through the open doors, missing the leftmost one by a handbreadth. Taro activated his suit's forceshield and flew in after it.

The forceshield over the cargo-doors was a lot stronger than the one on the Consensus airlock; going through it was like leaping through a curtain of cold fire.

He curled, tucking in his head whilst telling his implants to bring him to a relative stop.

It worked, sort of: he hit the far wall, rolled up it, then hung there, spread-eagled upside down, getting his breath back. The landing might have gone better if he'd remembered to turn the lifter-harness off first. Better late then never. He touched the controls and felt its embrace loosen.

He grunted and slid down the wall, re-orienting to come up standing on shaking legs. The comabox had gouged the deck plating, then bounced off the wall, leaving a mark on the bulkhead and a dink in the corner of the box, to finally come to rest at an angle against the curving wall.

'Fuck', he muttered, and reached out with his mind. The box would've insulated Nual from vacuum and forceshields, but it didn't have any inertial dampening.

Nual's presence flickered at the edge of consciousness: she was still out of it. She might be injured, but just knowing she was in there, and alive, was a massive relief.

He crouched down to check the readouts on the box. The hacked bots who'd been reprogrammed to move it from storage to the airlock had also been told to start the wake-up cycle.

'Is she all right?'

Jarek's voice in his ear broke the faint contact with Nual. 'Think so. I'm just checking.'

'Any idea how long before she'll be in a state to make the shift?'

'Dunno. Wait a sec.' He had another look at the control-panel. 'This readout's saying, um, twelve minutes before she's fully conscious.'

'And she'll need a few minutes to get herself together after that. Shit. That's not ideal.'

''cos of the mass-driver, you mean?'

'Amongst other things. They tried to lob a whole bunch of junk at us with the 'driver just after you came aboard, and if we were still on the old vector it'd be hitting us about now. Fortunately we're not. The bastards don't realise how fast this ship can go when I really ramp her up.'

Taro glanced at the cargo-hold doors, now closed again. 'So there's nothing to worry about, right?' Of course, if the Consensus *did* score a direct hit on the *Heart of Glass*, Taro wouldn't know anything about it until it was too late.

'Your faith is touching – and not misplaced, fortunately. Looks like that glitch you set off is working; none of the weapons are firing on us. Presumably the mass-driver's intended to accelerate cargo, so it's on a different system. I think they loaded it up with whatever was to hand and sent it after us more as a *fuck-you* gesture than because it's an effective weapon.'

'Sounds like you've got things under control.' Taro hoped he had. There was something he needed to do down here before anything else intervened. He had a promise to keep.

Jarek snorted. 'Did I mention the ships on intercept courses? Pretty much every vessel within half a light-second is heading this way, Taro – and there's no way of knowing if any of them are on a suicide-trip.'

'But we're accelerating up from the main disc, ain't we?'

'Up, up and away. As soon as you and Nual are ready, we'll shift. Meanwhile, I could use you up here monitoring sensors and getting the comp on the case if we need to take evasive manoeuvres. I need to prep the ship for transit.'

'Uh, I'm sure you can manage without me—'

'Look, Taro, I know you're worried about Nual, but I could really use you on the bridge right now. You can nip back down in ten minutes and check on her—'

'No! I mean, I have to stay here.'

'Don't piss me about, Taro! We're not out of the woods yet.'

'I'm sorry, I'll come up as soon as I can, really I will.' He cut the connection and blocked incoming com. Jarek might not be happy but Taro's mission wasn't over yet.

While they'd been talking he'd been checking out the cargo-hold. Jarek had moved the beacon back from the doors once the Consensus' bots had got it aboard and passed over the controller for the force-cage.

The v-suit that'd been such a comfort in space felt stifling now he was on the ship. He double-checked the atmosphere, then ran a thumb along the neck seam and peeled back the hood. He took a big gulp of ship's air and shivered; when he breathed out his breath steamed. The ship's forceshield might have kept the atmosphere stable, but the ship'd lost heat while the doors were open.

He walked slowly around the cargo-hold. Despite the need to hurry, he wasn't eager to get close to the beacon. That might be down to more than an over-active imagination; beacons were shit-powerful artefacts and even enclosed in a force-cage, some of that power could leak out. Still, this one wasn't fully active yet – Vy'd said beacons didn't come online until they'd taken their first trip through shiftspace. After that, getting too close to one would prob-ably be fatal – and it would be too late to carry out Vy's last wish. Right now the consciousness-fragment of whichever male had im-printed on the beacon was dormant; this was the only time it could be overwritten.

Looking at the force-cage made Taro's eyes water – forceshields hurt the eyes; he knew that 'cos Khesh City was enclosed in one – though in this case the effect might be partly down to the beacon itself, a perfect sphere floating in the centre of the glowing orange cube. The swirling, multi-coloured surface made him feel sick whilst at the same time beguiling him; *keep looking*, it seemed to be saying silently, *keep looking and get sucked in* ...

Taro tore his gaze away; blobby after-images danced across his vision. He checked the floor for the cage controller, but there was no sign of it; Jarek must've taken it up to the bridge once he'd stowed the beacon. Taro wasn't sure how much use it would be anyway.

Did he really have to do this? If the Minister asked him, he could always say he tried – if he just flushed the chip, no one would know any better.

But he'd know, and Nual too, of course; he didn't keep secrets from her. She wouldn't condemn him – she'd understand. That would make it even worse.

He'd come too far not to finish this.

Vy had said an inert beacon couldn't harm him, provided he didn't actually touch it, but a forceshield strong enough to contain a beacon was another matter. Good job he had his own forceshield,

281

though it was a pretty fucking feeble one in comparison. It'd just have to be strong enough—

He rolled the hood back up, guiding the smart-fabric over his head. The visor hardened as it slid down over his face. He opened his cache, shaking his arm until the empty dataspike fell onto the floor, then shaking it some more until the fingernail-sized gold chip dropped out. He caught it, wrapping his hand protectively around the tiny object, and made himself walk towards the force-cage. He refused to think about what he was about to do, but found himself wondering about the female component in the beacon: was it conscious? If it was anything like the transit-kernels, whose pain Taro could feel first-hand when he and Nual were together in the shift, then it was insane, beyond sense or salvation.

He stopped when he saw the bottom of the force-cage, his guts loosening and his heart thudding. Even through the v-suit, the power leaking from the shield was tickling the nape of his neck and making his teeth ache. He focused on his hands. *Do it quick and smooth, no hesitation.*

He turned on the suit's shield and thrust his hand through the force-cage.

He heard himself scream, but before he could register the pain he opened his hand, exposing the chip.

Afterwards, he decided he must've imagined the tickling sensation across his hand – after all, he was wearing a v-suit and had hardened palms. Vy had said something about 'strange attractors', laughing when he mentioned the phrase, like it was a joke. It was no joke now; Taro could sense it for himself; he could sense the chip being drawn into the beacon.

Something threw him back, hard.

His mouth was open and his head hurt. His hand hurt too. His head and hand hurt because … because …

<Taro?>

<Nual! Are you all right?> He made himself close his mouth and open his eyes. No time to rest. He was too uncomfortable to sleep

anyway, what with the headache and the pain in his hand, and the unpleasant squishy warmth lower down.

Nual was bending over him. He managed a smile for her.

She projected, <*I'll be fine in a while. What about you? What did you just do?*>

Mind-speech didn't allow for evasion. Nual picked up the edge of his returning memories and dived straight in. Taro rode the sudden, disorientating rush as she absorbed a brief summary of his insane mission to the Consensus and his encounter with the beacon. Then the cargo-hold, and the pain, came back. He realised what the unpleasant sensation around his groin was: he must've crapped himself when the beacon knocked him out. Well, nothing he could do about it now. Good job he was still wearing the v-suit.

Nual's voice was gentle in his head. <*We need to shift, don't we?*>

<*We need to shift. If you can.*>

<*I can. Can you?*>

<*I'll manage.*>

<*Does that suit have a com?*>

<*Yeah, why? Oh I see.*>

<*Yes, you had better com Jarek to tell him we're ready.*>

Taro didn't feel ready, and Nual didn't look it, but they didn't have much choice.

Before he made the call, Nual helped him stand; she was using a mixture of Angel implants and Sidhe control to keep going. He used his own flight ability to take some of the strain as soon as he was upright. He avoided using the hand he'd put through the forceshield, though it didn't hurt so much now. That was probably down to her, too, blocking the pain. All that mattered right now was that they manage to initiate transit before the Alephans took them out. Once they were in the shift their messed-up bodies wouldn't matter; when he made a transit in unity with Nual, Taro lost all awareness of the physical world.

There would be hell to pay later, of course; there always was, one way or another.

When the suit put him through, Jarek responded at once, 'I

don't know what the fuck you've been playing at down there but we need to go, now!'

'I know, I'm sorry; I'll explain later. Nual's ready and so'm I. Just start the countdown: we're on our way.'

CHAPTER THIRTY-EIGHT

Jarek addressed the floor in a slurred whisper: 'We really mus' stop meetin' like this.' At least he hadn't thrown up this time, though he thought he recalled the memorable sensation of all his internal organs making a bid for freedom from the nearest available orifice, shortly before his consciousness gave up trying to make sense of the senseless. He performed the usual post-shiftspace inventory of body-parts – everything was still more or less in working order – then made the long climb back up to vertical.

He'd been worried this transit would be even worse than the journey out to Aleph – after all, no one had ever made a transit direct from Aleph to Serenein. It had been bad, but it could have been worse. Either that or he'd managed to pass out before experiencing the worst bits.

He got to work restarting the ship's systems. Unlike normal transits, he didn't worry too much about coms; it wasn't as though anyone would be contacting them out here. Once he was confident the essential systems – life-support and the in-system drive – were green and everything else was on its way up, he eased himself out of his seat and made his way off the bridge.

Taro and Nual lay sprawled against the drive column. They were both unconscious. 'Oh shit,' muttered Jarek. He ducked round the ladder and bent down to make sure they weren't actually dead.

Taro was still wearing the hi-tech Alephan v-suit and lifter-harness, so he checked Nual out first. Yep, still breathing. She had a raw patch on the back of one hand and a bruise coming out on her cheek; neither looked serious.

He turned his attention to Taro. It took him a moment to work out how to unseal the suit – thank Christos the boy hadn't thrown up while they'd been in shiftspace. When he did manage to peel the helmet back he was greeted with a deeply unpleasant smell and decided it was probably best to leave Taro in the suit until he was capable of taking a shower.

Neither of them were showing any signs of coming round, so Jarek fetched the portable diagnostic unit from the medbay to find out how serious their injuries were. The results of the scan were reassuring: they were exhausted and physically stressed, but not in any immediate danger and neither had any significant injuries— No, scratch that. He ran the scanner over Taro again. Something had happened to his right hand; from the readouts it looked a bit like vacuum-burn. He couldn't see any rips in the suit; perhaps it was able to reseal itself? But the diagnostic wasn't quite what he'd expect to see for flesh exposed to space; it was more like neural damage. Not that he could do much about it without removing the suit, and that meant removing the lifter-harness first, a task that was beyond him right now. He decided Taro's hand wasn't going to get any worse if it went untreated for a few hours.

He added a dose of analgesic to the mix the scanner recommended, then administered shots to the pair of them. He wasn't up to moving them, so he put them in a position where they wouldn't choke if they threw up when they came around, then tucked a thermal blanket around them.

After that, he crawled off to get some rest.

Jarek slept for twelve hours straight, and woke to find Nual already up and about. Taro was semi-conscious, but she'd managed to get him out of the lifter-harness and onto the medbay couch, and had peeled his suit down far enough to uncover his hand. Jarek shuddered: the flesh looked like it had been boiled. His palm, hardened by the Angel mods, was untouched, and the edge of the damaged area was oddly precise, a perfect line around his wrist, stopping just short of the bloodless slash of his blade-sheath.

'Good to see you,' said Jarek to Nual. She still looked pretty rough. 'Are you well enough to sort Taro out by yourself?'

'I am. I was about to put a triage glove over his hand. The medbay also recommends we keep him sedated for the next few hours.'

'Good idea. Don't suppose you know how he came by that injury?'

'Actually I do, although I don't know why.' She didn't sound eager to share.

'I need to get back up to the bridge. Come and update me when you're done here.'

The *Heart of Glass* had re-entered realspace at the same relative location as the first time he'd come here, when he'd been slipstreaming the *Setting Sun*. That put them well out of range of the single inhabited world's defences, and the course Jarek had programmed before he'd slept took them even further away, to the Trojan point in the planet's orbit: beacons usually trailed the world they served at safe distance. He made some final course adjustments and ran a quick systems check. He should have time for a caf before they reached their destination.

A familiar smell greeted him as he came down the ladder. 'I was going to say you read my mind,' he said to Nual as he walked over to the section of the rec-room given over to the galley, 'But in your case ...'

She smiled at him. 'No arcane powers are required to work out when you need a caf, Jarek.'

As they sat at the table sipping their drinks, Jarek noticed the dressing on Nual's hand. 'That was where you wore your com wasn't it?'

'Yes. The males destroyed it so it couldn't be used to trace me. And I imagine they put me in stasis to stop me contacting Taro – and to keep me out of the way until they needed me.'

'Did Taro have time to fill you in on what they were up to?'

'From what I've worked out, they were either going to dissect my brain to find out what makes me tick, or else keep me on ice for use in a beacon.'

'In a *beacon*? How——?'

'That's how beacons are made, apparently: they are some sort of

287

unholy combination of male and female Sidhe consciousnesses.'

'My God – and there're nearly a thousand beacons in human-space. *Fuck*.'

'Quite. We went into this knowing we were walking a fine line with the Aleph males; if I'd known about my potential use as a beacon component I'd *never* have gone there!'

'No shit! But if they wanted you, why didn't they kidnap you while we were on the hab? Unless they were initially going to co-operate, then something changed their mind ...'

Nual frowned at her drink. 'I think you're right, and the logical conclusion is that it was something I did or said – most likely, it was because I admitted to having prescient abilities.'

'I wonder why they gave me the beacon and let me fly off after they took you. Without you, I was stuck at Aleph.'

'They were following the letter of the law – or rather, they were following a ruling by the Consensus: the one unifying factor that stops Aleph falling apart is the objectivity and ubiquity of the Consensus. Once the males agree on something in Consensus, that decision cannot be gainsaid unless they have reached a new decision – also in Consensus – that overturns it. It was on record that you were to get your beacon, and Taro was to be returned to you. They did that. They subsequently decided that I was to be de-tained, but that didn't change the earlier ruling. Having said that, I suspect your fate was being debated in the Consensus even as you and Taro were getting me out. They wouldn't have let you remain at large for long.'

'I'll bet. I think it's safe to say I won't be going back to Aleph in a hurry.'

'Me neither.' She gave a bitter laugh. 'Hindsight is a lot more reliable than foresight.'

Jarek smiled. 'Ah, you mean that old chestnut about seers not seeing something momentous coming?'

'That would be the one. I imagine it's as old as Sidhe abilities, perhaps older.'

Nual was troubled, he could tell. 'Is there something else you want to tell me?' he asked gently.

She pulled a face, the one she made when she was annoyed at herself. 'I had another flash, as I was getting Taro out of his suit.'

'I'm guessing it was as vague and unhelpful as they usually are?'

'You guess correctly: it was something to do with his part in things – something he's done, or is about to do—' She shook her head. 'Pah! Anyone who thinks precognition is a gift should try living with it. It's a wretched curse.'

Jarek had no answer for that, so he took a sip of his caf.

Nual did the same, then said, 'You wanted to know how Taro was hurt?'

'Yeah. It's a weird injury.'

'I believe it may have come from putting his hand through a powerful forceshield.'

'Why the hell would he do something like that?'

'I think he tried to touch the beacon.'

'He tried to *what*? Are you sure?'

'Not completely. His mind was somewhat garbled.'

'Then we'll have to ask him when he wakes up.' Jarek checked his com. 'We're almost in position. I should get back to the bridge.'

'Can I be of any use?'

'No, just rest up, and keep an eye on Taro. And don't go anywhere near the cargo-hold, obviously.'

While the *Heart of Glass* decelerated, Jarek took a few minutes to review the footage from the cargo-hold. Looked like Nual was right: Taro had fiddled with his suit, then walked up and put his hand through the force-cage. He'd been thrown back against the bulkhead immediately afterwards.

Jarek switched the camera to real-time feed. The beacon looked brighter than before its passage through shiftspace, but otherwise apparently unchanged. He located the control-box for the force-cage; the Alephans had warned him that once the beacon had been activated by passing through shiftspace he'd have to control the cage from up here. They had also assured him that the remote would work fine up to several hundred klicks, but Jarek wasn't inclined to trust them. He was relieved when his attempt to activate the force-cage resulted in it rising gently off the floor of the cargo-hold. 'Let's get you off my ship, you scary little bastard,' he muttered.

He made a few practice moves, getting used to driving the cage with only the on-screen view for feedback. Then he set the ship's forceshield to full and opened the doors.

He took his time getting the cage out of his hold; a mistake now might still be fatal, and after all they'd been through to get the damn beacon, that would really piss him off.

Finally, when the external camera showed the glowing cube at rest outside the ship and the cargo-hold doors were safely closed, he breathed freely.

He moved the ship off slowly, keeping an eye on the beacon. He'd reached five hundred klicks when the remote beeped to warn him it was about to lose signal. Jarek powered down the cage, then accelerated away.

So: beacon installed. He only hoped he'd done the right thing. The final stage was to link the beacon into the beevee network; until then, it remained invisible to the rest of the universe. Even as he thought that, the incoming com light blinked. *What the fuck?* He reached out to accept the call, only to have the light go out. What was that about? He interrogated the log and discovered that the incoming message had gone straight to Taro's com. He checked the message-tag: there wasn't one. That was *impossible* – then again, with the beacon outside the beevee network, getting any sort of message other than a direct call from the planet should be impossible. And this message had definitely come from out of system.

He needed to talk to Taro.

When he got down to the medbay he found Nual in the process of waking the boy up. He strode over and said, 'Can you hear me, Taro?'

Taro's eyes opened to slits, and he looked at Jarek with a mixture of confusion and alarm.

Nual responded, 'He's still a bit groggy.' *<Also, he is worried that he has made you angry,>* she added silently. *<Please do not cause him undue distress.>*

Jarek nodded to show he understood, then said out loud, 'Everything's fine, Taro. I just need to look at your com.' He lifted the boy's left wrist and accepted the pending call.

It was a succinct text message, just two words: *Thank you.*

'Now I'm really confused,' Jarek muttered.

He looked at Nual. She bent over Taro, then pressed a hand to the side of his face. After a few seconds he started and opened his eyes fully. Nual eased him up into a sitting position, half supporting him. 'Was that a message?' he asked shakily.

'Yes. Someone wants to thank you. Any idea who, or for what?'

Taro's face broke into a weary grin. 'It's Vy.'

'Vy? You said he was dead!'

'He is, sorta,' Taro said, 'but he's also in the beacon. And the beacon ... that's linked to Khesh.'

'You're saying that's who's thanking you? *Khesh?*'

'Yeah.'

'I think it's time you explained exactly what you did, Taro,' Jarek said, trying to keep his voice calm.

They listened silently to Taro's story.

Jarek couldn't be angry at the boy – he'd done a brave and honourable thing, and it wasn't his fault he hadn't had the chance to tell anyone what he was planning. If he had, they'd have had to agree with him.

When Taro finished he asked, 'So now this beacon has a one-to-one link with Khesh, is that right?'

'I think so.'

'And this is something independent of the beevee network, isn't it?'

'Yeah, reckon so.'

'And if you hadn't succeeded, the one-to-one link would be to whichever Aleph male imprinted on it?'

'Yeah, it would – it could still have been, but Vy must have been stronger, and he came out on top.'

'I'm not sure what the Aleph males thought they'd gain by having one of their own linked to the beacon – unless they've got shift-ships we don't know about and they wanted a route to Serenein.'

'It might have been nothing more than a desire to thwart Khesh,' suggested Nual.

'Those fuckers do like their pissing contests, don't they?' said Taro.

'Yeah, but what matters is that they failed. We've got our beacon. Now we need to head in to Serenein and share the good news.'

CHAPTER THIRTY-NINE

Although Kerin was desperate to leave the dungeon, she was faced once more with the banality of evil: this was not a part of the Tyr she knew, and without Urien to guide her she was likely to get lost. The last thing they needed was the Cariad wandering aimlessly around the lower reaches of the Tyr.

After she had calmed down, she stood for a while in the squalid cell, wondering how much had really changed. When she returned to her rooms she would be dealing with the same problems she had woken up to this morning. Above them, the night would be drawing on: the people of her world would be at home with their families, putting their children to bed, talking about the day with their spouses, living their small, ordinary lives as best they could, oblivious of what went on here. Most of them, anyway. One family, however—

She looked up at a scraping sound. Urien was standing in the doorway.

'Is he—?' she began, seeing the expression on his face.

Urien nodded.

'What have we done, Urien?'

'Let us return to your room before we discuss this further.'

On the way back, she received the expected respect from the few priests they encountered, which only made her feel worse. She could not shake the conviction that her fraudulent status had somehow become detectable to everyone she met.

Damaru was still out. Kerin got herself a drink, and offered Urien one. He accepted, and they sat down.

Then Urien said, 'To answer your question, I have made a mistake. Captain Siarl was innocent.'

'Did he have children?' She had to know.

'Two boys, I believe.'

'You had to spread lies about him too, did you not?' It was not an accusation; her earlier anger and frustration at Urien had evaporated, driven out by what she had witnessed. She needed to grasp the full implications of the night's foul work.

'Aye; we could not detain a monitor captain without giving a reason. When I checked his record I found that he was once accused of taking a bribe. It was the only irregularity, and I suspect the accusation was baseless, possibly even an act of malice. But it allowed me to put out a story that he was taken into custody today to answer charges of selling Tyr secrets to a subversive organisation.'

'What organisation? Please do not tell me you have been keeping the existence of such a threat from me!'

'The organisation in question does not exist, Kerin. In fact, I have yet to find the time to invent a name for it.'

'More lies,' she sighed. 'The further we go, the deeper we are caught in them.'

'Aye. I fear you are right. If I thought I could trust the other Escorai …'

'You told me you chose the best men for the job.'

'I thought I did, and in most cases I still believe that, but I do not see us being able to take any of them into our confidence in the foreseeable future. I simply cannot know how they would react.'

'I did not know how you would react when I returned from "Heaven" and told you how we had been lied to.'

'True enough. It was a brave act, Kerin; do not think I have forgotten that.'

His praise made her self-conscious, and she changed the subject. 'You knew I would insist on watching the interrogation, did you not?'

'I was not sure, though I strongly suspected it. I do know that if I had gone ahead without telling you what I was doing, you would never have forgiven me.'

He was right enough in that. 'Is my opinion really that important to you?' She knew they shared the same goals, but their very different backgrounds meant they had different ideas about how to achieve them – or rather, Kerin had very little idea. And that ignorance chafed.

'It is. I see in you something I lost many years ago, before I climbed upon the backs of my fellow priests to reach my current position. In some ways I envy your purity of vision. In others … it frightens me, for if we are to succeed then you must learn to accept some bitter truths – such as the need to sometimes allow innocents to suffer and die in order to safeguard the future.'

'Oh, I am learning.' Her earlier ire shamed her now. She saw how Urien's choice to keep certain details from her was a mercy; those burdens he did put on her were intended to teach hard but necessary lessons. 'I am sorry I have been such a surly student.'

'It is understandable.'

'Have you ever lied to me, Urien?' Again it was not an accusation; she knew in her heart that he would not deceive her without good reason. But she needed to know.

'No.' His answer was emphatic. 'And I never will. However, on occasion I have chosen not to expose you to certain truths. I am sorry to do even that, and I look forward to the time when I will not need to.' He looked up at her. 'You are the map to my moral heart, Kerin.'

Kerin felt herself blush. How hard his job was! One man trying to comprehend, and ultimately control, everything that went on in the Tyr … not just hard, all but impossible. Yet she had to believe he – *they* – could succeed. 'Thank you,' she whispered. 'Did you— Did you get anything of use from Captain Siarl in the end? Did he mention this Aelwen again?'

'He did: I think she is someone he and his mysterious friend knew when they were a lot younger, a woman of higher status his friend had feelings for.'

'And did he name his friend?'

'No. Siarl's link to this man ran deep. I got the impression they had known each other for a long time, and Siarl was the older of the two: Siarl said something about trying to keep him out of trouble even as a boy. I also believe he has recently fallen out with his friend, though I am not sure why. I thought it might be over a woman, possibly this Aelwen, but he also appeared to think his friend was going against the will of the Skymothers. From the intelligence I have so far gathered, I believe there is a priest of Fenland origin amongst Siarl's associates, though I cannot immediately see how a priest would fit either of those possible causes of conflict. I need to do further research.'

'And do you think there is a conspiracy?'

'The one good thing to come of this evening is that we have not uncovered any indication of organised dissent. Siarl doubted, and so, I believe, does this friend of his, but I think that is as far as it goes. Of course there may be other threats, but we need not fear these Fenlanders.'

'What about the house Siarl visited?'

'Aye, we should send— What is that?'

Kerin turned in her chair to follow the direction of Urien's gaze. The screen on the console was blinking. She puzzled out the text: *Incoming message*. 'Someone from above is trying to contact us,' she said.

'So it appears. You cannot find out who, can you?' asked Urien.

'Not without Damaru's touch to wake the console.'

Urien stood. 'I will go and look for him,' he announced, and left without another word.

Kerin found herself staring at the flashing words, mesmerised by the mindless rhythm. She was not ready for another crisis, not yet. Maybe when she had had some sleep ...

She jerked awake as her half-closed eyes let in the image of Captain Siarl's broken body.

A short time after that, Damaru burst into the room and headed straight for the console. As he leaned over her, Kerin got a whiff of a sweet, fruity smell and noticed something sticky smeared around his mouth. 'Damaru,' she said.

He paused, possibly expecting to be scolded.

'I need you to find out who that is before we, uh, accept their message. Do you understand?'

Damaru nodded, and pressed a couple of keys on the control pad.

As he did so, Urien spoke from behind her. 'I have had reports of him wandering into the kitchens late at night in search of treats, so I looked there first.'

Kerin turned and gave the Escori a brief smile of thanks, then looked back at the console. Most of the text now displayed meant little to her; *Heart of Glass* was the only thing she could read; the rest looked like random letters and numbers. Then, in smaller letters at the bottom she made out the words *Captain Jarek Reen* – the name the Sidhe had called Sais.

Sais had shown her how to use the 'com' function. She accepted the call herself, earning a mildly annoyed '*Huh!*' from Damaru as he realised he was not going to get to play after all, even though the console was finally doing something interesting again.

The text disappeared and she found herself looking at the man she had married a scant season ago. He smiled his engaging, lop-sided smile, and relief flooded her soul. 'You came back,' she said warmly.

For the space of several heartbeats he did not respond. Then he said, 'I did. It's good to see you, Kerin. Is that Damaru I can see half in shot?'

'It is.' Kerin found such disembodied conversations odd, and this one had an additional peculiarity, for Sais' image froze after he spoke.

She was about to speak again, when he said, 'How's the good fight going?'

'I – *we* are making progress. Sais, is something wrong? You are pausing before you speak.'

Again his image stayed unmoving for several heartbeats. Then he said, 'Sorry, Kerin, I should have explained. There's a time delay because I'm still a long way out.'

'How far?' Not that his words would mean much to her; her only understanding of the concept of 'space' was to acknowledge that it was too big for *anyone* to fully comprehend.

'We're outside the range of the orbital defences,' Sais said. 'I transmitted the override code, but I didn't get an acknowledgement. Is something wrong with the weaponry?'

'Aye, I think there is – the Sidhe came back, nearly a season ago now, and they wrested control of the sky-weapons from Damaru. He has not been able to regain it again, though he has tried. He says that he can no longer see the rock-throwers.'

Another pause, then, 'That's not good – but presumably he managed to trash the Sidhe first, or we wouldn't be having this conversation.'

'He says he burnt them with, uh, *cutting light*. Do you know what that is?'

The face on the screen looked quizzical for several moments, then Sais nodded. 'Yes, I've got an idea, but I'll need to check. Listen, Kerin, does Damaru know if the weapons are still offline?'

'Off—? Ah, if you are asking whether they will turn on you … I am not sure.' She turned to Damaru, who had been following the conversation with interest, and said, 'Damaru, is it safe for Sais to approach? Will the weapons try and hurt him if he does?'

'Do not think so.'

'He needs you to be sure.'

'*Cannot* be sure.'

'Can you find out?'

'I told you, I cannot *see* them.'

Kerin turned back to the screen, but Sais was already speaking again. 'It looks like you've lost contact with the weaponry. Kerin, I came here to give you something, but if Serenein's defenceless, we need to sort that out first. Assuming those defences really are down and we can approach safely … Listen, we need to discuss our next move. Can you stay near the console and wait for me to get back in touch?'

'I will remain here and hope to hear from you soon, husband.'

It was only after she had ended their contact that she wondered who he had meant by 'we'.

CHAPTER FORTY

'"Husband"?' Taro said incredulously. 'Shit and blood, she's your *wife*?'

When Jarek had told them about his adventures on Serenein, he'd missed out that particular detail.

'Yes, Taro, technically Kerin is my wife.'

'Fuck me.'

Jarek said defensively, 'We were married under Serenein law—'

'So, is there like, some little baby – what'd she call you? Oh yeah, *Sais*. So are there like l'il baby Saises running around?' Taro knew he shouldn't be finding this funny, but he couldn't help it.

'No, Taro, there aren't. I've only known Kerin about six months. It was a marriage of convenience, for both of us.' He held up a hand as Taro opened his mouth. 'And no, I didn't go to bed with her.'

Taro decided to let that one lie.

Nual asked, 'What are we going to do now? Will you risk going closer?'

'I could try and ping the weapons again, but I didn't get a response the last three times, so there's no reason to expect one now. Something's definitely up; I just don't know what. Everything was working fine when I was here a few months ago; in fact, according to the *Setting Sun*'s ship's log, the crew ran a major diagnostic on the system and found everything in good order.'

He added, 'Though I've only scanned a fraction of the decoded data, it looks like the *Setting Sun*'s memory-core includes full specs for every artificial object in orbit around Serenein – which makes sense, given that ship used to maintain the tech around here.

There's bound to be full details of the planetary defence system in the files *somewhere*.'

'Would it help if we looked?' asked Nual.

'Yeah, it would: it's a hell of a lot of data, and the indexing's a little idiosyncratic, but if both of you see what you can find out, we can cross-reference our findings.'

Searching through data wasn't Taro's idea of fun, especially as he was still a pretty slow reader – up until a few months ago he'd never needed to do much more than recognise the names of bars and count the punters' money. But though the stolen download from the *Setting Sun*'s comp had some prime info, like Jarek said, there was a shitload of data to wade through to get to what they needed. He joined Nual in the rec-room and left Jarek to bring the *Heart of Glass* up to the edge of the area covered by the orbital weaponry. Taro soon found that Jarek hadn't been kidding about the arse-backward indexing.

They'd been scanning the files for more than an hour when Nual said, 'I can't find anything in here to cover this situation; how about you?'

'Nothing—' and she was a lot more comp-savvy than him, Taro thought; she'd've used search-agents and all that shit.

'Let's see how Jarek's getting on,' Nual suggested.

Back on the bridge, Jarek agreed. 'I've had another look too: it appears that the only way to shut down the weapons is to transmit the override code or to use the console in the Cariad's room – and neither of those options are currently working.'

'What about this "cutting light" Kerin mentioned?' asked Nual.

'I reckon that's the point-defences.'

'That's different to the orbital defences, ain't it?' Taro asked. He thought he'd come across a reference to that somewhere.

'It is. The orbital defences are mass-drivers mounted on launch platforms. They fire high-density projectiles – not actual rocks, but I can see how Damaru got that. The defence grid is made up of thousands of these platforms orbiting Serenein, forming a halo that stretches out from the planet for half a light-second.'

'Pretty solid cover, then?' said Taro, trying not to think about what would happen if they got in range and the weapons *were* working.

'Oh yes. The point-defences are more local: they're laser emplacements on the counterweight at the top of the beanstalk and on the transfer-station partway down. There's a fair amount of debris in this system – the locals actually have a religious festival when the rain of "falling stars" is at its heaviest – so the Sidhe had to put in measures to protect the beanstalk.'

'And it's those defences that shot down your evac-pod when you were escaping from the Sidhe ship, which is how you ended up on Serenein in the first place?' Taro asked, fitting the pieces into place in his head.

'Yeah. Fortunately the point-defences are orientated to deal with stuff coming in from space, rather than dropping off the transfer-station and heading down to the planet, so they just ripped my smartchute, rather than holing the capsule itself. Still led to a pretty rough landing ... Actually, I'm surprised those lasers were powerful enough to destroy a shiftship, but I guess if Damaru waited until it was close, then managed to get all the weapons to turn on it together, and kept them focused until he got through in multiple locations   '

He paused, frowning, then said, 'Shit! I've just had a really nasty thought. I need to speak to Kerin again.'

'So, have we decided whether we're going in or not?' Taro didn't remember them actually discussing that.

'Do we really need to, given the risk if the defence grid is active?' said Nual. 'After all, we have planted the beacon; correct me if I'm wrong, but linking it into the beevee system requires us to return to human-space anyway.'

'It does,' said Jarek, tapping one finger on the console, 'but that's not the point. Kerin has got to have control of the defence grid if she's to stop the Sidhe retaking Serenein.'

'She said her son destroyed the last Sidhe ship with the point-defences, and those *do* work,' said Nual.

'They did, but the point-defence system isn't designed to take out whole ships, which is why I need to speak to Kerin again.'

As Jarek reached for the com, Taro said, 'You gonna introduce us to your wife this time?'

Jarek hesitated. 'I guess I should.' He didn't sound eager.

'Both of us?' asked Nual softly.

'Yeah,' said Jarek a little reluctantly. 'Both of you.'

Kerin answered his call at once. 'Are you coming here?' she asked.

'Still working that out. Uh, Kerin, can I ask you something?'

'Of course.' Jarek had the call on flatscreen, so Taro couldn't see Kerin clearly, but she didn't sound too happy.

'When Damaru used the cutting light to destroy the Sidhe ship, did you see anything from down there?'

'I did not, but there was much talk of a light, high up in the sky, on that night.'

'Right. And how about since?'

'It is odd that you should ask that, for there have been reports of flashes in the sky ever since.'

'That's what I was afraid of.'

'What do the lights signify? They have caused much confusion here. People believe them to be portents of doom.'

'They might be right. Damaru wouldn't have been able to completely destroy the Sidhe ship, but he must have done it enough damage that it broke up. The problem is, the bits are still in orbit – floating around in space above you – and those flashes you're seeing are the point-defence lasers – the cutting lights – going off, to destroy any of the debris that gets too close to the beanstalk – your silver thread. If they don't, one of the bits might hit it.'

'And that would be bad?'

'Yes, very bad.'

'But we still see the lights: surely that means these point-defences are continuing to do their work? Though ... the lights have become less frequent of late.'

'They have? That's my worry: the point-defences aren't designed to fire continuously; they're only meant to cope with occasional small stuff. Anything big, like the Sidhe ship, should have been trashed by the orbital weapons before it got anywhere near Serenein.'

'You are saying these point-defences are failing?'

'Not exactly failing, but as the system loses power it has to become more selective about what the lasers fire on.'

'Can you fix this?'

'I'm— We can try. But we'll have to come in and dock with the beanstalk.'

'Sais,' asked Kerin, 'you have twice said "we" now. Who is with you?'

'Ah, yeah. Sorry: I'm being rude. I have a couple of friends here – allies in our fight.' Jarek motioned to Taro, who came over and smiled at the tired-looking woman on the screen. She might have been pretty once, but she'd obviously had a well shitty life. 'Kerin, this is Taro.'

There was still some signal-lag, so it took a moment for Taro to see Kerin's expression change. He'd bet she'd never seen anyone quite like him before. 'Hi,' he said, giving her a big, friendly grin.

She got over her initial surprise and smiled back gravely. 'Good evening to you, Taro.'

Taro stepped back to let Nual come forward. 'And this,' said Jarek, 'is Nual.'

Kerin was silent for longer than the second or so it took for a message to get there and back. Then she said, 'Forgive me, but ... the way you look, I am reminded of the Sidhe I have seen.' She spoke hesitantly, trying not to offend.

Nual said evenly, 'You are correct, Kerin, and it is because I am Sidhe – but I am working against my sisters, with Taro and Jarek.'

Jarek added hastily, 'Nual really is on our side, Kerin.'

Kerin said, 'I need to think about this.' Then she ended the call.

Jarek swore under his breath.

'So, what now?' asked Nual. 'If she doesn't want our help because of me, then I'm not sure we have any choice but to leave.'

'Kerin's a smart woman,' Jarek said. 'She hates the Sidhe, but she trusts me. She's just a bit surprised, that's all.'

'It ain't like Nual could influence her over the com,' said Taro, 'but I guess she don't know that.'

The incoming call light came back on a few minutes later. Taro and Nual moved back to let Jarek take the call.

Kerin said, 'I am uncomfortable that you have an ally who is Sidhe, but I have had to accept a number of things I am uncomfortable with lately. If you are willing to help, then I would be grateful for your aid.'

'That's why we're here,' Jarek said. 'Now, let's work out what we can do, shall we? Personally, I'd risk the defences and come in to check out the status of the beanstalk, but this isn't just up to me; I'll only do it if my companions agree.'

'Of course,' said Kerin.

Taro looked at Nual, who said slowly, 'If Kerin wishes it, we should help. We are fighting the same enemy.'

'I'm in too,' said Taro.

'So that's a "yes" then. Right, Kerin, we'll speak again when I'm closer – assuming those weapons really are inactive! I'll keep the channel open so you can call me if you need to.'

'I will be here.'

Jarek minimised the call and swivelled his couch. 'You two can stay on the bridge if you like, but only if one of you gets me a caf first. I think I'm going to need it.'

While Jarek plotted their approach, Taro and Nual carried on going through the Sidhe files. They'd have been more comfortable in the rec-room, but if everything did go to shit, there was an unspoken agreement that they'd see it coming and go out together.

Finally Jarek said over his shoulder, 'We're going in.'

Though Taro caught his breath, there wasn't much to see – just space, big and black outside the dome, and Jarek's hands, flying across the controls in here.

When the planet itself came into view, a distant bright half-circle, he watched it for a while, but after several minutes had passed and they still hadn't been blown up, Taro risked speaking. 'Er, I notice we're not dead.'

'Well spotted. If the defence grid was going to fire on us, it would have done so by now.'

'Top prime.'

'Yeah, but that's not our only problem. I need to show you something.' The holocube display changed as Taro and Nual approached, to show Serenein at the bottom and the beanstalk growing up from it; the lump of the counterweight was at the top, with another lump, presumably the transfer-station, a little way below it. 'That's a real-time projection, magnified and enhanced so you can see everything. We'll actually be coming in on the planet's nightside. Now, watch this.'

A blinding barrage of flashes went off in the space around the beanstalk.

'Shit!' said Taro, 'is that the point-defences?'

'Sort of – they're currently firing about once every hour or so. What you just saw is a sim: I asked the comp to light up everything in the debris cloud that will, at some point in the next year, be in range of the beanstalk lasers. The cloud's smearing, spreading out to orbit the planet, so the calculations aren't perfect, but it gives you an idea. And that's just the big stuff; we're still too far out to pick up any micro-sized motes.'

'And we gotta fly through all that shit?' Taro breathed.

'Yeah, we do.'

'So we're gonna take it easy, yeah?' In Taro's experience, Jarek wasn't always one for taking the slow and steady course.

'We'd have to go really slowly to significantly reduce the risk of taking a hit. If the point-defences are starting to fire selectively, we need to get in there quickly and fix them – they've only got to screw up once for something to get through and take out the beanstalk.'

Taro had a sudden thought. 'Aren't the point-defences gonna fire on us when we get close? I mean, won't we look like a big lump of debris heading straight for the beanstalk?'

'Fortunately there's an approach corridor,' said Jarek. 'Provided we come in under power, on precisely the course from the *Setting Sun*'s comp, the defences will register us as a friendly ship, and not fire. But I'll need to run some more sims, to make sure none of that debris out there's going to trigger the lasers near us when we make our final approach … Or hit us before we even get that far, for that matter. And yes, I could use another drink.'

'I'll fix a round,' said Taro. This situation was way beyond his own meagre piloting abilities.

By the time he got back, he could see the central habitable area of green and brown between Serenein's massive ice-caps. Jarek was hard at work at the comp, but he paused long enough to give Taro a smile when he put the caf down. 'Thanks, mate. This is where it gets really tricky.'

CHAPTER FORTY-ONE

Lining up with a transfer-station on a beanstalk wasn't a straight-forward manoeuvre at the best of times, let alone with the added dangers of crossfire and space debris. Though the comp would do the calculations, Jarek needed to provide the correct inputs, and monitor the *Heart of Glass*'s vector. He normally ran the comp on silent mode – its smug voice bugged him – but now he switched on voice activation: there were some alerts he couldn't afford to miss.

It was a while before he had time to drink the caf Taro had brought him, but once the comp came back with the answer he'd been hoping for, he allowed himself a brief time out, thanking Taro for having the forethought to use a bulb rather than a mug, so the caf was still warm. He decided against telling his companions that he'd managed to plot a debris-free course, in case that jinxed it. He wasn't going to say they were safe until he was sure they were. He kept an eye on his readouts, but as he drank, he found his mind recalling his first visit ...

He'd slipstreamed the *Setting Sun* on spec, following a tip-off about this independent tradebird that allegedly disappeared from the shipping-lanes for up to three months every couple of decades. At the time he'd assumed it was a freetrader outfit who'd found a new – and possibly lucrative – transit-path. He already knew the Sidhe were still around, thanks to Nual, but he'd left her on Vellern nearly seven years before and his level of paranoia had dropped to wary caution.

Serenein's orbital weapons hadn't fired on him at once, and he'd been oblivious to the planet's defence grid, too busy tailing the *Setting Sun* and waiting for them to spot him and ask what the fuck he thought he was up to ... He remembered being puzzled that they hadn't commed him yet.

Then the weapons had opened up – or rather, one lone platform had fired one single projectile, and his basic countermeasures had defeated what he'd thought at the time was a not-so-smart-missile. Afterwards, of course, he'd had to reassess his opinion of the defences; it was much more likely the Sidhe ship had over-ridden the weapons and then initiated that one ineffectual attack, which had been enough to disconcert and distract him, so when the human pilot of the ship had commed him, claiming his vessel had sustained damage and needed help, Jarek had taken the distress call at face value. He'd rushed in – and promptly been captured. And that's when things turned really nasty ...

'Proximity alert.' The comp's synthesised voice startled him, and he dropped the bulb. 'Where?' he asked, scanning his console.

The comp obligingly maximised the source of the alarm: an extensive shower of debris motes.

The ship's nav-shields were good, but there was a limit to how much they could push aside, and at this speed even objects too small to see could tear a hole right through the ship. He'd been banking on the wreckage being in large lumps. It looked like he'd been wrong.

Time for some emergency evasive tactics; the view changed from the sliver of Serenein's globe currently in sunlight to the darkness of space.

Jarek looked back down at his display and ramped up the shield on the planet-ward side. They were definitely going to clip the edge of this debris cloud. In the clarity of cold panic he wondered if there might be something in Taro's opinions on the advantages of neurolinked flying. Jarek had always maintained those extra milliseconds of reaction time wouldn't make much difference to a freetrader ... he hoped the next few minutes weren't about to prove him wrong.

Fortunately, he knew the *Heart of Glass* inside out; he could fly her blind, if he had to. He ignored the warning display – he already knew they were close to operational parameters, thanks very much; some of the crap the shields were pushing aside was large enough to send faint judders through the ship. Instead, he concentrated on the sensors, hardly daring to blink, constantly assessing the debris cloud, tweaking the ship's course second by second, trying to keep as close to his planned vector as he could; if he strayed too far off, the comp projections he'd so painstakingly programmed would no longer be accurate, and he was likely to find himself in the path of something big enough to cut right through the shields and take them out in one hit.

More juddering, more flashing lights, more verbal warnings but nothing more serious, thank Christos.

As they cleared the cloud he let himself exhale. He could feel the eyes of his two companions focused on him.

'You might want to suit up,' he said, failing to sound quite as casual as he'd intended.

'V-suits?' asked Taro. 'We really in that much shit?'

'Hopefully not, but … just do it, all right?' He didn't have the energy for complicated explanations, not while he was still glued to his sensor readouts.

'We only have two suits,' said Nual quietly, 'yours, and the one Taro acquired at Aleph.'

'Yeah, so you two suit up—'

'What about you?' said Taro.

'As I was saying, you two suit up and find the patch-kit. It's in the engineering locker.' When they didn't respond, he added, 'Please, just do it. If we do get a breach, you're going to have to fix it, ideally quickly enough that I don't regret not being in a suit.' Despite his years in space, Jarek sometimes forgot how dangerous hard vacuum was; having grav-tech that kept you pinned to the floor and dealt with most minor hazards lulled you into a false sense of security. He made a mental note to invest in another suit as soon as they got back to human-space. Assuming they got back to human-space.

'We're on it,' said Taro, following Nual down.

Just after they'd left the bridge, the comp announced, 'You have deviated from the calculated course into a high-hazard area.'

'No shit,' he muttered, and made a hurried sensor-sweep: the comp was right, of course. He cut his speed slightly; it might throw the original calculations, which would mean more work for the comp, but it would also give him more time to react. Following Jarek's order, the comp grabbed the incoming data and went to work on a new vector to get them back on their original heading without hitting anything big.

Taro's voice came over the com, 'Er, sorry to disturb you, but we've got the kit. Where d'you want us?'

'The rec-room's fine for now.' From the heart of the ship they'd be ready to go in any direction … maybe not so useful if the bridge took a hit, but in that case he'd most likely be fucked anyway.

The comp stated: 'Unable to calculate course.'

'You *what*?'

'Please restate query.'

'Fuck it,' murmured Jarek, and interrogated the comp via the manual controls. *Never a machine empath around when you need one—*

Ah, that was it: there was no course that wouldn't bring them dangerously close to something that could kill them. Fucking marvellous. Right then, time to work out the least bad option. Dodging the big stuff had to be the priority, and if that meant hitting more clouds of motes – so be it.

He cut across the comp's attempts to make him pay attention to its warnings, and selected the least scary-looking option.

'Things might be about to get a bit hairy,' he said over the com.

'We're standing by,' said Taro, his voice terse.

No point trying to scrub more speed; by the time he'd decelerated enough to make any difference they'd be through. Or not. If he still believed in God, he'd be praying right now.

A series of small vibrations shook the ship. Sweat prickled over Jarek's forehead as the shields went amber. A fraction of a second later, the comp, sounding totally unconcerned, stated: 'Warning. Hull has been breached.'

'Fuck! Where? How badly?' he shouted.

'Please restate query,' said the comp calmly.

Jarek forced himself to speak slowly and carefully: 'What is the location of the hull breach? How big is it?' He couldn't hear the rush of escaping air – but then, he couldn't hear much at all over his pounding heart.

'A double breach has occurred,' the comp advised him. 'The entry and egress points are between two and three millimetres in size. Both are located in the cargo-hold.'

Taro's voice came over the com. 'D'you need us to—?'

'No, we'll leave them for now – just don't open the door to the cargo-hold!' He gave silent thanks to the nameless ship designer who'd decided to wrap the ship's cargo-hold around the living quarters and provide inner pressure-doors.

The sensors were showing them nearing the edge of the current cloud. Though the comp wasn't indicating any large hazards ahead, there was always the exciting possibility of more motes he'd not spotted yet.

As his breathing began to return to normal, Jarek realised why there was so much debris – the Sidhe ship must have chosen the same course he had, so when it got blown up, that's where most of its remains had stayed. Blindingly obvious, once he stopped to think about it. He'd know better next time.

They were decelerating hard now, ready to match velocity with the beanstalk and as Jarek watched, the planet moved slowly back into view. The surface below was dark, though the beanstalk's counterweight was still in sunlight. He called Nual and Taro back to the bridge.

'Sorry to be a bit short with you earlier,' he said as Taro flew up through the hatch.

'No worries. Thinking I'm gonna die makes me tetchy too,' Taro said with a grin. 'How're we doing?'

'We're coming into the area of space protected by the point-defences,' He didn't see any point in mentioning that someone – Damaru, maybe *accidentally* – might have messed with the settings on the beanstalk's defences, possibly even nullifying the approach

311

corridor he was about to fly them down. They weren't going to turn back, whatever happened.

In some ways, this last section was the easiest: once inside the point-defences, they shouldn't have to worry about running into debris. Jarek still hunched over the console, ready to take evasive action if the lasers did fire on them.

So far, so good. He glanced up through the dome: the comp's simulation indicated that spot there would light up, in three seconds, two, one—

—and there it was, a quick flash of silver.

'What was that?' asked Taro, sounding distinctly twitchy.

'That was the most reassuring sight I've seen in a while,' Jarek said with a smile. 'The comp predicted the lasers would fire on some debris, and they just did.'

'Thank fuck for that.'

'You said it!'

The beanstalk was in shadow now. Ahead, the plain cube of the transfer-station was a dark lump, with the bulk of the *Setting Sun* a larger and less regular lump attached to one side. Neither showed any lights. The Sidhe ship was a top-of-the-range tradebird, half the age and ten times the size of the *Heart of Glass*. Last time he'd been here he'd only cared about getting away, but now he was looking at it, he reckoned they could really use a ship like that.

But first things first ...

He took full manual control and brought them in, initially using a real-time projection in the holocube as a guide, overlaying a false-colour image on the display to avoid getting too close to the currently invisible beanstalk cable. The last few metres were reassuringly anti-climactic and he docked the *Heart of Glass* at the end of the *Setting Sun*'s command corridor without a hitch.

Once he had a green light on the airlock seal, Jarek put his hands on the pilot's console, leaned forward and let out a long, loud sigh. As he straightened he caught sight of the time: that little episode had taken more than three hours. It had felt like a tenth of that – or possibly ten times as long.

When he stood up, Taro was already there with a fresh bulb

of caf. 'I knew I kept you around for something,' he said with a smile.

Taro affected a look of mock hurt. 'Actually, we've been making ourselves useful-like: we took our minds off being shit-scared by reading the *Setting Sun*'s files. We've dug up some real prime info.'

'Tell me while I drink this and get ready.'

Taro and Nual followed him down to the rec-room, where he gathered together a few items.

Nual said, 'We think we know how the incoming Sidhe ship dealt with the defence grid: there's a way of completely shutting down the weapons, rather than overriding them, and until they're reset the defence grid is totally inactive – it won't accept *any* instructions, not from the Cariad, nor incoming ships.'

'Any idea how to get it back online?'

'You just have to enter a code – that's the good news. The bad news is that you need to do it on the "cold-start console" – but what and where that console is ... I'll keep looking for information on it, but we were concentrating on the point-defences.'

'Fair enough. And what's the news there?'

'You can access them from the transfer-station.'

'That's a good start.' He led the way back into the rec-room.

'And they're solar-powered.'

'Not so good. Solar is pretty low-output ... but then, it's also low-maintenance, and normally the lasers just have to pick off occasional dust motes. I guess solar makes sense, given how long this set-up gets left to its own devices. The problem is the debris from the ship Damaru blew up is going to orbit the planet until it either falls low enough to burn up in the atmosphere or else gets zapped down to nothing by the point-defences, and that'll take *years* – and there're other systems on the transfer-station that need that power too.' He sighed. 'I guess it's no wonder the point-defences are running down.'

'So what're we gonna do?' asked Taro.

'I need to think about it. Right now I've just remembered I forgot to pick up my gun from my cabin,' he said. 'Back in a mo.' He expected the *Setting Sun* to be completely locked down, just as he'd left it, but with the Sidhe, it paid to be paranoid.

He decided to take his needle-pistol, rather than just relying on tranq, and the answer came to him as he strapped on the holster. 'We need to hook up an alternative power source,' he announced as he re-emerged from his cabin. 'A fusion plant would do it—'

'—and there's one of those on the *Setting Sun,*' finished Nual.

'Precisely.'

They made their way down the exit corridor into the *Heart of Glass*'s personnel airlock. As the door closed, Jarek said to Nual, 'I'm guessing you'd have told me if there was anyone aboard.'

'You're correct: there are no conscious minds on the *Setting Sun.*'

'Good. Then let's go.'

The readouts were all glowing a cheery green. The door opened onto a familiar corridor, dimly lit by hazard lighting.

'So, we gonna go check out the engine room?' asked Taro.

'Yeah …'

'You don't sound sure,' said Nual.

Jarek had been thinking about his nascent plan to mesh two very different systems, one of them a fusion reactor. Having the full specs was a necessary starting point, but he was only a passable engineer, while Taro and Nual were total novices. And you only had to make one mistake with a fusion reactor …

'I'm certain that connecting the *Setting Sun*'s power supply up to the point-defences is a good idea,' he said, 'but I think we might need some help to do it.'

CHAPTER FORTY-TWO

Ifanna told Escori Garnon what she had experienced – or rather, not experienced – whilst in the Cariad's presence, then *Gwas* Maelgyn asked her to wait outside the room while he spoke to his master. They had not said she should remain standing, so she sat on the top step, careful not to look at the man at the bottom of the stairs who lounged against the wall, his crossbow propped up beside him. She could not hear much through the thick wooden door. Just as her eyelids were beginning to droop, the door opened and she jumped to her feet as Maelgyn came out, looking serious.

'Is all well, *Gwas*?' she asked nervously.

He favoured her with a smile. 'I believe it will be, *chilwar*.' He led her out of the tavern and back to the shuttered house, and this time, though Ifanna tried to find the courage to ask him what he intended – and more specifically, how she fitted in with his plan – he walked in silence. He had the air of a man holding fast to a secret. But when they reached the house, he bade her goodnight with the same tenderness he had shown when he had first helped her in the alley, and she was glad she had not asked, for to do so would be to doubt him.

Before she went to bed, she dragged the crib from the bedroom into the smaller room. That night she slept soundly.

Gwas Maelgyn had said only that he would be back, not when, so when she awoke the next day she fetched water for herself, keeping a look-out to ensure she was not observed, and put some lentils on to soak. As she washed, she quietly rejoiced at the change in her fortunes: she had arrived in the city expecting to die and be damned here; even the prospect of becoming a slave to the desire of strangers had been an attractive one compared to that.

Yet now, a mere three days later, not only was she no longer in fear for her life she was both free and under the protection of an important man, a man who valued her. She only wished *Gwas* Maelgyn would speak of the future, for though she was happy here, Ifanna knew she could not stay in this house forever.

She ate when noon came; she needed to look after herself, now that her life had turned around. She said a prayer of thanks over the food, but aside from that, she barely considered the Skymothers; her former deep devotion belonged to her old life.

Feeling restless after her meal, she wandered from room to room. She came across a sampler-frame, tucked under one of the seats in the parlour, and took the embroidery upstairs, where she risked opening the shutters a crack to let in some light, though she was careful to sit back from the window so she could not be seen. The half-finished design showed birds and animals in a ring around a figure who, though incomplete, was recognisable as Turiach, in her guise of Hearth-Mother. Ifanna spent a while trying to carry on where the dead seamstress had left off, concentrating on the flowers, but her stitching was clumsy, and she soon put the sampler down and stared out at the view of blue rooftops and bluer sky. Her lack of such homely skills had always been a disappointment to her mother.

Maelgyn came as the shadows were beginning to lengthen, identifying himself with his usual knock. Ifanna nearly tripped in her haste to let him in.

As soon as she closed the door behind him he said, 'You should gather what possessions you wish to take from here, *chilwar*. We feel it prudent to move you to different accommodation.'

'Is this the will of your Escori, *Gwas*?' She was not sure how she felt about coming to the attention of such an important man. Flattered, aye, but also anxious.

'We reached that decision after some discussion,' he said sagely.

'I will fetch clothes,' she said. Not wanting to keep him waiting, she grabbed a couple of skirts and blouses, the first that came to hand, and tied them into a bundle.

As he ushered her out, Maelgyn paused to put the latch down, and Ifanna experienced a brief moment of uncertainty to be leaving her sanctuary. But her unease quickly gave way to elation. She only had to look at Maelgyn's face to know that something glorious was afoot. This time she did not wait for permission to take his arm; he made no comment at her presumption, and even briefly covered her hand with his own.

They took a different route, though it also led to a tavern, this one small and genteel; its true nature was not apparent at first for the handful of old men in the main room appeared to prefer tea to beer, though they still watched her curiously when Maelgyn went up to talk to the red-cheeked matron who ran the place. After a few moments, Maelgyn came back and led Ifanna through a side exit and up some stairs to a short corridor. He opened the second door on the left, and Ifanna found herself in a small, neat room containing a bed, a storage chest, a chair and a washstand.

As Maelgyn closed the door her curiosity got the better of her. '*Gwas*, please, what is going on?' she asked.

'Great things, *chilwar*,' he told her with a gentle smile, 'great things. You will know more in good time, but I will say this now: all my life I have been denied the chances I deserved, but finally – *finally!* – this is changing.'

'Because of your Escori?'

'Aye. Garnon is a good man – a great man! – but even he cannot be expected to acknowledge everyone who answers to him individually, no matter how loyal and hard-working they may be. Yet now … now everything will change. And we – you and I – are at the heart of that change.'

His words lit a fire inside Ifanna, and she had a sudden, ridiculous desire to throw her arms around the priest. She resisted it, and instead said earnestly, 'Just tell me what I must do.'

'For now, wait here. I will return when I can.' He turned to go, then paused. 'Have you eaten today?'

'Some lentils earlier …'

'I will arrange to have food sent up: Mistress Dorwena can be trusted. For now I must return to the Tyr.'

And with that, he was gone.

The owner brought thick soup and black bread to her door soon after. The woman made no conversation, but gave Ifanna a smile. Though the food was good, as Ifanna ate her joy subsided. If only she could know what was going on in the Tyr! Her thoughts turned to the Cariad – or rather, to the woman who wrongly claimed that title. Ifanna felt a growing ire at having humiliated herself so in front of a false goddess.

When night fell Mistress Dorwena brought a taper to light the lamps; from the noise when she opened the door, the bar below had livened up somewhat. Ifanna kept the shutters open for a while, but the light attracted nightbugs, so she closed them.

Finally she lay down on the bed and slipped into a dream of swimming in the river at Nantgwyn, the water cool on her naked body. The riverbank was lined with priests, all of whom looked on silently, appraising her. She felt no shame, only a wicked joy.

A sudden noise startled her awake, and even as her heart leapt into her mouth she recognised the priest's characteristic knock. 'Come in, *Gwas*,' she called, rubbing her eyes.

Maelgyn entered in a flurry, closing the door quickly behind him.

Ifanna looked at his face and sat up rapidly. '*Gwas*, what is wrong?' she asked, her heart hammering.

'We have been betrayed,' he said grimly.

'Betrayed?' Her heart rate redoubled. 'Who has betrayed us?'

'Captain Siarl was taken, and now it is only a matter of time before the Tyr's inquirers discover all he knows.'

'And what— What *does* he know?'

'Very little, thank the Five, but he knows my name, and yours too. Urien will send men to the shuttered house – perhaps they have already searched it! Escori Garnon was right to tell me to move you! But now I am implicated, too. I cannot return to the Tyr—'

'Then run away with me!' Even as the words left her lips Ifanna was amazed at herself.

As was *Gwas* Maelgyn. 'Run away? With *you*?'

Before she could lose her nerve Ifanna continued, 'Aye, *Gwas* – I am a fugitive already, and now you are too. We could go—'

'Go where?' His voice was ragged, desperate.

'I will follow wherever you lead,' she replied at once.

For a moment Maelgyn was silent. Finally he said, 'You would do that – leave with me?'

'Aye, *Gwas*.'

Something passed through him; despite his priestly immunity Ifanna sensed how deeply her offer had moved him. Then he said, 'I need a drink. To calm my nerves.' He turned and walked out again, his back stiff and upright.

Ifanna stared at the door, her mind in turmoil. She was sure he felt as she did! Yet it was almost as though he was running away from her. She began to wonder if he would actually come back; and if he did not, what would she do?

Her heart leapt when he returned, bringing a flagon and two cups.

As he kicked the door closed behind him he asked, 'Will you drag over that chest please, *chilwar*?' His voice was high and brittle.

Ifanna got up and did as he asked; the chest was empty, and not very heavy. Maelgyn put the flagon and cups on its flat top, then brought over the chair. Ifanna sat across from him, on the bed. She forced herself to stay silent while he poured drinks for them both. The wine was the best Ifanna had ever tasted, though she had no great affection for its effects, and she sipped hers while Maelgyn gulped his down and refilled his cup.

'I will not run away,' he said finally, his voice full of the bravado of drink. 'No. That is not how it will be, however much— For now, we are safe here. In the long run Escori Garnon will protect us. And when the time comes, we will make our move.'

She knew better than to ask what he meant; Maelgyn obviously had a plan, and he was supported in this by his master, so that must be enough for her, for now. But she did ask softly, 'And when will that time be, do you know?'

'I do not.' Maelgyn drank again.

319

'So until then, you will stay here?' Something had changed between them; there had been an unspoken shift of power.

He felt it too. 'Aye,' he whispered.

Ifanna looked into his eyes as she asked, 'With me?'

His voice was barely audible when he replied. 'Aye. With you.'

She sensed it then, priest or no: she saw herself as he saw her – as a goddess.

Even as she put down her drink and got to her feet she felt a brief flash of contempt: she was so much stronger than him! But her doubts were easily drowned in the wonder of being seen as an object of worship ... and in darker, baser feelings she could no longer deny.

He watched her step up to him, holding his cup as though it were some talisman against her – against what they both felt. She reached out, and when he did not at first respond she drew his head towards her, pulling him to her belly. A shudder went through him, and she felt the word he breathed against her.

'*No* ...'

As he exhaled, she took a breath in, swallowing the last of his resistance as she did so. Her whole body throbbed now, and he had no choice save to dance to the rhythm of it.

The cup slipped from his hand.

CHAPTER FORTY-THREE

Despite everything, Kerin ended up dozing at the console. Damaru, concluding he stood little chance of playing with the technology while his mother sat beside it, went and lay down on his bed.

Urien left on an errand of his own before Sais called back to say he would be coming to help – accompanied by the Sidhe he claimed as a friend.

After that conversation she was briefly angry again: it appeared that the lessons this long night had to teach her were not yet done. But she calmed down, after a period of reflection; if there truly was a Sidhe on their side that could change everything, and for the better. And if this 'Nual' was not a true ally, then all was already lost. For now, Kerin had no choice other than to trust her husband's judgment.

When the tally-candle began to burn low Kerin found herself relaxing, despite the uncertainty; though noisome memories from the dungeon tried to intrude on her inner view, she made herself ignore them. She suspected such images would disturb her dreams for a long time.

'Kerin?'

At first she assumed it was Urien returning, and she had missed his knock. Then she realised the voice came from below her drooping head. She snapped upright.

The text on the screen had been replaced by a view of Sais' head and shoulders. 'I was worried for a moment there,' he said.

'I was just resting.'

'Uh, yes, sorry – I forgot what time it was.'

'No matter. Have you reached the *Setting Sun* safely?'

'We have, and we've been assessing the situation. We have a solution to the problem with the point-defences, but it's complicated.' She remembered that look; he was about to tell her something she would rather not hear.

She sighed. Whether she liked it or not, she would know the full story. 'Explain, please.'

Kerin could not pretend to understand everything he said, and she was sure he was giving her the simplified version. No doubt her own attempts to describe the wonders of Dinas Emrys to a villager from Dangwern would sound equally patronising. But she did grasp two things at once: that the solution needed to be applied quickly, and that it would require Damaru's help. Her first instinct was to refuse, especially when Sais explained what could happen if the source of the power they needed was not handled carefully.

'I don't want to take any chances,' he concluded, 'not when I can have a miracle-worker to back me up.'

Kerin knew this for fact, not flattery. He did have skyfools up there, lying in the deep sleep the Sidhe put them in to transport them. But those boys would never cooperate with a stranger who brought them to consciousness in an unfamiliar place. In their panic, they might even employ their powers, with potentially disastrous consequences.

'If that is the only way, then I agree,' she said at last, 'and I will come with him.'

'I was taking that as read. As for how you'll get up here ...'

Kerin had assumed she and Damaru would need to ascend the silver thread, though that was likely to alarm anyone who witnessed the carousel's unscheduled ascent, but Sais told her this would not work – it would take too long, and the lack of power at the top meant the carousel might not be able to safely enter the transfer-station. He did have an alternative plan, which required the cover of night ...

After Sais finished the call, Kerin hurried over and woke Damaru. She was not sure how well she explained what Sais needed him to

322

do, but once she had stressed the new and interesting technology he would have the chance to investigate he was happy to help.

She called for Urien, who arrived soon after she changed back out of the Cariad's robes. He was considerably less enthusiastic than Damaru about the plan, but he had to agree with Sais' logic.

'The console will remain active,' Kerin told him. 'You need only select the option to make a call, and Sais or I will answer.' She took Urien through the basic operation, just as Sais had done for her, what felt like a lifetime ago.

'Is it essential that I stay here?' he asked. 'I was beginning to make progress following up the late Captain Siarl's associates.'

She should have known better than to believe he would spend any of the night actually sleeping. 'It would be best for you to remain at the console for the time being; Sais says it is possible that some action may be required down here in addition to what we must do above.'

Sais would call when he got nearer; until then she had time to find out what Urien had uncovered. 'Should we be concerned about these potential rebels?' she asked.

'I have the name of the captain's associate; as I suspected, it is the Fenland priest. He is a mid-level administrator, competent enough in matters of record-keeping, but otherwise unremarkable. He works in the division that deals with correspondence from the provinces. It appears that he was the priest who first saw the letter requesting that the second girl be judged by the Cariad – I say "appears" because that letter has conveniently disappeared. I cannot think that a born bureaucrat like Maelgyn would be so careless as to lose such an important document accidentally.'

'Which backs up his guilt. Will you have him detained?'

'I intend to issue a warrant for his arrest, when I have the time. To be honest, I rather hope he runs. Trying a priest for sedition on such flimsy evidence would be complicated, and potentially disruptive. I have sent men to the house where the escaped witch may be hiding; her testimony could be enough to condemn him. Not that I am likely to hear much news while I am cut off from the rest of the Tyr guarding your console,' he added, a little grumpily.

'I know,' she said sympathetically. 'That is one of the matters I intend to raise with Sais: I know he has portable devices which can speak to each other at a distance. Perhaps he can give us some of them.'

Kerin left Urien examining the console and got Damaru ready to go. Sais called shortly after, and Urien handed control back to her.

'The north side,' he repeated, after running through her instructions.

'Aye, facing towards the mountains. We will see you there soon.' She stood up and said to Urien, 'I hope that while we are gone you will be bored enough to get some rest.'

'I am sure I will find something to occupy myself,' he said drily. 'Your task is more important than this minor unrest. If I had prayers to send with you, I would.'

She and Damaru left via the hidden passage. When they emerged from the storeroom, she led him on a little-used route that took them upwards. They met no one until they were nearly at their goal, when a high-ranking priest of Medelwyr emerged from his rooms and spotted them. 'What in the name of the Five are you doing up here, woman?' he thundered.

Kerin did not have to fake her alarm, but she had her response ready: 'Please, *Gwas*, the Consort ...'

The priest's gaze fell on Damaru, who had stopped a little behind Kerin.

Out of the corner of her eye she saw him fidgeting. Before the priest could say more, she continued, 'He came to our kitchen in search of a snack – he does that often, *Gwas* – and then he made clear his intent to visit the highest balcony of the Tyr. My hearthmistress asked me to accompany him, for though he is unlikely to come to harm she—'

'Aye, of course, of course, I see,' the priest said, more kindly. 'Your name and hearth?'

Kerin resisted the urge to smile as Gwellys am Penfrid came back into service.

They reached the top of the final staircase and Kerin felt the cool night breeze on her face. She hurried Damaru down a short corridor to the open balcony. Dinas Emrys, City of Light, fanned out far below, spreading from the base of the Tyr, though at this hour she could see little other than the grid-work of light-globes that lined the streets. To her right, the sky was already growing pale; they needed to be gone before dawn. She looked up, and thought she could make out a starless patch overhead. Holding onto the stone balustrade with one hand, she leaned out and waved.

Damaru gasped, and Kerin immediately turned to him, but he was staring out beyond the balcony, at the two figures floating in the air there. They appeared wreathed in shadow, darker than the night itself.

She shivered involuntarily as one of them spoke: 'We thought we'd come and find you, to make sure we got the right balcony before bringing the ship down.' She recognised the voice as that of the boy, Taro.

'Maman, they fly!'

She turned to her son and said, 'Aye, Damaru, they do.' Another miracle about which Sais had been quite matter-of-fact.

As the two figures came closer, the boy asked, 'All right if we land? That way we can be ready to go soon as the ship's in position.'

'Aye, of course,' Kerin said, pulling at Damaru's arm to get him to move back with her.

The pair of them landed together, light as thistledown, and beyond them she could now see the dark bulk of Sais' ship, which was descending rapidly. Though it was large enough to blot out the view, the vessel was almost silent; even listening carefully, Kerin could hear only the faintest hum.

In the light of the passage she got a better look at Sais' friends. They were bare-headed, and both wore dark, tight-fitting suits with no seams or joins; their strange clothes covered them from neck to toe; over these they had cloaks which appeared to absorb any light that fell on them. As she had thought when she saw him on the screen, Taro was not much older than Damaru – but he was taller than anyone she had ever seen. His hair was artfully messed, and he had somewhat the air of a dandy, which made Kerin smile, and put her more at her ease.

The same could not be said for his companion. She hung back slightly, as though not wanting to attract attention to herself, though such beauty was hard to miss – yet when Kerin looked again, she thought the Sidhe's aura of majesty appeared somehow *diminished*.

She felt a tense smile crease her face. She said to the woman, 'My son robs you of your powers, does he not?'

'He does,' she replied tersely.

'Right, who's going first then?' The boy's jollity was forced, and it failed to hide his unease at the exchange.

'I will,' Kerin said, 'provided Damaru can see me at all times.' As she spoke, a square of light suddenly appeared in the dark belly of the ship where a door had opened.

'Don't worry,' said the boy, 'he'll be able to keep his eye on you! You happy to come and stand between us? That's it. Now, turn around and hold your arms across your body like this, so we can lift you.'

'Must I turn my back on Damaru?'

'It don't make much difference which way you face. We just thought you might want to see where you're going.'

Her son was watching her, looking puzzled. She said to him softly, 'I must fly across to Sais' ship now, Damaru.'

'I want to fly too!' he said petulantly.

'You will, my lovely boy, just as soon as everything is ready for you.' She did not want to imply distrust by saying she needed to make sure it was safe first. He appeared satisfied with that, and Kerin followed Taro's instructions. She forced herself not to flinch when the Sidhe woman touched her, but she did gasp when they lifted off and floated free of the balcony, thinking she was about to slip; but they had her firmly, if not comfortably, in their grasp. As they left the balcony the boy had to duck to avoid hitting his head.

They floated free of the Tyr, the night-breezes whipping at Kerin's skirts. She was glad it was still too dark to see much, else she might have been tempted to look down.

The distance was no further than the dozen or so steps across her chamber, but Kerin was still relieved when they landed on the far side. 'Welcome aboard,' said Taro. He added, 'This ain't the usual entrance, but we had the doors open anyway, to soak up a bit of the local atmosphere.' His tone implied there was something amusing in this comment, but Kerin could not see what.

Before she could ask about Sais, the pair had left and were already halfway across the gap. Damaru was standing by the balustrade, staring over at her.

'Let them carry you across, Damaru,' called Kerin softly.

They landed on either side of him, and Damaru suffered Taro to take his arm, but when the Sidhe tried to touch him he shrieked, the sound painfully loud in the night air, and pulled his arm away.

'Damaru, please,' implored Kerin.

'No! She is *bad pattern*,' he cried, and took a step back.

Kerin hoped he would not bolt. 'Damaru, listen, my lovely boy: she is not like the Cariad – she is Sidhe, but she is on our side. She is Sais' friend.'

Damaru said nothing, and Kerin could see his hurt look.

'You know, Damaru,' she said sternly, 'that I will not come back there, so you have no choice but to come to me. And you have already said how much you look forward to seeing the technology above again. But to do that you must let the S— you must let Nual touch you. Do you understand?'

Damaru made a show of turning his head away from the woman, though he stood his ground.

'Try again,' said Kerin to the others.

Kerin saw Damaru tense his entire right side when the Sidhe took his arm, but he neither moved nor spoke.

His face was the picture of distaste as he was flown across the gap. He pulled away as soon as they let him go.

'Right,' said Taro, with a sigh of relief, 'let's get you two up to the bridge.'

CHAPTER FORTY-FOUR

'It's great to see you, Kerin.' Jarek opened his arms and gave her a hug; she looked exhausted. 'You too, Damaru.' He knew better than to try touching the skyfool, who was peering past him at the ship's controls. Nual and Taro had gone back to the cargo-hold to finish applying the patches over the hull breaches, which was just as well, because there wasn't room for five people on the *Heart of Glass*'s bridge.

'I am happy to see you too,' said Kerin. 'Damaru, will you not greet Sais?'

'Hello Sais,' said the boy.

Jarek sat down again. 'I hope you don't mind, but I'll be flying the ship while we talk. You can stand or sit, whichever you prefer.' Once they were underway, he said, 'So here's what we need to do: first, we have to physically link the fusion plant on the *Setting Sun* to the point-defence system on the transfer-station. Second – and this is where Damaru comes in – we need to rig up some sort of power conversion unit, so the reactor's output can help power the lasers.'

'The fusion plant and the reactor – they are both names for the same technology?' asked Kerin.

'Yeah, sorry – there're a fair few technical terms. Just ask if I say something that doesn't make sense. I suggest you and I get to work on the cabling – that's pretty straightforward, at least initially – while Taro and Damaru check out the situation in the transfer-station. We're going to need Damaru's special talents to work out what needs doing and how to do it safely.'

'Would it not be better if I accompanied Damaru?' said Kerin, 'or you, if this task requires knowledge I do not have. He knows you.'

'I realise that, but Taro's been reading up on the tech in there, so he's got the knowledge to help Damaru. There's another reason too: because of the problems with the power supply, there's no gravity in the transfer-station.'

'And gravity is what sticks people to the world?'

Jarek grinned. 'Yeah, basically.'

'And why—? Oh, I see, because Taro can fly. But Damaru cannot—'

'I've got a suit he can borrow that will keep his feet stuck to the floor. Taro will be his back-up, in case he has any issues with the lack of grav, and he can be Damaru's gopher – sorry, fetch and carry anything Damaru needs to do the job.'

'I see. And what will your other companion be doing during this time?' asked Kerin, her tone deceptively mild.

'Nual will be on the *Setting Sun*'s bridge, shutting down the reactor and monitoring the ship's systems to make sure we don't accidentally do anything we shouldn't.'

'Ah yes,' said Kerin stiffly, 'being Sidhe she can operate the ship. Though without Damaru's talent ...'

'Nual knows the *Setting Sun*.' Jarek didn't mean to snap, but he didn't want to discuss how Nual had come by that knowledge; it would lower Kerin's opinion of Nual even further. 'Right, if you're happy with the plan, let's sort out that suit for Damaru.'

He led the way down to the rec-room. Nual had very sensibly retired to her cabin, leaving her v-suit draped over the couch next to Taro.

'Hey, Damaru, how you doin'?' said Taro, springing to his feet. Damaru ignored him.

Kerin went over and made a show of examining the suit. Damaru trailed after her, and his interest picked up once he saw this was no ordinary item of clothing but a piece of wearable tech. Taro and Jarek looked at each other over their bent heads and smiled. Jarek decided it was safe to leave them to it.

329

Back on the bridge Jarek checked their course; he'd had to ascend at a shallow angle and then loop back in again in order to use the safe approach corridor. Looking outside, he saw that the top section of the beanstalk was already in sunlight again, and as the ship got closer he noticed how the counterweight and transfer-station both shone; they were completely coated with solarfilm, providing easy, eternal energy. He had to admit that the Sidhe thought bigger and longer-term than humans; they'd always been as interested in the control of space as in the control of people. Augmenting their maintenance-free solar system with fusion would mean occasional refuelling and checks on the reactor, but that fitted in with Jarek's plans for regular visits to Serenein from now on.

He kept half an ear on the proceedings below. From the sound of it, they were making some progress – at least he hadn't heard any tantrums yet.

He brought the *Heart of Glass* round so the *Setting Sun* came into view. The Sidhe ship looked comparatively tawdry against the bright solarfilm-covered transfer-station. He thought about calling Kerin and Damaru up to see the unusual sight, but it sounded like Taro was teaching Damaru how to use the v-suit, which was rather more important.

He lined up with the *Setting Sun*, and docked, then put the ship into standby and went back down. Nual emerged from her cabin as Jarek stepped off the ladder. Jarek was pleased to see they'd got Damaru suited up, though from Taro's expression he guessed it had been an uphill struggle.

Taro and Nual boarded the *Setting Sun* first. As Jarek followed with Kerin and Damaru he could see the tension in Kerin's face; the last time she'd been here she'd had her will stolen by one Sidhe and killed another; Kerin herself had been shocked by the deep and single-minded hatred she had displayed.

Once on board, Taro fell into step beside Damaru. It sounded to Jarek like they were getting on all right, even if much of Damaru's conversation sprang from a naked curiosity which would have been downright rude coming from anyone else.

While Nual made her way to the bridge he led his party to the

Setting Sun's cargo-bay. The room was dominated by a double row of comaboxes. Beyond them the loading doors were open to the dark transfer-station; though the station had shut down to save power, being docked to the *Setting Sun* meant it had kept its atmosphere, even if the temperature was on the low side.

'So, those got Consorts in then?'

Jarek started at Taro's question, and saw Kerin's brow furrow. 'Yeah,' he said slowly, 'that's them.' He had a good idea what Kerin was thinking: how the abilities of the sleeping boys could come in really handy in his fight against the Sidhe; and how, if he wanted to use them like that, there wasn't a lot she could do to stop him. 'Let's go through to the transfer-station,' he added hurriedly.

Or rather, to the edge of it. Once they reached the threshold of the massive shadowy room he asked Taro, 'All set?'

'Yeah,' Taro said, brandishing the toolkit he'd taken from the *Heart of Glass*.

'Be careful,' he told him. The capacitors might be low on charge, but they could still be dangerous.

'We'll be fine,' Taro said confidently.

Kerin went over and spoke with Damaru briefly; it looked to Jarek like the boy was eager to get to work.

The two boys took their first steps into the transfer-station, their suit-lights flashing in the darkness. Jarek said softly, 'Don't worry Kerin: he's only a comcall away.'

'Aye,' she said. Turning to Jarek she added, 'I wanted to ask you about your coms. It would be useful for us to have some of them below.'

'I'll see if I can sort that once we've fixed the point-defences. Are you all right to leave Damaru and Taro to it now?' Jarek didn't want to hassle her, but they had several hours' work ahead of them, and the lasers only had to let in a large enough spec of debris with the wrong trajectory ... He'd heard the spacers' legend – hopefully just a spacers' legend! – about a broken beanstalk that had wrapped itself around the equator of the planet it had been built to serve, cutting deep into the world's surface like a wire through butter.

'Aye. Let us go,' Kerin said after one last long look at the retreating figure of her son.

As they walked out of the hold, he asked, 'How are things going down there anyway?'

'We are progressing, slowly. The old Cariad encouraged mistrust and intrigue, and her ways still hold sway in the Tyr. Outside, the falling fire has passed, of course, though there was another, lesser ailment that came as it left.'

'A new disease?'

'Aye, a flux; quite unpleasant, though rarely fatal.'

'Oh.' He felt sick.

'What is it, Sais?'

'That might have been my fault,' he admitted.

'Your fault? How can a disease be your fault?'

'Serenein has been isolated for a long time. I could have brought that disease with me without realising it. I could've just been a carrier, or maybe I had a really mild case myself, but your people wouldn't have had any immunity. If I'd been in my right mind I might have thought of that at the time – and if I hadn't been so distracted this time ... *damn*. Well, it's not too late. We've been pretty thoroughly decontaminated recently, but all of us should get checked out in the *Setting Sun*'s medbay before anyone leaves the ship.'

'That sounds like a wise precaution.'

They had reached the engineering locker, which was actually a decent-sized storeroom. It didn't take Jarek long to collect the right tools. He checked the schematics on his com.

'Right,' he said, 'we need to lift the deck plating along the route of the central bus to expose the trunk cabling. I'll explain what and why if you're interested, but it's basically just a matter of taking up a load of panels.'

Once they'd got started, Kerin said, a little apprehensively, 'You said you had a gift for me – for us.'

'Yes, I do. It's a beacon, a device that can link you into human-space.'

'So my world will no longer be lost?'

'Exactly. Here, take this please—'

She lifted the first panel from his hands and propped it against the wall behind her. When she turned back to face him her expression was thoughtful. 'Is Serenein the first such isolated world to join the many worlds of humanity?'

'Yes and no. After the Sidhe Protectorate fell things went a bit crazy. Some systems suffered a catastrophic collapse; others were out of contact for decades, even centuries, although they were eventually rediscovered. But none of the systems we've found so far were deliberately hidden the way yours has been. Though the rest of humanity didn't know about them, their inhabitants generally knew there was someone else out there.'

'So there could be other lost worlds, as yet undiscovered?'

'It's possible.' He carefully lined the screwdriver up with the furthest screw, then paused before pushing it home, thinking about how much he should actually say to her.

Kerin said, 'Sais, do not think to save my feelings; you wonder if the Sidhe had more than one source of Consorts, do you not? You have explained what happens to the boys, that they become – I forget the word—'

'Transit-kernels. You're right; I'm sure that at one time there were more worlds like this, because shiftships were more common in Protectorate times, and the Sidhe would never have relied on a single location to breed their shift-minds. But that was then; these days I'm pretty sure it's just Serenein.'

'Which makes my world valuable, for all the wrong reasons.' When he glanced up at her, Kerin's expression was grim. 'I am sure the people of human-space will not simply give us what we ask for out of kindness. What do we have to trade, Sais? If the answer is "our children", then I do not wish this gift you have brought. I will not replace one unseen tyranny with another!'

'Kerin, that was never the plan,' Jarek said, bending over the panel again.

'Then just what was your intended fate for my world?' She sounded almost aggressively sceptical, a far cry from the meek woman who'd saved his life when he first arrived on Serenein.

'Surely in this universe of plenty, a backwards world like mine is of little interest?'

'Actually it is,' Jarek said firmly. 'We have this system – we call it beevee – which allows communication between different worlds ... but it does more than that. The whole economy of human-space is based on it – specifically, on its capacity.'

'Its *capacity*?'

'Sorry, I'll explain. These beacons, like the one I've got for you, allow a fixed amount of information to pass through them at a fixed rate, and they transmit it without any time-lag. The universe is short on constants like that. And every system has this capacity, because every system has a beacon. So they trade capacity – well, it's more *the promise* of capacity ... to cut a complicated story short, most people accept this capacity – *cap* – as the universal currency. They don't need to think any more about it than that. From your point of view, what you need to know is that just *having* a beacon gives your world an intrinsic value.' He pulled out the final screw with a flourish.

'So you give me a beacon, for nothing, and I trade its output for all the advantages of human-space? That sounds too good to be true!' said Kerin as she leaned forward to take the panel from Jarek.

Jarek moved along to the next floor-panel. 'You're quite right; of course there's more to it than that. If you're going to buy medicines, or much in the way of tech, you're going to need more than just the revenue your beacon's capacity can provide – but that's okay, because that leads me on to Plan B. Er, can you take these and put them in the tray in the toolbox?'

Kerin accepted the handful of loose screws, put them away, then waited for Jarek to continue.

'You remember I mentioned the beevee network?' he said as he began undoing the next panel. 'Well, to trade your beacon's cap – capacity – you need to be linked into it, and that's going to cause quite a stir – especially when people discover that your world has been going its own way since Protectorate times. They're going to be absolutely fascinated. Beevee transmits sound, and images too,

so they'll be able to see this amazing lost world for themselves –
that's a privilege they'll be more than happy to pay for,' he added
confidently. It helped that the Sidhe had already put surveillance
satellites in orbit, and instituted rules, like all acts of worship taking place under the open sky, to ensure the populace were easy to
observe.

'So what you are saying is that our backward nature is our main
asset ...'

'Yeah, that's right,' said Jarek slowly. Somehow his big idea
didn't sound so brilliant when he said it out loud.

'Sais, we are not some sideshow for others to gawp at! We are a
world, we are many thousands of people – we may not have great
knowledge or magical machines or all the advantages your people
have, but our lives are no less valid!'

'I *know* that, Kerin' he said, 'and I'm not trying to belittle you,
but you have to understand how human-space is likely to react
to Serenein. Most people live full and comfortable lives without ever leaving their home world – but they do crave novelty.
Entertainment is *big* business.'

'But only while we remain primitive? *That* is the feature which
makes us of interest, is it not? But it is exactly such isolation and
ignorance I seek to end.'

'Yes and that's the catch.' He turned his attention to a recalci-
trant screw on the current panel. Once he'd freed it, with Kerin
remaining silent he said, 'This is all optional. Until I register your
beacon, it isn't tied into the beevee network, so if you don't want
me to do that, I won't.'

'Would people want to come here, if this world interested them
enough? You say travel is rare, but it must happen, must it not?
For you are one such traveller.'

'In the long run yes, there might be enough interest for people
to come out here. Probably tourists, and possibly other traders, if
I—'

'Sais, the situation below is very delicate! The arrival of strangers
from the sky ... I shudder to think of what effect that might
have.'

'As I say, it's all optional. You could veto visitors. There are pan-human Treaties in place that allow systems to remain physically isolated if their inhabitants prefer it that way.'

'Good. But in that case, how would the benefits we might buy come to us?'

'We can use the revenue from the cap and beevee rights. I'll organise whatever you need and bring it to the transfer-station. In the long run, maybe I can also pick up items for trade – handmade stuff, embroidery, pots, that sort of stuff. It'll fetch a good price because it's unique to Serenein, which makes it rare. We can exchange the goods when the carousel makes its annual ascent of the silver thread at – what's it called again? Oh yeah, Sul Esgyniad – or more often, once you've got people to accept changes to their old ways.'

'Assuming I manage to do that. But Jarek, surely all this selling of "rights" and trading them for Serenein's requirements will distract you from your fight against the Sidhe?'

'Don't worry; I'll be using people I trust, and I've got access to lawyers who'll draw up watertight contracts—' he looked at her face and grinned an apology. 'Sorry, we'll get *written agreements* to make sure you and your people won't get exploited.' He held up the next panel. 'I've already made a few initial enquiries – discreetly of course. And if you do link in your beacon, you'd have full control over the feed to the beevee company: people would only see what you let them see.'

Kerin took the panel, then hesitated, her eyes clouded. 'This decision is too important to be made in haste,' she said slowly. 'I will need to think about it.'

CHAPTER FORTY-FIVE

Getting Damaru into the v-suit had tested Taro's patience and taken most of the trip back up to orbit. The boy was more interested in playing with the tech than in wearing it. He felt the fabric, fiddled with the backpack and stuck his hands down the legs to try and reach the boots.

After Kerin had tried and failed to talk Damaru into getting dressed, Taro hit on the trick of taking his own suit off and making a game of putting it on again: 'C'mon Damaru, bet I can get into mine quicker than you can get into yours!'

Damaru was up for that, until he got distracted by Taro's extra hi-tech suit. Taro carefully explained he *had* to have that particular suit, because it was the only one that fitted him, and Damaru's lip quivered – at which point Kerin had a few sharp words to say ... which brought on a minor sulk—

—until Damaru noticed that Taro was very conspicuously getting dressed, at which point he was back on side again.

As Damaru bent over to pull his own suit up, Kerin caught Taro's eye and said quietly, 'My son is not the fool people think, but he does select carefully what he sets his mind to.'

Taro understood. Damaru reminded him of Vy (on a bad day) – which made sense, given they were both male Sidhe, more or less.

They still had a few minutes before they docked, so Taro decided to take Damaru through the operation of the helmet and com – not that they expected to need them, but if something *did* go wrong and they had to suit up fully there wouldn't be time for

337

lessons. Plus it stopped Damaru trying to fiddle with the settings on his – or worse, Taro's – suit. Damaru wasn't wild about having his head enclosed, but the whole voice-in-the-ear thing tickled him so much that Taro had a job to get him to fold the helmet back when they heard Jarek coming down the steps.

Nual hung back when they boarded the *Setting Sun*; staying in the background to avoid pissing off Damaru and his mother. For once, Taro was glad when she didn't try to mindspeak to him, because he didn't want her to know how hard he was trying not to think about how she knew so much about this ship ... Taro had only met the *Setting Sun*'s human pilot briefly. He hadn't liked him much. He'd liked what'd happened to him even less ... though it hadn't been entirely Nual's fault: after all, he and Jarek had let her do it ...

Before Damaru went into the transfer-station Kerin had a few quick words with her son. Even though he was raring to get at the tech, he gave her his full attention, at least for a little while, and Taro found himself remembering Malia, the woman who'd brought him up, before she'd been murdered. He swallowed, trying to clear his tight throat. Kerin turned away, probably so the boy couldn't see her worried expression.

'Right, this is it,' Taro said cheerfully, 'suit-lights on!' and he stepped across the threshold, taking small, shuffling steps to stay in contact with the deck. He kept an eye on Damaru's feet; he wasn't sure the boy understood how complicated things could get if he lost his grip and started to drift off. Damaru spent a while watching his hands float in front of his face and brushing at his halo of hair; Taro was glad he'd thought to tie his own, longer hair back.

'Tummy feels funny,' complained Damaru.

'Funny as in "sick"?'

'Just ... funny.'

'You let me know if you're gonna p— be sick, right?'

'Right.'

Taro really hoped Damaru had it under control: nothing ruined your day quite like floating vomit.

The further in they got, the colder the air became, and Taro was glad of the insulation provided by his suit. Their breath steamed in the beams of their lights. Damaru drew closer; Taro suspected he found the huge dark room as spooky as he did.

Working out which bit of identical wall they needed to head for led to a few false starts, but by counting support struts he finally homed in on the section his com was indicating. 'We'll get this open together, and then I'm gonna point out a few things you need to know,' said Taro, trying to sound like he knew what he was on about. 'After that, just ask if there's anything you want me to look up. Oh, and don't touch the stuff I tell you not to. In fact, don't touch *anything* until I say it's safe.'

'Energy,' Damaru said hungrily. 'Behind here.'

'Oh yeah. And it's enough to hurt you, even if it ain't enough to do what it needs to.'

The maintenance panels were supposed to slide out of the way, but they obviously hadn't been opened for a long time and they were very stiff. It took both of them, pulling together, to get the first one moving. Taro's injured hand throbbed but whatever drugs the medi-glove was releasing were doing a prime job of keeping the pain at bay.

When they pulled back the final panel they revealed a set of four dark-brown squares, about a metre wide. The surfaces were ridged, to vent excess heat from the capacitors inside. Taro double-checked the diagram on his com against the tangle of wires and cables packed in between the capacitor covers: yep, this was it.

Damaru was watching him intently, waiting for his word. He smiled at the boy, and said, 'I'm gonna take you through what we've got here – what comes in, what goes out, what you can disconnect safely and what you really don't wanna touch. Then it's over to you.'

Though Damaru appeared to have listened to Taro's instructions, Taro still tensed the first time the boy reached for a cable. When nothing happened he relaxed, sending out a stream of white breath. Kerin was right: Damaru could be pretty smart, if he wanted. Taro only had to explain something once, and the boy had it – in fact, he'd actually worked out some of the set-up before Taro had finished looking it up on his com.

They ran into a few practical issues once they started using tools on the cables: neither of them had done anything like this in normal gravity, let alone in micro-grav, and more than once Taro found himself fielding a pair of pliers or waving aside an errant bit of wire. And it was bloody freezing in here, so they had to work with their suit gloves on, making some of the delicate stuff a bit tricky.

It was going to be a long haul, but looking at the expression on Damaru's face, Taro was certain they'd get there: the crazy kid was as happy as a stoned rat.

Nual had not realised quite how strong the antipathy was when male and female Sidhe met in the flesh. Being in Damaru's presence blocked her arcane senses, effectively blinding her – and made her skin crawl. No doubt she had the same effect on him. Despite this, there was an attraction there which, whilst not as strong as the repulsion, was more disturbing – if she were to be totally honest with herself, the sensations he sparked in her were not entirely unpleasant. In some ways, that was even worse. She told herself he could not help being what he was, any more than she could change her own nature ...

And here she was surrounded by reminders of that nature. Not so long ago she had read the mind of the human pilot of the *Setting Sun* – no, more than that, she had *subsumed* his mind, taking everything he was at the moment of his death. To do that, she had had to seduce him. She had had no other choice; the man had been too damaged by his Sidhe mistresses for her to read him normally. And it had worked: the pilot's memories were part of her. Nual had told herself she had his knowledge, but not his soul; yet being here, in the place he had thought of as home, she was not so sure. Everything she saw, everywhere she looked, triggered a rush of associations, from the bed where he had pleasured his Sidhe lovers to the personalised set-up on the ship's main control panel in front of her. Even the comp's voice was modulated to sound like one of the man's mistresses, though that particular problem was easily fixed, and she did so at once.

The sensations awakened in her by being in the pilot's personal space were disconcerting, and she could not afford any distractions. Though the routine she needed to run was a variation on the standard pre-transit power-down, there were important differences. She needed to apply herself fully to the problem, and for that, she must shut out her darker thoughts.

Only when she was sure everything was progressing as it should did she allow herself to relax a little. Her unease was still present – and with it now came a sharp, sweet taste deep in her throat. This wasn't merely an unfortunate stolen memory: this was foresight.

Of what, though?

The sense of narrowing options almost overwhelmed her for a moment, but the details remained infuriatingly vague.

When intuition fails ... try logic. What would be the worst thing that could happen right now?

There was one obvious answer. A Sidhe-driven ship didn't need a beacon to exit from shiftspace, so theoretically it could turn up anywhere. However, the nature of the translation through shiftspace meant a ship usually arrived near the point where any other recent visitors had dropped into realspace.

Nual turned the ship's sensors on the arrival point the *Heart of Glass* had used. There was nothing there. She got the comp to scan a wide volume of space around that point, allowing for the distance a ship arriving any time in the last four hours might have travelled since. That was all clear too. She extended the search, running the simulation all the way back to the *Heart of Glass*'s original arrival. She knew Jarek would have been running scans of his own until flying through the debris cloud took up all his attention, but there was no harm in double-checking.

Once again there was nothing.

She left the sensors trained on the exit point; if anyone did arrive, she'd know at once.

If whatever was tugging at her subconscious wasn't the arrival of the Sidhe, then what was it? Could it be to do with Taro? He and Damaru were dealing with forces that could kill if not handled carefully ... but he knew that, and he would be careful. And this didn't feel like something that affected only her lover. This time the infuriatingly nebulous sense of impending doom encompassed all of them.

She was distracted from her brooding by a system message: the shutdown was entering the final stage. Could the problem be with the reactor itself? She reran her earlier diagnostics. The board was still green. Not that, then.

Something to do with the planet below, perhaps? No, that wasn't it either – but thinking about Serenein did distract her for a moment. She found herself wondering about how it would be to live as the Cariad. There was something to be said for ruling an adoring people, caring for them while being worshipped unconditionally. It would be a lonely life, of course, never having contact with your own kind, having no one to confide in – not that she herself had any contact with the Sidhe, at least not if she could help it. But she did have Jarek – and Taro, of course—

She was so wrapped up in her thoughts that she nearly missed the single line of text scrolling across the bottom of the flatscreen monitor. Then the taste of ginger almost overwhelmed her.

As soon as she had control of herself again she let her hands glide over the board, guided by instincts not her own. She needed to be absolutely sure of this.

Finally she drew a long, hissing breath and commed Jarek. 'They're here,' she said.

'Who's here?'

'The Sidhe.'

'Fuck. You're sure? I mean when you say *here*—'

'I'm sending their current vector to your com now.'

There was a short pause. Then, 'Holy shit! Are you sure you've got this right? No offence, but you're not a spacer—'

'No, I'm not,' she said caustically, 'but I "knew" someone who was, and I know *exactly* how to use the instruments on this ship.'

'Ah, yeah, I guess you do. Sorry, Nual. But those coordinates put them inside the defence grid!'

'I know.'

'So how the hell did—?'

'I have absolutely no idea. They're coming in on a totally

unexpected vector. But it looks like they will be here in less than two hours. And they're in a big ship – a lot larger than the *Setting Sun*.'

'Right, I'm coming up to the bridge. I'll com Taro.'

Jarek arrived with Kerin in tow. 'I guess the point-defences will have to wait,' he said grimly, 'we need to get the defence grid working and destroy that ship.' He turned to Nual. 'Earlier you said something about the weapons being controlled from something called a cold-start console – have you managed to find out any more about that?'

'I have,' she said. 'It's not exactly a console; it's more a standalone comp. I think it's a failsafe, in case a Cariad goes rogue. An incoming ship can transmit a code to this comp from outside the range of the defences, and once that code is verified, the comp sends out a signal which takes the grid completely offline. Nothing the Cariad can do from below – or any later incoming ship can do from above – will have any effect on the defences.'

'So how do we get them working again – I assume it *is* possible to reactivate them?'

'It is. Someone needs to enter the correct counter-code into the cold-start console, which then transmits the reset signal to the defence grid to reactivate it.'

'That sounds simple enough – assuming we have the code.'

'That's the first problem: it looks like the reactivation code is also the shut-down code: the defence grid can only be reactivated by the code that shut it down. And whilst the *Setting Sun* would have had *a* valid shut-down code, once the Sidhe knew the ship was lost, they will have come up with a new set of codes, which we *don't* have.'

'We don't know that—' Jarek broke off as Taro and Damaru arrived and the boy went straight over to his mother, muttering something inaudible. Taro moved to stand next to Nual, who was relieved he didn't kiss her like he usually did; Kerin's already healthy distrust of the Sidhe would only increase if she discovered that Nual had a human lover.

343

Taro said, 'Sorry we're late. What'd we miss?'

Jarek recapped. It sounded even worse, second time around.

Taro gave a taut grin and said, 'I guess we can't just run away?'

'No,' said Jarek, 'we can't. Even if I were willing to give up control of the beanstalk without a fight – which I'm not – they're going to come after us and kill us anyway.'

'Yeah, that's what I thought,' he said. 'Just had to ask. We gotta understand all our options!'

Jarek said, 'We should try to find the original code in the *Setting Sun*'s files.'

'It's worth a try,' said Nual, though she was not sure it was.

'But if that don't work, I guess we'll need to, like, hack this cold-start console?' asked Taro.

In the brief silence that followed, all eyes turned to Damaru.

Kerin said softly to him, 'Were you listening to that, my lovely boy? Do you understand what we wish you to do?'

'Kerin.'

When Kerin looked up at her interruption, Nual felt the full force of her distrust and barely restrained loathing. She tried to ignore it, and continued, 'Kerin, you're right that we need Damaru to do this, but you need to be aware of the other problem.'

'What other problem?' asked Kerin carefully.

'The location of the cold-start console: it is on the outside of the transfer-station.'

'Outside as in, in space?' she asked, swallowing.

'Yes,' said Nual. 'A rogue Cariad would have access to machine empaths like Damaru, who could hack the codes for her. What she would not have is a v-suit. She couldn't access the cold-start console.'

Kerin looked at Jarek. 'Sais, you have told me that what is outside here will kill us. I know you have those special suits, but even so, I would not wish to put my son in such danger.'

'Neither would I, ideally,' said Jarek, 'but I can't see any alternative. And he wouldn't be alone: I'd go with him.'

'Is there really no other option?' Kerin was deeply conflicted:

Nual sensed that she feared for her child, but also acknowledged that he might be their only hope.

There was a warning trill and Nual looked down at the new message.

Finally Jarek broke the anxious silence. 'Please tell me that's good news.'

'I wish I could,' she murmured, 'but it isn't.' More loudly, she continued, 'The Sidhe ship has launched a fast shuttle and it is already drawing ahead of the main ship. Whatever we are going to do, we have to hurry.'

CHAPTER FORTY-SIX

Maelgyn was reticent at first, but Ifanna knew his heart; she had only to persuade him to follow it. She thought he murmured something that sounded like, 'This time it will be perfect—' but then he surrendered to her fully, and words were no longer needed.

As they were joined, Ifanna sensed the glorious truth: she was not only *his* goddess; if his plan came to fruition, she would be *everyone*'s goddess. Here was a wonder undreamt of, and it redoubled her passion for him. She began to wonder if what she was feeling was worthy of the word 'love' – whether it was or no, she knew now that she had a greater destiny than she could ever have hoped.

Afterwards, he turned away from her without a word. She touched his shoulder and he flinched, shaking her off, but he did not tell her to go, and she took comfort in that. She lay stretched out next to him on the narrow bed, tight against the chilly wall on one side, but touching warm flesh at hip and shoulder on the other. Her wounded side pained her, and her mind was in turmoil, but eventually, she slept.

She awoke to hear Maelgyn call out nervously, 'Who is it?'

The voice at the door was muffled. 'I have a message from the only true Escori.'

She felt Maelgyn relax at the man's words. 'Wait a moment, please!' He threw himself from the bed, flinging the covers back over her, then hurried over to his discarded undershirt. He dragged it over his head as he crossed the room.

As he opened the door a crack and began a murmured conversation, Ifanna sat up and pulled the covers around her against the chill. The grey light of dawn leaked through the shutters while she waited for Maelgyn to conclude his business.

When he turned back to her he had a large pack in his hands and for a moment she wondered if they were going to run away together after all. Last night, that would have been a dream fulfilled, but now her sights were set higher.

He pulled a cloth bundle from the pack and threw it towards the bed. 'Put this on!' he commanded. He was careful to keep his back to her.

'Have I caused offence?' she asked quietly, worried.

'Just get dressed, please.'

She unknotted the bundle to discover a heavy cloak, wrapped around more items: a skimpy robe similar to the one she had been given in the Tyr, this one adorned with braid and embroidery, and a small bag containing combs and cosmetics. 'Am I to be disguised as a Putain Glan?' she asked, looking down at the little pots of colour.

'You are,' Maelgyn said shortly. He was pulling on a red-trimmed robe.

'And you will be disguised too,' she said lightly, 'as a priest of Carunwyd.' She did not voice her thought: Carunwyd was the goddess of love; that was an apt disguise indeed. She finished lacing her robe under her breasts and spread out the other items on the bed. She selected the largest comb and ran it through her tangled hair, wincing as it snagged on the knots, then caught up the full length, twisted it and secured it on top of her head. She used the smaller combs to tidy some of the trailing strands. She was worried the effect was not going to be particularly enticing, but when she glanced up she saw Maelgyn watching her, a cup in his hand. Though she could not be sure of his expression in the dim light, she could tell that he wanted her again.

Keeping her voice neutral, she said, 'I have no skill in painting my face: what do you wish me to do?'

'L— Leave that for now,' he stammered. 'Time is short.' He lowered his eyes and drained his cup, then said, 'We must leave at once.'

'For the Tyr?'

'For the Tyr, aye.'

She could not see his face clearly, but she could feel his emotions, and what she sensed both frightened and aroused her. There was a wildness, as though something long caged had been released, but at the same time he was trying hard not to give in to her, building barriers to re-establish the distance between them. She resolved to chip away at those barriers, slowly and carefully, until she was able to release the side of him she had seen briefly in the night. Then they could be happy together, she was sure of it.

They donned their cloaks and left. Ifanna hesitated before taking his arm, then decided to risk it. He tensed, but did not tell her to let go. As they hurried through the growing light of morning it occurred to her that his apparent coldness might be nothing more than nerves at what they were about to do.

They turned into the steeper, richer thoroughfares leading up to the Tyr, and she said quietly, 'Maelgyn? Is there any part of the plan you can tell me? I will understand if not, but I wish to do my part to the best of my abilities.'

'You are to take over a role currently held by one with no right to it,' he said tightly.

Ifanna had half-expected him to chide her for not using the priestly honorific and when he said nothing, she smiled to herself, buoyed by such intimacy. 'That is what I hoped,' she responded. 'After all, if the mask must be worn by a mortal woman, it should be one with talent, should it not?'

'Precisely,' he breathed. She thought he was relieved that he did not have to state his intentions openly.

'Then I must ask something else: what of my promise to you?'

'W— What promise?' he asked, looking worried.

'When first we met, you forbade me to use my powers.' Arguably she had already broken that promise – but no, he had wanted her as much as she wanted him; no compulsion had been needed there.

'Aye, I did.' From the sound of it he had forgotten his earlier words, which annoyed Ifanna for a moment. Then he continued, 'You are free of that promise, provided it serves our cause.'

'Thank you.' She added softly, 'I would keep any promise I made to you.'

When they reached the Tyr he led her down a side-passage near the entrance, then knocked on one of the doors using a similar sequence to the one he had used at the shuttered house. Someone called out and they went into a small room. The walls were lined with shelves holding more scrolls than Ifanna had ever seen in her life, maybe hundreds of them. Escori Garnon stood before one of the two desks in the middle of the room. Two monitors, possibly the same men who had been with him at the tavern, waited at the back of the room.

'She has not painted her face,' said the Escori.

Maelgyn responded, 'There was no time.'

Ifanna forced herself not to take offence at being talked about as though she were not there.

'Hmm. Hopefully it will not matter, given the early hour. You will need to keep your cloaks on anyway, to hide your weapons.'

'Weapons, *Gwas*?' said Maelgyn

The Escori ignored the question, continuing, 'Gwaun and Onfel will accompany you. They are worth two men apiece. I had hoped to recruit more to our cause, but as we are, unfortunately, having to move sooner than I had anticipated, I have procured a crossbow for you. Onfel, kindly show Maelgyn how to use the weapon.'

The monitor came over and demonstrated; the mechanism appeared simple enough. 'Return it to us to reload, *Gwas*,' the monitor advised.

'So I will definitely be using this?' Maelgyn sounded worried.

'You will. Your task is to shoot the false Cariad – fatally, if you can, but if you do not succeed, one of the monitors will finish her off. They will be using their own first shots to incapacitate the Consort and Urien – the Consort will of course be released when this is over. As for my fellow Escori ... I have some questions to ask Urien.' For the first time he looked at Ifanna and said, in a wry voice, 'If the new Cariad permits it.'

Ifanna's heart raced. Should she answer? She met his eyes, at the same time circling her breast to show she meant no disrespect by such boldness.

From his expression, this was the right response. 'Can I trust you, Ifanna?' he asked quietly.

She held his gaze. 'You can, *Gwas*,' she responded earnestly.

'Good: I sense that your heart is true,' he said after a moment. '*Chilwar*, you will carry a weapon too, then, and when the other three have fired theirs you are to give your crossbow to *Gwas* Maelgyn, so he may keep control of the room while my monitors reload. Do you understand?'

'I understand, *Gwas*.'

'Remember, *chilwar*, though your powers are a curse, you may transcend that burden by using them in a just cause – and this *is* a just cause.'

She realised he was giving her permission to use her witch's talents to help kill the false Cariad. 'Thank you, *Gwas*,' she said quietly.

'And you Maelgyn: is everything clear to you?'

'Aye, *Gwas*.'

'Then you should be going – Urien will be wondering where his records have got to.'

As they left, Ifanna could not help but ponder what part, if any, Garnon was to play in these momentous events, save to take credit when the night's grim work was done. She put aside the unworthy thought; after all, Maelgyn said Garnon was a great man.

As they moved deeper into the Tyr further doubts assailed her. She found herself glad they would not be killing the Consort; though her faith was worn down to a small knot of hope and guilt, she did not wish to be party to the murder of such an innocent soul … and now she considered it, she suspected that the false Cariad was under Urien's control, which made her innocent too; it was a shame she had to die.

Maelgyn was obviously uncomfortable; he had not only to hide a crossbow under his cloak, but also to grapple with the pile of scrolls that provided their excuse for visiting the Cariad. Ifanna noticed that he kept his eyes down whenever they passed anyone on their route through the Tyr. The few servants they saw circled their breast for him; the priests nodded an acknowledgement. If anyone was curious to see outdoor cloaks worn so deep within the Tyr, they did not say.

When they reached the doors to the audience chamber, Ifanna's apprehension increased. She remembered her first time here – and how so much had changed, in a few short days.

The monitors on the door started to question Ifanna's presence, but Onfel interrupted them, saying, 'Does no one brief anyone properly these days! Have you only just come on-shift?'

'Aye, captain,' the monitor said, looking uncomfortable.

'Then you should know that Escori Urien requested these scrolls' – he gestured at Maelgyn, who kept his head bowed – 'and the Cariad requested this woman. It is not for me – or *you* – to question either the Escori's request or the Cariad's, is that clear?' He glared at both monitors, who stood as straight as they could.

'Now, will you open the doors and call the inner guard so we may replace him?' he barked. When the monitors exchanged glances Onfel said, 'Do not tell me you are not even aware of the changes in this morning's rota?'

'Aye, of course sir; my apologies,' one of the monitors said quickly. His companion opened the doors without further question.

Ifanna had been wondering how they were to cross the chasm, but when they entered the chamber she was relieved to see a slender, rail-less bridge in place.

'Take care crossing, everyone,' said Maelgyn unnecessarily.

Ifanna wondered if his thoughts matched hers: that they were about to enter divine territory. If they were mistaken, Heavenly retribution might well be waiting for them.

But they crossed without incident, and no such retribution greeted them on the far side. Maelgyn put the scrolls down and they paused for a moment outside the door to the Cariad's room. Ifanna resolved to use her powers against the false Cariad only to incapacitate, not to harm her.

One of the monitors opened the door, and the four of them rushed in.

There was movement ahead, someone turning rapidly—

—the *twang* of multiple crossbows—

—and the person they had thought to surprise, Escori Urien, was facing the door as though expecting them. He was sitting in a seat of strange design, and he too had a crossbow in his hand. There was no one else in the room.

All this Ifanna took in during an endless moment of frozen panic. Even as she was trying to work out what to do, one of the monitors fell to the floor, clutching his belly. Urien dropped his own weapon, which also clattered to the ground, and for a moment his head drooped, and Ifanna caught sight of the bolt, sticking out of his shoulder. But he straightened again almost at once, as though determined not show weakness.

Ifanna, remembering his cold condemnation at her judgment, decided to try and attack Urien's mind, but though she strove to catch his eye, his attention was focused on the remaining monitor, who was fumbling to reload his crossbow. Ifanna looked around and her gaze alighted on Maelgyn. She realised he had not fired yet; the tip of his crossbow wavered uncertainly.

As Ifanna looked back at Urien, his eyes met hers, and she knew at once that this was not someone on whom her powers would ever work. She did catch the echo of one of his thoughts: something that had puzzled him had become clear the moment he saw her face.

'Ah, Maelgyn.' Urien's voice was breathless with pain, but it was still loud enough to make Ifanna jump. 'I appear to have misjudged the situation. Still … that is one mystery solved. Siarl was right. She *is* your daughter.'

She is your daughter.

A roaring began in Ifanna's ears. She saw Maelgyn's grip tighten on his weapon.

I am his daughter.

I am his DAUGHTER.

The roaring grew, and she turned and shot Maelgyn in the chest. As he fell, she glimpsed the monitor behind him bending over his own crossbow and she sent out a great wave of formless pain. The man let go of his weapon, clutched at his head, and went crashing to the ground. Ifanna ignored him. She flung her crossbow away and rushed over to … to—

She threw herself down beside him and screamed, 'Tell me it is not true! Tell me!'

Maelgyn's gaze was already clouding. 'You— You are everything she should have been. I am so sorry—'

'No!' she cried, 'please, no—'

His eyes closed, and he managed one last word, as soft as a breath: 'Aelwen …'

Someone nearby, speaking so quietly Ifanna could barely hear him over the roaring in her ears, said curiously, 'And Aelwen was your mother, was she not?'

The roaring grew to fill the world and Ifanna scuttled backwards until she came up hard against a wall. She fell onto her side, hugging her knees so tightly to her chest that she thought her body would break – she *wanted* it to break, for it had betrayed her …

… and yet it did not, and the roaring grew louder, until she had no choice save to start screaming, just to drown it out.

CHAPTER FORTY-SEVEN

Taro and Kerin accompanied Damaru and Jarek to the *Setting Sun*'s cargo-hold while Nual stayed on the bridge, searching the ship's comp for the code to unlock the weaponry. The shuttle would reach the beanstalk in just over half an hour. Jarek had voiced all their thoughts when he'd cursed and said, 'I just wish we had some way of knowing who's on that shuttle and what they're up to!'

'If wishes were feathers, we would grow wings and fly to Heaven,' Kerin said, and at the blank looks, explained, 'It is something my mother used to say. There is no point worrying about what we cannot know, Sais.'

Normally he lived his life by just that sort of maxim, but with his enemies closing in and his friends looking to him for leadership, it wasn't much use to him right now. His state of mind wasn't improved by having to wear the v-suit that had once belonged to the *Setting Sun*'s pilot, and from Taro's expression, he didn't much care to remember the man either – but they could worry about the emotional baggage later; right now they needed to concentrate on surviving the next couple of hours.

When they reached the *Setting Sun*'s hold, Kerin persuaded Damaru to shuffle into the transfer-station until he was free of gravity, so Taro could hoist him up by his armpits. He let out an alarmed squeak, quickly followed by loud giggles. 'I can fly!' he cried delightedly as Taro bore him off, 'I can fly!'

Taro responded, a little breathlessly, 'Yeah, so you can.'

Jarek wasn't travelling by Angel; he'd dug out his old propulsion-pack from the *Heart of Glass*. It had been a couple of years since he'd done any zero-g work; he used the trip across the darkened transfer-station to get some practice – better to screw up in here, in private, than out there in space. He'd only managed to get halfway across by the time the others touched down at the airlock on the far side.

While Taro waited for him, he got Damaru sealed up in his v-suit. Then he gave Jarek a hand to crank the door open and, stuck to the deck again, suit-lights blazing, they shuffled into the airlock in single file. There was a certain farcical element to the proceedings, but Jarek couldn't stop thinking of how damn long everything was taking. They had nineteen minutes until the shuttle arrived, and counting.

As soon as Taro closed the inner door, Jarek started cranking the outer one, just far enough to let them all through. It opened tantalisingly slowly, showing a slice of space and, far below, the globe of Serenein itself, with its ice-locked poles and crumpled band of habitable land around the equator. They killed their suit-lights, then Jarek exited carefully. When he turned to help Damaru the boy looked terrified, and Jarek could hear him breathing hard over the com.

'Damaru,' he said, 'come to me – it's all right.'

'The beyond, it does not stop!' he muttered frantically.

'I know – try closing your eyes.'

'No! Feel funny!'

'All right then, keep your eyes open, but Damaru, *look at me*.'

Damaru's terrified gaze locked on Jarek.

'That's good. Now, listen to me! You have to come out here because this is where the tech is. Do you understand?'

Silence.

Jarek switched to the private channel. 'Taro, just lift him up, slowly.'

'He don't sound happy, Jarek.'

'No, but if he really couldn't handle space he'd have done something drastic by now – I know him: he'll deal with it when he has to. We just have to take it easy.'

Jarek needed Damaru with him for more than the boy's technical abilities: the Sidhe would scan for sentiences as soon as they were in range, just as Nual had done; Damaru's presence would shield him, and that was the only way to make sure the Sidhe didn't head straight for them – and the cold-start console.

Of course, if they hung around the airlock too long the Sidhe wouldn't need to rely on their powers to spot them; all they'd have to do was look.

Taro said over the open channel, 'I'm gonna lift you up now, Damaru, and we're gonna fly, just like we did inside. You keep looking at J— You keep your eyes on Sais now, and everything'll be fine.'

Damaru flinched when Taro's arms snaked around him, but he didn't resist. Jarek kept smiling at him, encouraging him, as Taro lifted Damaru clear of the airlock and floated out. He could still hear Damaru's harsh breaths, and Taro's face, visible over his shoulder, was set in a frown of concentration.

So far, so good. 'Now we're going to fly again, Damaru,' Jarek said calmly. 'You just keep looking at me.' He thumbed the controls on his chest and began to move slowly up the side of the transfer-station. Taro matched his pace. He was wearing his shimmer-cloak and the bottom corner had partially wrapped round his leg, creating the disconcerting illusion that Taro's knee was missing. Jarek looked away.

Suddenly the light brightened as they came into full sunlight. A fraction of a second later, the v-suits' visors darkened automatically. Damaru cried out, and began to struggle in Taro's arms.

'Whoa! Whoa! Whoa!' said Jarek, 'don't panic, I'm still here!'

Damaru's head was twitching from side to side, and even through the darkened visor the rolling whites of his eyes were visible.

Jarek could see Taro was having to fight to keep hold of him. 'Damaru!' he said sternly, deliberately mimicking Kerin's tones, 'calm down!' At the same time he opened his arms in a welcoming hug. 'I'm still here, I'm still with you. Do you hear me, Damaru?'

Damaru's panicked flailing eased off a little, though not before he'd managed to accidentally head-butt Taro, who responded with the sort of language Kerin probably wouldn't want her son hearing.

Jarek said, 'That's it, Damaru, you're doing really well.' He surreptitiously checked the time. Thirteen minutes.

Jarek's com chimed. He took the call, and was relieved when Nual announced, 'I have found the unlock codes: there are three possible combinations. I'm sending them to you now.'

'Got them. What happens if I try all three and we don't get a result?'

'Nothing, as far as I can tell. There is no additional security: either you enter the right code and the grid reactivates, or you don't and it doesn't.'

'That's something, at least – I was worried we'd have to get it right first time, or be locked out forever.' Not that the approaching Sidhe ship wasn't incentive enough to succeed quickly. 'The shuttle's twelve minutes out, according to my suit timer. How about the main vessel: is it still incoming?'

'It is, and I've got a visual on it now: it looks like a military transport ship. Though it is probably wise to assume it is armed, I do not believe the Sidhe would be stupid enough to use space weaponry near the beanstalk.'

'Let's hope you're right. Though a military transport also implies trained soldiers ...'

'Quite possibly.'

'Just what we need. Right, we're nearly there. Jarek out.' They'd travelled most of the way up the side of the transfer-station. Above them was the distant, shining rock of the counterweight, and beyond that, the star-scattered darkness of space.

'Where to now?' Taro asked as they reached the 'top'.

A good question. Jarek's suit inertials would direct him to the right panel, but all he could see was a shining expanse of solarfilm. 'Let's get clear of the edge, and then you can put Damaru down. We'll cover the rest of the way on foot.'

'Yeah, 'cos I need to get back inside, ready to repel boarders.' Taro was trying to make a joke of it, but his voice showed his nerves.

'Here's as good a place as any.'

Taro touched down more gently than Jarek did, and kept his hands hovering above Damaru's shoulders in case the younger boy needed any help. Jarek said, 'Right, Damaru, flying time's over; you'll have to walk for a while. Remember how you walked inside, always keeping your feet pressed down? That's how you have to walk here too. Do you understand?'

'Understand.' He wobbled slightly, then stood stock-still.

Jarek said, 'That's great, Damaru. Now just stay where you are while I clip this on.' As he shuffled over to the boy he found the solarfilm didn't provide as good a grip as the decking inside the transfer-station; they'd need to watch that.

Once Jarek had attached his wrist to Damaru's with a long tether, Taro said, 'Here, Jarek, take this.' He held out a small dark roll of cloth.

'Isn't that Nual's shimmer-cloak? Won't she need it?'

'We thought it'd be more use to you out here.'

'Thanks.' Jarek grinned at him and clamped the bundle under his arm.

Taro pulled his own cloak tight around him, half disappearing into its dark folds, then took off. 'Good luck,' he said over the com as he flew back towards the lip.

'You too.'

Jarek double-checked his suit readouts and looked around, orienting himself. His heartbeat sped up when he spotted a wavering star off to one side: the Sidhe shuttle, coming their way. How good were the shuttle's sensors? Could it spot them from this range? Time to use Taro's gift; no point in making it easy for the Sidhe bitches. He unfurled the cloak – which turned out to be easier said than done without gravity – and fastened it round his neck, then smoothed it down over his suit as best he could.

He turned to Damaru, who was standing motionless, his elongated shadow streaming away across the bright surface. 'We need to get going, Damaru,' he said. 'You just walk slowly, same as you did inside the transfer-station with Taro. I'll be right beside you.' He'd have had a better chance of hiding Damaru with the cloak if he'd been able to stay behind him, but he was pretty sure the boy would panic without having someone to focus on.

'Too big.' Damaru's voice was barely audible over the com.

'Don't look, Damaru. Keep your eyes down, like this.' Jarek bent his own head, exaggerating the gesture to encourage Damaru to follow suit. 'Good! That's the way, Damaru. Now focus on the place you're about to put your foot, then move that foot.'

'Darkness there ...'

'Yeah, that's just your shadow. Ignore it. Try the other foot now.'

Their progress was excruciatingly slow. Damaru held himself hunched over, his arms pressed to his sides, as though shouldering the invisible weight of the void. His breathing was just this side of panicked.

Jarek could see the beanstalk cable ahead, a slender line of silver against the darkness. The shuttle would arrive in – he checked his com – seven minutes. His shoulders tensed further.

Finally they reached the right panel. Fortunately it was only about ten metres from the edge – if they'd had to cross the entire top of the station they would have been in trouble – but that wasn't so good from the point of view of remaining out of sight of the approaching shuttle.

'Right, we're here, Damaru. You just stay still. Keep looking at your feet; I'll open up the console.'

The panel had a pair of latches on one side. Jarek crouched, careful to keep his feet flat, and tried to undo the first, but it wouldn't budge. He reached into his pack for a set of grips and tried again. By the time the latch finally moved, Jarek had cramp in his hand and burning shins from holding himself in one position. Everything was so much more complicated without grav. He straightened carefully. Damaru was still staring at his feet. Jarek took a shuffling step to the side, crouched down again and went to work on the other latch. He was expecting the panel itself to give him grief too, but it slid back relatively easily to reveal a shallow hole about a metre square and a quarter of a metre deep. At the base of the hole was a raised cube with handles on either side of it. He guessed those handles were designed for the user to hook his – or rather *her* – feet through. As Jarek slid back the inner cover to reveal the screen set into the top of the cube he noticed Damaru looking on with interest. 'Do you want to come over and sit down, Damaru?' he asked.

After a few seconds of fruitless and dangerous flailing from the boy, Jarek activated his pack, picked Damaru up and lowered him over the hole. Damaru didn't complain, and he put his feet in the restraints as Jarek directed, then crouched down over the screen. Jarek landed next to him and scrunched himself up awkwardly to keep the soles of his feet in full contact with the solarfilm. He pulled a hardened flat-comp out of his pack and handed it carefully to Damaru, who'd already located and uncovered the plug socket. Old, clunky tech, but solid, and vacuum-proof. Jarek let out a quiet sigh of relief when the console's screen lit up, displaying the words READY FOR INPUT.

'Damaru, we've got some codes; we're going to try them first, so you might not need to do much at all. Shall I enter the codes into the comp for you?'

'No,' said Damaru possessively.

'Do you – er – do you know how to use a keyboard?' Jarek asked carefully.

His voice full of pride, Damaru said, 'I have learned my letters and my numbers!'

'That's great,' Jarek said, meaning it. 'Before we go any further, I'm going to spread this over us.' He draped Nual's cloak around Damaru's shoulders – it wouldn't hide them completely, but they were both sitting down so it would help keep them from any casual observers.

Damaru entered the first code.

No response.

The same with the second.

According to Jarek's com, the shuttle was less than a minute away, though he couldn't see it – presumably it was occluded by the transfer-station. That was fine by him; it couldn't see them either.

Damaru tried the third code, but again it had no effect.

Looked like he was going to get to play after all. Jarek said, 'Over to you, Damaru.'

CHAPTER FORTY-EIGHT

Kerin would have found it easier to dislike Nual if the Sidhe had not been making such an obvious effort to be patient with her – she must be frustrated by Kerin's ignorance of the workings of the *Setting Sun*, yet she was doing her best not to show it. And she had been so apologetic when she had interrupted the lesson because her 'agent' found the codes Jarek needed.

Nonetheless, Kerin breathed a sigh of relief when Nual left her alone on the ship's bridge. For a while she watched the coloured dots in the cunning projection Nual had set running. It was hard to believe those glowing patterns represented the approach of their doom.

Her thoughts returned to Sais' offer: while her instinct was to be appalled at the idea of the lives of her people being reduced to mere entertainment, she had to admit this option did have the advantage that it kept outsiders from her world – assuming Sais had spoken truly when he told her that those who held power in human-space would respect Serenein's sovereignty. She did not think he would deliberately lie to her; but she did worry that he might not know as much about such matters as he thought he did.

It had occurred to her, when they first set foot on the *Setting Sun*, that she could simply ask Sais to take her and Damaru away with him. They could leave their problems behind and make a new life elsewhere. She had no idea whether he would agree to that, but it did not matter; she had entertained the possibility for no more than a heartbeat. She would stand – or fall – with her world.

A soft chime sounded; the accompanying message confused her

for a moment – until she identified the *dirtside console* as the console in her room. After another short delay while she found the correct command to accept the message, Urien's head and shoulders appeared on the main screen. 'Ah, Kerin,' he said. 'I was beginning to worry my call would go unheard.'

'No, I am here. What is wrong with your shoulder Urien? That looks like—'

'A crossbow bolt? It is. But the bleeding has stopped and the wound does not pain me greatly.' His pale face belied his words. He told her succinctly about the attempted coup, concluding, 'This ingenious chair saved me – that, and my decision to borrow a crossbow from one of the duty monitors.'

'And what was the final fate of the rebels?' Kerin asked.

'The priest and one monitor are dead. The other monitor and the girl are only incapacitated – I am afraid you will need new bedsheets, for I had nothing else to bind them with. I have retracted the bridge, so no one can reach me here, but I hope to see you back soon, not least because of your skills as a healer.' His voice was breathy and weak.

'I look forward to seeing you in the flesh again too,' she said, hoping she would not be too late.

'May I do anything to help effect the repairs from here? After all, I am not going anywhere.'

'We have things under control, at least for now, but I will call again if we need your help. Just rest and relax, Urien – and do not take any action that may reopen that wound!'

Though she would not burden him further with the details of the situation up above, if it looked like the Sidhe were about to retake the transfer-station Kerin resolved to warn Urien, so that he might flee. Not that she expected he would.

Taro had never really got his head round this 'keeping fit' fad, possibly because for most of his life he'd been too busy just staying alive. As he cranked the airlock shut behind him he could feel the sweat being sucked up by the v-suit. He allowed himself a few seconds to catch his breath before he got to work on the inner door.

As the door eased open his suit-light lit the familiar figure waiting for him on the far side, floating just above the floor. He was
pleased to see Nual had appropriated one of the Setting Sun's v-
suits for herself; it might have some use as armour if it came down
to a hands-on fight. He tried to com her, but her suit's com wasn't
routed through the *Heart of Glass*'s system; something else they
hadn't had time to sort. Instead, he projected, *<Hi!>*

<Hello yourself.>

Taro tried not to get distracted by the intoxicating closeness of
mindspeech.

Behind her, the transfer-station was in total darkness; the *Setting
Sun*'s cargo-hold doors were shut, sealing the ship off from the
transfer-station. He opened the airlock door just wide enough to
get through, and squeezed out. *<Any chance you could give me a
hand getting this door closed again?>* he asked.

<Of course.>

As they straightened after cranking the door, she grabbed him
and he felt himself sucked deeper into her mind. He tried to ask
<Have we got time for this now?> but her response was to pull him
in tighter, and he gave himself up to it ... then her mental hold
relaxed.

<Sorry,> she projected, *<I needed to hide your presence.>*

<From them out there?>

<Yes. Someone just tried to scan us.>

<Did they spot us?>

*<She is not that powerful, so I was able to shield myself without too
much effort. I believe I hid you too.>*

<So she ain't got no idea we're here?>

*<Correct. Her scan will have picked up one human, on the bridge of
the* Setting Sun. *Jarek's ship is docked to it, so she should assume that
she is sensing him.>*

<So they won't go looking for him anywhere else?>

*<Exactly. They will be here at any moment, Taro. Are you
ready?>*

<I'm ready.>

*

Jarek had watched Damaru with tech before, but he'd never seen anything quite like this. Except for his fingers, the boy was totally still. He had a half-smile on his face and a glazed look in his eyes. It was almost as though his consciousness had entered the machine – and given what he now knew about male Sidhe, it probably had.

It was ironic really, Jarek thought: the main threat Serenein's space weaponry was designed to meet was not stray humans like him, but a concerted effort by the males, should they ever find this place. Yet here it was, being brought back online by a Sidhe male!

Jarek had another look around; while Damaru was deep in communion with the tech, his only function was to watch the boy's back. A flash above caught his eye and set his heart racing, but it was gone before he could focus on it. He told himself not to panic: it was only the defences, doing their job. If anything, that should reassure him.

<She has dropped the scan.>

<So we don't have to stay like this?> Not that Taro objected to being held close by Nual.

<We don't, but we may as well for now. We do need to get some height though.>

They rose slowly to hover just below the transfer-station's ribbed ceiling.

Taro started as a faint tap sounded through the hull. *<That them docking?>* he asked.

<Must be. I think the Sidhe flying the shuttle was the one scanning; she dropped the scan just before they closed. That implies there is just the one.>

<Pure blade. And you reckon she's not that powerful?>

<I cannot be completely sure, but no, I do not think she is – that would make sense: this is a reconnaissance mission. She is expendable.>

<So you could take her?>

<Possibly. But she is likely to send mutes in first.>

Taro knew about the mutes, the Sidhe's human slaves: they had

had their voices and wills stolen by their inhuman mistresses. He shuddered.

<We should turn off our suit-lights,> suggested Nual.

The resulting darkness was total, and Taro had to resist the temptation to hold Nual tighter in response. There was another faint tap, this one slightly louder. *<What was that?>* he asked.

<I am not sure. But I am going to risk a scan of my own.>

Before Taro could object Nual stiffened in his arms. Then she exhaled. *<Yes, just one Sidhe, and about half a dozen mutes. The mutes are entering the airlock; she is still on the shuttle.>*

<You said mutes're pretty crap, so they should be easy meat.> Not that Taro was comfortable killing mutes, given the poor fuckers didn't have much choice about acting as Sidhe cannon fodder.

<We cannot assume anything, Taro. The ones we had on the mothership were just menials, but I am sure they can be conditioned to do other jobs.>

Taro heard a new sound: someone was cranking open the inner door of the airlock. A beam of light played across the floor below them. Taro made himself breathe evenly. As the door opened he and Nual released their hold on each other and drifted a little way apart. The boarding party took the time to open the door fully, and then rushed in, way too quickly. They immediately lost their footing.

Taro swooped down and grabbed one of the stumbling figures. He felt a momentary resistance as the mute's v-suit tried to hold its wearer to the floor, then he had him – and it was a him, too. For a moment the mute was too surprised to react, then he began to struggle. He was a bulky cove, and the v-suit made it hard to get a good grip. Time for a change of plan. Taro corkscrewed upwards; as he turned, he let go, flinging the mute away from him. The man cartwheeled off into the darkness in slow motion, his suit-light tracing a lazy arc. One down – or at least out of the way.

Two things registered on Taro's consciousness at once. One was a dark and sensuous echo in his head. The other was a bright flash out in the real world.

He sussed the outside event first: *<They've got guns!>* he projected.

<Apparently so.> Though Nual's response was calm, Taro knew that what he'd just sensed was the brief, unholy pleasure she'd felt as she took the life of her mute.

<Thought mutes were too dumb for guns,> he projected.

<Apparently we were wrong.>

The world outside his head was moving with a pleasing precision and slowness, and he and Nual were already closing in on the second pair of potential victims, sweeping down wide and fast. The remaining mutes had got their collective act together and had their feet firmly anchored, so no chance of another snatch and grab. Just before the suit-light of the mute he was heading for briefly blinded him, he saw a raised hand, holding a weapon of some sort—

He jinked to the left, expecting a shot, but none came. Perhaps the cloak had hidden him, though with all this zipping around it was a bit of a liability. Too late to worry now. He adjusted course, coming in at head height, and slashed down and across, aiming for the mute's neck. The blow connected, tearing suit and flesh, but Taro was already gone.

Taro's target was wobbling comically, hands clasped to his neck; Nual's second mute had lost his grip on the floor and was running on air, a slow spray of blood fountaining out from him. Taro could see there were still more than two unharmed mutes: three? No, four, at least – and they weren't running away. The fight wasn't over yet.

Damaru's hand moved, a slight twitch of the fingers, though his face remained blank. He did it again. Jarek watched, fascinated, looking between the boy's hand and his eyes.

Total stillness, then another tiny jitter. Was Jarek imagining it, or was the boy looking somehow more *here*, more present in the real world, than he had been?

The jitter became a tapping and Damaru blinked, once. Slowly but steadily, he began to type.

Jarek held his breath. The screen remained blank.

A frown flitted across Damaru's face. He tapped a finger on the flat-comp, three times. His gaze softened.

'Come on,' murmured Jarek, 'You can do it.'

Taro shrugged his cloak out of the way and went in for another run. This time he got a solid hit: the mute was distracted by his two companions, who were dying messily around him, and he didn't see his attacker until it was too late. He turned just in time to give Taro a clear target. The blade sliced deep into the mute's throat, and blood spattered Taro before he could get clear. For a moment the scene was washed in red, until his suit absorbed the liquid and his visor cleared.

Nual was still struggling with her mute, but Taro, assessing the situation, decided she'd got it covered. He checked the door again: only one there now, a female, standing with her back to the door, nervously pointing a small pistol out into the dark. The hovering globs of blood appeared solid in the crazy flash of suit-lights, so the view was a bit muddled, but it looked like the door she was guarding was beginning to close. The last mute must've decided to leg it.

Taro was about to let Nual know the good news when her voice exploded in his head: *<Behind you!>*

And something slammed into his back—

CHAPTER FORTY-NINE

Tap, tap, tap.

Jarek tried not to get irritated or impatient: if this was what Damaru needed to do, he should just let him get on with it.

Damaru gave up tapping the corner of the comp and started typing on the keyboard again, giving each key a solid *thunk*. Code entered, he lifted his fingers from the keyboard like a virtuoso ending a performance. As he did so the display on the inset screen changed.

CODE ACCEPTED.

'Yes!'

Damaru started at Jarek's exclamation, jerking his head back and blinking.

'Sorry, Damaru, I didn't mean to startle you – it's just … You've done *really* well, Damaru. Really well.'

The screen displayed a new message: DEFENCE GRID RESTART IN PROGRESS.

Jarek grinned wildly, feeling some of the tension drain out of his shoulders. 'I'll get up first, Damaru, then I'll help you. Understand?'

'Understand.' Damaru sounded tired but happy.

Jarek levered himself up and straightened slowly. He glimpsed something out the corner of his eye, and his brain initially assumed it was another defensive flash, but it didn't look quite right, so he turned his head.

Halfway between the console and the edge of the transfer-station a suited figure was shuffling towards them in a crouch. It was pointing a gun in their direction.

Jarek whirled – and realised his mistake at once, as his feet lost contact with the solarfilm. He twisted in the air, his hand going to his chest.

The figure was raising its weapon.

Jarek slapped the controls for his pack, feeling the jets kick in.

He glimpsed a shimmer of silver rain, and something tugged briefly at the edge of his cloak.

His foot connected with Damaru's shoulder and the boy squealed. He needed to provide cover for him. 'Stay calm, Damaru!' he said authoritatively. 'Stay calm, and hunch down, low as you can!'

He went for his gun, which, like his attacker's, was a needle-pistol: the choice of spacers who didn't take prisoners.

The figure fired again, and missed again. Jarek saw the way its – *his* – arm jerked wildly as he took the shot: he obviously wasn't used to fighting in micro-g, where recoil and inertia were issues, even with a needle-pistol. Neither was Jarek, but at least he under-stood the problem. He needed to get a stable footing before he could risk firing back.

He descended diagonally to land in front of Damaru, though he misjudged it slightly and the tether-line pulled taut as he touched down. Damaru yelped in his ear and the line pulled Jarek off true, jarring his left shoulder. He swivelled on one foot, slamming the other one down hard to get a good seal on the solarfilm.

Now he and the man were face-to-face. Jarek realised he was looking at a mute. They fired at exactly the same moment.

Later he realised it was Nual's cloak that had saved him, but at the time all he knew was that the mute's shot went wide, and his didn't. A wound blossomed like an obscene red flower across the man's chest and he staggered backwards, lost contact with the deck and began to float off. His sedate progress into space contrasted with the frantic, futile motions of his limbs. Jarek felt momentarily sick.

Damaru was still mewling over the com.

'Don't panic, Damaru, we're fine now,' said Jarek as he turned back to the boy. Damaru's feet were still caught in the restraints, thank Christos; his tethered arm had been pulled straight by the tension on the line, while his body wriggled to compensate. He looked like he was doing some sort of bizarre dance, and for a moment, Jarek laughed out loud.

Then he saw a second figure, off to one side, raising a gun.

Nual started to fling aside the body of the mute she had just killed, then changed her mind. She brought it round as she turned, using the dead flesh as a shield while she flew towards the mute who had just shot Taro. She hadn't had time to examine the weapons the mutes were using, but she was pretty sure Taro had taken a hit from some sort of high-powered stunner. He was just about conscious but a second shot could kill him.

With that thought came fear. The Minister altered his assassins to stop their instincts impairing their efficiency; when she had first awoken with the Angel mods seven years ago, Nual had been furious at his imposition. She had lost count of the times since that she had been grateful for it. The fear she felt now was not for herself, but for Taro, and part of her resented that – but not enough to make her hesitate.

Taro had been shot by the mute he had flung away earlier; the man had hit the ceiling and stayed there, clinging on with one hand, pointing his gun with the other. As Nual hurtled up to him he shot at her; light flashed and the mute she was using as a shield spasmed in her arms.

Then she was close enough to make eye contact. She froze him: he was conditioned to obedience and would have willingly become her slave – after all, she was far more powerful than the Sidhe who had sent him on this mission. Mutes were bred to serve, and to worship power.

Nual had no time for that. She stopped his heart, ignoring the rush of another life despatched, then discarded the first mute's body and flew back to Taro. Only one mute remained standing, covering the now-closed door. Nual had hoped to board the shuttle and take on the Sidhe pilot, but that was not going to happen now.

Taro turned limply in the air. He had been trying to hold onto consciousness until Nual reached him. <*Bollocks*> he thought, thoroughly irritated, and passed out.

This attacker had got closer than the first one: the bastard had been smart enough to use the distraction to sneak up on them, and he was also smart enough to work out that his gun worked differently out here – either that or he just got lucky. His shot hit Damaru in the arm, and the boy screamed and threw both arms up.

One of Jarek's feet came loose from the deck as he turned to face the new threat. Damaru was completely defenceless, and somehow Jarek needed to draw the mute's fire. He pushed off and threw himself in front of Damaru. What might have been a dramatic dive in gravity became a slow, cumbersome drift, but it had the desired effect: the man – another mute – refocused on him. Jarek realised he'd only get one shot, so he needed to make it count. Before the mute could switch his aim, Jarek fired, and hit his leg, shredding his kneecap. Even as the mute's foot was kicked out from under him by the force of the shot, Jarek, experiencing the equal but opposite reaction, sailed inexorably back towards Damaru.

He tensed, though when the impact came it was gentle, barely more than a nudge. Damaru's wails took on a more panicked note, but he stayed connected to the deck. Jarek bounced away again, then he got his free hand to his chest and activated his pack. As he began to reorient he called over the com, 'It's all right, Damaru.' Not that he was sure it was; it would be a few frantic heartbeats before he was in a position to find out if he was lying.

The second mute had continued to fall forward, and come to rest at a bizarre angle, like a human letter T, with one foot still attached to the solarfilm. Not that he was at rest: he shuddered and twitched as he died a slow and painful death, blood and air puffing out of his ruptured suit into the vacuum. His gun floated serenely above him.

Jarek looked away hurriedly, instead scanning his surroundings to make sure there weren't any other nasty surprises. The first man had stopped moving and come to a halt some way off; there was no one else in sight.

Once he was sure they were in the clear, he turned to Damaru. Like the doomed mute, Damaru was attached to the deck by only one foot, but his movements were a lot more energetic; he was hugging his arm to his chest and gyrating crazily, his free leg kicking out at nothing.

Jarek landed, then tried to get Damaru's attention, waving his hands at him and calling, 'Damaru, I need to see! Please, let me see where he shot you.'

Damaru continued to wail and thrash about, which was not helpful.

'*Damaru!*' he ordered, 'let me see your arm!'

'Hurts! Cold!'

'I know, I know – show me your arm, Damaru. Please.'

Damaru stopped flailing, though he kept a rigid hold on his injured arm. Though the wound itself didn't look too serious, he also would be experiencing vacuum-burn. Unlike Taro's highly advanced Alephan one, his v-suit didn't have an emergency force-shield.

Jarek briefly cursed his decision not to bring a suit patch-kit with him; the tools they needed to do the job plus the propel-pack's controller had taken up all his carrying capacity. He thought he heard the chime of an incoming com over the boy's wails, but it would have to wait; Damaru didn't have much time. There was only one option left.

'Damaru!' he shouted, loud enough to distract him, 'you have to *shift*. You have to—' *What did Kerin call it? Oh yeah*— 'You have to move the pattern, Damaru. Do you understand me? Move the pattern to get back inside. *Now!*'

Damaru stared at him, his eyes full of pain.

'Do you understand what I'm saying? Damaru, you have to get away, back inside!'

Damaru blinked.

'Move the pattern, Damaru. *Move the pattern!*'

Something began to blossom in Jarek's head. *Flexing . . .*

The universe disappeared – a moment of panic, too brief to register – then returned.

Minus Damaru.

The rope tether was still attached to Jarek's wrist; it ended in a frayed cut. And Damaru was gone – where to, Jarek couldn't say. He straightened, and looked around. No sign of the boy, which was a good thing. Hopefully.

Movement made him flinch – he'd almost forgotten the dying mute. He turned carefully, got his footing, then took aim and then shot the top of the poor fucker's head off. The mute jerked, then swayed to a graceful halt in a cloud of freeze-dried blood.

Jarek was confused when he glimpsed something on one side of the headless man – he'd been sure the first mute was dead ...

No, this wasn't a body: something big was rising up over the edge of the transfer-station. Even as he put together the pieces, the shuttle advanced smoothly, flying just above the shining surface; its darkened screen turned transparent, and before Jarek could look away—

—he was caught in the gaze of the female Sidhe sitting in the pilot's chair.

Oh Christos, no! Please, not again!

CHAPTER FIFTY

'Sais, the ship is turning! Can you hear me, Sais?' Still no response. Kerin wondered if she had failed to operate the controls correctly. She looked back at the display, where the dot representing the Sidhe ship had changed course. Whether this was a good thing or not—

The thought died in chaos.

She lost all awareness of the world. She was a soul suspended above an unthinkably deep abyss—

Before she could panic, she was snatched away from the glimpse of madness; the room reasserted its existence around her. As it did, something appeared in the corner of her vision, then fell. Kerin knew this sensation, and even as her eyes were refocusing in the aftermath of the wrenching weirdness, she was searching for the source of the effect, looking around …

… and then down, to the figure lying on the floor.

The last pieces of the world fell into place and she tumbled from her seat, crying, 'Damaru!'

Behind the clear mask Damaru's eyes were screwed up tight, his mouth open. She grabbed her son, wanting to get him out of the strange suit, to tell him that she loved him, and that he was safe now. Then she saw his arm.

He suffered her to examine him. Kerin recognised the mark of the weapon that had caused the damage, and was hugely relieved to find that it had scored only a glancing blow, just below his elbow. The wound was not deep, but it looked odd, as though the flesh were already dead.

She unsealed the suit and peeled it back from his head. Damaru took a big gulp of air. His eyes were wet, his mouth pulled down into a grimace. He focused on her and held out his undamaged arm. She bundled him to her, hugging him close and murmuring calming nonsense.

When the console buzzed again, she was tempted to ignore it. But it could be important, so she stood up, letting Damaru keep hold of one of her hands.

<Yes, it is you. As I thought.>

The Sidhe's voice was crystal clear in Jarek's head. He didn't respond. He was too busy trying to fight her using the tricks Nual had taught him: nonsense rhymes, repeated phrases heavy with irrelevant meanings—

<I have some of your sister's recordings, you know. Such a loss.>

Fury rose, and before he could help himself he thought back, *<Fuck you, you—!>*

<Oh! Now I wonder who taught you to mindspeak, Captain Reen?>

His brief pulse of anger had allowed her to get her mental hooks in deeper. That was why she'd done it, of course. And now he'd revealed ... *Nothing, hide your thoughts think of nothing at all, nothing-nothingnothing.*

<Sorry, you will have to do better than that. Given how much you don't want me in your head, I think we should most definitely have a little chat. It will have to be brief, sadly, and probably terminal, for you—>

Something dropped in front of the shuttle, cutting off the contact—

—no, not some*thing*, some*one*. The pale grey v-suit was stained with splotches of red. Jarek's overloaded mind was still rebounding from the Sidhe's mental hold, trying to make sense of what was happening, when his com chimed.

He accepted the call.

'Sais?'

'Kerin?' Now he was really confused.

375

'Nual says, uh, that you must go to the shuttle airlock and let yourself in.' Kerin said carefully. 'After that, she says, you know what to do.'

Of course the suited figure was Nual. Even if the curves hadn't tipped him off, the blood should have been a giveaway. 'Tell her yes, I'll do that,' he said after a moment. 'Is Damaru—?'

'He is safe, with me.'

'Thank Christos.' Jarek took off, flying round the shuttle, careful not to look towards the front, where Nual hung motionless.

Kerin said, 'She says it would be a good idea to hurry. She is not sure how long she can maintain her hold over the other Sidhe.'

'Tell her I'm hurrying!' He approached the rear airlock. 'This had better not be locked,' he muttered as he came to a stop, but it wasn't; the shuttle was a standard personnel transfer model, with no additional security.

He opened the outer door. The 'lock took what felt like an age to cycle. When the inner door opened he pulled the cloak around him then rushed in, gun-first.

Movement—

—he dodged, squeezing off a shot. Something hit the side of his head, spinning him around. But there was no pain, and he was still on his feet, though his vision was starred along the right-hand side – the shot must have grazed his visor. He wheeled back round, then fired again, wildly, trying to keep his opponent off-balance until he could work out what he was up against.

The gun clicked empty. *Shit.*

He glimpsed a shadowy form, and, out of other options, he charged, hitting soft, female flesh – another Sidhe? No, a Sidhe wouldn't need to resort to firearms; this was a mute, just a mute. He had to get her gun and shoot the Sidhe. The Sidhe was the real threat here.

Sheer momentum forced the mute back, but his attack was unfocused and his attempts to disarm her ineffectual. Beyond the mute he glimpsed a jigsaw image of the darkness of space, and the pale figure outside the ship.

The mute came up short – and so did he. They both fell, tripping over something. He lost his grip on her as he went down.

Someone grabbed his wrist – the grip was sure as death, and he felt the contact, *felt* it, in a way that told him instantly this was not the mute.

Suddenly it wasn't about overcoming his opponent; it was about escaping his worst nightmare – but he was already on the floor. A dark shape loomed over him. She had hold of one of his hands but he still had an arm free. He brought it round to punch her, and hit something hard, scraping his knuckles and jarring his wrist. Shit, whatever that was, it wasn't her!

His wrist was released, but before he could act, a fist in his groin replaced any rational thoughts with agony. He tried to curl in on the pain, only to find something sliding across his body. By the time he was able to think straight again, the Sidhe had straddled him, kneeling across his upper chest, her knees grinding into his armpits.

She punched his forehead; the visor took the brunt of the blow. He wondered where the mute was – and more importantly, the mute's gun. The Sidhe hit him again, harder, using both hands together. Though he was dazed, he suddenly realised she didn't *want* the mute to shoot him; this kill was hers. She couldn't get a firm purchase on his mind, not through the suit, and given he sure-as-shit wasn't going to look at her, she would have to try another tack. So, she was going to break his visor. The predator needed to get through the hard shell of her prey in order to finish him off ...

He bucked hard, trying to dislodge her, but he'd just had his balls pummelled, and his body hadn't caught up with his mind yet. He managed a feeble thrust – briefly, repulsively, reminiscent of a different intimacy – and then she hit him again. The visor shattered, covering his face in hard-edged fragments. He squeezed his eyes shut as a hand swept across his face, scooping the pieces of broken visor out the way. Then her fingers were on his flesh, almost gentle as they caressed his cheek. And she was in his head, pulling his mind free of its futile, terrified defence, ready to annihilate it—

The relentless mental advance halted; at the same time, in the outside world, he felt the Sidhe's body jerk. She went rigid, then softened and collapsed over him. Something wet and foul-smelling spattered his face. He used a hand to wipe his eyes, and opened them to see the Sidhe's head — or what was left of it — lying next to his. He hurried to struggle out from under the weight of dead flesh, then pushed the body away, gagging, and looked around.

The mute had lowered her gun and was staring out of the window at Nual, her face slack with mindless adoration.

Jarek realised he was next to the pilot's chair. So that was what he'd tripped over and then punched earlier. He used it to pull himself to his feet. Nual turned her head to look at him and smiled, and he met her eyes.

<Are you all right?> she asked, projecting concern.

Jarek, his mind still raw, winced at the mental contact, but he made himself respond, *<I'm fine, thanks to you.>*

<I would have got here earlier, but I had to make some emergency suit repairs.> She held out her two wrists, both patched over the slits from where her blades emerged. *<Did she hurt you?>*

He knew which 'she' Nual meant. *<No. What did you … do? To her, I mean.>*

<I dominated the mute and told her to kill the Sidhe.>

<Ah. I see.> Nausea bubbled. *<And now?>*

<The mute is mine. However, she is also … damaged.>

Jarek decided he didn't want details. Absurd, hysterical relief was coming in hard on the heels of the horror. *<You know why the Sidhe won't win?>*

<I suspect you are about to tell me.> You'd never have guessed from Nual's dry mental voice that she'd just taken one life and subjugated another.

<Because for all their big plans, when it comes down to it, they just have to make it personal.>

CHAPTER FIFTY-ONE

Kerin saw the incoming ship die, but only because she happened to look up at exactly the right moment. She had relayed Nual's message, and was turning her attention back to Damaru. As had happened before when he moved the pattern, he was befuddled and exhausted, but she wanted him to stay awake until she had had time to treat his wound.

Kerin had not been paying the display much attention, though it had been running all the time. It showed the incoming ship as a blue dot; the ship's path, which curved round and back on itself where the Sidhe had turned and run, was a faint yellow trace. Now Kerin spotted something new: a halo of red points of light flared into life around the dot representing the Sidhe ship; smaller lights detached themselves from these and sped towards the ship. A moment later, the display flared, then died away. The incoming ship was gone, replaced by empty space.

Kerin had a sudden urge to laugh. Damaru looked up woozily, and she smiled at him. Then she called Sais, to tell him the wonderful news.

When Taro awoke, Nual was there, which was pleasant, but not a surprise. He wasn't surprised to wake up in the *Setting Sun*'s medbay either. What was a bit odd was finding everyone else there too.

'Nice of you all to come visit me,' he said, although they were actually busy with the medtech, rather than clustering around his bed in a suitably concerned manner.

Jarek said, 'Ah, you're awake. Stay there, I've got something for you.'

Taro raised a quizzical eyebrow but Jarek had already gone. He asked Nual, 'How long was I out?'

'A little over an hour.'

'Right.' He didn't feel too bad in himself, just a bit numb and tingly in places. 'Guess we won then?'

'We won.'

'And we're having a party in the medbay to celebrate?'

'Not quite. Kerin is patching Damaru up after he took a glancing shot and had a close encounter with hard vacuum.'

'Ouch. He all right?'

'He'll be fine. We have also been getting ourselves checked out, to make sure no one's going to pass on any pathogens to Kerin's people.'

'And are we?'

'Not according to the medbay readouts.'

'Top prime.'

'Can you sit up?'

'Think so.' He could probably have managed by himself, but he was happy to have Nual give him a hand. 'So what'd I miss?' he asked as he settled back against the cushions.

'Once I knew you were out of danger, I went after the shuttle – which was just as well, for the Sidhe on board had found Jarek. We dealt with her – she was not that powerful, but she had some training in mental combat. In the end I had to use a mute against her.'

'Another mute to add to the body-count, eh?' He was half-joking, though he knew it wasn't funny.

'This one is still alive, though not entirely sane. We put her to sleep, after I read her. I discovered the reason we did not spot the Sidhe ship: it was already here. It had been waiting at the edge of the system, and when we arrived they moved in slowly, presumably waiting for us to prove the defence grid was down – something they suspected, but were not about to risk confirming the hard way. Once they knew they would not get shot at, they sent a scout ahead, and she put down two mutes outside – I presume as insurance in case Jarek had managed to access the *Setting Sun*'s computer and find out about the cold-start console.'

'Which of course he had,' said Taro. 'So they knew Jarek was here – or was that only when they saw the *Heart of Glass*?'

'I think they already suspected Jarek was behind their loss of contact with Serenein. They wanted him alive, to find out what he knew. The Sidhe on the shuttle was hoping to get some useful information from him. The main ship had already turned, and was powering up to leave the system, so the lone Sidhe may have planned to land on Serenein and lie low until the others returned.'

'So they'll definitely be back?'

'Serenein is too valuable to them. They will not give it up.'

Jarek returned with a bulb of caf which he presented to Taro with a flourish. 'My round,' he said magnanimously, ruining the moment by adding, 'actually, I've got an ulterior motive. We need you up and about as soon as possible. We've still got to fix the point-defences. You're with Damaru.'

'Oh yeah. I'd almost forgotten about them.' Taro groaned.

They went back to work on the capacitors in the transfer-station. When Damaru didn't need him Taro swept his light around, checking for bloodstains. He thought he saw some near the door, but there was no sign of any bodies. He knew enough about shipboard waste reclamation to work out where the dead mutes had most likely ended up. He decided not to think about it.

Once Damaru had worked out what was needed, Taro helped him go through the *Setting Sun*'s engineering locker to find the right bits, after which Damaru set to work building what looked to Taro's uneducated eye like a box of cables decorated with lumps of useless crud.

They stopped for a meal of ship's mush – Taro tried *really* hard not to think about the mutes as he ate it – after which he took a quick catnap while Damaru was busy tinkering.

When he woke up Jarek was there, muttering over the doodad

box with Damaru. Taro checked his com. He'd been asleep for *six* hours; it was nearly fourteen hours since they'd seen off the Sidhe.

'Need any help there?' he asked.

'Actually we're nearly done.'

'Right. I'll just go and—'

'She's asleep in your cabin, Taro. Don't wake her.'

'Oh. Guess I'm back to being caf-boy, then.'

'Thought you'd never ask.'

Taro got back with the drinks to find Jarek and Damaru just heading back to the *Setting Sun*'s bridge. 'We need to look up a few things on the ship's comp before Damaru goes home,' Jarek said.

Taro asked Damaru, 'You finished your box of tricks then?'

'Aye.'

'Prime. So, what's the hurry?' he asked Jarek.

'Things are bit volatile down on the planet. Kerin and Damaru need to get back.'

Whatever his feelings about the late pilot, Taro had to admit that the bridge of the *Setting Sun* was his idea of travelling in style. Only one corner of the room had any actual ship controls in; the rest was a luxurious cabin complete with ents units, luxury gaming rigs, a top-of-the-range multi-gym and a massive bed. There was even a massage chair and a small bar area. 'Er, is that Kerin?' Taro pointed to the figure sleeping in the massage chair.

'Yeah – do you mind waking her up and seeing if she needs a drink or food? Oh, and tell her we'll be done in time to get her back under the cover of night.'

Taro sighed in a put-upon way and went over to wake the woman.

When Kerin wandered off to find some food, Taro asked Jarek, 'Shall I wake Nual too?'

'Go on, then – but can you both come straight back afterwards?'

Taro did his best not to sound offended. 'What're you trying to say?'

When he got back with Nual, Damaru was still at the console, and Kerin and Jarek were deep in conversation.

'I cannot make a decision yet,' Kerin was saying. 'Not until I know how things stand in the Tyr.'

'Fair enough.' Jarek hesitated, then said, 'And what about the Consorts?'

'Sais, I believe you will take one of the sleepers with you, regardless of my wishes.'

'I'm sorry, Kerin, but their abilities are just too useful to leave untapped in our war against the Sidhe. I will take only one, though.'

'And you will leave the rest of the boys to sleep in peace, and do everything in your power to keep the one who goes with you safe?'

'I promise I'll keep him out of danger, if I can.'

In the awkward silence that followed that qualified remark, Taro found himself thinking about the sleeping boys. He hadn't realised Jarek would want to take one, but it made sense. As he said: they were too useful. But if Damaru was anything to go by, they could also be a right royal pain in the arse – and the boy they chose wouldn't even have a 'maman' to keep him in line. Taro hoped Jarek had some sort of plan to make the boy behave.

Damaru looked up, and Kerin asked, 'Are you nearly done, my lovely boy?'

At Damaru's nod, Jarek said, 'Guess it's time to get you back. Then Taro and I have some cables to finish rerouting.'

Taro turned to Nual. 'How come you get off engineering duty then?'

'I'm going to Serenein.' Seeing the look on his face, she added, 'Don't worry Taro, it is only for a while. We have some unfinished business down there.'

CHAPTER FIFTY-TWO

As they descended the stairways of the Tyr Nual was grateful for her shimmer-cloak. Fortunately it was still early, and there were not many people around. Pressing herself against the wall and pulling the cloak tight was usually sufficient, although one servant did stop dead and stare in confusion. Fortunately Kerin was far enough ahead not to notice Nual briefly grasp the man's hand and look into his eyes; he would have a bit of a headache when he recovered his senses, but no memory of Nual at all.

Kerin's room was large and, by the standards of what Nual had seen so far, relatively opulent. However, it also smelled awful, possibly due to the presence of two dead bodies, both male. In addition there were two live but deeply unhappy ones: a man, gagged and trussed up in a torn sheet, and, in the other corner, an adolescent girl, bound in another sheet. The man was awake; the girl semiconscious. Nual, curious, dipped into her mind, then recoiled from what she found there.

She hung back as Kerin rushed over to the only live, unbound occupant, an elderly man whose bald head was covered in tattooed writing. His face was pale, except for two spots of colour high on his cheeks, and he had a crossbow bolt sticking out of one shoulder. As Kerin bent over to examine the wound the man looked past her.

'Ah,' he said, 'you ... must be Nual.'

Though his voice was feeble and feverish, she sensed his mixture of curiosity and apprehension. She gave him a respectful nod. 'That's right. And you must be Urien.'

'Maman, I want to sleep now!' Damaru was standing by the smaller of the two beds, which had had its covers stripped off.

'Use my bed, Damaru,' said Kerin.

Damaru made a *harrumph* of irritation deep in his throat, shot Nual one last hostile look, then thumped down on the larger bed and rolled himself up in the covers.

'Urien,' said Kerin in a businesslike tone, 'I must draw the bolt immediately.'

'I imagine that will hurt,' he commented tightly.

'Not as much as you think. I have a spray here to numb the pain.' Kerin began to rummage in the bag she had brought from the *Setting Sun*. Nual cast an eye over the two dead bodies. One was a guard, like the bound man; he was lying in a dried pool of what was presumably his own blood. The other wore robes like Urien's, though less ornate. They were coloured red, rather than Urien's green. He had a crossbow bolt sticking out of his chest.

Nual realised Urien was still watching her, both out of curiosity, and to distract himself from what Kerin was doing. 'The guard is my work,' he said, 'it took him ... a while to die. The other ... she shot herself.' More quietly he added, 'She had not known ... he was her father.'

That explained the girl's deep well of self-loathing. 'Is she drugged?' Nual asked softly.

Urien addressed Kerin. 'I hope you do not mind ... I gave her one of your sleeping draughts. Although she showed little inclination to stir, even without ... the draught.'

Kerin said, 'A sensible precaution, Urien. I think we should keep her sedated for the moment.' She looked around, then said, 'Urien, you must lie down on Damaru's bed. When I remove the bolt, you may not be in a state to converse for a while, even with the sky-medicine. So, before we go any further, I need to ask you who you think was behind the attempted coup.'

'Escori Garnon, almost certainly.'

'And if it was Garnon, what do you think he will do now that nearly a full day has passed and there has been no sign of life from within these chambers?'

'I cannot ... be sure.'

'I can,' said Nual quietly, looking meaningfully at the trussed-up guard who was staring, wide-eyed, over his gag at her. When the other two turned their attention to her she added, 'If nobody objects.'

'That would be ... most useful,' said Urien. 'Kerin?'

The other woman hesitated, then agreed as well.

Nual bent down next to the man and dived into his mind. He put up little resistance and it did not take long.

As Kerin laid out what she needed to treat Urien on the table next to the bed, Nual said, 'Your suspicions are correct: the man Garnon is behind this. He intended to wait to see how things turned out.'

'Always was brazen,' commented Urien, who had got himself up onto the bed.

'We must deal with him quickly, then,' said Kerin.

'Absolutely. At this hour he should ... still be in his chambers.'

Nual said carefully, 'And is this a problem you are happy to leave me to solve?'

Urien gestured vaguely to indicate it was Kerin's choice.

She said, 'I am, aye. Do what you must.'

Urien whispered, 'We need to ... make an example of him.'

'I understand,' said Nual. 'What about this man?' She pointed to the guard. 'I will need him to guide me to Garnon's room. After that—'

'If you can avoid taking any more lives,' said Kerin coldly, 'I would appreciate it.'

The guard, Gwaun, was right: Garnon might be brazen, but he was no idiot. He had two of his most loyal men standing guard outside his room, and they were understandably surprised when Gwaun turned up after having been missing for a day, accompanied by the Cariad herself. Naturally, they opened the door without question.

Garnon was alone in his bedroom. He too was surprised. 'I was beginning to worry,' he said, looking from one to the other. 'Am I to understand that Onfel and Maelgyn did not survive?'

Neither Gwaun nor the Cariad responded, and Garnon began to look a little uncertain. He addressed the Cariad. 'Are they still in your room, then, *chilwar*?' A pause. 'That *is* you, is it not, Ifanna?'

<No,> Nual reached for her veil. *<It is not.>*

When the Cariad swept out of Garnon's chambers a short while later, she was alone. After she left, the monitors argued about whether to close the door, which she had left open in her wake, until one called out to the Escori, '*Gwas*, can we get you anything?' When they received no answer, he plucked up courage to go inside, where he found his fellow monitor sitting on the floor of the antechamber, glassy-eyed and mumbling.

Escori Garnon himself was sitting up in his bed. At first the monitor thought nothing was amiss – then he looked at the Escori's face, which was frozen forever in an attitude of awestruck terror. His hands were bent into claws that gripped the counterpane as if it were the only thing that could save him. It could not, of course.

Nual took off the robes of office, and with no one to witness them, she and Kerin dragged the two bodies out of Kerin's room and rolled them into the chasm. Nual suspected they would not be alone down there. Then she and Kerin did their best to clean up, though the Cariad's room still stank, despite their efforts. Nual sensed Kerin thawing a little; she had expected Nual to claim such unpleasant chores were below her.

By the time they were done, Urien had recovered enough to sit up. Nual listened to him and Kerin talking with interest, and answered the few questions they had for her. She had never been in on discussions about the future of an entire world before. Afterwards, Urien, who was chafing at being kept away from his sources of information, insisted he was well enough to go out, though Kerin made him take a wrist-com with him. He only needed to be shown how to work the device once.

Then Kerin put on the Cariad's robes and went out to announce the name of Garnon's successor.

*

Just two days ago, Kerin could not have countenanced being in the same room as a Sidhe. How much had changed!

Garnon's replacement entered the audience chamber at noon, as he had been instructed. Kerin's knowledge of Dinmael came largely from Urien's trove of information: he was relatively young, with a strong streak of personal integrity. That was one good reason for choosing him. The other was the late Escori Garnon's negative feelings for him, as uncovered by Nual. Dinmael would be eager to prove himself a better man than his power-hungry predecessor.

He looked suitably awed when he entered, and when Kerin asked him to cross the chasm on the bridge, he hesitated before circling his breast and complying. Kerin suspected he had not expected to be called onto sacred ground.

He made to kneel as soon as he was on her side of the chasm, but Kerin told him to remain standing. She could see he was shocked by that; it felt unholy not to offer obeisance to the Skymothers' representative on Earth.

Without any preamble, she said, 'There are three, sometimes complementary, reasons to become a priest. There are those who seek the certainty of faith, and who take solace in unquestioning belief in a higher power. There are those who desire knowledge and personal power, and see the priesthood as a way to achieve these aims. Finally, there are those few who wish to help their fellow man.

'I cannot imagine anyone rising to the rank you are about to attain with their faith intact; you will have seen too much that is bad in people to believe fully in divine goodness. And you will enjoy the power you wield; that is only natural. However, you must never forget your responsibility to those below you, because you do not just rule your sect, you help rule this world.' She paused.

Realising he was expected to speak, Dinmael said resolutely, 'Aye, Divinity. I will do my best.' He looked predictably confused: he had expected formal ceremony, not thoughtful observations.

Kerin felt her lips curve into a bitter smile. 'Dinmael, look at me,' she said softly.

He did, reluctantly. He would see only the Cariad's veil, hiding the face of his goddess.

Kerin continued, 'You are used to thinking that you – that all the priests – command your own small domain, with the permission of the Cariad.'

'As you will it, Divinity,' he murmured.

'No,' said Kerin firmly, 'not so. Not any more.' Kerin reached up to lift her veil, and the priest gasped, circling his breast and averting his gaze.

'Dinmael!' commanded Kerin. 'Please, do not look away!'

She saw his expression change when she drew the veil aside to reveal a very un-divine countenance.

'As you see, I am no goddess.'

'Is ... Is this some sort of test?' he stammered. 'Or an illusion—?'

'No. I am as you see me: a mortal woman. Yet I rule – *we* rule, I and the Escorai, as allies. That is how it must be now. If you cannot accept that, then' – she smiled, a little grimly – 'you should not accept this job.'

'I ... Forgive me, but there were rumours. I did not want to believe them—'

'No doubt some of them were lies; others, however, were quite true. That does not change the fact that we must work together to guide our people.'

'But— But the miracles of the Tyr, what are they if not divine?'

'They are devices, and I *do* have control of them, something you would be wise to remember in the coming days.'

'*You?* But you are a mortal woman ...' He swallowed. 'Is this Urien's doing?'

Kerin sighed. 'Urien is my staunchest ally. He is *not* my master. You will have to get used to taking orders from mortal women, Dinmael. Can you do that?'

Dinmael's expression worked through disbelief to cautious, if somewhat bemused, acceptance. Finally he said, 'Has it always been thus?'

'No, Dinmael, it has not. For many years we were ruled, cruelly, by an outsider, though she was no goddess. That unjust rule is over. It is time for us to take control of our own destiny.'

Dinmael digested what she had said. Then he asked, 'If I cannot accept this strange and unlikely truth, then what? Will you have me killed?' He sounded more amazed than fearful.

'No,' said Kerin shortly, 'but you will not become an Escori, and I can promise you that you will leave here with no memory of this conversation.'

On cue, Nual stepped out of the shadows.

Dinmael's eyes widened in further confusion.

'*I* am not a goddess,' Kerin continued, 'but my companion here can do everything the woman who once occupied this throne could.'

Nual turned to Kerin and said, 'He hasn't lied to us yet.'

'Good,' said Kerin. 'Then let us find out if he ever will.'

The other three Escorai were summoned an hour apart. Urien reported that the Tyr was already abuzz with news of Garnon's fate; the senior priests were predictably apprehensive about being called into the Divine presence.

Like Dinmael, they reacted with confusion to Kerin's frank confession.

After that, it was over to Nual, who probed their minds to determine their basic intent, after which she wordlessly showed each Escori an edited version of the truth about Serenein; the main detail she omitted was the fate of the Consorts. Where needed, she carried out a limited degree of programming.

Though the Escorai of Carunwyd and Medelwyr gave no trouble, the Escori of Turiach, the last to be called in, had been planning dissent. Nual put him to sleep and told Kerin her findings.

'Can you influence him to be loyal?' asked Kerin. She briefly considered summoning Urien to ask his advice, before realising that she already knew what he would say.

'Not without impairing his ability to do his duties.'

'But you could stop him being a threat without killing him?'

'Yes, I could make him docile and obedient. He would be no use

390

to you as an Escori, but he would be alive – even happy, in a way. He would not know what he had lost.'

Kerin examined her options, and quickly acknowledged how few they were. 'Aye, do that, please,' she said at last.

After Nual was done, Kerin called monitors into the audience chamber and instructed them to remove the inanely smiling Escori and turn him out on the streets of the city. She knew his vacant face would join Siarl's agonised one in her nightmares.

Naturally Urien already had a replacement in mind. He also approved of her treatment of the failed Escori. 'The people could use a little fear,' he said tartly.

By the time they finally returned from installing the new Escori of Turiach, it was evening. Damaru was awake; when he stared suspiciously at Nual Kerin realised how much her own attitude to the Sidhe had changed in just one day. She took no joy in her son's dislike, although she was more relaxed when Damaru was present to offset Nual's powers. But there was a link between her and Nual now, if only in their shared complicity.

'Did you wish to rest now?' she asked Nual, who looked exhausted. 'Damaru will most likely wander off soon.'

'No, thank you; I want to get back tonight. And we cannot wait any longer for this.'

Kerin had to agree. The final imposition was the worst, but it was also the most vital.

CHAPTER FIFTY-THREE

She remembered flinching away from a man, but being too weak to resist when he bound her. She remembered the horror of recollection breaking over her, and wishing desperately she could forget it again. Then she remembered being given a sweet drink that brought the oblivion she craved.

She had washed in and out of consciousness for some time; after a while there had been voices, not inside her but outside, which meant she was alive. She tried to hide from them, because she was not sure she wanted to live.

Yet she could not ignore the fact that she had survived.

Ifanna opened her eyes. Above her was a stone ceiling. Was she still in the Cariad's chamber? Or was this a cell? She was constricted, wrapped in a bed-sheet, and there were loops of something around her wrists, but she was no longer tightly bound. Her body ached from having lain on a hard stone floor, and she was abominably thirsty. She began to wriggle free of the sheet and bindings, then stopped as she noticed the finely made cup next to her. She reached out tentatively. The cup appeared to have water in. Was it for her? Was it safe? The worst that could happen was that the drink killed her, and that was still a prospect she would welcome. She pulled the cup across, raised herself on one elbow and drank. It tasted like water, pure and cool.

The drink brought her fully to her senses and for the first time she realised she was not alone. She struggled to sit up, and saw that this was indeed the Cariad's room. A boy watched her from the strange revolving seat Escori Urien had been sitting in. He had an open, innocent face, and she reached out to get a sense of who and what he was, but her regard slid off him like water from oiled cloth. The attempted contact sparked off odd, complex feelings, some of them echoing other feelings she had had recently; so wrong, so very wrong—

'Can you stand up?' He asked the question as though he had no idea how she might answer, and was genuinely curious.

It came to her who he must be and she went to make the circle, then stopped. The gesture meant *nothing*.

The boy's brow furrowed, and he said again, more slowly, 'Can you stand up?'

'I will try,' she said, her voice shaking. Why not? Lying on the ground wishing she were dead was no way to spend the rest of her life.

It took a while, for she was weak, and kept getting tangled in the sheets. The Consort watched her silently, his expression between impatience and curiosity. When she finally got to her feet he said, 'Come with me.'

'I— Please, I have to know something.'

The boy stared at her; of course he would not react like anyone else. But the question was one she had to ask before she faced whatever fate the future held for her. 'Is ... is Maelgyn dead?'

Seeing the boy's confused expression, she added, 'The priest who came here, with the monitors. Is he dead?'

'Dead. Aye.' The boy spoke as though it was a foregone conclusion. Perhaps it was. She had known the truth in her heart; to hear it confirmed lifted some of the weight from her – though she knew that was not how she *should* feel.

The Consort continued, 'We must *go!*' He half-walked, half-capered across the room and pulled open the door. He did not wait to see if Ifanna would follow.

She took a last look around. Aside from the strange seat and oddly decorated wall behind it, the room was ordinary, though well appointed. She followed the Consort out. The boy led her back to the audience chamber, and Ifanna felt fear wash over her, which redoubled when she saw the woman standing there wearing the

393

Cariad's black and silver robes. But the woman's head was bare, and her face was as ordinary as the room where Ifanna had awakened. She stood next to the throne, one hand resting lightly on its high back. Whilst the front of the great chair was ornate, the back was plain. The imposing façade was not made to be viewed from this side.

The room beyond the throne was dim and, as far as Ifanna could tell, empty.

The false Cariad spoke, her voice more heavily accented and less resonant than the last time Ifanna had heard it. 'Do you wish to live?'

What a question! Had she asked if Ifanna *deserved* to live, she might have been able to answer more easily. She had committed a terrible sin of the flesh, then repeated it – and then she had committed murder. Of course she did not *deserve* to live.

But that was not the question.

The woman did not appear to mind waiting for her answer: she just stood there, her face composed but not unfriendly. From the corner of her eye Ifanna saw the Consort leaving. For all the unease he inspired in her, she found herself half wishing he would stay. And in thinking that, she had her answer.

'Aye. I want to live.' Then she added, more tremulously, 'If ... if that is permitted.'

The false Cariad said mildly, 'If we thought you deserved to die, you would never have woken up.'

Ifanna could not fault the sense in that.

'And what would you want your life to be?' the woman asked.

Ifanna stared at her. 'I do not understand.'

'It is a simple enough question: have you never asked it?'

'I— Such choices are not for me to make.'

The woman smiled, and there was something in that smile that said she too had once thought that way. 'Imagine they were. What is your heart's desire?'

'My heart's desire.' Such a phrase! So might a lover speak; a lover who was true, who was not ...

Nausea clawed at her throat, and she saw the false Cariad's

alarmed expression, before it was blurred with Ifanna's own tears. She put out a hand to tell the woman to stay back, that she did not need her help, though actual words were beyond her. She fought for control. Finally, she regained it.

She blinked hard, and rubbed her eyes. When she looked again, she saw something that might be pity in the false Cariad's face, and wondered if she knew the full, vile truth. No, she could not – no one could know that.

Ifanna said shakily, 'You spared my life, when I was judged.'

'I did. And now, in return, I ask that you answer my question: what do you want of that life?'

'I want ... I want to serve the Skymothers, to be good—'

'No!'

Ifanna jumped; this was the first time the woman had raised her voice. 'Ifanna, if you lie now, you *will* die here,' she continued emphatically, 'Though I may lack the power to see into your heart, I believe there is strength in you. I *want* to believe it – I want you to prove me right, Ifanna. So answer me *truly*.'

'I do not know what I want! I knew what I wanted before: to be loved and cherished, and to know that I mattered to ... someone. To the Mothers, if not to anyone down here. But that was then, before ... and now I have no surety. I no longer know what is true! I no longer know anything.' Ifanna fought hard, but the tears were back.

To her amazement, the woman smiled. 'An honest answer,' she said, 'and that is a start.' The false Cariad took a pace back. 'Now, come here, please.' She beckoned – a casual, friendly gesture – then stepped back again.

Ifanna had no idea what the woman wanted of her, but she walked forward as the false Cariad continued to walk backwards, slowly, all the while looking at Ifanna. When she passed the throne, she took her eyes off Ifanna's face, looking to one side, and at the same time, she made a small gesture. Ifanna followed the motion, looking in the direction she indicated.

There was another woman on the throne, and this one was far from ordinary. She sat at her ease, one ankle resting on her other knee. Her hair was shorn, and she wore the strangest clothes Ifanna had ever seen. Despite this, her beauty burned like the sun.

Ifanna opened her mouth, then closed it again. Finally she stammered, 'I— I do not understand.'

<*Then allow me to enlighten you.*>

Kerin went back to her room to wait for Nual to do what she had to do. It was not a process she felt comfortable witnessing, especially as its success was far from guaranteed. While she waited, she considered the pieces of the puzzle that made up Ifanna's life. That the girl had been duped and used, she had no doubt of. Yet Ifanna had also killed both her husband and her father. As for why? That was between Ifanna and her conscience.

The door finally opened, and Nual came in, looking utterly drained. She left the door open, and Kerin held her breath, releasing it when Ifanna ventured in. Kerin smiled at her; Ifanna's answering smile was uncertain. Then the girl looked around the Cariad's room, as though seeing it for the first time. She asked, 'The Consort ... where is he?'

'Damaru has gone in search of supper,' Kerin said. 'We should probably consider getting some food for ourselves soon.'

'Aye,' said Ifanna, then, sounding slightly surprised, 'I am very hungry.'

Kerin went over to the clothes-stand and lifted the headdress off. As she handed it to Ifanna she said, 'You will find it changes your voice; you may wish to practise alone before you use it for any rituals.' She looked the girl up and down. 'I think you are tall enough that you will not have to wear those awful lifts in your shoes, which is a mercy.'

Ifanna looked at the headdress in wonderment, then at Kerin. 'Will we be sharing this room?' she asked.

'I think one of your first decrees should be that the Consort who has been living with you should get his own room. And a housekeeper.'

'I think so too.' Ifanna smiled fully for the first time.

'You should try on the rest of the robes, then go and ask for food to be brought. We can talk further while we eat.'

'Aye,' she said, 'I will.'

Nual called over, 'The ship is on its way down. I need to go and meet it.'

'I will guide you out,' said Kerin. She led Nual to the hidden passage. They left Ifanna fastening her robe.

When they were out of her earshot, Nual said, 'The girl is seriously damaged; I couldn't do much to deal with that, certainly not in one session. But she will always obey you, just as the Escorai will always obey the woman who wears the Cariad's robes.'

'Good,' said Kerin shortly. Though she accepted the price of progress, she had no desire to dwell on how they had achieved this victory. 'May I take you to a lower balcony? We are less likely to encounter anyone that way.'

'If you wish.'

They carried on in silence until they came to the passage leading out, when Kerin asked, 'Will they come back?'

'Yes.' Of course, Nual had not needed to ask who. 'But not for a while. They have lost three ships here, and that will be a major blow. They will want to marshal their strength before they make another move on Serenein.'

'And I want to be ready.'

'I hope you will be.'

Kerin wondered if she was going to ask about Sais' offer to integrate her world into human-space, but they reached the balcony without her mentioning it.

Nual stepped up to the edge. 'Good luck, Kerin.'

'You too. And Nual: thank you.'

Nual sprang into the air without another word.

Kerin watched the Sidhe's shadowy form disappear into the darkness.

CHAPTER FIFTY-FOUR

When Kerin commed Jarek, Nual had just come aboard. Once pleasantries had been exchanged, she asked, 'So both sets of defences are working fully now?' She was in her chamber; Jarek saw someone, presumably the girl who would be taking on the Cariad's role, walk past behind her.

'That's right. The lasers are back at full power, and the defence grid's entirely under your control.'

'Good. Thank you. And the cold-start console can no longer be used to shut down the defence grid remotely?'

'That's right. Damaru has disconnected it from the rest of the system, so any future attempts to deactivate the defences won't work.'

'Also good. That just leaves the matter of the beacon.'

'Yes.' Jarek kept his tone neutral. 'It does.'

'Am I right in believing that the Sidhe would wish to destroy any such means of putting us back in contact with humanity?'

'In theory, yes, although beacons aren't easy artefacts to damage. But the Sidhe have no idea there's one here: even if the ship we destroyed did notice us dropping off the beacon before we gave them something else to worry about, they couldn't have told anyone – no beacon means no beevee.'

'But all that would change if we were to – what did you call it? – link in our beacon?'

'Everyone would know about you then, yes.'

'Everyone.' Kerin's expression was unreadable. 'And the people in the rest of human-space, they would really be willing to pay to watch us go about our lives?'

'Like I said, you'd generate a lot of interest, and from that, a lot of revenue.' Jarek resisted the temptation to try and steer Kerin towards accepting the beacon. It had to be her decision.

'And if people came here because they wanted to see this place for themselves,' continued Kerin, 'if they ignored the laws that told them not to approach my world, and did not heed any warnings we sent out: what would happen if we used our planet's defences as a final deterrent to such persistent curiosity?'

Jarek drew a deep breath before he said, 'Serenein is a sovereign state. This system is your territory. Provided you inform the rest of human-space of the laws that hold here – and the measures you'll be using to enforce them – you'd be within your rights to fire on any unauthorised ship that approaches your world.'

Kerin digested this. 'You once referred to the power that the Sidhe wield as a hidden empire ...'

'I did, yes.'

'Then I have made my decision.'

When Taro woke up, Nual was still deeply asleep. She needed to be fully rested before they shifted, so he left her sleeping and got up. He found Jarek at the galley table.

'So, where are we?' Taro asked, fixing himself a caf.

'Most of the way to the beacon.'

'What did Kerin say?'

'She said "Yes". Her main priority is keeping the Sidhe away. If Serenein's existence is common knowledge, and if anyone in human-space can tune into the feed Kerin supplies, then if the Sidhe do turn up here they'll expose themselves to public scrutiny. They'd never do that.'

'Prime. I'd hate to have gone through all that shit for nothing. So we're gonna claim it's a lost world we dropped in on after a normal transit got arsed up?'

'That's the plan. There's some precedent for that; not all beacons were linked into the network when it was first set up.'

'Sounds good to me. I guess we just gotta hope whoever checks our logs for the beacon address don't look too closely at where we were before Serenein ...'

'... which is why we're going back to Vellern. I'm hoping the Minister – or whichever Khesh avatar does the technical stuff – can edit the *Heart of Glass*'s logs for us.'

'Why don't we call him and ask? Might be worth doing that anyway, just so's we don't get any shit from Traffic Control when we arrive.'

'Good idea. I assume you've still got that message he sent to your com? If you bring your drink up to the bridge we'll see if we can get a connection from there.'

Taro handed over his com and let Jarek link it into the ship's systems. It took a while to do the business, and when they finally got a response it was just a voice, one they recognised at once.

'Yes, what is it?'

'We're on our way back,' said Taro. He mouthed to Jarek, '*It's the Minister*,' and Jarek nodded. 'We was wondering if you could smooth things over with Traffic Control at your end.'

'I imagine so.'

'Thanks – listen, it's kind of freaky just having your voice. Any chance of visuals?'

'Sorry, no, not with this connection.'

Jarek leaned forward. 'What do you mean by that?'

'And hello to you, Captain Reen. I mean: this is not that type of beacon.'

Jarek said carefully, 'I wasn't aware there were different types of beacon.'

'It is a bit esoteric, but yes, not all beacons are the same.'

His voice deceptively mild, Jarek said, 'But this beacon can still be used for beevee, can't it?'

'Unfortunately not.'

'*What?*'

'Voice only, I am afraid, point-to-point. However, your lost world can talk to me – and through me to you – and I will freely relay your messages to them.'

'But we can't link Serenein into the beevee network?'

'Not as such, no.'

'The terms of our deal—'

'The terms of our *deal* were that I would give you the means to get to Aleph and they would give you a beacon. This is what happened.'

Taro flinched as Jarek punched the console, sending his bulb flying, before stalking off across the bridge, trailing curses.

Taro found he was surprisingly calm. He managed to keep his voice even when he said, 'I can't believe you fucked us over like this.'

'I did exactly what I said I would.'

Taro thought about Aleph and its 'Consensus'. With male Sidhe, it was all about the letter of the law, or the exact wording of the promise.

'Now you've seen what Aleph is like,' continued the Minster coolly, 'do you really think the Alephans would have given you a functional beacon and let you link it in to the rest of human-space?'

'No, but *you* knew that—'

'I strongly suspected. I did not *know*.'

'You could've told us!'

'If I had, would you have gone to Aleph?'

Of course they wouldn't. 'You're meant to be on our frigging side!'

'I am; we are fighting the same fight. You are free to use this beacon to speak to your contacts on Serenein. Had an Alephan male imprinted on it, you would not have that option.'

'You're a total bastard, you know that?'

'Yes: this is not news to me. It should not be news to you.'

Taro looked at Jarek, who was glaring at the com, his face crumpled with fury. Taro wondered if he was going to give the Minister a piece of his mind, before realising no, he wasn't, because the best he could hope to achieve would be to piss him off. And the worst? Jarek's expression reminded him who actually owned the *Heart of Glass*.

The Minister continued calmly, 'You will have no trouble when you return to Vellern – assuming you do not try and cause any. We are allies, after all. Now what is that human saying? Ah yes, I remember: *Better the devil you know—*'

Taro cut the connection.

The fall of the Hidden Empire begins in

QUEEN OF NOWHERE

coming in 2012 from Gollancz

ACKNOWLEDGEMENTS

This book made it into print thanks to the usual suspects and the new recruits who gave honest and comprehensive feedback, sometimes in ridiculously short timescales: Emma O'Connell, Nick Moulton, James Cooke, Susan Booth plus, of course, Tripod (currently consisting of Dr James Anderson, Mike Lewis, Andrew Bland, Bob Dean and Marion Pitman). Thanks to Dr Mark Thompson of the University of Hertford for emergency orbital mechanics and thought-provoking suggestions of an astrophysical nature. Also to my husband Dave, less for plot advice this time than for keeping me sane when shiftspace and deadlines conspired to eat my brain. And last but not least, my ongoing gratitude to Jo Fletcher, who I was lucky enough to have as an editor for my first four books.